IN THE SHADOW OF THE WALL

GORDON ANTHONY

IndePenPress

First published in Great Britain by Pen Press an
Imprint of Indepenpress Publishing Ltd
25 Eastern Place
Brighton
BN2 1GJ

ISBN 978-1-907172-47-2

Printed and bound in the UK

A catalogue record of this book is available from
the British Library

Cover design Jacqueline Abromeit

For Alaine

Acknowledgements

I would like to thank Gavin Barton, Moira Gee and Ken Wayman for reading the first drafts of the story and for their encouragement and support. Special thanks are due to Moira Anthony and Stuart Anthony for their constructive criticism and comments, some of which I actually listened to.

List of Characters

Agrippina – Aquila's wife.
Albinus (Decimus Clodius Albinus) – Governor of Britain.
Anndra – head man of Broch Tava. Brude's father.
Atticus - a gladiator.
Aquila (Gnaeus Vipsanius Aquila) – a Roman knight.
Barabal – Seoc's sister.
Basillus – a tribesman of the Votadini, a Roman captive.
Batix – a Roman slave.
Brigid – a Roman slave, Batix's wife.
Brude – a warrior of Broch Tava.
Brutus (Marcus Septimius Brutus) – Brude's Roman name.
Caitlin – a woman of Broch Tava.
Caracalla – elder son of the emperor.
Carallus – a Brigante tribesman, interpreter for the Romans.
Caralugnus – a Romano-British nobleman.
Caroc – Blacksmith in Broch Tava.
Castatin – Mairead's son.
Cato (Tiberius Servilius Cato) – a Roman cavalry officer.
Cet – a warrior of Peart.
Cleon – a Greek, freedman of Aquila.
Colm – Brude's boyhood friend.
Cruithne – a warrior of Broch Tava.
Curtius (Gaius Lollius Curtius) – a trainer of gladiators.
Danaidh – Nechtan's nephew.
Decimus – assistant to Philo.
Drugh – a warrior of Dun Nechtan.
Eairsidh – Nechtan's son.
Farinus – a medical orderly in the Roman army.
Festus (Lucius Vipsanius Festus) - Aquila's son.
Fionnlagh – Mairead's father.
Fothair – a warrior of Peart.
Frontius – a gladiator.

Frual – a warrior of Broch Tava.
Gartnait – head man of Peart.
Geta – younger son of the emperor.
Glabro (Publius Cornelius Glabro) – a Roman senator.
Gruoch – a carpenter.
Iomhar – a warrior of Broch Tava.
Irb – a warrior of Broch Tava.
Josephus – a gladiator.
Julia – a Roman slave.
Julia Domna – wife of the emperor.
Kallikrates – a trainer of gladiators.
Longinus (Appius Claudius Longinus) - a Roman nobleman.
Lentulus (Lucius Fulvius Lentulus) – superintendent of gladiator school.
Lucius - See Festus.
Lulach – a thatcher.
Lutrin – a warrior of Broch Tava, adviser to Colm.
Macro – a trainer of gladiators.
Mairead – Brude's childhood sweetheart.
Marcella – a slave girl.
Marcus Arminius - Roman freedman, estate overseer.
Mata – an interpreter with the Roman army.
Mor – Brude's mother.
Moritasgus – a Brigante chieftain, cousin of Caralugnus.
Nechtan – chieftain of the Boresti.
Niger – a landlord, an ex-soldier.
Oengus – a warrior of Peart, son of Gartnait.
Philo (Appius Flaminius Philo) – a centurion of marines.
Pollio – a gladiator.
Poppaea – a Roman woman.
Porcius – a tribune in the Twentieth Legion.
Priscus (Gaius Folconius Priscus) – commander of the Twentieth Legion.
Propertius – owner of a gladiator school, a rival to Lentulus.
Rufus (Sextus Arminius Rufus) - a Roman senator.
Sarcho – a gladiator.
Seasaidh – Seoc's youngest sister.

Seoc – a warrior of Broch Tava.

Seoras – elder tribesman of Broch Tava.

Severus (Lucius Septimius Severus) – emperor of Rome.

Talorc – a warrior, brother of Nechtan.

Tertius (Quintus Aemilius Tertius) – commander of Rome's legions in Germania.

Tiberius Arminius – a Roman freedman.

Trimalchio (Publius Vipsanius Trimalchio) – owner of the gladiator school.

Tygaeus – a physician.

Valerius – a gladiator.

Varro (Gaius Ampulius Varro) – a Roman senator.

Veleda – a druidess.

Vipsania – Aquila's daughter.

The tribes of northern
Britain c. 196 AD

CAERENI
SMERTAE
DECANTAE
CREONES
VACOMAGI
TAEXALI
MAEATAE
CALEDONII
Dun Nechtan
BORESTI
Peart
Broch Tava
DAMNONII
VENICONES
Antonine Wall
VOTADINI
SELGOVAE
NOVANTAE
Hadrian's Wall
BRIGANTES
Eboracum
Londinium

A.D. 209

Brude stopped when he saw the Wall. He had half expected that it would disappoint him, seeing it again for the first time in more than twelve years. Back then he had been young, hurt and frightened and to his inexperienced eyes it had seemed a wonder of construction, immense and strong. Now, he was older and, having seen the marvels of Rome, he had thought the Wall would not match his memories of it.

It did. He saw now that it was just as impressive as he remembered it. From the hilltop he looked across the valley, down at the fort, laid out in the familiar rectangular pattern, teeming with soldiers, travellers and traders. Outside the fort was the long, straight road, which ran parallel to the Wall, and the great ditch with its high banks of turf. Clustered along the south side of the ditch were the scattered and rather bedraggled dwellings of the local inhabitants, those who depended on the fort for their livelihood. No doubt some huts were the homes of the soldiers' unofficial families.

His gaze travelled upwards, to the top of the opposite slope. There he saw the Wall itself. He could make out the small figures of the patrolling sentries, idly walking up and down on the wide pathway at the top of the Wall. And he saw the gateway with its square towers dominating even the vast fort.

Beyond the gate was home.

To get there he had to go down the hill, through the fort and talk his way past the gate. He tugged on the halter rope he was holding, clicking his tongue to encourage the mule to follow him. Laden with his personal belongings and a variety of trade goods, the mule picked its way carefully down the slope after him.

His feet sank into the spongy grass and bracken of the hill-side as he made his way down to the road. He made no effort to conceal himself but walked slowly and casually, just another itinerant trader. There was no point in concealment anyway, he knew. The gaps where the mighty ditch was bridged were few, and each one led directly to a fort. The only way to cross through the Wall was with the permission of the Romans.

There was a small queue at the fort's south gate. Some locals were hassling the guards, trying to gain an audience with the garrison commander about a grievance, which seemed to involve the actions of some off-duty soldiers. Brude stayed back a little, standing behind a large wagon laden with sacks of grain, waiting patiently while the centurion who had been summoned by the guards took some notes and eventually persuaded the aggrieved locals to leave the matter with him. He told them to come back the following day. They departed reluctantly, still muttering about the injustice done them, but in their own language, not in the broken dog Latin they had been speaking to the centurion. Brude could make out a fair bit of what they were saying. He had no interest in their problems but even having walked the length of the province he still enjoyed being able to listen to the British tongues after so many years of hearing little except Latin and Greek.

He watched the next man, the owner of the wagon, being waved through with the guards taking little more than a cursory interest in the contents of his wagon. They exchanged some friendly banter with the man who was obviously a regular visitor.

Then it was Brude's turn. He smiled as he walked up to the guards, hoping a friendly approach would ease his passage but the soldiers dropped the amicable faces they had worn for the wagon owner and eyed him with suspicion.

There were four of them, though Brude knew that the fort was probably home to at least one cohort of around five hundred men. One of the sentries barred his way now, his large, oval shield held ready and his javelin held at an angle, which, while not overtly threatening, indicated that it could quite easily become so.

2

"What's your purpose?" he demanded brusquely. His accent was quite harsh, one that Brude vaguely recognised as being from the eastern parts of the empire.

"I wish to go north," Brude replied calmly, making sure that the man could see he was holding no weapon, but also that he had a sword at his right hip.

"North? Across the Wall?"

"That's right."

"You need special permission for that," the guard told him. The man studied Brude carefully. Brude was dressed in long woollen trousers and a linen shirt with a woollen topcoat and cloak. The clothes looked more British than Roman but were of good quality, if slightly worn. On his feet he had soft leather undershoes and old army sandals with thick soles and hobnails. His hair was straggly, in need of cutting, but was styled in the Roman fashion, not the long hair of a native Briton. The gladius slung at his right hip suggested he was an ex-soldier while the heavily laden mule was typical of a trader.

To Brude's amusement, the guard showed some confusion at the mixed messages of his appearance. Keeping his voice even, he asked, "So who do I need to see to get permission?"

The guard turned, walking back through the gate to have a brief discussion with the centurion who shot Brude a dark look. The two of them came back, watched by the other guards who looked as though they were anticipating some fun at Brude's expense.

The centurion was a grizzled veteran in his forties. He carried the vine staff indicating his rank with the easy nonchalance of many years' service. When he spoke he did not have the same accent as the guard. Brude reckoned the man was probably a time-served legionary ranker who had been promoted to a command in the auxiliaries. The centurions were the backbone of the Roman army and Brude knew nobody attained that rank without being a very competent, and very tough, soldier. "You want to go north?" the centurion asked.

"That's right, Centurion." Brude let him know he knew his status.

"Not many people are allowed to pass through the Wall these days," the centurion said in his gravelly voice. Brude recognised the tone of someone sensing an opportunity for a bribe. "What's your name and what's your purpose?" the centurion wanted to know.

"Marcus Septimius Brutus, freedman in the service of Gnaeus Vipsanius Aquila. I have goods to trade and my employer wants some examples of native art for his collection." It was a poor lie, and Brude knew it, but it was better than telling the truth.

The centurion eyed him warily. Brude had announced he was a freedman, an ex-slave. Using the *nomen* Septimius meant that he had probably been given his freedom by decree of the emperor, whose family name that was. Brude could practically see the thoughts going through the centurion's mind. He also recognised that the centurion was canny enough to know that Brude could have traded his goods for trinkets and artefacts from any number of British tribes south of the Wall and passed them off as pieces from beyond the borders of the empire. The centurion decided to try another tack. "Do you know why this Wall is here?" he asked, giving a slight backward jerk of his head to indicate the great barrier behind him.

Brude decided to let the centurion have his say. "To guard the frontier?"

The centurion barked what obviously passed for a laugh. "To guard the frontier? Oh no, my lad! We don't have enough men to stop an army crossing it if they want to, and anyone in a boat can sail or row round the ends of the Wall any time they like. The imperial fleet's supposed to stop them doing that of course, but they're usually as much use as a eunuch in a brothel, if you take my meaning." He shook his head as if exasperated at Brude's ignorance. Brude grinned at the weak joke. "No, the Wall is here to stop people going north in case they are supplying weapons or money to the enemies of Rome, or planning some sort of rebellion." He held Brude's gaze. "You're not planning some sort of rebellion, are you, laddie?"

"I'm a Roman citizen," answered Brude, holding the centurion's gaze firmly.

4

Brude's expression let the centurion know that he would not be intimidated easily. The centurion nodded thoughtfully. "Search the baggage!" he snapped to the guards. He watched as two of the soldiers laid down their shields and javelins then began unstrapping the bags and packs from the mule. Brude made no protest but watched as they laid out the assortment of pots, cooking utensils, cloths, brooches, beads and rings that made up his stock, scattering them across the roadway while the centurion studied him as much as the baggage. One of the men found the small pouch of copper and silver coins that Brude had carefully stashed at the bottom of one of the sacks. The soldier tossed it to the centurion who caught it deftly, untied the drawstring and tipped out some of the coins into his palm. He raised a quizzical eyebrow.

"My emergency stash," explained Brude.

"That all you've got?"

"If you can find any more, you can keep it," Brude told him in a tone which he hoped conveyed that the small bag contained all his wealth. He was about to suggest that the centurion might want to keep the money in exchange for letting him pass but one of the soldiers unpacking his bedroll gave an exclamation of surprise.

"What is it?" the centurion demanded.

The man pulled out a short, wooden sword that had been wrapped in Brude's blanket, together with a small leather package. He handed them over to the centurion.

The centurion hefted the wooden sword, feeling its weight. When he looked at Brude there was some respect in his eyes. "Is this what I think it is?"

Brude nodded. "Given to me by the emperor himself."

"And this?" He indicated the small leather case.

"My papers of manumission."

The centurion nodded. "All right, lads. Pack it all up again." He handed the case and the wooden sword to Brude. "I expect you won't bother too much about any warnings of how the Picti treat strangers?"

"I can take care of myself," Brude assured him. He picked up his blanket, carefully wrapping the wooden sword and leather case in it. These were the symbols of his freedom, the proof that he was no longer a slave but a free man, a Roman citizen.

It took the soldiers a few minutes to re-pack the mule. Brude fastened his bedroll onto the beast, grabbed the halter rope and gave the centurion a questioning look. The soldier nodded. "Follow me. I'll see you through." He led Brude to a small building just inside the gate where a scribe etched out details of who Brude was and what he was carrying. "There's a tax of six sesterces on the goods," he said in a disinterested tone.

The centurion counted out the coins from Brude's small bag then handed the rest back to Brude who counted out another twenty sesterces which he gave back to the centurion. That left only a few coppers but he doubted he would have much need for them where he was going. "For your trouble," he told the soldier.

The centurion nodded his thanks then led Brude through the fort, one of the guards falling in behind. Brude did not pay much attention to his surroundings; he had seen army camps before and could probably find his way round this one blindfolded. All of his attention was on the northern gate. He found his heart was beating fast at the thought of getting through. He knew he was the subject of some curious looks from the soldiers he was passing but he ignored them.

The centurion said softly, "You'll need the tribune to agree to open the gate."

"I'm sure you'll be able to persuade him," Brude replied.

"You've still got time to change your mind. They're a troublesome lot, the Picti. Been raiding down here for years, ever since that fool Albinus took the legions off to fight the emperor." Brude nodded. Decimus Clodius Albinus had been governor of Britannia when Brude was a boy. He had stripped the province of most of its soldiers to support his attempt to become emperor. He had lost the war and so, by definition, was a fool. Ever since, the fractious British tribes had been rising in sporadic revolt, with the Picts and tribes from Hibernia raiding the coasts and sallying across the Wall while the outnumbered Roman troops marched from one part of the country to another, quashing resistance where they found it. The Romans were still in control, but only just, and whenever they stamped on the locals in one part of the province, trouble broke out somewhere else. Brude listened with interest as the centurion went on, "Still it'll all be sorted now the emperor is on his way here."

That nearly stopped Brude in his tracks. He had deliberately kept away from the main roads and settlements on his way north. It had made the journey longer but it meant he had been able to avoid trouble. By cutting across country, he had avoided confrontations with any tribesmen seeking to liberate his possessions and do away with another Roman. But it also meant he had heard little news of what was going on. "The emperor is here?"

"Not yet, but he will be soon," the soldier told him with grim satisfaction. "He came over with three legions at the end of last year. Going to sort the locals out and make sure they stay sorted. About bloody time, if you ask me. Bloody Brigantes have always been uppity." The Brigantes, Brude knew, were the major tribe in this part of the province, holding sway over the mountainous country south of the Wall, all the way to Eboracum. While the tribes in the far south of Britannia were almost thoroughly Romanised, the Brigantes, along with the fierce tribes of the western fringes of the province, were constantly causing trouble. In the years since the province had been stripped of much of its army, they had become bolder, raiding Roman settlements, burning homes, stealing cattle, goods and women, and ambushing any Roman traders who dared to travel without a sizeable armed guard. Despite Britannia having been a province of the empire for a hundred and fifty years, some of the locals seemed determined not to become civilised. But if the emperor was really coming here, the Brigantes were likely to find themselves well and truly under the Roman heel before long. Britannia, a tiny and relatively poor province on the fringes of the empire, had always needed at least three legions to keep the populace in order. Brude took a perverse pride in that. Rome only had around thirty legions to control its entire empire and no fewer than three of them were needed to keep this province in line. The Britons had had it easy for the past thirteen years but now that the soldiers were back in force, the emperor would no doubt make a show of imposing order again. It made Brude even more determined to escape the confines of the empire.

They reached the gate at last. The centurion told Brude to wait while he went to speak to the tribune. Brude stood beneath the immense gateway, its two square towers flanking the huge oak doors, which were barred firmly shut. Behind him, the guard shuffled idly while on the towers another guard, javelin resting on his shoulder, looked down with interest to see what was going on.

The tribune, a young man, barely into his twenties, walked down to meet Brude, the centurion accompanying him a pace behind. The tribune, Brude knew, would be the son of a wealthy family doing a stint of military service as a prelude to a life in politics. Technically the centurion's superior officer, he would be inexperienced and would almost always look to the more experienced man for guidance. With his sculpted breastplate and crested helmet, he looked every inch the martial hero until Brude looked at his face and saw how young he was. "You want to go north?" the tribune asked him in a puzzled tone.

"That's right, sir. Trading trip, sir. I've paid the toll." Brude tried to sound as if he expected to be allowed through with no arguments.

"The northern tribes are really not very friendly," the tribune said. "For a Roman citizen to go there is very dangerous. Especially just now."

"Cut your balls off as soon as look at you," the centurion added cheerily, bringing stifled laughs from the nearby soldiers.

"I can take care of myself," Brude said evenly, trying to stare the young tribune down.

8

"The centurion says you won the rudis?"

"Four summers past," Brude confirmed.

"Then I expect you *can* take care of yourself," the tribune conceded.

Brude just gazed at him calmly, daring him to refuse permission. After a moment the tribune backed down. He signalled to the soldiers manning the gate. "Let him through!"

Brude exchanged a nod of mutual respect with the centurion, tugged on the halter rope and walked steadily forwards as one of the huge wooden gates was pulled inwards. He passed through the shadows of the gateway. Heart pounding, half expecting the tribune to change his mind, he made his way out to the other side.

He had made it. He was going home.

A.D. 196

Colm and Brude were going to war. They were sixteen years old and felt invincible. Like all the men, they had painted their faces and bodies with the blue war dye, daubing each other with swirling lines and circles, tracing images of bears, horses and eagles across their chests. They admired each other, laughing as they painted themselves. For the march, Brude was wearing a linen shirt but he left the front untied so that his painted chest and belly could be seen. When the time came for fighting he would discard it so that he could face the enemy with his upper body bare. To complete his battle gear he was carrying a large, round shield and a long spear with a wickedly sharp iron blade fixed to the tip. He had worked on its edge for days, rubbing and oiling until it was so sharp he could have shaved with it. If he had been old enough to have any beard worth shaving.

He stood among the crowd of warriors savouring the applause from the assembled villagers, trying to see whether Mairead was watching him, but at the same time trying not to appear as if he was looking for her. Instead he saw his mother kissing his father farewell and he joined in the chorus of cheers that greeted the gesture. Brude's father was the head man of the village, a wealthy man who owned nearly twenty head of cattle. Now, dressed in his bronze breastplate which gleamed like gold in the summer sun and carrying a mighty sword at his waist, he was about to lead his twenty-eight warriors on the greatest adventure of their lifetime.

Nechtan himself had come all the way from his fortress in the hills, bringing a huge army of over ninety warriors. Nechtan, acknowledged among the Boresti as the mightiest warlord of the tribe, had called the leaders of all the villages to set aside their squabbles and join him in the march south. For the news had reached them that the Romans had sailed away, across the sea, leaving only a handful of soldiers to guard their province. The time was ripe for the tribes of the Pritani to go south to plunder the wealth of the undefended towns. Nechtan, sitting astride his horse, had told them that the men of the Venicones, the Damnonii and the Selgovae would join them in the greatest army the Pritani had mustered in nearly twenty years.

Brude felt proud to be a part of such a great adventure. He and Colm had talked of little else in the past days. They had practised with their spears and shields, copying the older warriors, the battle-scarred men who plastered their hair with lime to shape it like the mane of an angry horse. The two boys had dreamed of the deeds they would accomplish and the Romans they would kill.

Now Colm stood beside Brude, grinning broadly as he waved to someone in the crowd. Brude followed his gaze and saw Mairead, standing in the shadow of the great broch, a garland of flowers in her long hair. She gave them a smile and Brude smiled back. Colm frowned when he saw Mairead was looking more at Brude than at him.

Mairead was a couple of years younger than the two boys but they had grown up together. Colm was two months older than Brude and liked to take the lead in most things that they did together, which was just about everything. Though they were like brothers, Brude, as the younger, usually let Colm have his own way. He knew that Colm, who had lost his parents when he was quite young, liked to prove he was better than everyone else. He always wanted to win at everything he did. Most of the time Brude did not mind that. Colm was taller than he was by half a head but Brude was stockier and stronger. Despite that, he usually let Colm win when they wrestled. Usually, but not always.

Mairead, by common consent, was the most beautiful girl in the village. She had reached the age where she should marry.

Everyone seemed to take it for granted that she would marry Colm before long which meant he would be the next head man, for Mairead was the daughter of Brude's grandmother's cousin. The Boresti, like all the Pritani, inherited through the female line. Only men could rule, of course, but even though Brude was the son of a head man, his mother was not of a noble line, so he would not follow his father in that position. It did not bother him. He was young, strong and happy, and he was off to war to become a hero. What more was there to wish for?

They gathered on the wide, open space north of the broch. Its mighty tower, the height of twelve grown men, dwarfed them all, casting a long shadow in the morning sunlight. It was the wonder of the coast, built by Brude's great-great-grandfather after the Romans had come and gone many years before, built to offer protection for the villagers should the Romans ever return. They never had, so the broch had never been needed as a defence. Its two concentric walls, each as thick as a man is tall, formed an impregnable fortress, providing a safe haven for people and animals alike. With only one small entrance and a platform at the high summit from which defenders could hurl rocks and spears at any enemy, the broch was a symbol of the power of the Boresti. The village of Broch Tava had grown and flourished in recent years. Brude's father was accounted a good leader, for the people prospered under his rule. He was not the mightiest lord of the Boresti but he was the only one who had a broch to defend his people and the whole village took pride in that fact.

Now Nechtan, the mighty warrior, lord of lords, led them in a prayer to Belatucadros, god of war, seeking his blessing on their venture. Then he drank from a horn full of ale, tossing it loftily aside when he had drained it. They all cheered as he waved his arm, urging his horse to turn and set off westwards.

The army followed, accompanied for some way by the villagers. Colm ran to Mairead and gave her a kiss, waving happily to her as he rejoined Brude in the marching troop. "I'm going to marry her when we get back," Colm told him. Mairead's father, Fionnlagh, who was marching a few paces ahead of them, turned to give Colm a studied look before glancing at Brude. Brude looked away, turning his head in time to see Mairead blow him a kiss. He grinned at her like an idiot and tried to blow a kiss back, but couldn't because he was holding a spear in his right hand and had a shield strapped to his left arm, so all he succeeded in doing was knocking the spear against his head. Colm laughed at him but Brude did not mind for he had a secret. He knew that Mairead would not marry Colm. She had told him so last night when she had given herself to him. Brude knew that she was waiting for him to return, not for Colm. Brude knew that his friend would not be happy, but that was a problem for another day. Today they were marching to war and he was a real man with a woman waiting for him to return a victorious hero.

They marched inland, skirting the flat-topped slopes of the hill they called the Law before heading out to the wide plain which lay between the shining Tava away to their left and the hills to their right. Some distance inland to their right was the old hill fort where their ancestors had once lived but the place had been long abandoned, unused since the Romans first came and drove the Boresti from it.

The plain was fertile land, heavily wooded but dotted with small farmsteads and cleared fields. Every few miles another man would come to join the march, leaving his family behind to tend the land and the livestock. There were some women in the army too, their cheeks decorated with swirling painted designs, armed like the men with shield and spear, just as eager to fight. Brude somehow felt more intimidated by the women than the men. He remembered asking his father once why some women went to war with the men. His father had laughed and told him that it was to stop the men running away. "No man wants to appear a coward in front of the women," he had said. Then he had added, "And some of them are bonny fighters as well." Brude could well believe it.

It took them two days to reach Peart, where they could cross the river. Here the Tava was narrow and fast, but fordable in some places. The people of Peart under their head man, who was called Gartnait, had even built a wooden bridge so the army could cross without getting their feet wet.

Peart was a large settlement, nestled around the river in a valley between hills and cliffs. There was great rivalry between Gartnait and Brude's father but Nechtan called them together, telling them to put aside their quarrels, so they publicly embraced, then drank some ale together.

That night there was a great feast. The cattle raids were joked about and nobody came to blows, so keen were they all to join the war. They had stormed across the northern wall in the year Brude was born. Nechtan, Gartnait and Brude's father had been young men when they had joined that last great raid. As the ale and uisge flowed, they told of how the Romans had run before them and how they had freed the Selgovae from the yoke of the invader. Brude listened to the tales avidly though he remembered his father boasting of these exploits once before. He recalled his mother whispering to him that in truth the Romans had all gone south long before the Boresti had crossed the wall. Brude did not mind. The stories were good, some of them funny once he had some ale inside him, and boasting was the warrior's way. One day soon he would have stories of his own to boast about.

Colm and Brude got very drunk. They slept in the open, only waking when Brude's father kicked them to their feet and told them to get moving. Hung over and thirsty, they staggered after the army, most of who were not in much better shape. Men and women dropped out regularly to throw up before hauling themselves to their feet again and rejoining the march. Brude had never felt so ill in all his young life but somehow he kept walking. By mid-morning Colm announced that he could no longer carry his shield, so Brude picked it up, strapped it to his own back and carried it along with his own weapons.

The army's march was so strung out and disorganised that Nechtan called a halt by mid-afternoon when they reached a small stream that meandered through a wide valley. Most of them simply collapsed and lay where they fell. A few hardy souls got fires going so that they could cook some broth and some meat but there was barely enough to go round, so many of them went hungry. Brude's father, himself looking a little the worse for the excesses of the previous evening, managed to get some meat for the two boys. He sat with them while they ate. "Did you find yourselves some women last night?" he asked.

Brude felt embarrassed and simply shook his head while Colm confessed they had been too busy drinking. Brude's father laughed at them. "Next time, don't waste the chance."

The march continued, the army straggling in a long, winding column over the hills and through the valleys. There were few settlements here but a handful of men of the Venicones joined the march, eager to take part in the plundering.

Four days out from Peart they reached the remains of the old Roman defensive lines. Brude marvelled at the height of the turf wall and the carvings on the broken stones that had once lined its foot. In some places the wooden palisade, although mostly rotted away, was still partly visible. Now, it provided some ready-made firewood for them.

Clustered round their fires for the evening, the boys listened to the tales of the Romans. Some of the older men said they could remember when the Romans had built this wall. They insisted that it stretched from one side of the country to the other. Brude thought that was unlikely. He knew how the storytellers liked to exaggerate. Nobody could build a wall that long, he thought, but he held his peace, even when someone said that the next wall was even longer, even higher and made of stone.

"Do you think that's true?" Colm asked him that night as they lay down to sleep. "About the wall, I mean?"

"What? That it's made of stone and stretches right across the country? I'll believe it when I see it."

"It can't be true," Colm said fervently.

Brude said nothing. As a child he had always been told he asked too many questions, always trying to understand how things worked or why things happened. Often the answers did not satisfy him. It was only now that he was older, no longer a child, that he was starting to understand that his father and the other older men did not know everything. He wanted to ask someone about the wall of stone but he knew none of the men of the Boresti had ever seen it and he did not know any of the men from the other tribes well enough to know whether they would answer him truthfully. He decided he would have to wait until he saw it for himself.

On they marched, soon entering the lands of the Damnonii where Nechtan warned them all not to steal anything or otherwise harm the inhabitants, for the Damnonii were going to join them. They saw little sign of them though and the never-ending march continued as it had before. Brude's feet were aching from the constant walking and the soles of his shoes were starting to fall away. He felt exhausted yet at the same time fitter than he had ever felt before. He was pleased that he was able to keep up the pace better than most. Still, walking barefoot would slow him considerably so he scrounged some goat's hide from a farmstead they passed and fashioned a crude pair of new shoes, which were uncomfortable and gave him blisters.

The hills grew steeper and higher as they continued southwards. Now their column was joined by warriors from the Damnonii and soon they were greeted by the people of the Selgovae as well, until Brude could not count how many were in the army. His father told him he reckoned there must be over five hundred men altogether. What chance did the Romans have against such a host?

They made their way through the deep, dark forests of the Selgovae, always keeping away from the eastern coast now, for that was the land of the Votadini who were known to be friendly to the Romans. Colm derided them for that. "How can any of the Pritani befriend the Romans?" he asked aloud.

"It is difficult for us to understand," Brude's father conceded, "but when the Romans are living just beyond the next hill, perhaps it is as well not to upset them too much."

Brude and Colm both looked at the southern hill as if expecting to see Romans cresting the summit. Brude's father laughed aloud. "I didn't mean that hill," he chuckled.

Nor the hill after that, nor the one after that either, as it turned out. The march went on. The deeply wooded slopes slowed their progress but there was, at least, plenty to eat, for the forest was full of game and the Selgovae were good hunters. They ate well, enjoying the slower pace which allowed their aching muscles to recover slightly. Brude lost count of how many days they had been walking, but he knew it was past midsummer now. When the forest at last came to an end, they marched across open hillsides, crossed bracken-covered moors and valleys, splashing across streams and shallow rivers.

To Brude's surprise, they stopped early one afternoon. Then the word filtered back that they were to rest, eat and sleep for the wall was less than three hours' march away. "We'll set off at nightfall," said Brude's father to the men of Broch Tava. "Stick together." He looked hard at Brude and Colm. "And you two youngsters stay close to me."

At this time of year there would only be around six hours of darkness so they had a long wait ahead of them. The men of Broch Tava sat together, or lay on the ground, resting against rocks. Some of them lit a cooking fire but there was not a lot of food left, so the best they could do was produce a thin broth.

There was a quiet tension in the air. Fionnlagh told them that the Selgovae had warned that the Romans often sent patrols out north of the wall so they had to lie low. "We've got scouts out watching for them, but it's best not to make too much noise or too much smoke from cooking fires," he warned them.

Brude felt his stomach churning. Even though he was tired after the days of marching, he was unable to sleep. He decided to go for a walk to see what the other tribes were doing. Colm was lying on his back with his eyes closed so Brude left him in peace. Much as he loved Colm like a brother, he knew their friendship would be unlikely to survive when they returned home and Mairead married him instead of Colm. He did not want to hurt his friend but could see no alternative. He decided that, once they were on the way home with their plunder, he would speak to his father about what to do.

He wandered along the banks of a small stream where he found a group of men and women from the Selgovae cutting down some trees and stripping the trunks to leave only the stumps of larger branches. He watched, fascinated, for a few moments, then asked one of them what they were doing.

The man laughed at his ignorance. "Making ladders to climb the Wall," he said. "You stick the trunk against the Wall and climb using the stumps of the branches."

Brude looked at the three crude ladders the Selgovae had already made. One of them was the length of four men and the others were not much shorter. He was about to ask why they had made them so long but decided he did not want them to laugh at him again, so he wandered back to where the men from Broch Tava were resting. He told his father what he had seen but the older man was not impressed. "We can climb the wall with our bare hands, I'm sure," he said dismissively. "Like when I caught you and Colm trying to climb the broch when you were boys."

"The Selgovae seem to know what they are doing," persisted Brude.

"Oh, I dare say they'll be able to climb quicker with their ladders," his father conceded grudgingly, "but we'll manage fine without them."

Brude was not convinced, but he knew not to argue otherwise he would be told that his father was older, wiser, and more experienced than he was, so he said no more. He recalled the northern wall that the Romans had abandoned and how impressive it had been even though it was little more than earth and turf. He worried that a wall of stone might be even more formidable but he supposed that his father was probably right; stone walls had plenty of gaps for finger and toe holds so they would be able to climb it no matter how high it was. And it was unlikely that there would be any Romans trying to stop them, because who would stand to face such a huge force? He reasoned that the Romans had already shown they could not face the Pritani otherwise why would they have abandoned their northern wall? The Romans, Brude decided, must be very frightened of them if they cowered behind stone walls. He felt a lot better now, even managing to snooze for a couple of hours in the warmth of the fading sun.

By nightfall they were all on their feet, weapons checked and eager to go. The moon, almost full, was rising, casting its baleful light over the rugged terrain they had to cross. Nechtan made a short speech, encouraging them to stick together so that they could share in the spoils. He told them that beyond the wall were rich pickings from undefended farms and villages. He said that he was sure the Boresti would show the other tribes how to carry out a real raid. He promised them gold, cattle and women and they cheered him loudly, spears held aloft.

Brude's father led the men of Broch Tava on the night march, which, despite the pale light from the moon, soon turned into a difficult and dangerous journey. The ground was uneven and treacherous. In the dark they could not see where they were treading, so men would stumble, cursing, or twist their ankles in hidden rabbit holes. The approach to the wall was supposed to take only three hours but the sky was already growing lighter and the birds were chirping to greet the dawn by the time the army ground to a halt at the foot of a dark slope, which appeared to Brude to be no different from the many others they had climbed during the night.

They crouched, hushed to silence, in a stand of ash trees. Colm and Brude, both now stripped to the waist, squatted beside Brude's father near the front of their group. They looked up the steep hill and there, in the shadowy half-light, Brude saw the wall.

Suddenly he realised why the Selgovae referred to it as The Wall. It was not just a wall; it was immense. It snaked along from left to right as far as he could see, always on the highest ground, following the contours of the land regardless of how steep the slope was. Ahead of where they lay, just off to their left, was a small tower rising above the crenellated parapet of the Wall itself, a darker patch against the lightening sky. Peering anxiously at the tower Brude thought he saw a dark shadow move on its summit.

Without warning, the Selgovae were on the move, bursting from where they had hidden at the foot of the slope. They ran up the hill, carrying their long tree trunks, several men to each one. Others carried long lengths of coiled rope over their shoulders. There were no war cries, no cheers, just men and women running as fast as they could up the steep slope, but the Roman guards must have been alert. Before the Selgovae had got half way to the Wall Brude saw a flame leap from the top of the tower, It began to wave backwards and forwards and he heard the shouts of alarm. He realised that someone was holding a burning brand, making an unmistakeable signal.

All at once Nechtan's voice boomed along the tree line. "Boresti! Come on!" They yelled in response, jumped to their feet and charged up the hill towards the Wall.

Brude was tired before they got to the Wall but he was still one of the first to reach it, his young legs driving him up the slope ahead of the others. In the gloom, he tumbled into a deep ditch, coming to rest in a heap at the foot of the Wall. He clambered to his feet as other men blundered after him. The cheering from the Boresti had subsided as men saved their breath for the run up the steep slope but Brude could hear others still shouting away to the left. He flung himself at the Wall but quickly realised he would not be able to climb it carrying his spear and shield. He wondered what he was supposed to do with them, then he discovered that he could not climb the Wall anyway. In the growing light he saw that it was not built of dry stones like the walls he was used to. The way Broch Tava had been built required the careful balancing and interlocking of many stones, using their own weight to hold them in place, larger stones at the base, using gradually smaller ones as the height increased. But this wall was made of carved blocks of stone, smooth and regular, with no gaps for fingers or toes to help him climb. There seemed to be some sort of mortar between the blocks, holding them firmly in place. Frustrated, he slapped his palm against the sheer stonework, helpless with rage. He recalled the Selgovae laughing at his ignorance as he realised with a pang of disappointment that his father and Nechtan, men he looked up to, knew as little of the Romans as he did.

The rest of the Boresti reached the foot of the Wall where they stopped, bemused and uncertain. To their left, the Selgovae were attacking the gateway in the tower but here in the ditch where they were clustered there was no gateway to attack and no way to climb the smooth stones. Away to the left, some of the Selgovae were scrambling up their makeshift ladder poles and Brude, looking to the west, saw that the Damnonii were doing the same. Only the Boresti had no way of getting over the Wall.

There was no point in waiting for the other tribes to get over, for the ladders could only hold one person at a time. Even then, they had to be held in place by other men at the foot, to prevent them twisting and throwing the climber.

Nechtan yelled, "Form a human hill!" He began pushing men into place, half a dozen against the Wall, facing outwards, another row in front of them to lift their comrades up to form a second tier. Brude looked hesitatingly at the idea. It would take at least three men standing on the shoulders of those below before the fourth could even hope to reach the parapet. He, for one, did not want to be at the bottom of that weight.

Colm, looking helpless and confused, asked him, "What do we do?"

"We get a rope," Brude decided. He pushed his way through the crowd and ran towards the Selgovae. As he ran, the thought came to him that it was just as well the Romans were not on top of the Wall because the Boresti would have had no option but to retreat. Fortunately, apart from the man in the watchtower, there did not seem to be any sentries at this bit of the Wall.

He reached the back of the crowd of Selgovae warriors who were still waiting their turn to climb. There were only six ladders, so scaling the Wall was a slow business. He looked for men with ropes but they had been among the first to clamber up and even now they were tying one end of each rope round the crenellations of the parapet, dropping the loose end over the Wall to let their comrades haul themselves up. Brude shouted up to one of the warriors on top of the Wall who had not yet tied his rope, yelling at him to take the rope along to the Boresti. The man laughed and began tying it to the parapet where he stood. One of the men standing next to Brude also laughed. "Get your own bloody rope," he snarled.

"All right, I will," Brude retorted. Slinging his shield over his back, he barged forwards, pushing through to grab the end of the falling rope. There were shouts of protest and someone grabbed his shoulder but he shrugged it off and leaped forwards, planting his feet against the stone. Grunting with effort, he hauled himself up the rope. It was awkward and dangerous trying to climb with his long spear in his hand but he had seen that the Selgovae were managing it, so he made the best of it, slowly dragging himself to the top. He dropped his spear over the parapet, using both hands to heave himself over, half expecting the warrior who had tied the rope to start an argument with him. But the man had gone to join the other tribesmen who had climbed the Wall and were now charging into the watchtower. Turning, Brude began to untie the rope. "Get off!" he yelled down at the next warrior. He hauled the rope up, jerking it out of the hands of the warrior below. Hurriedly, he reeled it in, hauling it over the parapet. As quickly as he could, he unpicked the crude knot, coiled the rope around his shoulder, retrieved his spear, then ran along the walkway to where his tribesmen were.

He had no idea how long he had taken but it could not have been long. By the time he reached the point on the Wall above where the men of Broch Tava were gathered, the first men using the human climbing frame had just reached the parapet. Further along, some enterprising men had tied their cloaks together into a very crude rope. Somehow, they had managed to throw it up, looping it over a crenellation so that both ends fell to the ground. One brave man was clambering up the makeshift rope, fervently praying that none of the knots would unravel.

Brude fastened his own rope firmly round the nearest crenellation. He dropped the loose end over the Wall. Peering down, he saw his father catch it, pull to test it, then begin to climb. Only then did Brude turn to look around at his new surroundings.

The sun was up now, revealing the land stretched out beyond the Wall, much the same as the land on the north side except for the road that ran, straight and true, parallel to the Wall itself. Beyond the road was another wall, of turf this time, near the height of two men. Beyond that was a ditch, then another turf wall.

A sudden yell of triumph reached his ears. He span to see the Selgovae surging through the gateway. Some of their men had obviously fought their way down inside the tower and opened the gates. In moments, they were through the small tower, fanning out across the open space, charging over the narrow roadway that spanned the walled ditch, then heading south and east in search of plunder. To the west, the Damnonii, fewer of them, were running to join the Selgovae, pushing and jostling to get across the ditch before heading south, clearly intent on climbing the hills beyond the Wall.

Brude felt embarrassed that only the Boresti were still trying to cross the Wall. He waved the first men towards the watchtower. "There's a way down in there," he told them. Grinning gleefully, they set off at a run. Just then, his father reached the top of the rope. Brude laid down his spear to help him climb over the parapet. He got a hug and a slap on the back. "Well done, lad!" his father said.

Now the warriors below were running for the open gateway as an easier route through the Wall rather than over it. Colm climbed Brude's rope, grinning like a madman as he clambered over to stand on the walkway. Clapping him on the back, Brude's father said, "Come on the two of you, we'll get left behind if we stay here. Let's go down."

Brude silently thought that the Boresti had already been left behind but he followed as they hurried to the watchtower, able to walk three abreast on the top of the Wall. Brude was amazed at the incredible feat of construction. He could scarcely conceive of how much effort and skill it must have taken to build such an astonishing fortification, but he seemed to be in a minority; everyone else was in too much of a hurry to pay much attention to the Roman engineering.

They went through the open door, into the gloom of the watchtower where they immediately came across two bodies. One was a warrior of the Selgovae, lying crumpled at the foot of the stairs which led to the upper level of the tower. The other was a Roman soldier who lay on his back, a jagged wound on his neck, staring up at them with blank, unseeing eyes. Brude tried to ignore the corpses but he was struck by the armour the Roman wore, protecting his upper body. He paused to take a closer look, touching the metal plates which inter-linked, each one attached separately on to the leather shirt beneath. Brude's father thumped him on the shoulder, telling him to leave the corpse. "It's been well plundered by now," he said, thinking Brude was trying to find some coins or jewellery. To Brude, the armour was worth more than any gold or gems and he was considering trying to strip it from the body so that he could keep it for himself. Such a prize would be almost priceless. He reckoned the Roman must have been a wealthy man. His father, though, did not allow him the time. More warriors were flooding in to the tower and heading for the south side so Brude reluctantly left the fallen Roman and ran down the wide wooden steps.

Bursting out into the sunlight he came across another fallen Roman who was also wearing the segmented armour plates. Brude had a sudden, sobering thought that it was unlikely two wealthy Romans would be on guard duty in a remote watchtower. Which meant that this armour was probably common among the Roman soldiers. He had heard tales of how the Romans had conquered the Pritani generations ago and that their soldiers all wore suits of metal but he had thought those were exaggerated tales. Now, he was not so sure. The Pritani usually fought without armour, a shield being their only protection apart from their skill. Only the very wealthy sometimes wore breastplates but most warriors felt it was a point of honour not to wear protective armour. Brude knew the warrior code but to his mind, the Romans were more likely to win if their men could withstand the spears and swords of the Pritani. It was an unsettling thought.

Colm dragged him out of his reverie by thumping him on the back. "We did it!" he shouted happily. "We're here!" He danced a little jig in celebration.

Nechtan arrived, on foot because his horse had gone lame on the night march. Briskly, he ordered them to gather at the road. Brude's father called for the men of Broch Tava to follow him and, after some confusion while they sorted themselves out, they set off in high spirits, down the gentle slope to the road. Only Brude was subdued. To him, the assault on the Wall had been a shambles. Now that they were on the other side, they seemed to have no clear plan as to what they wanted to do next because it took Nechtan some time to gather the men where he wanted them. Then, instead of crossing the wide ditch, he led them along the road, heading to the west. Brude heard him say to his father and the other village leaders, "The Selgovae have gone east and the Damnonii have gone south, so we'll go this way. Then we won't have to share any spoils we take."

Brude snorted a breath of dissatisfaction with this plan. Nobody heard except Colm who nudged him and asked what was wrong.

"The Selgovae know what they are doing. Look at how they crossed the Wall before us. If they're heading east they must have a reason. And we should stay off the road. We are trapped here between the Wall and the ditch."

"Who cares?" Colm said dismissively. "There aren't any Romans about anyway."

"Didn't you see that fire signal?" Brude asked him, keeping his voice low. "Look, you can see another watchtower away along there. The guards were signalling to somebody."

"Well if there are any Romans, we'll soon see them off," Colm said confidently. "If you're afraid you can always stay here," he added mockingly.

"I'm not afraid," Brude snapped back, "I just think going this way is a bad idea. We should at least send some scouts ahead."

"Nechtan knows what he's doing," Colm asserted.

Brude wasn't so sure.

They set off at last. Brude had to concede that walking along the road meant that they made much better time than going across country. It ran dead straight, taking them up a long, gentle rise, always around five hundred paces from the Wall to their right. They soon reached the next watchtower where, seeing several figures on its summit watching them, Gartnait of Peart led some of his men to try to attack it. They soon hurried back. The solid oak door had been barred and the Romans were throwing javelins and dropping rocks from the top of the tower. With no way of breaking down the door, the men of Peart were forced to make an ignominious retreat. Worse still, Gartnait himself was injured, a dropped rock having smashed through his shield, breaking his arm, then falling onto his foot and crushing his toes. He bore the pain stoically but could not continue the march. Nechtan sent him back to where they had crossed the Wall with instructions to guard the tower to make sure that they all had a way back. Gartnait was not happy, but Nechtan promised him an equal share of whatever plunder they took so he hobbled off, supported and half carried by four of his men.

The rest of the Boresti went on, cresting the small rise only to see that the road dipped slightly before rising again a few hundred paces away. They had barely started on the gentle downward slope when the leading men came to an abrupt stop, causing the straggling column to bunch up, cursing, as men stopped suddenly. The warriors quickly dispersed to either side of the paved road, peering ahead to see a group of horsemen on the road, just where it reached the top of the next rise. The horsemen reined in, stopping to watch the assembled Boresti. More appeared until Brude counted twenty of them, all on large horses, much bigger than the small horse Nechtan had ridden on the long march.

Nechtan waved his sword in the air, bellowing an incoherent war cry which was soon taken up by the whole tribe. They stepped purposefully forwards, shields held in front of them, spears at the ready. The horsemen did not wait to meet them but turned and rode off quickly, vanishing almost immediately over the crest of the low hill. The Boresti laughed and cheered, boasting of what they would have done to the horsemen if they had caught them. Even Brude was caught up in the excitement. The Romans had not bothered trying to fight although he could scarcely blame them; twenty against over a hundred and fifty was hardly a fair contest, even if the twenty were on horseback.

Nechtan led them on again but this time they marched in a line rather than a column, the men of Broch Tava on the right flank near the Wall, tramping over the tough, tussocky grass, while Nechtan was near the left, on the road. All of them were watching ahead keenly for more signs of the Romans. Nechtan, much to Brude's satisfaction, at last sent a handful of men running ahead as scouts. These warriors jogged along the road, down into the small depression then climbed the far slope. They came to a sudden halt when they reached the crest, then quickly turned and ran back, moving much more quickly and urgently. Nechtan called a halt, waiting for the men to return. Standing on the grass some thirty paces from the road, Brude could not hear what they said but he did not need to for Colm nudged his arm and pointed to the road ahead. "Look! More of them," he said excitedly.

The Boresti watched silently as a column of marching Romans came into view at the top of the rise. Marching two abreast, each man carried a large rectangular shield that covered practically his whole body and each had a long javelin over his right shoulder. Brude saw that they were indeed all wearing the incredibly tough yet flexible segmented armour. Their legs were bare but the sound of their marching feet tramping on the cobbles of the roadway could be heard even from a distance of two hundred paces. At a shouted command, the column halted with every man stamping his foot at the same time. Another shout and they all turned in unison to face the Wall. Then they began marching, but this time the men on the road nearest to the Boresti stayed practically still, marking time while the whole column swung around them, wheeling on to the grass between the road and the Wall to form two ranks of men facing the tribesmen.

Brude tried to count how many men were in each row but lost count and had to start again. Like many of the tribesmen he was almost mesmerised by the smooth efficiency of their manoeuvring. The Romans acted as though the Boresti were of no account. Now they moved their arms, revealing that they were each carrying two javelins, not one as Brude had thought. Each man now held one javelin in his left hand, which also supported the huge red and yellow shield, while the one in his right hand was clearly ready for use. They stopped, standing still watching the tribesmen.

Then the horsemen reappeared, this time on the other side of the ditch. They rode past at a swift canter, soon disappearing behind the high turf wall, which hid the ditch from view. Brude wondered what Nechtan would do. The Roman infantrymen were blocking the road ahead while the horsemen were obviously aiming to get round behind the Boresti. They could cross the ditch at the watchtower where Gartnait had been hurt, then come up behind the tribesmen. It was as Brude had feared. The Boresti were trapped between the Wall and the ditch.

There were really only two choices; attack or retreat. To Brude, there was only one choice. To go back now would be a disgrace.

Nechtan obviously agreed. He raised his voice so that all could hear him. "There are only one hundred of them! We have half as many again! And we are Boresti!" The Boresti cheered, waving their spears aggressively. One of the women, bare-breasted, her upper body almost entirely blue with war dye, ran forwards, shaking her spear at the Romans. Nechtan yelled, "Belatucadros is with us, so let us show these Romans what it is to fight real warriors. They have the high ground, but we shall soon take it from them!"

Brude, despite his misgivings, was caught up in the excitement. He felt no fear, for his friends were with him. He saw Colm's eyes shining, heard his cheering and knew that he was doing the same himself. Nechtan was right. No matter how impressively the Romans might march, they were outnumbered and could not hope to stop the Boresti.

Then the cheering subsided as it became clear that the Romans had other ideas.

There was another shouted order from the neat ranks. The first Roman line began marching down towards the Boresti, moving in unison at a slow, steady pace, forsaking the slight advantage afforded by the shallow slope. The second rank followed a few paces behind. Brude suddenly felt doubt grip him. Why were they attacking? They were outnumbered and had the advantage of the high ground yet they were marching down to meet the Boresti. They made no sound. There were no war cries, no waving of spears, no yells or taunts. The silence of their steady advance was unnerving.

Nechtan bellowed his war-cry and the tribesmen answered it, yelling at the top of their voices, banging spears against their shields, letting the Romans know they were ready. The Romans paid no attention, simply marching on, not a sound coming from them in reply.

Deciding to seize back the initiative, Nechtan yelled the order to charge. The tribesmen responded eagerly, cheering as they ran towards the enemy, racing to be the first to kill a Roman. Brude, although he was fast and knew he could have outstripped most of his neighbours, obeyed his father's shouted reminder to stayed close to him on his left side. Colm was to Brude's left, screaming like a madman while others ran ahead, jostling and barging each other in their eagerness. Mairead's father Fionnlagh, normally a placid man who tended the village's sheep, was just ahead of Brude, yelling as fiercely as any of them.

They got to within fifty paces of the Roman front rank when the Romans stopped, drew back their right arms and hurled their javelins. In the time it took them to do that, the first tribesmen had closed the gap to within forty paces. The javelins struck home with awesome power. Men fell, screaming, or tried to catch the javelins on their shields, only to find that the long iron spikes pierced the wicker and hide with frightening ease to strike at the unprotected flesh beneath. Still running, Brude watched in horror as any men who had escaped injury when they managed to catch the spears on their shields, found they had no choice but to drop their shields to the ground because the Roman javelins had bent on impact, the long iron tip protruding through the shield while the wooden haft bent at a right angle, dragging the shield down, rendering it useless. With discarded shields, the men had no protection against the next volley of javelins hurled by the second rank of Romans while the first rank crouched to give them room to throw. Brude saw Fionnlagh go down, a javelin taking him in the chest, showering blood. Brude yelled to cover his fear as he ran past the stricken warrior, knowing he was dead and that Mairead now had no father.

Then the first Roman rank rose to their feet to fling their second volley. By this time, Brude, leaping over fallen men, dropped spears and discarded shields, was barely twenty paces from the Romans. He saw a javelin hurtling straight at him. He dodged to his right, flinging out his left arm to knock the javelin aside, somehow catching its flight so that the point did not actually hit his shield. Colm yelled in pain as the javelin crashed into his arm, side on. Brude ignored him and kept running.

The final volley of javelins from the second rank of Romans flew over his head but he knew that the awful weapons had done terrible damage to the charging tribesmen. Their attack was disjointed, broken apart by the volleys. Ahead of him, a few men reached the Roman ranks only to find a wall of shields with the sharp, shining blades of short swords gleaming in the spaces between the soldiers. The Romans, still eerily silent, stepped forwards in unison, working together to meet the charging tribesmen head on.

And the carnage began.

Using their enormous shields to batter the tribesmen down, the short swords stabbed repeatedly forwards. While the Boresti flailed and jabbed extravagantly with their spears, trying vainly to breach the Roman line, the Romans were economical with their thrusts, the sword blades biting home then withdrawing. Men fell, their blood covering the grass. Women as well, for the Romans treated them no differently. Then Brude saw his father swinging his own sword uselessly against the shield of the soldier in front of him. Brude, scarcely aware of anything apart from the men on either side and in front of him, flung himself to his own right, aiming for the narrow gap between the shield of his direct opponent and the man facing his father. Jabbing his spear overhand, he yelled in triumph as the wickedly sharp point caught the Roman in the neck, releasing a fountain of bright red blood.

Time seemed to slow. Brude's father leaped into the gap as the Roman soldier fell. He swept his sword in a wide arc to knock over the man to his right. Brude heard the sound of his iron sword ringing on the man's armour, cutting through the din of battle. He made to follow his father into the gap but was battered by the huge shield of the Roman to his left. He lost his footing as he was thumped again with incredible force, the metal rim of the shield catching him just above his left eye. He stumbled, felt his knees go weak and fell to the ground. As he dropped, he saw that his father was now confronted by the entire second rank of Roman soldiers. He tried to call out, to tell his father to run, but could only manage a strangled croak. He landed on the fallen Roman soldier, rolled helplessly, his vision obscured by blood streaming into his eyes. He hit the ground, lying awkwardly face down on the grass, his legs twisted and entangled with the limbs of the Roman he had killed. Without warning, a huge blow hit him as someone crashed down on top of him, then something hard struck the back of his already battered head.

Everything went black.

A.D. 209

Peart looked more prosperous than he remembered. From the height of the hills overlooking the wide valley of the Tava, he gazed down and saw the village nestled beside the river, surrounded by a strong wooden palisade. Smoke curled up into the afternoon sky from the large roundhouses. Cattle, sheep and goats dotted the lush fields and people were everywhere, going about their daily lives. By the standards of the empire, it was a poor place but it compared favourably to other Pritani villages Brude had passed on the long walk north from the Wall.

He wondered how much it would have changed. He had discovered that the Selgovae, once a proud people, were virtually gone, their lands and the people themselves now ruled by the Votadini who were ever friends to the Romans. The leaders of the Votadini used Roman goods, drank Roman wine from Roman glasses and some of them even had Roman-style houses with walls of brick topped by clay roof tiles. They were not part of the empire but they were friends of the empire. The rich men of the Votadini became richer while, as was ever the Roman way, the poor became poorer. The Wall, Brude thought, cast a long shadow.

Would Gartnait of Peart be like that, he wondered. Was he, too, now trying to be a Roman? Brude looked to his right, towards the east, and saw the Tava, sparkling in the spring sun, broadening as it went. There, away in the distance he thought he could make out the black finger that was Broch Tava, standing like a sentinel on its hilltop at the wide mouth of the river. It was very distant, almost lost in the haze, and he might have been mistaken but he told himself he was nearly home. The thought filled him with a mixture of emotions; anticipation and apprehension in equal measure.

Tugging the mule, he set off down the hill towards Peart, cautiously eyeing the darkening clouds to the west. If he was lucky he would reach the village before the rain started and would be able to get shelter for the night. Not that he wasn't used to sleeping outdoors but warmth and shelter were always preferable.

The sky was overcast by the time he reached the gates of Peart. Two warriors stood there, watching him approach. He knew they would be suspicious of his appearance. His hair was still a lot shorter than any Pritani would wear and his sandals were definitely Roman. He had put away his Roman sword, wrapping it carefully in his bedroll beside his wooden rudis. His only visible weapon was the small dagger at his left hip. He had, though, acquired a long, roughly hewn staff that he used as a walking aid and which would serve as a more than adequate weapon if need be. He didn't think he'd need it; most villages welcomed travelling tradesmen.

The guards were cautious but not unfriendly. One of them led him into the village to meet the head man. Brude followed calmly, making sure he gave friendly smiles to the villagers he passed. Most of them watched him curiously as he went by but he soon had a small group of followers, mostly children.

The head man's home was a large roundhouse, bigger than the other dwellings, wattle and daub walls rising from a stone foundation, the conical roof made from turf laid over long branches, a thin column of smoke rising from the central hole at the apex. Another guard stood there, spear angled across his body. He ducked inside the low doorway when Brude's guard told him that a travelling merchant had arrived to pay his respects. A few moments later, the head man came out to greet his visitor, followed by a group of young men and an older woman. Brude recognised the head man immediately. It was Gartnait who stood in front of him.

Even after nearly thirteen years Brude knew him. He was older, well over fifty, with his long, braided hair greying, his skin wrinkled and flabby around his neck and face. He was plump, his belly large beneath his well-sewn clothes, a golden torc about his right arm. He had rings on every finger. His left arm, though, Brude noticed, was badly misshapen below the elbow and the fingers of his left hand were arched like a claw, unmoving. He looked Brude over as he opened his right palm in welcome. "Greetings, stranger," he said. "I am Gartnait, son of Oengus, head man of the Boresti of Peart. And these are my people."

Brude nodded at the formal welcome. "Greetings, Gartnait," he replied. "I am Brude. I bring goods to trade and news from afar. May I shelter in your home for the night?"

Gartnait nodded. "Of course. Your name is Brude, you say? That is a Pritani name, is it not?"

Brude had anticipated the question. He had not given his father's name because he did not want news of his return to reach Broch Tava before he did and also because he could not be sure how he would be welcomed if they knew who he was. Even within tribes, the Pritani often quarrelled amongst themselves and he had no idea what the present relations between Peart and Broch Tava were like. To deflect the issue, he said, "I have several names, for I have travelled a long way. Brude will suffice."

"And where are you from?" Gartnait asked.

"Most recently, Germania. Before that, Rome."

There was a murmur from the assembled villagers. Even Gartnait looked surprised. "You have been to Rome?" His eyes narrowed slightly. "The Romans are no friends to us."

"Nor to me," said Brude, "but I bring some of their goods which I will trade for shelter and some food."

Gartnait nodded. "Then welcome. Let us see your goods and then you shall eat with me and tell me of your travels."

A woman brought a stool for Gartnait to sit on. Many of the villagers sat on the ground in a semi-circle around the doorway to the hut while Brude unpacked some of the packages fastened to his mule. Anxious to conclude this before the rain arrived, Brude took out some of the smaller, more valuable items and presented them to Gartnait; some rings of gold, brooches and a fine leather belt with an ornate buckle. He added a small brass cooking pot, then carefully unwrapped two finely crafted red pottery beakers, which brought a sparkle to the eyes of the woman standing behind Gartnait.

There was some obligatory haggling before Brude accepted a fine new cloak and some warm, woollen leggings in exchange for the beakers and pot. He presented the belt and some brooches to Gartnait as a gift and they clasped hands to seal the deal. Brude could have traded more of his goods to the other villagers but, in truth, he wanted to keep most of what he had left, so when the first drops of rain began to spatter on the ground, he used that excuse to pack up his wares. He unpacked the mule and Gartnait had some men carry the baggage into the large house. Another man took the mule away, promising to see it fed and watered, so Brude ducked into the house at Gartnait's invitation.

The interior was gloomy, lit only by the central fire and the light admitted by the two doorways, which were on opposite sides of the hut. The smell of wood smoke and damp earth recalled memories of his boyhood, much of which had been spent in houses like this. They sat in a circle around the fire, Brude sitting on Gartnait's right. He was introduced to the others. Three of the young men, two of them scarcely more than boys, were Gartnait's sons, while four others who joined were leading men of the village who were accompanied by their wives. There were two young girls aged around ten who were Gartnait's daughters. The old man told Brude that he had another son, his oldest boy, Oengus, who was away on a hunting trip. The woman who had been so taken by the Roman beakers turned out, as Brude had suspected, to be Gartnait's wife. She was short and plump with a happy demeanour, though she scolded the serving girls into dishing up broth and meat for the guests.

Brude exchanged greetings with everyone, knowing he would be unlikely to remember all their names. Gratefully, he accepted a wooden goblet of ale from one of the serving girls. They toasted Belisama, the goddess of rivers, who was important to the people of Peart, and then toasted Taranis, god of storms and thunder, so that the rain now pouring down would be no more than a simple rainfall.

Brude enjoyed the broth and the tender strips of lamb that followed but was careful not to drink too much. He remembered the first time he had been to Peart all those years before and he was determined not to suffer the same sort of hangover.

During and after the meal, he told them news he had picked up from the Votadini as he had passed through their land on his way north but what they really wanted to hear about was Rome. Eagerly, they all plied him with questions. Was it really the largest city in the world? How big was the empire? Did the emperor really sleep on a bed of feathers? He spun them some tall tales, knowing they would discount half of what he said anyway, for it was the Pritani custom to boast and exaggerate their stories and they would assume he was doing the same. In truth he only had to exaggerate a little for Rome was so different, so far beyond their experience, that they could scarcely comprehend the wonders of the empire.

The subject turned to memories of warfare and Gartnait, the ale loosening his tongue, recounted the great raid, which had taken place when his youngest son was still a young boy. Brude sat still, listening intently as the old man said drunkenly, "Many of our kinsmen did not return but those that did, came home wealthier than any of the Boresti before us."

Acting as innocently as he could, Brude asked, "Your raid was a success then?"

"For those who came back, aye, it was. But I led forty men away and only nineteen of us returned." He stared into the fire while the other men nodded sadly, lost in their memories.

"But you returned with much plunder?" Brude asked, smiling.

"More than we could have hoped," Gartnait agreed. "Peart is now mightier than ever before."

"Did the Romans not pursue you?" Brude persisted. "That is their usual habit."

Gartnait shrugged. "We heard they struck at the Selgovae and burned many villages but they never came this far."

"Too scared of us!" laughed one of Gartnait's young sons.

Brude ignored the laughter and changed the subject. "Can you tell me what other villages there are near here? I have heard that the land of the Boresti is large and I would like to see as much of it as I can. Are there villages further along the river?"

Gartnait gave a snort. "There are some farms and small places. The next place of any size is Broch Tava, out where the river joins the sea."

Brude detected an undercurrent of animosity in Gartnait's words. "Perhaps I will go there. Do you know the head man?"

Gartnait frowned as he took another swig from his beaker. He looked at Brude darkly. "His name is Colm. He is not to be trusted. You would be best to avoid Broch Tava."

Colm.

Brude's heart missed a beat. So Colm had survived and had returned to become head man of the village. He was aware of mutterings from the men around the fire at the mention of Colm's name. Willing his emotions into check, showing the blank expression he had learned to adopt many years ago, he asked Gartnait, "You think he would cheat me?"

"Colm would cheat his own mother if he still had one. He dreams of becoming leader of all the Boresti. He even asked to marry one of my daughters so that he can have a son who will become head man of Peart."

"He is not married then?" Brude was surprised; the secret fear he had nursed for almost thirteen years may have proved unfounded.

"Married! Of course he is. He's got a son as well. He just wants more. He wants everything."

"He doesn't like to lose," Brude murmured absently.

"What's that?" Gartnait asked him.

Brude covered his mistake as best he could. "He sounds like someone I once knew. Someone who didn't like to lose."

"That's Colm all right. Each year he takes more and more from those who live near him, and he builds his village all the time. He has over seventy warriors now."

Brude raised an eyebrow in surprise. Few villages had more than a handful of warriors for they were the elite, the men who owned the most cattle, the richest men who spent their time hunting and practising the arts of warfare. When the Pritani went to war, the bulk of the fighters came from the ordinary villagers, farmers, herdsmen and fishermen who swapped their ploughs and nets for spears to follow the warriors into battle. To have seventy warriors was unusual to say the least. That was an extra seventy mouths to be fed by the rest of the village.

Gartnait shook his head sadly then brightened up. "But let us talk of better things than Colm of Broch Tava. Tell me of the women of Rome. Are they beautiful?"

Brude span some more stories until it grew dark, then he was given a space beside the wall, a mattress stuffed with old straw and a blanket. He lay awake, unable to sleep, while the rain pounded down. He thought about Colm. And Mairead.

The morning dawned bright and chill with light clouds floating high in a pale blue sky. The air was filled with the smell of the damp earth after the overnight downpour but it promised to be a good day for travelling. After a breakfast of porridge, Brude packed his goods onto his mule. Some women gathered round and he traded a few trinkets for some dried meat, bread, honey and a small bag of salt. Then he threw on his new cloak, fastened it with one of the many brooches he had left and said his farewells to Gartnait and his family.

A small crowd of children accompanied him to the bridge, scampering round his feet, pestering him with questions about where he was from and what he had seen. He laughed them off and crossed the long wooden bridge to the north bank of the Tava, turning east, out past the high cliffs and onto the river plain.

He took his time, enjoying the peace of the springtime countryside. Bees were buzzing from flower to flower and the blossom filled the apple trees. It had taken him so long to get here that he wanted to savour every moment. The thought of reaching Broch Tava still brought some trepidation but he remembered the words of Cleon, his friend from the home of Aquila in Rome. Cleon was a Greek, an ex-slave and a follower of the teachings of Epicurus. Whenever Brude was worried about something, Cleon would smile his friendly smile and tell him he should not concern himself about things he could not affect. "What is, is," Cleon would say. "Deal with things when you meet them but don't worry about what might or might not happen." Brude would always reply that it was easier to say that than to do it and Cleon would always agree. "But it helps to try," he would say with a happy smile.

Brude wondered what Cleon was doing right at that moment. He imagined his friend eating his hearty breakfast before dragging out his scrolls and tallies, ready for another day of recording the household's business affairs. He smiled at the thought. Cleon was always happy and at ease with the world. The only time Brude had seen him sad was the day they had said goodbye, nearly three years ago, when tears had run down Cleon's cheeks as they clasped hands for the last time. Of all the things and people he had encountered in the empire, Brude missed Cleon the most. He wondered whether the old Greek would be happy if he was here now, in the lands of the Boresti, far away from all the comforts of Rome and living among the savages he had heard so much about. Brude laughed to himself at the thought. Cleon would claim to be content anywhere, he knew, but would admit to preferring to be content in comfortable surroundings.

Brude walked along the wide plain, the hills away to his left, the Tava, much wider and deeper now, off to his right, hidden behind the trees. By the time he reached Broch Tava the river would be about two miles wide and merging with the open sea. He mentally kicked himself. A mile was a Roman measure, one thousand paces, not a term the Pritani would use at all. He was no longer a Roman, he told himself. He did not feel Roman. All the time he had been there, he had known he was Brude, son of Anndra of the Boresti, a Pritani warrior. Yet the closer he got to home, the more Roman he felt. The feeling had come to him again last night, sitting with Gartnait and the men of Peart, one of them by birth yet not one of them. It was an uncomfortable feeling.

He went back to studying his surroundings. There was a trackway of sorts but he decided to avoid that. The plain was very fertile, good farm land, with several farmsteads and isolated houses scattered across it, all the way from Peart to the hills west of Broch Tava. He was not in the mood to meet any of the locals because he wanted peace to savour his journey home, so he led his laden mule through the scattered woodland, leaving the trackway to the south. Knowing the dangers for any lone traveller, whether following a track or not, he unwrapped his gladius and looped the strap over his left shoulder so that the sword hung at his right hip. It felt comfortable and reassuring.

He stopped at mid-day, making a cold camp in a wide clearing beside a shallow stream, which burbled its way cheerily through the trees. He left the mule to graze, knowing it was unlikely to wander off, and sat down, leaning against a birch tree to eat some of the bread and honey. The sun was warm now so he took off his cloak, laying it on the ground beside him. He closed his eyes, listening to the sounds of the woodland surrounding him. Soon, he drifted off to sleep.

He woke with a start, unsure what had roused him. The sun had not moved far; it was still early afternoon so he must have only dozed for a short time. The mule was still nearby, stripping some leaves from a small bush. Rising to his feet, he went to fetch it, looping the halter rope round a branch to make sure it did not run off. He looked around carefully, eyes and ears straining for signs of what had woken him, some sound that was out of place. It could have been a passing deer or fox, he thought, or even a wolf though that was unlikely. He was not bothered by that, for wolves rarely attacked people, especially in the springtime when other food was plentiful. A bear would be a different matter entirely. If it was a bear, he would have no option but to flee. He glanced at the mule. Whatever it was had not spooked it. He checked the wind, little more than a slight breeze wafting from the west. So if there was something approaching he guessed it was coming from the east otherwise the mule would have been more concerned.

He decided to fetch his cloak and staff and set off again, chiding himself for being scared of shadows but he had barely taken two steps when he saw movement as some men came out of the trees on the far side of the stream. He stopped and looked at them. There were three of them, long-haired and painted with blue dye, dressed in wool and leather. They were carrying spears and the leading man also had a sword, a symbol of high status, strapped to his waist, but they wore no helmets and carried no shields. They had seen him, so came out of the trees cautiously, checking to see whether he was alone. As they walked into the sunlight, he saw that one of them, a short, dark-haired man, was leading a bull, a magnificent long-haired beast with wide, sweeping horns and a ring through its nose. The third man was also leading a rope. At the end of it, hands tied together, was a young boy of around ten or twelve years of age.

He knew them now. They had been on a cattle raid and had stolen someone's prime bull. And, for some reason, they had taken the boy as well.

Satisfied that he was alone, the three men splashed across the shallow stream. The leader, a man in his early twenties, stopped a few paces away and looked sneeringly at Brude. "What have we here? A stranger in the lands of the Boresti?"

Brude smiled as pleasantly as he could. "My name is Brude."

"And where are you from, stranger?" Brude saw that the man was eyeing the sword that hung at Brude's right hip, greed clear in his expression.

"Many places," Brude replied cautiously. He had no desire to get involved in a fight, especially against three armed men, but the young man's arrogance annoyed him and he felt his own anger rising. He masked it with his practised blank expression. He looked at the other two men. The short one leading the bull was young as well, probably under twenty, and had the look of a born follower. The other man was taller, well muscled with strong arms bearing many painted designs, his long hair braided, his eyes sharp and watching carefully. He, Brude thought, was probably the most dangerous of the three if it came to a fight though he seemed willing to take his lead from the man with the sword who was probably his lord. Brude looked back at the swordsman. "And who are you?"

The man glared at him as if Brude should have known him. "I am Oengus, son of Gartnait," he replied. "I expect you have heard of me." His eyes blazed a challenge.

"Not until yesterday," Brude said. "Your father said you were out hunting." He looked pointedly at the bull and the young boy. "Successfully, it seems. Who's the boy?"

"Nobody," snapped Oengus but the boy lifted his gaze to look at Brude. Defiantly, he said, "I am Castatin, son of Colm of Broch Tava."

Oengus rounded on the boy, snapping at him to be silent. To the tall man holding the boy's tether, he said, "Fothair, if he speaks again, hit him. Hard."

The man named Fothair nodded in acknowledgement but without enthusiasm. He turned to glare at the boy, jerking the rope to make the lad stumble and nearly fall.

Brude stared at the boy as he struggled to regain his balance. Castatin, son of Colm. The son of his friend. The son of the head man of Broch Tava. He tore his gaze away and looked Oengus in the eyes. "Let the boy go," he said firmly.

Oengus laughed at him. "Are you mad? He is a hostage for his father's behaviour. And I do not take orders from wanderers like you."

Brude held his arms at his side, his palms open and facing Oengus. "Then let us trade. You can take the mule and all that is on him except my personal gear. You can even keep the bull. Give the boy to me."

Oengus did not even consider the offer. "I have a better idea," he said. "You give me the mule and your sword and I'll let you live." He hefted his spear, holding it in two hands, the point an arm's length from Brude's chest.

Brude glanced at the others. The short man was grinning in anticipation, the tall Fothair was watching carefully, his face expressionless but his eyes alert, while the boy Castatin was staring, eyes wide, at Oengus. Brude looked at Oengus again, his arms still at his side, ignoring the threat of the spear. "I do not want to fight you," he said.

The short man laughed while Oengus grinned mockingly. "If you are afraid, then give me your sword and I will let you go."

Brude looked at him calmly. "I am afraid," he admitted. "Afraid of breaking my oath."

Oengus frowned. "Oath? What oath?"

"I made a promise not to kill any more. So release the boy and we'll all go our separate ways."

Fothair said, "Oengus, we have no time for this. Leave him and let us go home."

"Do you think I am afraid of this wandering merchant?" Oengus snapped, his eyes never leaving Brude's face.

"No," Fothair said, "but he does not seem afraid of you either. Come, we have what we wanted."

"I want his sword," Oengus hissed between gritted teeth. "Last chance, merchant."

"You are a fool," spat Brude. "Your friend has more sense than you."

Without warning, Oengus roared a challenge and lunged with his spear, aiming for a quick killing blow that would drive the point of the blade into Brude's chest. Brude, ready for the attack, swayed back, twisting his body and moving lightly on his feet. With his left hand, he grabbed the shaft of the spear just behind the blade as it shot past where his chest had been only a moment before. He pulled, dragging Oengus towards him and crashed his own right shoulder into Oengus' chest. Oengus gasped as the blow took all the air from his lungs. He let go of the spear as he fought for breath but Brude's fist thumped into his stomach and he doubled over only to meet the shaft of the spear as it swung viciously upwards. It caught him on the face with a loud smack, breaking his nose and jerking his head back, blood spraying in the air. Brude's fist caught him again, smashing into the side of his head to send him sprawling to the ground.

Brude span, facing the other two men who were looking at him in awe, unable to comprehend how Oengus had been felled so quickly. The man called Fothair released the rope holding the boy and gripped his spear with both hands. Brude saw that he was afraid, yet determined to support his lord. "We'll get him together, Cet," Fothair shouted to his companion. The short man, eyes wide with fear, also readied his spear. He circled to Brude's left, leaving the bull, which, alarmed by the smell of blood, bellowed in protest as it trotted off to the stream.

Brude said nothing. The time for talking was past. Oengus had been caught by surprise but these two were ready for him. He dismissed Cet, concentrating on Fothair who jabbed his spear forwards, aiming for Brude's eyes but not over-committing himself as Oengus had done. Brude smiled the smile of a wolf. He hefted the spear he had taken from Oengus into his left hand, holding it two-thirds of the way down its length, clamping the lower part against his left thigh. With his right hand he deftly pulled his short sword from its sheath, twirling it to hold it underhand, the point towards Fothair.

The tall man watched the blade as Brude waved it gently, keeping the tip moving. Then he stepped forwards, whipping his left arm so that his spear crashed against Fothair's own spear, knocking it wide to expose his left side to Brude's sword. The blade lunged forwards, aiming for Fothair's neck. The tall man let go of his spear, staggering backwards to evade the deadly thrust. Brude saw the boy Castatin dive forwards, crouching on the ground behind Fothair so that the tall man fell over him, arms flailing as he crashed to the earth.

Brude turned again, looking for the man Cet, who was trying to get behind him. The young man stopped when he saw Brude face him, fear etched in every part of his face. "Drop your spear," Brude told him. Cet did so immediately. "Now go help your friend in case he chokes on his own tongue."

The man called Fothair was struggling to his feet, groping for his spear but Brude quickly sprang to stand over him. He jabbed his own spear downwards, letting the blade strike the ground barely two fingers' breadth from Fothair's nose. "Don't be stupid," Brude told him.

Fothair exhaled in defeat. He lay on his back, looking up at Brude standing over him. "What now?" he asked.

"The boy comes with me. You can keep the bull."

"Oengus will not forget this," Fothair said.

"I hope not. If we meet again I hope he has more sense than to try to kill me." He turned to the boy and beckoned him over. The lad approached warily, his face shining with excitement. Brude lifted his tied hands and easily cut away the bonds with the sharp blade of his sword. "Are you all right?" he asked the boy.

Castatin nodded. "That was amazing. Where did you learn to fight like that?"

"Rome."

"That's a Roman sword, isn't it? My father told me about them. Are you a Roman?"

"No," Brude told him. "No, I'm not a Roman. I'm from Broch Tava."

Castatin was full of questions, most of which Brude answered sparingly or not at all. The boy was tired but excited and talked incessantly. Brude let him ride on the mule, unloading one large pack which he strapped over his own shoulders. They headed for the track for it was the fastest way to get to Broch Tava and Brude now wanted to put as much distance as he could between himself and Peart. "You should have brought the bull," Castatin chided. "It was my father's stud bull. I was supposed to be watching him but they caught me last night."

"I'm sure your father can get another bull. It's not so easy to replace a son."

Castatin looked doubtful. "It's his favourite bull," he said. "He'll be very angry."

"Then he can be angry at me. Has he still got a temper?"

Castatin looked at him, puzzled. "Do you really know him?"

"A long time ago. Before you were born." He hesitated, unsure whether to ask the question he had to ask. "What is your mother's name? Maybe I know her as well."

"She's called Mairead. I'll be head man when I'm older because of her."

"I remember," said Brude softly as his dreams evaporated.

They reached the track and headed east towards a low line of hills. He knew that when they reached the top they would be able to see the last hills before Broch Tava, including the flat-topped Law. He knew now that the Law had once been a volcano, which gave it its peculiar shape. Why, he wondered, had he had to travel so far to learn about something so close to home? In the lore of the Boresti it was a holy place, possessed by spirits and fire demons and was shunned by mortals.

Castatin suddenly yelled in delight and pointed up the track. Brude saw a group of riders galloping down the slope towards them, raising a small cloud of dust as they came. They were riding horses, not the small war ponies he remembered. He had rarely seen so many Pritani horsemen together at one time. There must have been nearly twenty of them. "It's my father!" Castatin squealed with glee.

Brude stopped and waited as the riders reined in a few paces from him. There was Colm, still tall, still dark-haired and handsome, swirling blue designs painted on either cheek, dressed in fine linen with a bronze breastplate on his chest and a long sword at his hip. He glared at Castatin then at Brude and Brude saw that Castatin's joy had turned to concern. He had expected the boy to run to his father, but he stayed seated on the mule, biting his lips nervously. From behind Colm the riders, all armed for war, fanned out to surround them.

Colm nudged his horse forward, approaching slowly. He looked at his son. "Are you harmed? Who was it who took you?"

"I am fine, Father. It was Oengus of Peart who stole your bull and took me. This is Brude. He rescued me."

Colm's gaze snapped to Brude who smiled back at him. "Hello, Colm. It's been a long time, hasn't it?"

There was a moment's puzzlement in his eyes, then Colm's jaw dropped and the blood drained from his face. "Brude?" he whispered. "You can't be Brude. Brude is dead!"

Brude laughed, rolling up his right sleeve to reveal the tattoo on his forearm. It was a swirling design signifying his coming of age, the only tattoo he had ever had. "I got this the same day you got yours."

Colm sat there on his horse, his eyes darting from the tattoo to Brude's face, his mouth open, unable to speak. At last he composed himself. Brude was ready for a warm greeting, a clasping of hands, a brotherly hug. Instead Colm just said, "You are alive, then? After all these years?"

"It's taken me a long time to get home," Brude said. "You have done well while I was away, I hear. You have a fine son and people tell me you are head man now."

Colm nodded. He did not seem to know how to respond to Brude's sudden reappearance. Realising his men were looking at the two of them curiously, he remembered his manners. "I'm sorry, this is quite a shock. You obviously have a story to tell us. I'll have some men escort you to my… to our village. I'm sure your mother will be pleased you have returned to us." Without giving Brude time to respond or ask any questions, he then looked at Castatin. "Where's my bull?"

"Oengus still has him," the boy replied nervously. "They're not far away, though. They're going through the woods toward Peart. Only three of them. I can take you to where we left them."

Colm shook his head. "You are going home." To Brude he said, "I will leave four men to escort you. I have some cattle thieves to catch."

"If you find them, do me a favour."

"What?"

"Don't harm the man called Fothair. The tall one."

"What is he to you?" Colm demanded.

"Nothing. But he seems a good man."

"I'll bring them all back in chains," Colm snarled. He quickly told four riders to stay with Brude and Castatin, then jabbed his heels to his mount's flanks and led the rest of his men along the track. Brude watched him go, bemused by the reception Colm had given him. He didn't know what he had expected, but it wasn't that coldness.

"He doesn't seem very pleased to see you," Castatin said.

"It will take him time to get used to it," Brude replied. "After all, I've been dead a long time."

A.D. 196

Brude was being crushed. He tried to open his eyes but only his right eye responded and all he could see was darkness because his face was pressed against the ground. His left eye was caked shut. He made an attempt to move his arms, to push himself up but he felt weak and dizzy and there was something heavy lying across him. His throat was parched and his lips were dry and cracked. He had to get up. He groaned with the effort as he managed, at last, to free his left arm. He reached up to feel his face. There was a crust of what he knew must be dried blood all down the left side, clogging his eye shut. He ran his fingers up to his forehead, feeling a damp stickiness.

Then he heard voices. He could not make out the words but there were people nearby. Or were they far away? His befuddled brain could make no sense of his surroundings but he tried to call for help, to wave his arm, to let them see he was still alive.

The pressure weighing down on his back was suddenly eased. He knew that whatever was on top of him was being lifted off. Then it was gone altogether, allowing him to roll to his side, to let his right eye see daylight. He immediately wished that he was blind again. The weight that had been on him was that of his father's corpse. Anndra of the Boresti now lay on his back, his unseeing eyes staring skywards, just like the dead Roman sentry they had seen in the watchtower. Brude lay there, staring at his father, feeling numb all over. His father had worn a fine breastplate of bronze, which was battered and bashed, but what had killed him was a stab to his throat where the flies now gathered round a raw, open wound.

Brude was hauled to his feet, staggered, nearly fell, and got a slap on his face for his trouble. Strong arms dragged him away and he was dimly aware that he was passing more bodies lying scattered across the grass. Then he was unceremoniously thrown to the ground where he lay still, unable to move. "Get up!" a voice hissed in warning. "Get up or they'll just kill you." Hands reached for him, supporting him until he managed at last to sit up. "Here. Drink!" Someone held a clay beaker to his lips. He swallowed, desperate to quench his thirst. The water was tepid and unpleasant but he drank it all. Then he looked up and saw a man he recognised but whose name would not come to him. "You'll be all right," the man told him. "I think you took a nasty blow to the head, but you'll survive."

Gradually Brude's senses recovered. He felt better when more water came, brought by a Roman soldier, allowing him to wash the dried blood from his face. After some cautious rubbing, his left eye was freed from the congealed blood and he was able to see reasonably well.

What he saw dismayed him.

There were thirty-four of them, all men, most of them wounded, although none too seriously. Four Roman soldiers stood guarding them while other Romans wandered the battle-field, checking for survivors. Brude saw that any fallen tribes-man who was too badly wounded was simply despatched by a thrust of the short Roman swords. One more tribesman, his right hand mutilated by the loss of three fingers and limping badly, was brought to join the prisoners. The rest were either dead or gone. There was a cluster of bodies where the two battle lines had met but most had obviously been killed when they turned to flee. The corpses, both men and women, were scattered in a long line, heading back over the rise and, he supposed, beyond that. It had been more a slaughter than a battle, for the actual fighting must have lasted only a few moments while the Romans had thrown their javelins and then marched forwards, swords stabbing in those terrifying, short, brutally efficient killing thrusts.

He tried to count the corpses but he had such a headache that he had to give up. All he was able to count was the number of Roman dead because they were laid out on the grass only a few paces from where the prisoners sat. There were only four of them, lying on their backs still wearing their armour. He looked at his companion, a man from Broch Tava whose name suddenly came back to him. He was Frual, one of the village's best fishermen. Brude recalled that he had two children, with a third on the way. He was a quiet man, strong yet gentle and not given to too much boasting. "What happened?" Brude asked him.

Frual shrugged. "We lost. We couldn't break their line and they just killed us. Most of the men ran when you and your father went down. We thought you were dead."

"Colm! Did you see what happened to Colm?"

Frual shook his head. "He's not with us and I don't think he's among the dead here, but the Romans chased us all the way back to where we crossed the wall. The horses got a lot of men as we ran and when we got to the tower there wasn't enough space for us all to get out. Nechtan got away, and so did Gartnait, but a lot of us were stuck on this side of the wall. Then the Romans caught up with us and we laid down our weapons." He looked apologetically at Brude. "It was either that or be killed."

"Maybe Colm got away then," said Brude.

"Forget him," Frual told him roughly. "We have to look after ourselves now."

A wagon arrived, pulled by two large horses. The Romans gathered all the weapons and armour they could and began piling them on to it. The prisoners, though, were prodded to their feet and marched westwards along the road. Brude felt weak and dizzy but Frual helped him and it turned out that they did not have far to go. Beyond the next rise was a large Roman fort, enclosed within a massive stone wall. Brude realised that this was where the sentries had been signalling. No wonder, he thought, that the Romans had found them so quickly. He suspected the Selgovae must have known how close the fort was, which was why they had headed in the opposite direction, leaving the Boresti to bear the brunt of the Roman attack. He felt he should be angry about that, but all he felt was numb and empty.

They were herded into a large building made with walls of brick with small, high windows and only one door. There was little talking. They sat or lay on the bare floor, tired, hurt and lost. Brude tried to sleep but Frual kept him awake. "Not good to sleep after that bang on the head," he told him. "You might not wake up." Brude must have dozed off anyway and when he awoke he saw by the change in the angle of the sunlight coming through the high windows that it must be afternoon.

They were brought some food and water. A little while later a young soldier came in and spoke to them in a language they could make out though his accent was strange and some words were unfamiliar. He told them that he was called Carallus and they were now slaves of imperial Rome. Then he told them all they had to strip, bathe and have their hair shaved. "You may bring disease here," he explained. So they were marched out, forced to strip naked and pile their clothes onto a fire which had been lit in an open space within the fort. Then they were given cold water and some hard, grainy soap to wash with, always under the eyes of the Romans. Many soldiers came along to watch in a disinterested sort of way. Brude saw some who wore fine red cloaks and solid breastplates. He could tell these were important men but he got a cuff on the back of his head from a soldier who barked at him in Latin. Carallus translated, "Keep your gaze lowered, slave."

After they had washed, their heads were shaved which to most was the worst part of the day for the Pritani were proud of long, strong hair. It showed their virility and to lose it was a source of shame. "It will grow back," Carallus reassured them. Once they had all been shaved, they were examined by a small man who was, according to Carallus, a doctor although he did little to help the wounds they had other than to wrap some linen bandages round them. Then they were given short tunics to wear before being taken back to their large cell room.

Another light meal of plain oatmeal gruel and some water was brought to them as evening came. There was barely enough to go around but one of the men, a large warrior called Drugh, one of Nechtan's men, insisted that they all share the food equally. Nobody argued, despite the hunger; they were all in this together.

They had no blankets and nowhere to sleep except the hard, beaten earth floor so they lay down and tried to sleep, though some men whimpered because of the pain of their wounds or the loss of their freedom. Brude did not cry, not even when he remembered his father's death. He wanted to, but no tears would come. Instead, he burned with a deep resolve that he would escape this captivity and return to Broch Tava to marry Mairead. It was the only thing he could think of that kept him feeling alive.

Brude soon learned that escape would not be easy. They spent a week cooped up in the fort, during which time two men died when their wounds became infected. They discovered that Carallus was a Pritani, from a tribe who lived far to the south, which was why he had the job of speaking to them. Drugh, the big man who had become their nominal leader, asked him once why one of the Pritani would fight for the Romans. Carallus just shrugged. "The pay's good," he said. "And you get regular meals."

Then one morning they were taken outside, heavily guarded, and the Romans put them in a long coffle, iron rings fastened about their necks and linked together with long iron chains. They could move their arms and they could walk but they had to keep together for if any man did not keep pace or changed direction, his neighbours were dragged by the neck chains and choked.

So began the long years of Brude's slavery.

They walked along the road behind the Wall, prodded by the guards if their pace flagged. At night they were taken inside the nearest fort and Brude began to realise just how many soldiers the Romans had. They had heard that most soldiers had gone away to fight in some other part of the empire but there were still hundreds of them in the forts along the Wall, every man armed and armoured with enough iron to make a Pritani a wealthy man.

They turned south, sometimes handed from one guard party to another. Some of them were now starting to pick up a few words of Latin. Brude was able to recognise the words for water, food, orders to get up, march, stop and rest. They all knew the word for slave, for they heard it constantly. They were just *serui*. They had no names as far as the Romans were concerned.

The roads ran straight across the countryside, passing through villages and even large towns, many of them with streets laid out in orderly, rectangular patterns and surrounded by high walls. Sometimes they spent the nights sheltered in barns but mostly they slept outside, shivering in their short tunics even though it was high summer. "Lughnasa today," said Frual one morning as they sipped the small ration of water and ate the dried oatmeal biscuits they were becoming used to. "I don't suppose we'll be celebrating, though."

Brude wondered how Frual knew it was Lughnasa; he had lost all track of time. He also wondered how Broch Tava would celebrate the summer festival this year when so many of their warriors were dead or captured.

The march went on, much further than the trek they had made from Broch Tava to the Wall, yet the going was faster for the Roman roads allowed them to cover long distances easily. Brude noticed small stone markers at the roadside every so often; strange, unfamiliar symbols scratched on them. He supposed they marked some sort of holy place but on a much smaller scale than the high-standing stones the Pritani used.

Day after day they marched, the Romans never allowing them any chance of escape. Brude whispered to Frual and some others that he thought they should try to overpower the guards one night, even if it meant all of them attacking in unison because of the restricting coffle. Nobody greeted his suggestion with any enthusiasm. "Where would you run to?" one man asked. "Even if you could get out of the chains, you'd soon get caught again."

"I heard they kill runaway slaves," said another man gloomily.

Drugh told Brude to forget his plan and the march went on.

As they travelled further south the towns grew larger and became more prosperous. Brude marvelled at the sight of enormous buildings built of stone and brick, or even gleaming marble; some with huge round columns supporting triangular cornices decorated with incredibly lifelike painted statues. They made Broch Tava seem crude in comparison. And as they were marched through the towns they heard the people muttering and pointing, calling them "Picti" when they saw the blue painted designs on their faces and bodies. The paint was fading, its bright colour lost, but was still clearly visible, still marking them as Pritani warriors.

After eighteen days they reached the biggest settlement Brude had ever seen. He heard the Roman soldiers call it Londinium although that meant nothing to him. After an overnight stay, locked in a large storehouse, they were shepherded out to the river where the wharves teemed with people and noise. They were marched onto a huge wooden boat, where they were shackled in the hold. Even Frual, who was a good sailor and knew his way round boats, had never seen a boat as large as this. Other slaves were brought in and shackled alongside them, including some women and children. When they thought the guards were far enough away, they exchanged whispered words and learned that most of the newcomers were of the tribe of the Brigantes who lived south of the Wall but had never sat easily under Roman rule. One of them whispered to Frual that the Romans were struggling to keep the Brigantes under control as most of their soldiers were across the sea, following the Governor of Britannia who had proclaimed himself emperor and gone off to fight the other claimant to the imperial throne. "It didn't do us much good, though," the man conceded. "They stomped on us pretty hard."

"Rome has two emperors?" Brude asked him.

The man laughed. "Not for too long, I expect. One of them will kill the other one eventually."

The voyage was a misery of darkness and terror as the ship pitched and rolled its way down the wide river and out to sea. Brude, like many of the others, was sick but had no choice except to lie there, filthy and stinking, praying for the awful movement to stop. When it finally did, they were all led up on to the deck where they were told to clean themselves up as best they could before being led off through the busy harbour town and out again onto a road for yet more walking.

The summer sun was hot, hotter than the Boresti were used to. They suffered in the heat, as did some of the children who were treated no differently to the adults by the guards. These men were not dressed as soldiers but they were armed and just as harsh. They certainly watched the slaves just as closely as the soldiers had done and there was no chance of anyone escaping. Even if they could, the Boresti knew now that to get home they would have to cross the sea. What chance was there of that for an escaped slave?

It took another six days of walking before they were herded into a large wooden enclosure on the edge of a town, which boasted a massive wall and gate towers built from stone that looked almost black. That evening they were brought plenty of food, water to wash in and clean tunics. They were ordered to wash off as much of their body paint as they could, so Brude scraped and soaped and scraped again until his skin was pink and raw and the blue marks were faded almost to nothing, leaving only the small tattoo on his right forearm. For Brude, it was not too bad but for most of the older men who had used the blue paint for years, their skin remained stubbornly tinted even when the patterns could no longer be made out. Many had tattoos which would never come off.

There were other slaves already in the stockade. One of them, an older man with his hair starting to turn grey at the temples, approached Frual and asked which tribe he was from.

"Boresti," said Frual.

"I knew you were from the north, from all that paint," the man said. "Nobody but the northern Picti use that nowadays. I am Basillus of the Votadini."

Brude eyed the man cautiously. He remembered his father talking about the Votadini who were said to be friends of the Romans. Frual didn't seem to bother. He and Basillus exchanged what little news they had. Basillus, it turned out, had been a slave for over ten years. "It's not so bad if you're careful," he told them. "Keep your mouth shut, your eyes averted, your expression blank. Don't step out of line and you'll be fine. The Romans work their slaves hard but you'll get fed and watered and they even let you have the run of the women slaves."

"I've got a wife back home," said Frual.

Basillus laughed amiably. "You won't see her again, my friend, not unless your master gives you your freedom."

Brude was suddenly interested. "Slaves can be freed?"

Basillus looked at him sharply. "Yes. It happens quite a lot in the empire, lad."

"How? How do we get free?" Some of the other slaves were listening in now.

Basillus held up his hands in front of his chest. "Don't get too excited, my young friend. You're just a boy and obviously impatient but look at me. I've been a slave for ten years and I'm not near getting my freedom."

"But it is possible?" Frual asked.

"It's possible," Basillus conceded. "It's easiest if you're a house slave, of course. A field slave doesn't get much chance to earn money or perform important services for their master."

"Is that how you get your freedom?" Brude asked insistently. "You perform some service for a Roman?"

Basillus was the centre of attention now and he looked un-comfortable. He sighed. "All right, here is how it is," he said. "There are a few ways it can happen. If you can save enough money, you can buy your freedom, but that can take a lot of years."

Money. Brude had seen coins before. His father had once had a few silver coins. They had all been fascinated by the tiny pictures and strange symbols. They were a convenient way to carry silver around but quite prized. His father had exchanged them for some goats.

Basillus went on, "But getting money means you need to be in a place where you get the chance to earn some. Like I said, a house slave has a better chance. Or sometimes a master will free a slave who has given many years of service. Sometimes they have to wait for the master to die and he leaves a will, setting them free."

Brude wasn't sure what a will was but this didn't seem like a quick option either. Unless... "So kill the master once he's happy with you," he suggested.

Basillus was horrified. "Whatever you do, you don't do that. Look, I said it wasn't so bad being a slave. You get food and shelter which is more than some people back home ever got, but if you so much as raise a finger to a Roman citizen you'll get a whipping or a beating. If you strike a Roman, you'll be killed. And if you kill one, every slave in the household is executed along with you." He paused, looking round at their faces. "This is no game," he said softly. "The Romans have no problem with a slave getting his freedom but they won't stand for a slave who doesn't know his place."

The Boresti were silent, made to think hard by his words. Only Brude spoke up. "Is there no other way?"

Basillus shook his head, smiling at Frual. "He's a persistent lad, isn't he? What it is to be young, eh?" To Brude he said, "Well, I didn't want to make things hard for you lot but even with most of your war paint cleaned off you look different to the Romans. As a rule, they don't like people who are different. If I had to bet, I'd say you've got a good chance of ending up in the arena. You can win your freedom there if you are very lucky."

They all gave him blank looks. "What's the arena?" one man asked.

"It's where you fight. For show. The Romans like to see people fighting."

"We can do that!" said Drugh happily.

The others laughed but Basillus did not join in the laughter. "You fight each other. Usually to the death."

There was a silence as a pall came over them. "To the death?" Frual asked.

Basillus nodded. "Usually. If you're a war captive or a criminal, they'll make you fight or they'll just cut you down if you don't. Sometimes they give you special training to become a gladiator, and then you might live a bit longer. A few win their freedom if they fight well. Very few." He looked round their worried faces. "I wouldn't count on winning your freedom that way. Better to hope for a job as a house slave and earn it."

Brude nodded sombrely. If the only way he could win his freedom was by killing his friends, he didn't think he could do that.

The slave market was held in an open space outside the stockade. They were paraded on a wooden platform to allow the audience of prospective purchasers to see them. They went up in groups of three or four, prodded by spears held by tough-looking guards. Sometimes a buyer would come up to inspect some of them, even having them stripped naked so that their limbs could be checked for sign of deformity.

They were unchained from the coffle but had leg irons put on, so when Brude's turn came to climb on to the platform he had to hobble up slowly, taking care not to stumble. There were two other Boresti with him, men he had only known since their captivity had started. Both of them were older than him.

He stood blinking in the warm sun, trying to look indifferent to his fate. He looked out at the audience, noticing that there were only two or three paying any attention to him or to the other men beside him. There were some calls, some waving of hands, then the guard jabbed him with the butt of his spear, indicating that they should make their way down the steps at the other side where more guards waited. Brude was separated from the others and led away to the side of the stockade where he was roughly pushed to join two men and a young woman who had been through the auction before him. He did not know any of them and none of them spoke any language that he understood. He looked round for Frual or any of the other Boresti but they were nowhere to be seen in the crowd.

A small man approached them, rubbing his hands, obviously pleased with himself. He was wearing a smart tunic and a wide-brimmed hat, and was accompanied by three burly guards. He spoke to them in Latin, but the only word Brude could make out was *serui – slaves*. The man waved a hand imperiously and one of the guards removed their leg irons while another fastened them into a coffle. At a word from the small man they set off, Brude at the tail end of the coffle, heading out of the stockade and back onto another of the seemingly never ending Roman roads. Brude tried to twist round to see where his friends were but he got a cuff on the head from the guard behind him. He realised that he had not even said farewell to Frual, Drugh or any of the others.

They were heading west and south and they walked nearly all day. By evening, they turned off the road onto a less well-made track, passing through fields of wheat and barley where slaves were busy gathering in the harvest. Up ahead was a large two-storey building with a red tiled roof. It was sur-rounded by several other buildings, all made of stone or brick with white painted walls which dazzled in the sunlight. They were marched round the back of the villa to an area that com-prised many small rooms facing inwards on to a large square courtyard. The rooms were cells with strong, plastered walls and doors with bars of iron. One at a time they were released from the coffle and pushed into a cell. Brude was last to go in and he found himself in a tiny space with no windows. The door slammed shut behind him and he heard the lock grate as it closed.

There was a ledge, made of stone, just wide enough for him to lie on; two blankets, old and smelly, and a wooden bucket in the corner. Nothing else.

Tired from the long day, still hungry and thirsty, he folded one of the blankets into a makeshift pillow, lay down on the hard stone shelf and covered himself with the other blanket. Through the small barred grille in the door he watched as the daylight slowly faded. His thoughts turned to his home, to his mother, to Mairead who would think him dead, and to his father. He began to shiver, suddenly unable to stop trembling. Tears came to his eyes and would not stop. He was just sixteen years old and he was truly alone for the first time in his life.

The villa belonged to a wealthy Roman named Sextus Arminius Rufus. Brude never saw him. One part of the villa was set aside for Rufus to use when he did visit, but that was a rare occurrence so the rooms were left empty most of the time.

Brude's life revolved at the whim of Marcus Arminius, a former slave who had been freed, taken his master's name and now ran the estate for him. He was assisted by a retinue of former soldiers who were only ever too happy to enforce his will, and by the small man who wore the wide-brimmed hat and who had overseen Brude's purchase from the slave market. He was another ex-slave who had taken the name of Tiberius Arminius. Rather timid and indecisive, he was the person responsible for allocating the slaves' duties on a daily basis in accordance with Marcus' wishes.

Brude soon learned that the advice he had been given by Basillus was worth following; he kept his mouth shut, his eyes down and never raised a finger to anyone. That way he escaped the beatings that some of the other slaves received. He was a field slave, the lowest of the low. To the Romans he had no name; he was simply a slave and that was what they called him when they spoke to him at all, which was usually only when the guards gave him orders. Even the freedmen, Marcus and Tiberius, were indifferent towards the slaves. Brude was learning that in Roman society everyone did indeed have their place and was expected to behave accordingly.

The other slaves were friendlier, of course, although at first only one of them could speak to him in a language he understood, a man in his thirties called Batix, a Gaul who had been a slave since he was a boy. Batix helped him learn to speak Latin and they would practise while out in the fields or in the orchards as long as they were out of earshot of the guards. Thanks to Batix, Brude was able, within a few weeks, to at least exchange some words with the other slaves. They were from all over the empire, some with dark olive skin, others with hair the colour of wheat, the likes of which Brude had never seen before.

They worked hard in the fields as long as there was daylight, doing whatever task Tiberius allocated to them but in many ways life was not so bad. For one thing, they wore no shackles, which Brude questioned with Batix. The older man said, "They know we won't run. There's nowhere for a slave to run to and if you do run, when they catch you, they just kill you. You get no second chances with the Romans."

Brude was tempted to try to escape anyway but he knew in his heart that Batix was right. Where would he run to? A life of hiding in the forests did not appeal to him. He owned nothing, not even the tunic he wore, so how would he survive alone? Still he dreamed, but he decided it would be better to learn as much as he could about the Romans and then find a way to get free somehow.

The slaves were allowed to congregate in the courtyard where they ate their meals and could sit and talk before the guards locked them in the cells each night. There were informal family groups among the slaves and though the men were supposed to be locked away separately from the women, the guards usually turned a blind eye if some couples were locked in a cell together overnight. Slaves were not allowed to marry but among themselves they performed their own unofficial marriages, which the Romans did not mind. Any children who were born were automatically slaves who would be able to work on the farm from a very early age. Batix had a young wife called Brigid, who was originally from Germania. The two of them allowed Brude to eat with them while they taught him the ways of life as a slave.

Much to his surprise, Brude learned to speak Latin quickly, paying special attention whenever Marcus Arminius or Tiberius spoke because they were freedmen who tried to speak Latin the way the Roman gentry did, not the coarse slang of the soldiers and slaves. Brude surprised himself by being able to detect the difference. He was tempted to try speaking to Marcus in an attempt to get a job as a house slave but he had seen another slave get beaten half to death for approaching Marcus in a way the overseer deemed inappropriate, so he bided his time. Tiberius was more approachable but even Brude, young and inexperienced as he was, recognised that the little freedman had no real influence.

Day followed day, month followed month, and the winter came. They celebrated the Roman midwinter feasts of Saturnalia with an extra ration of bread and some watered wine, which the master had graciously allowed them. It wasn't quite the Samhain feast Brude was used to, but it was better than their normal fare, which, though reasonably plentiful, was very plain.

The field slaves had less work to do in the winter as the days were shorter. They all liked that, even though they were cold for several months. When spring came, things changed and they were all soon exhausted with the ploughing and sowing through the longer days.

Brude turned seventeen. He was aware that he was filling out, his muscles becoming honed by the heavy manual work. Brigid assured him that some of the younger women would be glad to slip into his cell if he asked them but Brude was wary of that. He still dreamed of Mairead most nights even though he was a man now and he could not help but look at the younger slave women.

By midsummer, Brigid had encouraged one of the young girls, whose name was Julia, to join them at evening meal and sit next to Brude. Julia was shy but clearly fascinated by Brude. Brigid practically threw them at each other. Brude, feeling awkward and clumsy, cast an appealing look at Batix who just shrugged and gave him an encouraging smile. Brigid almost shoved Julia into Brude's cell that night. They made love clumsily but enthusiastically and Julia clung to him all night. She came to his bed every night after that. Brigid smiled, telling him he was a lucky boy to get such a young and attractive girl for himself. Brude felt as proud as he had ever done, walking tall and feeling invincible. Batix, although not meaning to, deflated him a little by telling him that because Julia was now nearly fifteen years old, she wanted to get pregnant; expectant women were generally given lighter duties and if she was really lucky she might even be taken to the master's house to act as a wet nurse if there were any babies in the master's family. Brude, feeling rather used, mentioned it to Julia that evening. She openly admitted it. "Of course," she said. "That's what all the women do. But I do love you," she added, putting her hand on his arm. Brude wasn't so sure now and that night he thought about Mairead again for the first time in several weeks.

He never learned whether Julia became pregnant, for only a few days later his whole world changed again. The slaves knew that something was wrong when the sun rose but the guards did not arrive to unlock the doors to their quarters. They sat, confused, isolated and scared, sometimes calling to one another softly, but nobody seemed to know what was happening. Brude was worried. The routine of life was never disturbed, so something serious must have happened. And if something serious happened in a Roman household, the slaves were always affected.

It was near the second hour when the doors were at last unlocked and swung open to reveal the unexpected sight of little Tiberius standing in the centre of the courtyard, an expression of pure misery consuming his lined face. He stood there, the brim of his hat doing nothing to hide his anxiety, looking at them, trying to compose himself. They watched him, silently, waiting for him to speak. When he did, his voice was cracked with emotion. "Your Master, Sextus Arminius Rufus, is dead." He waited for a reaction but there was none. None of the slaves had ever seen their master so his death meant nothing to them. They were slaves and knew better than to display emotion. Tiberius went on, "He has committed suicide following the victory of Lucius Septimius Severus over Decimus Clodius Albinus."

Brude sneaked a surreptitious glance at his fellow slaves to see whether any of them understood what this was about. He had no idea who the people Tiberius was talking about were. Few of the slaves showed any comprehension. Tiberius continued, "Septimius Severus is now Augustus Caesar and all the property of Arminius Rufus, including this estate, is forfeit to him. An imperial freedman has arrived and will now be in charge of this estate. You are all to come outside for him to inspect you."

Tiberius had to repeat the last bit and start to physically usher them outside before it sank in. As they made their way through the outer doors to line up outside the villa, Brude whispered to Batix, "What does this mean?"

The older man shrugged. "I don't know, but I expect it might not be good."

When the slaves were standing nervously in a line, Brude saw a troop of Roman soldiers emerging from the villa. They were escorting a large man in a toga who walked briskly over towards the line of slaves. There was no sign of the usual guards but Marcus Arminius was anxiously following in the man's wake. The new arrival cast a disdainful look over the slaves, then slowly walked down the line, casually looking each of them over. Brude kept his head down and his eyes firmly fixed on the ground so all he saw was the man's well-made sandals as he passed him. The man went back to where Marcus was waiting, hands clasped together, then beckoned Tiberius. There was a brief discussion before the man in the toga went back inside the villa, Marcus following after a short and hurried exchange with Tiberius. The little man came back, six soldiers with him. He walked down the line and as he went he pointed out some of the younger men to the soldiers who took them aside, sending the others back into the slave quarters. Brude watched Julia being sent back, then Tiberius reached Batix and Brigid. He sent Brigid back, hesitated over Batix but sent him back as well. He stepped in front of Brude and pointed to him before moving on.

A soldier grabbed Brude's arm and shoved him to where the other chosen men were standing under the watchful eye of the other guards. Brude glanced back over his shoulder in time to see Batix giving him a lost, hopeless look before being shoved out of sight through the door that led to the slave quarters.

In all, Tiberius selected twelve of the younger men. They were chained into a coffle and led off without another word, four of the soldiers accompanying them as escort. Brude saw Tiberius watching them and thought the little man's eyes looked full of tears though no words were spoken. Brude was once more on his travels. For the second time, he had been abruptly taken away from his friends without an opportunity to say farewell and this sudden break hurt almost as much as when he had been taken from his fellow Boresti after the slave market.

It was a long time before he was able to piece events together but from listening to the soldiers as they chatted on the march, he figured out most of it eventually. It seemed that the owner of the villa, Arminius Rufus, had been a supporter of Clodius Albinus, one-time Governor of Britannia, the man who had taken away the bulk of the legions from the province to support his bid for the rule of the empire. Albinus had set himself up as ruler of Britannia and Gaul but he had formally declared himself emperor of Rome when he fell out with Septimius Severus, who had also claimed the imperial throne. Some great battles had been fought between the armies of the two rival emperors and, obviously, Severus had won. Clodius Albinus had committed suicide and Arminius Rufus, his loyal supporter, had done the same, allowing the new, undisputed emperor to seize his property. Brude wasn't entirely sure but it seemed that the estate he had been working on was not the only such place owned by Rufus. Brude had already had trouble conceiving of one man owning an estate as huge as the one he had worked on and having so many slaves, but to learn that this was just one of his estates was even more difficult to comprehend. Brude wondered idly what he would ever do if he was that wealthy. Try to back the winner, he decided; Arminius Rufus had lost everything by supporting the wrong man.

They marched south, another leg in the long journey that took Brude inexorably away from his homeland. The soldiers who guarded them were talkative, chatting among themselves within earshot of the slaves. By listening carefully, Brude learned they were heading for somewhere called Hispania. The name meant nothing to him but one of the soldiers had been born there and was looking forward to returning. That made Brude think of his own home and family. He still felt the loss keenly and now, after only a year in captivity, he had lost his second family by being separated from Batix, Brigid and Julia. He decided that he would not suffer a loss like that again so he stayed distant from the other slaves on the march. He knew them all, of course, but he was not close to them and he was determined that it would stay that way. He reckoned he could survive on his own. Batix had taught him a lot about how to get by and, despite his youth, he had learned the lessons well.

It took weeks to march all the way to where the sea met the mountains and the season had turned by the time they got there, the trees shedding their leaves and the wind whipping up a chill. Brude overheard the soldiers discussing what to do. Apparently they had to cross the high mountains to get to Hispania and they were worried about being caught by winter snows. In the end, the soldiers requisitioned some warm clothing for themselves and the slaves before pushing on.

Brude thought he knew mountains but he soon discovered that what were mountains in his homeland were really only hills. The mountains they crossed into Hispania were jagged peaks, which towered to dizzying heights above them, the summits often lost in the clouds, their tops covered in snow even though winter had not arrived. The Roman road forged through the passes and the soldiers kept them moving at a wicked pace, fearful of being caught by snow. Fortunately, they made it through the mountains before the first snowfall of winter, eventually reaching a hilltop town on the coast that the soldiers called Saguntum.

After only a few days' rest they pushed on, now heading westwards, through more hills and valleys, following the Roman roads that Brude was so used to now. What he had also learned on this march was that the small stone markers he had thought marked holy places were actually called milestones. When he counted the paces from one to the next he was astonished to find that the distance was exactly one thousand paces at the soldiers' military pace and that the markings on them indicated how far it was to the next town or city. It was a revelation that staggered him and brought home to him just how organised and uniform the empire was. The Romans seemed to build everywhere. Roads, towns, cities, they stamped their mark on the countryside wherever they went.

Pressing on through the chill of winter, they reached Asturica, footsore and weary, early in the new year, before spring had started to turn the land green. The slaves were handed over to another group of soldiers. The guards who had accompanied them on the long journey from northern Gaul went off without a word; another lost farewell in the growing line of separations Brude was experiencing.

They found themselves in an enormous, strongly guarded camp which held over six thousand slaves. They soon discovered that they were there for a purpose and that purpose was to build. The town needed a new aqueduct so the new emperor was going to give it one. Army engineers and skilled masons would oversee the work but the manual labour was to be done by slaves and animals, which were treated much the same by the Romans.

The aqueduct had to cover a distance of twelve miles from a hillside spring to the city. The engineers had already plotted a route, the owners of the land the aqueduct would cross had been removed, either voluntarily or by force, and the stone was to be quarried from nearby hills then dragged into position by the slaves.

It was backbreaking work. Brude was assigned to the transportation teams. They used wagons, mules and oxen and he was shown how to use the incredible devices of rope and wood that the Romans used to lift heavy stones. Yet even with these, a lot of the work involved human muscle power to shift the huge blocks. His days turned into an agony of pushing, pulling, heaving and lifting, always walking a slightly longer distance as the weeks passed and the aqueduct grew longer and longer, closing on the town. He saw that the blocks were only the outer facing of the huge foundations and walls of the aqueduct. The Romans used what they called concrete to give the structure its strength, the stones being laid precisely around a central core of concrete, constantly watched by the engineers who had to make sure that the final result was a smooth gradient for the water to flow down at a regular speed for mile after mile.

A part of Brude recognised it as a brilliant piece of engineering but at the same time the greater part of him was usually too exhausted and concentrating on doing his own job well enough to avoid punishment to appreciate what they were achieving. The main object in his life was simply to survive.

He worked on the aqueduct all through the baking heat of the summer, all through the cold and snow of winter and then through the following summer. Men died from exhaustion, from exposure or from accidents when blocks fell or ropes gave way. Nobody paid much attention to the losses; slaves were plentiful.

By the end of the following winter Brude was twenty years old. His skin, once pale and white, was burned brown by the sun. He was strong, the muscles of his arms and legs more powerful than they had ever been. Above all else he knew how to survive as a slave. What he did not know was how he was ever going to gain his freedom.

By the following spring the aqueduct was nearly completed and some of the slaves began to speculate about what would happen to them. Brude was busy trying to think about how to get involved in some skilled work, perhaps carving the stone blocks or even learning how to sculpt the statues the Romans were so fond of. He was not sure whether he had the skill for it but he thought there might be a route to freedom that way.

Annoyingly, he could not think how he could ensure he was chosen for that type of work. Bribing someone might work but as imperial slaves they received no pay and some of the other, less savoury ways of ingratiating oneself with the overseers did not appeal to him.

As unexpectedly as ever in the life of a slave, things changed again. One morning, as they were finishing their frugal breakfast, a stranger appeared, accompanied by two armed guards. The man himself was big, hugely muscled but slightly overweight, his hair cropped short and almost entirely grey. In his prime he must have been formidable; even now he did not look the sort of man who would back down from a fight. His keen eyes surveyed the slaves as he wandered around, one of the overseers accompanying him and answering questions, which the man snapped at him. Every so often the big man would stop to examine a slave, sometimes nodding his head. When he did this the slave was sent to stand near the gate of the camp. Brude recognised another slave sale; the aqueduct was nearly finished so some slaves would be sold off.

The big man approached Brude who lowered his gaze as he had learned was safest to do. The man, though, reached out and lifted his chin, staring him in the eye. He asked, "Where are you from?"

"Caledonia," Brude answered, using the Roman name for the land north of the Wall.

The man's eyes studied him carefully. "One of the painted people, eh?" He seemed amused. "I'll try him," he said to the overseer. Brude was sent to stand with the other chosen men.

After an hour of careful selection the big man had pulled out nineteen slaves. He had them lined up in a row, then he stood in front of them. "I am Gaius Lollius Curtius," he announced in a deep, strong voice. "I am going to stand in front of each of you in turn and I want you to hit me." That got their attention. The man grinned. "Don't worry. If you do manage to hit me there will be no punishment. One punch, that's all you are allowed. If you hit me hard enough I'll take you away from this place."

They watched him intently, hanging on his every word. Life in the camp was hard and all of them wanted nothing more than to get away from there.

Curtius marched purposefully to one end of the line, where Brude stood fifth from the end. Curtius approached the first man and stood two paces from him, thrusting out his chin. "Hit me!" he barked. The man swung a clumsy fist and Curtius swayed back, easily avoiding the blow. The slave overreached and stumbled. Curtius caught him and steadied him, pushing him back into place before moving on to the next man. "Hit me!" he said again. Another wild swing missed, much to the amusement of the watching guards and of Curtius himself. He gave the slave a mocking smile before moving on.

The third man managed to clip Curtius' jaw with a straight jab. Curtius nodded, his eyes sparkling. He pushed the man back into place and moved on to the man beside Brude who tried the same jab but missed completely as Curtius ducked aside.

Then it was Brude's turn.

Curtius stood in front of him, blue eyes shining with enjoyment, daring Brude to hit him. He thrust out his chin and barked, "Hit me!"

Brude hit him in the stomach.

Curtius was astonishingly fast for such a big man and he nearly avoided the blow but Brude caught him with enough force to drive the wind from him and make him step back, doubling over. Brude quickly stepped back into line, remembering that he was allowed only one punch. To try another would be to invite punishment. Even now he was anxious that he had done the wrong thing, but Curtius had not actually said they should hit him on the chin, just that they should hit him.

The big man straightened up, rubbing his belly where Brude's fist had caught him. He grinned hugely at Brude. "Well done, lad. What's your name?"

"Brude." He was astonished. No Roman had ever asked his name before.

Curtius thought for a moment. "That's no Roman name. I think we'll call you Brutus." Then he moved on to the next man.

He went down the line but only three more men managed to come close to hitting him. At the end he picked out four men in total, including Brude. Then he counted out some coins, which he gave to the overseer. A clerk scribbled out a receipt while Curtius beamed at his four new slaves. "You may live to regret this, my lads," he told them gleefully. "But you'll be well fed, well clothed and well trained where we are going. You'll have names and if you are good enough, you'll have some respect. If you're really good, you'll be able to earn your freedom." He was looking straight at Brude when he said that and must have seen the sudden spark of interest in Brude's eyes. He walked closer. "Do you want to ask me a question, Brutus?"

Brude lowered his eyes. "No, Master."

Curtius grabbed his chin and lifted his head. "Yes you do. And that's the first thing you have to learn. From now on, when you're with me, you can ask questions. You are still slaves and you behave like slaves with others but with me you can ask a question as long as you ask permission first." He stared into Brude's eyes. "So what do you want to ask me?" He released Brude's chin from his iron grip.

"Do I have permission to ask a question, Master?" Brude asked him.

"Clever boy. Yes you do."

"Where are we going?"

"To Rome. To the amphitheatre. You are going to become gladiators." He paused to let that sink in, then he added with a laugh, "Even if it kills you."

A.D. 209

Broch Tava had changed. He supposed it was inevitable but, somehow, it seemed so different from the way he remembered it, not like his home at all. One of Colm's men had galloped ahead to bring word of his coming and of Castatin's safe return so there was a crowd gathering as they approached, villagers keen to see a man come back from the dead.

Most of the other riders had taken their lead from Colm and were rather cool towards Brude, barely speaking to him. One of them, a young man who introduced himself as Seoc, asked him who his father was.

"The old head man?" Seoc asked when Brude told him.

"That's right."

"I remember him," said Seoc. "I vaguely recall he had a son but I don't really remember you. I was just a kid when you all went off to war."

"You're making me feel old," said Brude with a wry smile. Seoc was in his early twenties so would probably have been around nine or ten years old when Brude had marched off with the war band. At that age Brude would hardly have had anything to do with him.

Seoc looked as if he was going to ask another question but Castatin interrupted with a question of his own. "How old are you?" the boy asked him innocently.

"Not as old as I feel," Brude told him. He saw Castatin looking puzzled as he tried to figure that out. Brude explained, "I'm the same age as your father."

"You don't look as old as him," Castatin told him.

Brude laughed. "Thank you for that," he said. He liked the boy, which he thought was only right as the lad was Mairead's son and her gentleness and inquisitiveness would have rubbed off on him. As they neared Broch Tava, Castatin grew anxious. He jumped down from the mule to run ahead. "I'll tell my mother all about you!" he shouted as he charged off.

They approached the village from the open plain on the north side of the hill that would take them to the broch with scarcely a climb. Beyond it, Brude knew, the land fell away steeply, down towards the river where most of the people lived. The broch sat on a spur of the hill overlooking the village. From the walkway at the top, it gave panoramic views over the river and the inland plain all the way to the northern hills. Only to the east was the view restricted for the very top of the hill was steep, uneven and covered with thick woodland. Now he could see that the broch still stood there majestically, jutting skywards like a squat, accusing finger, a thin curl of smoke from the hearth rising from its circular summit. When he had left, the broch was where his father had his seat and there had been only a couple of roundhouses outside because the villagers got much of their food from the sea so most of the dwellings were down on the flat river bank where there was also good grazing for their livestock. Now, he saw, the woodland near the broch had been cut back, creating wide fields on the open land to the north and west, some ploughed, some with cattle, freshly shorn sheep or goats. There were enclosures formed by walls made in a similar dry stone way to the broch, although much more crudely, with each stone delicately balanced, held in place by gravity and the weight of the stones above, not cemented to its neighbours at all. There was a skill to building these walls, or dikes as they called them, but compared to what Brude had seen in Rome they looked paltry and crude. Even the broch, which he had once thought the mightiest structure in the world with its immensely thick walls and the stones fitted neatly together, now looked less impressive.

In addition to the new fields, the broch had acquired a wooden stockade, stretching in a wide, rough circle, the pointed timbers high, sturdy and strong. Over the top of the high fence he saw the roofs of new buildings too, huddled round the broch. The village had obviously expanded considerably under Colm's rule.

Brude stopped to take the pack from his back and refasten it to the mule. He also unlooped his sword from over his shoulder, stuffing it firmly into his bedroll. Glancing up, he saw Seoc watching him. "I won't need it here," Brude explained. He took up his staff and walked on.

He was close now, a warm feeling of homecoming filling his senses. He had dreamed of this moment for so many years that he wanted to savour it. The crowd stood at the wide gate which led through the perimeter fence to the broch. He was close enough now to make some of the people out. There were men, women and children and he was struck by the realisation that a surprising number of the men were armed with sharp spears and sporting shields. He saw Castatin speaking to a woman who was crouching down to hug him and hold him. As Brude drew near, Castatin pointed back at him and the woman stood up to look at him.

He stopped, standing there in full view of everyone, only a few paces from her. His heart pounded faster as he saw her and knew her.

Mairead.

She was probably standing in roughly the same spot as she had been when he had last seen her, nearly thirteen years before, when he had marched away. That memory of her was still strong in his mind and seeing her again brought it back to him once more. She looked at him, her eyes wide, her lips parted in surprise and wonder. Castatin tugged her arm and she took a faltering step towards him. All Brude could do was stand there feeling stupid. The only words that came to him were, "Hello, Mairead."

"Brude? Is it really you?" Her voice was smooth as silk, yet full of strain and worry. She was tall for a woman, her long dark hair curling around her shoulders. She was no longer the girl he had left behind but a woman, a mother now, with a full figure and some worry lines around her eyes. She wore sparkling pins in her hair and a brooch of gold on her finely woven dress. Painted on her left temple, half hidden by her hair, was an intricate, swirling, blue pattern. She was still the most beautiful woman he had ever seen.

But she was Colm's wife.

She reached out with her left hand, gently touching his cheek, as if trying to make sure that he was really there. Her fingers traced a delicate line down his chin then back up to his short hair. Her touch was as soft as silk yet it burned itself into his skin. She stared at him, confusion written all over her face. He saw her eyes begin to fill with tears. "Brude?" she whispered. "Colm said you were dead."

Before he could answer there was a shrill yell from the gate as an old woman pushed her way through the crowd calling his name. Mairead turned and the spell was broken. Brude looked over her shoulder to see his mother running for him. He dropped his staff and went to meet her, arms wide. Unlike Mairead she did not hesitate but ran to him, throwing her arms around him, sobbing his name. He held her tight and felt his own eyes stinging. After an age she stood back, still holding tightly to his arms. She looked at him, then began sobbing, so she clung to him again.

Then others approached and some of the older women recognised him, calling his name. His mother at last let him go so that she could run her hands over his face. Then she pulled his head down to kiss him as if he was a small boy. He laughed and told her to stop because he was a grown man now. She laughed through her tears, telling him he would always be her little boy and she had missed him so she would kiss him as much as she wanted.

"Give the lad a chance to meet folk, Mor," said an elderly man with grey hair and a weathered face, gently tugging her hand. Then he held out his own hand and clasped Brude's hand in welcome. "It's me, Seoras. Your mother stays with me now. Welcome home, boy."

Brude remembered Seoras as a friend of his father's, one of the village elders. He had been left in charge of the village when the war band had left, Brude remembered. "Thank you, Seoras. It is good to be back."

The crowd was pushing in now so Seoras shouted at them to back off and give Brude space. "He's home and we've plenty of time to hear all about where he's been." He began pushing a way through the crowd. "Come on, lad, let's take you home."

Brude, with his mother clinging to his arm and trying to tug him through the crowd, turned to see Mairead. She gave him a smile that lit up her face as she waved for him to go. "I'll see you later!" she called. He could still feel where her fingers had touched his face.

Brude called to Castatin, asking him to bring the mule along. The boy eagerly ran to grab the halter rope and proudly march behind him. That gave Mairead an excuse to tag along if she wanted and, after a moment's hesitation, she followed. Most of the crowd came along as well, mainly women and children, while the spearmen simply looked on, rather bewildered. Seoras led the crowd in a procession through the gate, past some houses and out another wide gateway on the south side of the stockade. A wide, well-trodden path ran down the steep slope towards the main village and Brude felt a pang of loss at the realisation that the broch itself was no longer his home.

Seoras took them down the winding path to a large roundhouse at the foot of the hill. All the way there, Brude's mother clung to him, constantly asking him if he was well and what had happened to him. He assured her time and time again that he was fine and glad to be home.

They reached the house where Seoras ushered them inside, allowing Mairead to follow. He told Castatin to tether the mule outside and then come in. He ordered everyone else to stay outside then he waited for the boy before pulling down the goatskin flap that served as a door. "They'd all try to come in if we let them," he said with a smile. Brude had a momentary worry that all his belongings were on the mule and it was out of his sight but he told himself he was home now, not in Rome, and nobody would steal his things, especially not with so many people watching.

They sat at the central hearth where the fire always burned. Brude's mother fetched a pot to boil some water and brew a tisane while the others sat looking at each other, nobody quite sure what to say.

"I see a lot has changed while I've been gone," Brude said eventually. There was an odd tension in the air and Mairead looked as though she wanted to be there with him yet also to be somewhere else at the same time. Years of being cautious as a slave gave Brude the patience not to force questions on her, but he could not help constantly looking at her. She returned his gaze, studying him carefully but she was biting her lips nervously and kept her hands clasped in her lap.

"Never mind that, boy," said Seoras. "Where have you been all these years? We all thought you dead along with your father and all the others."

"No, I was only knocked cold. When I woke up I was a prisoner. I've been a slave of the Romans pretty much since then. It took me a long time to get back."

He gave them a very short, edited version of his first years as a farm slave and a labourer, then said, "After that I was taken to Italy, to Rome itself. I was there for a long time. A very long time."

"And we thank all the gods that you are back with us now," said his mother as she poured the hot water into wooden beakers, wafting the smell of crushed herbs to Brude's nostrils.

"And I must thank you for rescuing my son," said Mairead. "He tells me you fought three men."

"You should have seen him, Mother!" Castatin exclaimed enthusiastically. "He was amazing."

"It wasn't really that much of a fight," Brude said, trying to play it down. He remembered enough about the Boresti to know that a reputation as a fighter would be likely to bring challenges from young warriors who wanted to prove themselves and he had no wish to fight his own people.

As they sipped the tisane, Brude's mother insisted he tell them all the details of what had happened to him. Brude suddenly felt tired and emotionally drained. He was also reluctant to say too much until he learned more about what had happened in the village during the past thirteen years. There was an undercurrent here that he could sense but not explain. "There's not much to tell," he said. "I was a slave. All I could do was what I was ordered to do and hope to survive."

"But you got away?" Seoras asked. "Escaped?"

Brude shook his head. "The Romans know how to keep slaves. No, I was given my freedom."

"They let you go?" Mairead asked. "Why would they do that?"

"I was part of a group who entertained the emperor," Brude explained. "He was pleased and I was set free as a reward."

"You've met the emperor?" Castatin was impressed.

Brude smiled. "Not exactly met. But he was there watching, though I doubt he would remember me."

"Hush, Castatin," Mairead said. "Brude must be very tired after coming all the way from Rome. We should go now in case your father comes back."

At the mention of his father, Castatin fell quiet. Mairead drank her tisane quickly and then stood, thanking Brude's mother for the hospitality. She took Castatin to the door and Brude followed her outside. The crowd was gone but two young men were waiting, resting lazily on their spears. Brude raised a questioning eyebrow as Mairead turned to him. "Colm doesn't like me to wander off without protection," she said.

He heard the sadness in her voice and wondered what or who Colm thought she needed protecting from. He wanted to reach out for her, hold her and tell her that it was the thought of her that had kept him going during the long years of his captivity but she remained distant and aloof and he knew it would be a bad idea to do anything so forward while the two guards were watching. She gave him a sad look. "You're not the only one who has been a prisoner, Brude," she whispered softly. Then, raising her voice, so that Colm's men could hear her words, she said, "Thank you again for rescuing my son. I am grateful." She turned, leading Castatin by the hand, and set off up the steep slope towards the broch. The two young spearmen gave Brude an appraising look before following her.

Seoras came outside to stand beside him. "Be careful, lad," he said. "She belongs to Colm and he is not a man to cross."

"I have no intention of crossing him." But he stood there, watching the swing of her hips as she walked up the hill and he did not take his eyes off her until she disappeared from sight behind the trees that stood where the path turned.

Brude and Seoras unpacked the mule and took Brude's belongings inside where he presented his mother with a bolt of fine linen, a mirror with a silver back engraved with images of Roman goddesses and a gold brooch. She hugged him again, tears flowing down her cheeks until Seoras gently pulled her away and told her to prepare an extra bed for Brude. While she bustled away at one side of the house Brude dug out a small dagger with a finely carved handle of ivory which he presented to the old man. "Thank you for taking care of her," he said. "I've brought back enough things to make sure we live comfortably for a while. You can have anything you fancy, but I'd like you to have this."

Seoras turned the knife over, admiring the craftsmanship. "Thank you, but you don't need to give me anything."

"I know, but you didn't have to take her in, either."

Seoras shrugged. "It's been good for both of us," he said quietly. "My wife died only a year after you left and neither of us had anybody else." He glanced to make sure Mor could not hear him. "Anndra is dead, then?" he whispered.

Brude nodded. "Definitely. He was beside me when he fell."

"I'm sorry, lad. He was a good man. A good village head man."

Brude nodded again. The unspoken words were almost as audible as the spoken ones. Brude was in no doubt that Seoras believed that things were not so good with Colm in charge.

He rose with the dawn, going outside to fetch some wood for the dying fire. Once he had fed the flames, he brought in some water from the rain barrel at the back of the house and set it to heat up, then he went outside to wash. By the time he came back the water was warm enough for him to shave. He used a small razor, its handle the twin of the knife he had given to Seoras.

His mother was soon up and about, fussing over him, preparing breakfast. Seoras joined them for the oatmeal porridge that Brude knew he was going to have to get used to again. His mother was in her element, scooping more porridge into his wooden bowl in case he was hungry. He relaxed and let her get on with it, exchanging a look with Seoras who just smiled and shook his head.

After breakfast he decided he had better go to see Colm. He climbed the steep hill, stopping every so often to turn and enjoy the view. The village was spread out below him on the flat land beside the river, roundhouses scattered irregularly between the hill and the water. He saw people moving around, going about their daily lives. There would be corn to grind for baking, some women would be spinning wool or flax to make clothes, the old men would be fixing fishing nets or making lobster traps while others would be tending their small plots of land where they grew herbs and vegetables. Children were fetching water from the small stream which babbled down the hill near the path. Everyone would be working during the daylight hours to bring food into their homes. They would barter and swap so that everyone shared in the benefits. It was, he thought, no different to many such villages he had passed on his long walk north, but this place was special to him. This was his home even though he had spent almost half of his life, and nearly all of his adulthood, away from it.

Beyond the village the broad expanse of the Tava spread out below him, sparkling silver in the morning sun. The tide was out and he thought he could make out the dark shapes of seals basking on the sandbanks. He could certainly make out the tiny shapes of children wandering the rock pools along the sandy beach to the east, looking for crabs or shellfish. There were a couple of coracles, the occupants paddling with smooth strokes to get the small oval vessels out to deeper water where they would drop a net over the side while the gulls circled and screeched at them, waiting to catch anything the nets let slip. Fishing from a coracle was dangerous work, he knew, for the vessels were really meant for shallow water and could be easily swamped by large waves but the men worked in pairs, handling the tiny vessels expertly, as the fishermen of Broch Tava had done for generations.

Further inshore there was a small wooden boat with a solitary sail, manned by four fishermen setting off to try their luck in the deep waters of the estuary. The sight of the boat reminded him of Frual, who had been a captive with him for a short while all those years ago. He had been a fisherman before Nechtan and Brude's father had led him off on their great raid, never to return.

Brude looked across the river to the green hills and forests on the far side, which stood out in sharp relief, giving the impression he could almost reach out and touch them, though in fact they were two miles away. He breathed in the gentle breeze blowing in from the sea, enjoying the coolness of the northern air and the faint tang of salt on the sea breeze. After so many years in the heat of Italy it was a joy to climb a hill and not be dripping with sweat from the first footstep. He knew that when winter came and brought wind, rain and frost, he would be wishing for the heat again but, for the moment, he simply enjoyed the feel of the cool air on his skin.

Turning again, he clambered up the track, revelling in the feeling of being home. He approached the south gate in the new, unfamiliar stockade where, to his surprise, two spearmen were on guard. Like all villages, Broch Tava had its disagreements with its neighbours but few villages had warriors on guard all the time. Perhaps, he thought, it was in response to the kidnapping of Colm's son and the theft of his bull. And one thing Broch Tava did not seem to be short of were young warriors. Gartnait had said Colm had seventy men at his command, a frightening number for such a small place.

The two young men eyed him warily as he drew near but he was unarmed except for the short dagger at his waist and he smiled and nodded a greeting to them. They let him pass without question. He strolled into the stockade to have a proper look around. Yesterday's walk through had been a blur and he had paid very little attention to his surroundings.

Many people were already up and about and he saw that there were several buildings dotted around: two long, low buildings with thatched roofs; a few traditional roundhouses; some pens for animals and even a smithy where a big man with huge, muscular arms and wearing a long leather apron was already heating his tools while his young apprentice stoked the furnace with charcoal.

He circled the smithy, wishing a good morning to some women who were carrying baskets of laundry, then, stepping quickly aside to dodge two young boys who were chasing each other, waving short sticks, he entered the wide open space between the main gate and the broch. He headed for the broch itself. There were two more spearmen guarding the low doorway. One was the young man, Seoc, he had spoken to the day before and the other was just about the biggest man Brude had ever seen. He had the same bear-like physique of old Curtius but was taller, more than a full head taller than Brude. His face was covered in hair, his bushy eyebrows, moustache and beard merging to form a tangled mass that parted to show his mouth, leaving a small space for his nose and eyes. Even his bare forearms were dark with hair. Unusually for one of the Pritani he was wearing a long coat of chain mail, which must have been incredibly heavy to wear all the time. He glowered at Brude as he approached.

"Good morning," Brude said amiably. "I'd like to speak to Colm."

Seoc nodded. He nudged his companion. "Go tell Colm that Brude is here to see him."

The big man frowned then ducked and squeezed his enormous frame through the small doorway. Brude looked at Seoc questioningly. "Where did you find him?"

"Cruithne? He's one of Colm's new men. He comes from somewhere away to the west. He says they threw him out for killing a man." Seoc lowered his voice. "I wouldn't upset him if I were you. He'll break your neck as soon as look at you. And Colm likes him."

"I'll bear that in mind."

"Lots of brawn, not much brain, our Cruithne," Seoc grinned. "He said once that he wants to fight a bear because he thinks he's stronger." He shook his head, still grinning. "Mad as a stag at rutting time, he is."

A figure appeared at the doorway and Colm himself came out. The giant Cruithne followed him, resuming his post beside Seoc. Colm was all smiles, dressed in a fine linen shirt and leather trousers, gold rings on each finger and a golden torc around each arm. Smiling, he clasped Brude's hand eagerly. "Sorry about yesterday," he said. "Not much of a welcome for you, was it? It was a bit of a shock, I'm afraid, seeing you after so long when I thought you were dead. But we will make up for it because, tonight, we will have a feast to celebrate your return."

"There's no need for that," Brude told him. "I'm just glad to be home. Did you manage to get your bull back?"

"Of course!" Colm beamed. "And three new slaves into the bargain. It turned out to be a good day after all." He took Brude's arm. "Come! Walk with me a way and I'll show you what we've done here. The place has changed a lot since you left."

Colm wandered through the stockade, Brude at his side. The head man pointed out the long buildings that he said housed his warriors.

"You're building an army?" Brude asked him.

"I am making Broch Tava strong," Colm corrected him. "Already the farms and villages along the coast look to me for protection, even those more than half way to Peart. They all send a share of their produce here to Broch Tava."

Brude thought to himself that people were the same wherever he found them. Colm would have made a good Roman, and if the Romans ever did come back, no doubt he would be one of the first to adopt their customs in exchange for being allowed to stay as leader of his own little empire.

Colm was in good humour as he introduced Brude to Caroc, the smith, who growled a greeting in a gravelly voice before returning to his work. "He doesn't say much," Colm laughed, "but his work is excellent. He is of the Damnonii and they are the best iron workers of all the Pritani. Fortunately, I persuaded him to come here to help build our village into a real town."

They left Caroc to his work, circling to the back of the broch where Colm showed him the pens where they kept half a dozen pigs. There was another small building backing onto the broch with two more spearmen guarding it. They stood aside as Colm approached. One of them unbarred the door and pulled it open at Colm's signal. Colm ducked inside, gesturing for Brude to follow. The room was small and windowless, reminding Brude of slave cells he had experienced at first hand in the empire. He saw immediately that that was exactly what it was.

Three men lay on the hard, earthen floor. Brude recognised them, although they had been badly beaten. One of them looked at him with sullen eyes. It was Oengus of Peart. "You are keeping Gartnait's son as a slave?" he asked in surprise.

Colm nonchalantly kicked out at Oengus, forcing him to squirm back against the wall. "It's what he deserves. He stole my bull and my son."

"Won't Gartnait cause trouble for you?"

Colm laughed. He was enjoying this display of his authority. "I am stronger than Gartnait now," he said. "If he wants his son back, he will have to pay in cattle, gold or silver. But I doubt he will bother. He has other sons." He sounded as though he didn't care one way or the other what Gartnait did.

Brude looked at the other two men. Cet, the small man, had a swollen eye and was nursing his left hand. Fothair, the tall man, was lying down, eyes closed, only the slight movement of his chest showing he was alive. His clothes were ripped and bloody. Crude bandages had been wrapped round his chest and his left leg. Brude noticed that Colm was watching his face to see how he reacted, but Brude had been a slave for long enough to know how to maintain a blank expression. He had asked Colm not to harm Fothair yet he was the worst injured of the three. Brude reckoned that was deliberate.

Colm ushered him outside again, leaving the three men under the care of the guards. As they walked slowly back to the doorway of the broch, Brude had an idea. "Those slaves! Are they for sale?"

Colm was surprised. "What? Those three? Perhaps. For the right price."

"I could do with a slave," said Brude. "I'll need to build a place of my own and an extra pair of hands would be useful."

"If you can afford one of them, you can have him," said Colm. He sounded as if he was sure Brude could not afford the price. He seemed amused. Brude guessed Colm was setting a test of some sort and he suspected that he was probably failing it. Still, Fothair had been hurt because of him and he could not let it rest. "Why don't you come down to the village? I'll show you what I can offer," he suggested.

Colm hesitated. He was the head man and others should come to him, but Brude was supposed to be his friend and he was in a good mood so he agreed, although he signalled for the giant Cruithne to follow them.

At Seoras' house Brude asked his mother to bring some food and water for Colm, which she did less than graciously while Brude brought out a bolt of fine, red-dyed linen and some gold rings. Colm was impressed despite himself. He agreed that Brude could have one of the men for his personal slave. "I'll have the small man sent down," Colm told him. "I'd prefer to keep Gartnait's son myself."

Brude shook his head. "You can keep both of them. I'll take the tall one, Fothair his name is."

"He's half dead," said Colm scornfully. "He will probably die on you."

"I'll take that chance. I can always buy the other one from you if he does die."

"You have more of this stuff?" Colm asked, indicating the cloth and gold.

"Not much now you've got that lot," Brude admitted as amiably as he could. He knew that he had paid well over the usual rate for a slave but he felt he owed Fothair something. By now he was convinced that Colm had singled him out precisely because Brude had asked him not to. And although Colm's expression betrayed nothing, Brude reckoned he had known from the start that Brude had wanted to buy Fothair. All of this was a way for Colm to show Brude who was in charge.

Colm stood, passing the cloth to Cruithne to carry while he pocketed the gold rings himself. He looked at Brude thoughtfully. "Things have changed since you left, Brude, you have seen that. But you have changed, too. You are not the Brude I remember."

"That was a long time ago," Brude shrugged. "We were both very young then." He was tempted to say that Colm had changed too, except that Colm was basically as he remembered him. He wondered why they had ever been friends. Yet for the sake of that old friendship he said, "We all change as we grow older, Colm, but that does not mean we cannot still be friends, or at the very least not enemies." He did not give Colm a chance to reply. "Speaking of enemies, you should know that I heard the emperor has come to Britannia. The Romans may come here."

Colm gave him a mocking look. "Let them come. Their army left these lands many generations ago. When they come now, it is to bring gifts of silver and fine jewellery."

"The Romans have been here?" Brude was surprised.

"Of course!" Colm laughed. "They often sail up the coast. They stop here, from time to time, seeking our friendship. The Romans are not as strong as you imagine, Brude. And even if they do come as enemies, we are strong here. They cannot defeat us in our own home."

Brude stared at him. He was about to argue, to tell Colm of the things he had seen, to tell him that a Roman legion had over five thousand armed men and siege weapons that would soon demolish his stockade and smash even the thick walls of the broch in time. The broch offered spurious safety at best, Brude knew. When he was a boy, he had thought it was the strongest fortress in the world. Now he knew differently and his expert eye recognised that it was poorly sited. The high ridge to the south east blocked the view to the sea, even from the top of the tower where the watchmen could see for miles in any other direction. The ridge was too narrow for the broch to have been placed on its summit without a huge effort to dig out a flat base, so the men who had originally built the broch generations before had taken the easier option of building it on the flat land to the west of the ridge. Experienced Roman soldiers would soon have their siege weapons dragged to the top of the ridge, allowing them to shoot down onto the broch from the higher ground. Or they would take the longer option of waiting for the broch to run out of water because the nearest stream was a hundred paces away and people cooped up inside would soon be forced out.

Despite its failings, which were obvious to Brude, Colm apparently still believed the broch was a fortress. Brude wanted to tell him that if the emperor was coming he would bring more than one legion with him. The Romans, he knew, were masters at dividing and conquering their foes, which was why they often paid silver to men they thought might help them, or at least not oppose them. But if the emperor came in war, the Boresti would only have two choices; surrender or die.

He wanted to say all of this but he knew that Colm would not believe him, could not conceive the true might of Rome because he had never really seen it. Brude realised that his relations with Colm were already strained, although he did not fully understand why. Arguing with him now would not help and would probably change nothing anyway. "Maybe you're right," he conceded. "They probably won't come this far."

"Of course not. But one day I might lead another raid to plunder their villages and towns."

Again Brude looked at him in astonishment. "I don't think that would be a good idea. Don't you remember what happened the last time?"

Colm laughed. "Of course I remember. But next time we will go by sea. I intend building ships to take us past the wall. That way we can raid and be gone before they can catch us. Even the Romans can't put soldiers on the sea."

"Yes they can," countered Brude emphatically. "They have ships too, you know."

Colm was not impressed. "I can understand your fear, Brude. You spent a long time as a slave. You are bound to be afraid of the Romans. Not all of us are."

"Of course I'm afraid of them," Brude retorted. "I've seen what they can do. Not as individuals but as a people. They are far stronger than you think. That force that defeated our tribe thirteen years ago was only one small part of one legion. The emperor has thirty legions under his command and the empire is bigger than you can possibly imagine." Brude stopped because he was growing angry and he could see from Colm's expression that he did not, or would not, understand. "Oh, you can do what you like," he said disgustedly, "but don't count me in your plans."

"I wasn't intending to," replied Colm coldly. "Anyway, the last raid was not entirely a failure. Those of us who survived came back with enough booty to make us rich men."

Brude asked the question he knew Colm was waiting for. "How did that happen? I heard that everyone ran like scalded cats."

"Oh, we did," Colm admitted. "But later we went back and crossed the wall further east while the Romans were hunting down the Selgovae. We found a rich farmhouse and some very wealthy merchants. When we got back across the wall we bought lots of sheep, cattle and other goods from the Votadini. I came back with enough wealth to make me the most important man in this village and I've been head man ever since." He jabbed Brude's chest with his finger. "I don't intend that you will take that away from me."

Brude decided he had best try to make amends for his earlier outburst. He really had not meant to fall out with Colm like this, not on his first day back home. He took a deep breath. As calmly as he could, he said, "Colm, I just want to be home. I am pleased that you have done well for yourself and I bear you no ill will. I have no intention of doing anything more than living as peaceably as I can."

Colm gave him a satisfied nod. He still liked to win. "Very well, we shall speak no more of this. But there is one more thing," he said, a hint of iron in his voice as he pressed home his advantage. "I hear Mairead was here yesterday."

"Yes, she came to thank me for finding your son."

Colm nodded but his eyes were hard. "She's my wife, Brude. I want you to remember that."

Brude returned his stare and nodded. "I know that, Colm. I won't forget it."

Fothair was in a bad way. Brude and Seoras carried him down the hill as gently as they could but he was badly hurt and the journey was agony for him. When they reached Seoras' house Brude laid him on the bed he had asked his mother to make up, then set to tending his wounds. His mother insisted that was work best done by a woman but Brude assured her he knew what he was doing. He fetched some of his most prized belongings from his pack, a selection of delicate instruments and some small leather pouches, each one tied and with the name of its contents inked on the side. He set them out beside the bed. Kneeling, he stripped off Fothair's dirty clothes and washed his wounds. There was a jagged gash on the tall man's left side, at the foot of the ribcage and another, deeper stab wound on his left thigh. Brude checked them and, selecting a small pair of tweezers from his instruments, he carefully picked out the fragments of wool or cloth that had been forced into the wounds.

Fothair groaned. Brude took a pinch of some dried herbs from one of the pouches and told his mother to mix it into some hot water as a drink.

"What is it?" she asked.

"Something to make him sleep. Mix it well, please."

While he waited for the drink, Brude fetched some cloth from the one remaining bolt he had and asked Seoras to cut some long strips for bandages, then he began mixing together some more herbs from other pouches with warm water to make a paste to which he added a dab of the honey he had brought from Peart.

"What's all that?" Seoras asked as the smell of the herbs wafted through the cottage.

"Juniper and mint to help keep the wounds free of infection. Some comfrey to help heal the cuts and a balm to stop the bleeding." He worked as he spoke, making sure the paste was mixed to the consistency he needed.

His mother helped him lift Fothair's head and make him drink the bitter potion she had brewed. Fothair grimaced, trying to resist but Brude pinched his nose to make him swallow and the medicine went down eventually. Brude waited for a while to let it take effect, then went back to cleaning the wounds. The one on Fothair's side looked bad but was actually of less concern than the deep one on his thigh, which was still oozing blood. Satisfied that they were as clean as he could get them, Brude applied the paste he had mixed to each one then tightly wrapped them in the bandages Seoras had cut. "His bandages are better quality than my clothes," Seoras observed, trying to brighten the mood.

Fothair's breathing was steadier now. Brude checked him over and found that two fingers of his right hand were broken. He reset them, which made Fothair jump and cry out, then he attached some small twigs which he bound up as splints.

He knelt back, satisfied he had done all that he could. "We'll give him another drink in a few hours to keep him asleep. That's the best cure for him at the moment."

"Where did you learn all that?" Seoras asked him, impressed at Brude's competence.

"Rome," Brude replied. "I saw a lot of injured men and I watched the healers working. I even had to get some treatment myself a few times."

"I saw the scars when you were washing," his mother said. "How did you get all them?" Concern was evident in her voice.

Brude had not realised she had been watching him but he supposed that she would rarely let him do anything without watching him now that he was back after she thought he had been lost. He shrugged off the question. The scars were old ones. "I was in a few fights," he explained.

He watched Fothair throughout the day, checking for signs of fever and was grateful when there were none. He mixed another sleeping draught around midday, forcing Fothair to drink it to keep him asleep. By late afternoon the big man was stirring again and opened his eyes. He tried to speak but Brude made him be quiet until he had fed him some fish soup his mother had made, followed by some oatmeal cakes.

Fothair's eyes were brighter and more alert by the time he had finished but he was still sleepy from the drinks Brude had mixed and weak from losing blood. "Why are you doing this?" he managed to ask.

"You're my slave now," Brude told him. "I don't want you to die otherwise you'd be a waste of what I spent on you."

"The others? Oengus? Cet?"

"I couldn't afford them."

Fothair studied him for a moment, "Why me?"

"Because you're bigger, tougher and smarter than the other two. And because it annoyed Colm." Brude was a little disappointed in himself at how true that last bit was.

Fothair tried to laugh but gasped in pain when he did. "I suppose if I live it will annoy him even more," he managed to say.

"I'm sure it will."

"Then I'll try to live. But I don't think I'll make a very good slave."

Brude smiled and said, "I don't know whether I'll make a good master. I've never had a slave before."

"You won't have one for long either," Fothair told him. "I'll run as soon as I can."

"Wait until you're better before you try that. You won't run far in the state you're in just now."

Brude made him drink another potion and waited until the big man fell asleep, his chest rising and falling evenly.

"Will he live?" his mother asked him.

"If the wounds stay free of infection, I think he will. I've seen men survive worse." He had also seen men die from lesser wounds that had become infected, but he thought it best not to mention that.

"What is he to you anyway?" asked Seoras. "Do you know him?"

"I only met him yesterday," Brude said. "But I like him. And this is partly my fault. Colm did this because I asked him not to hurt him if he caught him."

"That sounds like Colm," Seoras agreed, his voice grim.

The feast was held outdoors in the wide space in front of the broch where the ground was relatively flat and even. Wooden tables had been set up on trestles around a massive cooking pit over which two freshly slaughtered lambs and a calf were roasting. Stools and chairs had been hauled from the houses and jugs of ale and *uisge beatha* were brought out. Colm sat at a long table, Mairead on his left, with Brude in the position of honour on his right. The hostility of the morning was gone and Colm was in expansive mood, especially after he had toasted Brude's return with a tumbler of uisge.

Brude was wary of drinking too much. He had been young when he left and had only rarely been drunk. During his years as a slave strong drink was a luxury usually denied him although he had in the later years tried some of the Roman wines. Still, he knew he was not used to alcohol, and certainly not to the potent uisge, so he decided to restrict himself to only sipping at some ale.

Practically the whole village was there, both the upper and lower parts of it. Excuses for feasting were always welcome and everyone wanted to take part. A group of young men began playing some music, beating on drums while two played wild, intricate melodies on small flutes. Brude saw Caroc, the smith, still frowning at everything, drinking from an enormous mug. Seoc was there and the giant Cruithne too. There were others he recognised now, mostly the older women. His mother reminded him of their names and who they were related to. She was sitting beside Brude with Seoras to her right but young Castatin wormed his way into a seat to sit next to Brude. The boy spluttered when he tried some uisge, tears coming to his eyes, much to everyone's amusement. "It does that to me too," Brude whispered to him.

The drink flowed as the sun slowly dipped to the horizon, turning the sky a glorious red. Torches were lit and candles were set out on the tables. The meat was carved and passed round, then more drink was poured. The music became more fragmented as the musicians grew more and more drunk and the evening air filled with laughter and the growling and yapping of dogs that prowled beneath the tables, fighting over dropped scraps.

Brude was happy. Not drunk, but happy and relaxed. Then Mairead leaned forwards and said, "Brude, you must tell everyone what happened to you. We are all dying to know and you will have to tell the tale a hundred times unless you tell us all now."

Brude looked across at her, saw that she really did want to know. Colm was not pleased but played the part of a magnanimous host and made no objection, especially when others joined in the demands for Brude's story.

Realising there was no escape, Brude skipped straight to the moment they had joined the Romans in battle. He told how he had attacked the Roman line, killed his man, then been hit on the head and seen his father fall.

"I saw you both fall," said Colm. "When Anndra went down, everyone panicked and the battle was lost. We thought you were both dead."

"And when I woke up it was over," said Brude. He told them that others had survived but he could not remember many names. He explained that he had been hit hard on the head but the truth was that his memory failed him after thirteen years. He remembered Frual and when he mentioned his name young Seoc spoke up, saying, "My father lives?"

Brude looked at him, saw the eagerness in his face. He remembered now. Frual had had two children, a boy and a younger daughter with a third child on the way. He saw that Seoc was harbouring thoughts that his father might yet return and wondered how he could tell him to give up any hope he had of his seeing him again. "He was alive after the battle," he said after a moment's pause. "But we were all separated shortly afterwards and I have not seen him since then. I'm sorry."

Seoc's face fell and he nodded sadly. Brude's mother leaned close to his ear. She whispered, "Seoc's mother died two winters past. He has two young sisters to care for now." Brude saw that there were indeed two young girls, aged about fourteen and twelve, both with long dark hair and flashing eyes. Seeing them, he was suddenly reminded of Frual.

Mairead prompted him to go on with his story so he gave them an abbreviated version of his time as a field slave, omitting any mention of Julia. Then he recounted the long march to Hispania and the building of the aqueduct. "It took a long time," he told them, "but it is quick to tell for each day was the same as every other. Then, when the aqueduct was nearly done, I was sold again and taken to Rome itself, a city like no other in the world."

"Is that where you learned to fight?" Castatin interrupted.

"My son tells me you are a great warrior," Colm said, his tone suggesting that he did not believe it. "He says you defeated all three of the men who took him."

Brude felt uncomfortable but could not avoid the question. Speaking softly, he said, "Yes, I was taught to fight in a special school where slaves were trained to give shows and to die for the entertainment of the people of Rome."

"That doesn't sound so bad," Colm said happily. "Any man of the Boresti can fight a Roman any day!" That brought some laughter but Brude wondered how Colm could so easily forget the slaughter that had happened on the one occasion he had met the Romans in battle and how he had turned tail and fled in fear. But Colm went on, "Cruithne there would love that life." The giant's hairy face broke into a toothy grin.

"Well, between the fights it was easier," Brude admitted. "We trained hard but we ate well and got plenty of rest." He paused, staring into the clay mug in his hand, swirling the ale thoughtfully. "But every time you entered the arena could be the last time and your opponent was also trained and wanted to win. So that is why, when I was given my freedom after one particular show that pleased the people, I made myself a promise."

A hush had fallen over the table. All eyes were on him. Even some of those further away were straining to hear what he was saying. "What promise did you make, Brude?" Mairead asked gently.

"I promised myself I would not kill again unless I had no other choice. That I would not even fight unless there was no alternative."

"You fought Oengus and his men!" Castatin piped up excitedly. "Whipped them in a heartbeat!"

"I didn't have a choice," Brude told him. "But I did not kill them. I didn't even hurt them that much."

The giant Cruithne stood up slowly, waving his beaker extravagantly. "I could beat you!" he roared.

Brude sat still, looking up at him. "Yes, you probably could," he said. "But I am done with fighting now anyway."

Cruithne frowned. Normally when a man was challenged he was honour bound to accept and if any man accepted Cruithne's challenge it gave the big man the opportunity to show how strong he was. But Brude just sat there, watching him. Confused by Brude's immediate acknowledgement of his inevitable victory, Cruithne glanced at Colm who gestured for him to sit down.

Brude watched him carefully. The giant warrior had had a lot to drink but there was something in his eyes, which suggested that he was not just the big oaf he made out. He was a typical, boastful Pritani warrior and his size made him formidable but, even though he sat down at Colm's gestured command, Brude thought the big man was perhaps no fool.

Castatin nudged Brude's arm, distracting him. "Did you kill many men?" he asked with the eagerness to hear of battles typical of a young boy.

"Too many," replied Brude sadly.

A.D. 200

The gladiator school was a few miles outside Rome, just off the Appian Way, to the south of the great city. By the time they got there, Brude knew Curtius as well as he had ever known any Roman. The man was a former gladiator himself, hard as nails and with a morbid sense of humour born of daily encounters with death. He allowed them some freedom when he could but they all knew he would be ruthless if they crossed him. His bite would be every bit as bad as his bark.

There were four of them under his guard: Brude, now called Brutus, a stocky German called Valerius, a Jew named Josephus and Sarcho, a tall, olive-skinned man from Africa who spoke little Latin. Curtius warned them not to get too friendly with one another. "You may have to face each other in the arena one day. It's not pleasant to be up against someone you like and have to try to kill them. Believe me, I know."

Josephus, small and quick with dark eyes that missed little, spoke up. "You had to fight a friend, Curtius? What happened?"

"I'm still here, aren't I?" Curtius grinned wolfishly. "You figure it out."

So they reached their new home and found it was large, surrounded by a ditch and high wall which had a high wooden walkway running round the inside perimeter where armed guards patrolled day and night. There were at least a dozen buildings inside the wall, including some well-appointed rooms where the head of the school lived and some basic quarters for the slaves who slept in separate cells but ate and lived in a communal barracks. Compared to what they had been used to in Hispania, it was luxury.

At breakfast the new recruits quickly learned that there was a pecking order among the gladiatorial slaves. As untried and untrained new arrivals, they were right at the bottom of it. Josephus, eyes sparkling dangerously, was about to object when they were pushed to the back of the queue for food, but Brude grabbed him by the shoulders, holding him back. Josephus muttered something in his own language but made no trouble, even when the other men refused to make space for them at the long wooden tables. Brude simply stood against the wall, balancing his plate in his hand while eating. The food – barley gruel, bread, olives, grapes and cheese – was a lot better than he was used to so he did not mind standing. He was not fond of olives but knew better than to waste any food that was available. Sarcho and Valerius followed his lead but Josephus tried to squeeze onto a bench between two other men who growled at him but eventually moved. Brude wondered whether he had made a mistake by not doing the same, especially when he got some scornful looks as the men filed outside in answer to a blast on a horn. If he had, he supposed he would find out soon enough.

They followed the gladiators outside where Curtius greeted them with a barrage of curses, telling the four of them to follow him. He led them across a small courtyard, through a guarded gate and into another yard. The place seemed to be filled with small courtyards, most of them floored with hard-packed earth. As they walked, Curtius pointed out the bathhouse, bakery and infirmary with solitary words and a wave of his hand.

In the second courtyard a man with short grey hair and wearing a long white tunic was sitting on an ornately carved stool, flanked by two armed guards. Two more guards stood at the edge of the courtyard, one on either side. Standing beside the seated man, wearing only a loincloth and sandals, was a large man with a shaven head. His muscled torso was tanned and criss-crossed with the fine white lines of many old scars. He gave the four newcomers a smile of eager anticipation as they followed Curtius across the small yard.

Curtius spoke to the seated man. "Hail, Lentulus. Here are the four new recruits."

Lentulus cast his disapproving eyes over the four men. "I hope they are better than the last lot you brought, Curtius. Another two died while you were away and the last one was defeated and badly wounded. He may never fight again."

Curtius ignored the jibe. "You know, it's hard to tell, but I think these four all have potential."

Lentulus waved him aside. "Let's get on with it then," he said impatiently. "Macro!" The shaven man bent down to pick up two wooden swords, tossing one to Josephus who caught it deftly. Curtius stepped to stand beside Lentulus' stool and turned to watch.

Macro held his own wooden sword and adopted a practised fighter's stance, gently waving the sword at Josephus. "Come on then, little man," he said. "Show me what you can do." Without warning he sprang forwards, his arm moving in a sweeping blow aimed at Josephus' head. The little Jew jumped backwards, nearly crashing into Valerius who backed away quickly. Macro leaped again, aiming another blow, which Josephus parried, still going backwards. He reached the wall and could go no further. Macro's arm moved with bewildering speed as he swung and thrust. Three blows Josephus frantically parried but the fourth, a whack to his sword arm, caught him hard and the fifth, a jab to the stomach could have done him serious injury had Macro not pulled the blow at the last instant. "You're dead," the shaven man hissed triumphantly. He backed away and Brude thought Josephus was about to hit him from behind until Curtius shouted the Jew's name and ordered him to stop. Curtius beckoned him over, telling him to stand in front of Lentulus while Macro strutted back to take his place beside Curtius.

Lentulus looked at Josephus appraisingly, then turned to Curtius and raised an eyebrow. "Thracian, do you think?"

"He's fast enough," Curtius agreed. "Not many can block Macro first time out."

"Thracian then," said Lentulus. He hesitated, "He's a Jew, you say?"

"He just has some funny rules about what he eats," said Curtius, trying to gloss over any potential complications. "Nothing to worry about."

Lentulus was not convinced. "Don't the Jews have some funny rules about not doing anything on one day a week?"

Curtius dismissed the objection. "If he doesn't fight, he'll be killed. End of problem."

Josephus cautiously looked at Curtius and said, "May I speak, Master?"

Curtius nodded.

"Some of my fellow Jews, who were taken into captivity with me, tried to observe the Sabbath," Josephus said. "They are dead. I am still here. You need have no worries about me."

Lentulus tilted his head to one side then gave a small nod. Brude thought the man probably didn't care much whether Josephus lived or died. "Next!" Lentulus shouted. Josephus was waved aside and Curtius told him to give the sword to Valerius.

Taking up his fighting stance again, Macro attacked Valerius. The German tribesman was not as fast as Josephus but he was stronger. He let Macro hit him, the sword raking across his chest, then lashed out with his own sword, forcing the big man back to avoid the blow. If Macro's sword had been real, Valerius would have been badly cut, but he simply ignored the blow from the wooden rudis and made his own attack. Macro grinned, attacked again. This time his sword rapped Valerius on the knee, making the German shout in pain. Still, he did not go down. "Enough!" Curtius shouted. Macro immediately backed away, leaving Valerius looking puzzled.

Curtius said to Lentulus, "Secutor, I thought. Samnite or Murmillo?"

Lentulus considered for a moment. "Murmillo," he said, and Valerius' fate was decided.

Sarcho was next but he did not last long. Macro changed his attack style, jabbing and thrusting the wooden sword, making the tall African dance to avoid the blunt end of the cylindrical wooden blade. Sarcho tried to block, was better at dodging but was concentrating so much on the sword that he walked straight into a left cross from Macro's fist. Sarcho collapsed, knocked from his feet by the strength of the blow. While he lay on the ground, trying to get up, Lentulus and Curtius discussed him.

"He's tall," observed Lentulus. "Retiarius probably. It would be better if he was a bit faster on his feet."

"He can learn," Curtius said.

"He'll die if he doesn't," observed Lentulus dryly. "Very well, Retiarius. That gives us a nice balance to the first three. What about the last one?"

It was Brude's turn. He picked up the wooden sword from where Sarcho had dropped it. The blade was short, about the length of a legionary's gladius, which Brude remembered so well, but this blade was a thick cylinder of smooth, polished wood with a flat end at the tip. The handle was basic, shaped slightly to fit his hand, which was protected a little by the flat crosspiece bars of the hilt. It was heavier than he expected. Macro grinned at him and adopted his fighting stance. Brude had watched the first three fights carefully and had already decided his tactics. He knew this test was not designed to kill them, simply to see how fast and strong they were. Or how well they could think.

He decided not to defend himself but to attack first, forcing Macro to step backwards to parry his sudden swing of the sword. His blows were clumsy, wild and inaccurate but if they had landed they would have done some damage. Macro twisted, dodged, then parried a blow that was aimed for his head. He tried to strike back but Brude blocked his thrust, lashing out with his left hand, hoping to catch Macro off guard the way he had done to Sarcho. The shaven man, though, was incredibly fast and he ducked away from the punch then jumped aside as Brude tried to kick him. Brude's foot missed by a fraction but he realised he had overextended himself. Macro's wooden sword smacked against his left leg as the big man danced round behind him. It hurt but Brude turned, swinging his own sword, trying to strike

Macro's back. He missed again. And Macro's sword was at his throat. "You're dead," the big man gasped, breathing heavily.

Brude dropped his sword. He turned to face Curtius and Lentulus, noticing that Lentulus was looking at him with keen interest. Brude quickly dropped his gaze the way a slave should, standing still while they openly discussed him as if he could not hear them.

"Fast and strong," Lentulus commented admiringly. "Thracian, do you think?"

"He's fast enough," Curtius agreed. "But I think he would be better as a Samnite."

Lentulus rubbed his chin thoughtfully. "You think so? I suppose he has the strength for that but he was very fast. He'd make a good Thracian."

"He'd make a better Samnite," Curtius insisted. "If he survives the training he could be very good indeed."

Lentulus nodded but did not seem convinced. He looked at Macro and raised an eyebrow. "What do you think, Macro?"

Macro looked at Brude, testing him with his eyes. After a few moments' thought he said to Lentulus, "I agree with Curtius. Samnite."

Lentulus nodded. "Samnite it is then. Excellent! One of each class. Begin the training immediately."

So Brude's fate was decided. He was to be a Samnite. Whatever that was.

"There are five main types of gladiator," Curtius explained. "We train them all here. Lucius Fulvius Lentulus runs the school and I am the *lanista*. I am in charge of the training. There are others, all experienced fighters, who help me. Macro, you've met. He trains the Thracian fighters."

They stood at the edge of yet another courtyard, a large one this time, the floor covered in sand. It was full of men training. At one side were a few who were practising with various weapons under the watchful eye of their trainers while armed guards stood close by. Elsewhere the men used shields and wooden swords in mock combat while closer to where they stood men were running, jumping, dodging mechanical devices which swung heavy wooden beams with frightening speed, or dancing along blocks of wood protruding from the ground, leaping as quickly as they could from one to the next. It was the strangest sight Brude had ever seen.

Curtius pointed to the men with the real weapons. "That's a Murmillo, the one with the fish crest on his helmet. Large shield, heavy sword, face guard, shin guard, armoured sword arm. Heavy and strong, the Murmillones are. Well protected but usually a bit slow because of the weight they carry. Brude glanced at Valerius who had been nominated to fight as a Murmillo. "Why a fish?" he asked Curtius.

"Tradition," Curtius replied without thinking. He went on, "Then there's the Samnite. Basically the same armour but uses the gladius of the legions and has a slightly different helmet. Still heavily armoured. These two are the Secutors, the chasers. It is their job to hunt down their opponents in the arena.

"Then the Thracian." He indicated another gladiator. "Hardly any armour, just the very small circular shield and the curved sword, the sica. Relies on speed and agility to defeat the armour of the Secutors." Brude saw Josephus nodding. The little Jew had shown that he was quick and would train as a Thracian.

"Finally the Retiarius," Curtius said. "No armour, just the trident and the net. Uses speed and the long reach of the trident. If he catches you in his net, you've had it." That was Sarcho's designated role.

"You said five types," Josephus pointed out. "That's only four."

Curtius gave him that wolfish grin they knew heralded a macabre joke. "The fifth kind are the dead ones. We get lots of those." He laughed aloud at the joke, which they soon discovered was a stock one at the school. Curtius looked at them all, his face serious again. "But before you learn how to fight, you must learn how to move. If you are fast, you must become faster; in thought and in movement. We will train you so well that you'll be able to catch a fly off the wall with your bare hand. If you are strong, you must become stronger, able to take the pain and stand in the sweating sun and keep on fighting no matter what." He lifted a hand, pointing at them, one at a time. "I warn you, many do not survive the training. Either you get killed here or, if I judge that you are not up to it, you'll be sent to the arena with the criminals and war captives. Either way, you're dead." He let that sink in, then said, "I expect at least one of you to fail the training, maybe two of you. That's normal. It's up to you to prove to me that you deserve to stay and become the best."

The training began. It was brutal, efficient and relentless. They ran, lifted weights, spent hours hacking at wooden poles with heavy wooden swords, jumped on rolling logs to improve their balance, and had to run a course which involved dodging swinging weights and beams. In the sweltering summer heat they were soon exhausted but the trainers gave them no respite, working them till they dropped. Brude had thought he was fit and strong but this was the hardest thing he had ever done and he never had a problem sleeping at nights. Often it was all he could do to stay awake long enough to climb into bed. His muscles ached from exertion and his body was bruised whenever he misjudged a swinging obstacle and caught a blow from one of the weights.

Despite the exhaustion, the training had its compensations. The food was varied and good and, if Curtius deemed they had done well, he would sometimes send one of the female slaves to their cell at night. That was about the only thing that could keep them awake.

In the barracks room they were soon accepted, although only if they kept their place in the pecking order. The experienced fighters were always at the head of the queue, sat together to eat and rarely spoke to the newcomers. Then there was a group of men who had fought a few times and survived and, finally, those who were untried in actual combat. Despite the warning Curtius had given about forming friendships, Brude soon discovered that many of the gladiators were close. Living together in such proximity, he supposed it was inevitable but, for his own part, he took care not to become too friendly with any of them, not even the three he had arrived with. He thought Josephus was mad anyway. The little Jew boasted he had killed half a dozen Roman soldiers in his homeland in what he called the perpetual struggle for freedom from the imperial yoke. He insisted he was enjoying the training because it would allow him to kill more Romans. He did not change his view even when Brude pointed out that most of the gladiators were slaves, not Romans. "I'll kill them anyway," Josephus laughed. "The Lord has told me that is my destiny."

Valerius was strong but slow-witted and Brude had little in common with him while Sarcho made no attempt to learn Latin and spoke to nobody, so Brude was happy to keep himself to himself. He concentrated all his energies on working hard at the training. He still recalled the words of Basillus, in the slave stockade four years earlier, about how a slave could win his freedom in the arena. That dream kept Brude going, drove him to become as fast and as strong as he could.

Like all of the gladiators, he took a few bruises and pulled some muscles. When that happened he would be sent to the infirmary where a Greek physician would examine him. If the physician said he should stop training, there was no argument until he was pronounced fit again. Brude quickly realised, though, that getting hurt deliberately to be allowed some days of rest was not a good idea because when he returned to training he had to work even harder to catch up with the others. If he was not able to train, it also meant that he was assigned other duties such as cleaning out the privies. After only a few weeks, most of them preferred to put up with the aches and pains, refusing to go to the infirmary unless they were genuinely unable to train.

It was three months before they were given any training in actual combat, three months of hard work, which improved their strength and their speed beyond anything Brude would have thought possible. He tried catching flies off the wall of his cell in the evenings. He never quite managed it but he felt that one day soon he might do it.

He learned more about the school as well. Lentulus was not the owner, just the manager who ran it on behalf of an ex-slave called Trimalchio who was, therefore, Brude's master. "You'll hardly ever see him, though," Curtius told him. "He pays for the running of the place and takes a share of the profits but it's just a hobby for him."

"He was a slave and he owns the school?" Brude was incredulous.

"Yes, he was a slave and he is now a very rich man indeed. He's a pompous ass, but he's a rich pompous ass and he owns more land than you or I could walk across in a day."

"How does a slave get to be that rich?" Brude asked him.

"Don't start getting ideas," warned Curtius. "First you've got to gain your freedom and then you've got to earn the money. Trimalchio has fingers in lots of pies and from what I hear he has an influential patron."

"But a slave can be freed and become wealthy?" Brude insisted, his mind once again racing with dreams of freedom.

"It can happen," Curtius conceded, "but most slaves die as slaves. Even if you do get your freedom, either by buying it, which you won't because you'll never be given enough money, or by winning it in the arena, like I did, you still stay poor."

"Poor but free."

Curtius looked at Brude seriously. "Look, Brutus, you've got some talent and, if I was a betting man, I might put money on you being good enough to win the rudis and get your freedom. But don't count on it. Aim for it and try your damndest and you might get there if you are very, very lucky, but this is a dangerous life. No matter how good you are, and you're not that good yet, believe me, you can have bad luck or you can get over-confident or you can simply meet someone who's better than you. When that happens, it can all be over."

Brude listened to the advice and promised he would work as hard as he could, but the dreams of freedom would not go away.

He also learned that while the threat of death was a constant companion for every gladiator, it was not as common as Curtius made out to the newcomers. There were twenty-six gladiators in the school, all at various stages. Those who were deemed ready to fight would only be taken to the arena perhaps three or four times a year and, even if they lost, death was not always inevitable. Gladiators were expensive to train and to keep and no lanista liked losing an experienced man so the school charged a lot more when a gladiator died. The magistrates who paid for, and supervised, the shows knew this, so would often let a gladiator live, especially if they had fought well and enough of the crowd called for them to be allowed to survive. On the other hand, they sometimes liked to show their generosity to the crowd by condemning a defeated gladiator to death. If the emperor was presiding, there was more chance of this happening because emperors liked to be generous to the people and money was no object for a man who ruled the empire. One more dead gladiator would make no difference to the emperor's wealth.

So every few weeks Curtius and Lentulus would go off to Rome with a few of the experienced men and, perhaps, a novice they deemed ready. Later that day they would come back, sometimes without one or two of those who had left. The bodies would follow later, brought on a wagon and the men would be buried in the small graveyard, which sat outside the school. Often they all came back, even men who had lost their fights. Brude saw that such men were welcomed even though the school had lost some reputation. Every gladiator knew that defeat could happen to any of them. There was no shame in it provided the man had fought well. That did not stop them fighting hard in training and constantly trying to outdo each other, to improve their standing in the group, but when it came to actual combat there was a feeling of togetherness, a fraternity of fighting men who looked out for each other because of the dangerous lives they shared.

By the time the autumn rains were turning colder and winter was approaching, Brude was given to Kallikrates, a Greek who had lost his left hand after a wound had become infected, forcing the physician to amputate it at the wrist. Kallikrates could no longer fight but he had been allowed to stay at the school to help train the other fighters. He was very good at it. He had fought as a Samnite and now he trained the eight men in the school who also fought that way. Brude was allowed to join the group and was initiated by being dressed in the armour of a Samnite, given a wooden sword and set against Pollio, the most experienced man in the school, who had fought nine times and won seven of the bouts.

Brude listened carefully as Kallikrates explained the armour. Wearing only a loincloth, Brude had an iron greave strapped to his left shin and a broad leather band fastened around his belly like an enormous belt. Next, the ornate crested helmet with its face guard was placed over his head. He could hardly see anything out of the eyeholes and the weight of the helmet was far greater than he had expected. A heavy linen sleeve was strapped to his right arm by leather bands, providing protection for his sword arm. Then he was given the rectangular curved shield, made from layers of plywood bound in iron, with a large, round iron boss at its centre. The shield was large enough to cover his body from the greave to his shoulder and was curved so that it provided almost full protection when held in front of his body. Lastly, Kallikrates gave him the heavy wooden sword then shoved him onto the sand of the training arena to face Pollio.

The fight did not last long. Brude was nervous, felt restricted by the helmet and was still trying to adjust the shield when Pollio attacked, using his own shield as a battering ram to knock Brude off balance. Pollio's sword cracked against Brude's helmet, sending a ringing through Brude's head. Dazed, he waved his sword in a futile attempt to hit Pollio who simply blocked it with his shield before knocking Brude over with another massive shove.

Brude crashed to the ground, jarring his head when the heavy helmet struck the sand and getting a crack on the ribs from the rim of his own shield. Lying on the ground, he felt Pollio's foot on his chest. Angry and disappointed, he let go of his sword and heard the laughter from the watching men. Kallikrates helped him to his feet and removed his helmet for him, a broad grin on his face. "We do that to every new man," he said cheerily. "It makes you realise how much you still have to learn."

More training and more mock combats followed. Kallikrates showed Brude how to use his shield as a weapon, not just something to hide behind. "The sword does the killing but the shield is what can really do the damage," the Greek told him.

He was pitted against novices from the other types, the Retiarii and the Thracians, once against Josephus who was making a name for himself among the Thracian fighters. He danced round Brude, lashing at him with his tiny shield and a wooden replica of the curved sica. Brude was adjudged to have lost that fight but it was a close contest, and he was pleased with himself that he managed to give the Jew a real test.

"You're very fast for a Samnite," Josephus told him after the fight.

"Not fast enough yet," said Brude. "I couldn't catch you with a single blow."

"Nobody's as fast as me," Josephus said happily, "but you were close a couple of times."

So Brude worked on his speed all through the winter. The cold, which others complained of, did not bother him. Compared to the winters he knew from his youth in Broch Tava, the Roman winter was just pleasantly cool.

He began to win some of the mock combats, even against men who had fought in the arena, and soon he found that he and Josephus were moving up the complex and unspoken social scale of the barrack room, even though neither of them had ever actually fought a real fight.

Then, on a day which he reckoned must be near to his twenty-first birthday, Curtius called him and Josephus out of training and told them they would be going with a couple of other men to fight in the arena. "I think you're both ready," he told them, "and so do your trainers. This is a small show in a town a few days' march down the coast so hopefully it will be a nice easy start for you."

Brude's stomach churned all day.

It took them over a week to get to Paestum, nestled on the Campanian coast south of Rome. It was the home town of a young senator who had just been elected as a praetor and wished to celebrate his success by giving a small show to the people of his home town. The emperor had given his permission so a small wooden amphitheatre had been hastily constructed on the outskirts of the town. Curtius, accompanied by two guards, had taken four gladiators, as instructed by Lentulus. They were to fight four men from another school, the school of Propertius, which, Curtius said, was one of the biggest around. "It would be nice to put one over those bastards," he told them cheerily. It had been arranged that each school would provide two novices and two experienced fighters. Brude and Josephus were the novices while Pollio and a tall Retiarius named Frontius were the experienced men.

Brude was nervous but Curtius sat with him and Josephus in the cramped space set aside for the gladiators beneath the rising rows of seats. He talked to them calmly yet reassuringly, reminding them of their training and instilling confidence. Then he went to meet the lanista from the school of Propertius, leaving the gladiators to listen to the sounds of the crowd gathering in the tiers of benches above their heads. Over the clumping of footsteps and the murmur of voices they heard a woman laugh. "Sounds nice," Pollio said.

"She probably looks like a goat," replied Frontius. Brude and Josephus laughed. Then the door opened and Curtius returned. He looked at Brude and told him that he would be up first, fighting a Retiarius.

Brude threw up.

Curtius checked Brude's armour, tightening the greave on his leg, checking the straps on the thick linen binding on his right arm, then fastening the wide leather belt that protected his belly. Finally he handed Brude his helmet and told him to tuck it under his arm. "You'll be fine," Curtius said. "Just remember, the trident you can dodge or block, it's the net that you have to watch out for. Get tangled in that and you're in trouble, so stay clear of it. Understand?"

"I remember."

"And try to get the crowd on your side. That way even if you get into trouble, they'll want to keep you alive." Brude had heard Curtius say that hundreds of times but, right then, it somehow didn't sound quite as reassuring as it had before.

Curtius led him out into the narrow corridor that led from the cells to the arena. In the dim light, Brude felt hemmed in, as if the walls were closing in to crush him. The noise of the crowd filtered down, adding to his nervousness. He had never fought in front of an audience before and the thought that he had to die for the entertainment of the Romans made him angry, yet the anger could not force out the fear.

There were armed guards in the tunnel and another man, tall, wearing a loincloth and sandals, who stood facing the entrance door to the arena. A lanista stood beside him. The gladiator's skin was black and Brude hesitated, fascinated by the sight. He had heard about the Nubians but never seen one before. The man turned to look at Brude, opening his mouth in a feral grin, his teeth pearly white against his dark skin. Brude struggled to keep the fear from his face. Curtius leaned close behind and whispered into Brude's ear, "His blood is red, the same as yours." Brude nodded, thankful for the reassurance. Curtius was telling him that the Nubian was just a man, whatever colour his skin was. Brude took a deep breath, trying to calm his mind, to think of nothing but the task in hand.

In the shadows of the tunnel, he had a closer look at his opponent. The Retiarius' only armour was an iron shoulder guard on his left shoulder and a long sleeve of linen down his left arm. He would be unhampered by the weight that Brude had to carry. He would have speed and the weapons he used would give him greater reach.

The weapons were handed to them. The Nubian strapped his wide net to his left wrist, had a small dagger wrapped round his waist then took his trident in his right hand, checking the wickedly barbed tines to make sure they were sharp. Brude was given his shield, strapped his left arm through the loops and took the gladius in his right hand. It was heavy, but not as heavy as the training swords they used so it seemed relatively light to his touch. Short and double-edged, it was designed for thrusting, the way the legions did their killing, not the wild swings of a barbarian long sword.

There was a fanfare of trumpets then a herald's voice called out, announcing to the crowd the beginning of the games being given by their own Publius Cornelius Glabro, son of Publius, by kind permission of the emperor, Lucius Septimius Severus. Brude barely listened. His heart was pounding and his mouth was dry, the taste of his own vomit still lingering. Then Curtius slapped him on the back as two guards pulled the doors open to let in a blaze of sunlight. The trumpets blasted again.

The Nubian strode forwards, out into the light with Brude only a pace behind him, walking out into an amphitheatre for the first time. The roar of the crowd met him.

The amphitheatre was both a surprise and a disappointment. The arena itself, oval in shape, was not sand but hard earth. It had walls of wood, too high to jump to the first row of seats from ground level and seats that rose in steep tiers. The people at the front were close enough to make out their faces clearly and hear their individual voices above the general hubbub. There were shouts of encouragement, clapping and cheering as the people anticipated the show. Brude tried to ignore them but saw that the Nubian was grinning broadly and nodding his head to people in the crowd, waving his trident in salute.

The two combatants walked to one end of the arena where Glabro himself sat with his friends and clients. The two gladiators gave the traditional salute, "We who are about to die salute you!" Brude heard the Nubian's voice, recognised the confidence in his tone, the conviction of victory. Glabro beamed proudly, waved at them to begin and they backed away from each other. Curtius helped Brude put his helmet on, making sure it was fastened tightly, rapping his hand on it when he was satisfied. "Remember your training," he said urgently. "Watch for the net." Then Curtius stepped back, as did the opposing lanista, each holding a whip and a short sword. There were four guards, armed with spears, and archers standing round the top of the arena wall. Gladiators, heroes to the crowd, were still only slaves. If they did not fight, or tried to attack anyone but each other, they would be killed without hesitation.

Brude looked at the tall Nubian, his muscled body gleaming in the sun with the oil he had rubbed on to make it difficult for an opponent to grab hold of him. He grinned again, showing the teeth whiter than any Brude had ever seen as he hefted his trident, holding it underarm, swishing the net with its weighted edges, making small casts to show Brude what was waiting for him.

"Fight!" shouted Curtius.

"Fight!" shouted the other lanista.

The Nubian cautiously approached Brude. And Brude suddenly found his fear gone as the months of training took hold. He watched the man's movements, looking for clues in his eyes and in the bunching of his muscles. He decided he did not want to die for the entertainment of the crowd, not here, not now. The noise of the audience faded from his senses as he concentrated. The Nubian's skin may be black as ebony but Brude remembered Curtius' whispered advice that he was just a man, the same as other men. He could bleed just the same as other men.

Brude put his shield across his body, kept the gladius low and close to his side then stepped forwards, taking small steps to keep well balanced. The Retiarius, with no armour to weigh him down, would rely on speed and agility to get past Brude's shield, use the longer reach of his trident to stab and thrust, fling his net to tangle Brude's arms and legs or even land it over his head to render him helpless. To win this fight, Brude had, somehow, to avoid the net and trident and get in close. If he could do that, the Retiarius had no protection. It was easier said than done. Of all the gladiator types, the Retiarius won more often than not.

The Nubian swung his left arm, casting his net high, trying to let it fall over Brude's crested helmet. Brude stepped backwards, raised his shield and the trident was suddenly spearing forwards to come under the rim of the upraised shield, aiming for his thigh. He jumped backwards, heard the lead weights of the net rattle down the shield and he was clear.

He backed away which brought some jeers from the crowd. He was a Secutor, a chaser. He was supposed to hunt the foe, not try to escape him. The Retiarius may have the advantage but the Romans liked their Secutors. Curtius had told him to try to please the crowd but Brude ignored them, concentrating instead on trying to win. Fighting well and losing did not interest him. He stepped forwards, waving his sword clumsily and ineffectually. The Nubian danced away, spinning in an effort to get out of Brude's line of sight. Brude turned his whole body, holding his shield close, keeping his opponent in view. The helmet, with its small eye holes and even smaller breathing holes was a great protection but also a great weakness for it was heavy and restricted his field of vision. He had to know where the Nubian was or he was a dead man.

Again the Retiarius cast the net, low this time. Brude easily dodged it, backing away to the sound of more jeers from the crowd. "Stick him!" a man's voice yelled to the Nubian from the front rows. The Nubian waved his trident to acknowledge the cheers. Brude resumed his fighting stance, stepped forwards to make sure he had room behind him and watched the man's eyes closely, trying to anticipate the next move.

The net came high again. Brude had already guessed it from the way the man's arm had started to move. As he had done before, Brude stepped back, raising his shield high to block the net. As he had done before, the Nubian lunged forwards with the trident, aiming for Brude's exposed left thigh and once again Brude jumped backwards to dodge the falling net. But

for his troubles. He dealt out more to his opponent who lived, despite having taken several cuts from Josephus' sica. Frontius, the Retiarius, also won, eventually taking down his Thracian opponent who lived, but was badly wounded, while Pollio had an epic struggle against another Samnite which seemed to last for ages and which ended with both men exhausted and bloody. Pollio got the upper hand at the last, knocking his opponent to his knees, but the crowd, pleased by the performance of both fighters, indicated to Glabro that the man should live.

Curtius was in such a fine humour at having so comprehensively beaten the men from the rival school that he gave each of them a few sesterces from the prize money. It was the first time Brude had ever received any money as a slave.

Their trip back was leisurely, principally because, apart from Brude, the others all had injuries which needed tending and had to walk slowly after they had been treated. Curtius took the chance to visit the local forum where he bought two more slaves who walked back with them in the slave coffle. When they did reach the school, they discovered Valerius was gone. "Wasn't up to it," Kallikrates told Brude. "Lentulus sent him to the arena to fight with the war captives." Which meant Valerius was dead, for the war captives were never allowed to survive, even the winners simply being thrown back at the next games.

By the time of the Saturnalia, the mid-winter festival, Brude had fought three more times and won each fight without receiving anything worse than a slight scratch. Two of his opponents had survived and the last had been alive but had put up a poor show so the crowd had demanded his death. Brude had delivered the death blow as quickly as he could, driving his gladius into the kneeling man's spine at the base of his neck. He had hated it and had nearly thrown his sword away in disgust but Curtius had snapped a warning and he had retained his composure, doing what he had to.

He and Josephus were now allowed to sit with the veterans in the barracks room. The little Jew was also making a reputation for himself in the arena. He claimed it was because his god was protecting him. Brude make the mistake of asking which god he was referring to. He was astonished to learn that the Jews only had one god, which seemed far too few to him. Kallikrates said, "All the Jews are mad, but they're not as bad as the Christians. We won't have any of them as gladiators. They refuse to fight."

Sarcho, the African, who still refused to speak much Latin even though he understood it well enough now, failed to return from a fight and, in the spring of the next year, Frontius was also killed. Brude started to realise that surviving for any great length of time as a gladiator was not going to be easy. He trained even harder, surprising even Josephus by beating the little man in a mock fight one afternoon.

Kallikrates gave him a word of caution. "You're good, Brutus, potentially very good, because you've got ice in your veins and you're faster than most. But Curtius has been putting you up against men he was pretty sure you could beat and you won't get away with that much longer. You're getting a reputation now and you'll find it a lot harder, so don't get over-confident. Even the best of us, sooner or later, has a bit of bad luck."

Brude soon discovered the truth of Kallikrates' words. His next fight was in Rome itself, in the great Flavian amphitheatre that some called the Colosseum after the colossal statue of the emperor Nero which had once stood nearby. Built on the site that had formerly been a private lake in the grounds of Nero's palace, the massive amphitheatre could hold over fifty thousand people, a huge crowd, more than Brude had ever seen in one place before. The arena itself was surprisingly compact but seemed hemmed in by the incredible height of the tiers of stone and wooden benches that rose skywards in a dazzling array of arches. It was a feat of construction that showed the power and wealth of imperial Rome. It also allowed the people of Rome to give vent to their desire to see blood.

Brude's opponent this time was another Retiarius, a tall man with golden hair, obviously an experienced fighter. Brude had won his first fights in quick order and was confident in his own ability but this battle lasted nearly fifteen minutes as they probed, parried, thrust and dodged, testing each other. After one frantic spin away from danger, Brude took a raking blow from the trident across the back of his shoulders. He could feel the stinging of the cut and the blood flowing down his back but he ignored the pain and managed to face his opponent again, much to the delight of the crowd. Sweat dripping from every pore, he drew on all his reserves of strength as he risked becoming tangled in the net to charge close to the Retiarius. The tall man, even without the weight of a shield and helmet, was tired too, and he was fractionally slow to react to Brude's attack. He avoided the deadly thrust of the sword but could not dodge the huge shield. Brude, putting all his effort into the blow, knocked him from his feet. Quickly kicking the trident from the man's hand, Brude stamped his foot on the man's chest and hissed, "Lie still! They'll let you live." He didn't know whether that was true but he hoped it was. The man had fought well and deserved to live. Brude looked to the imperial box where he saw the emperor himself, bearded and wearing a toga, sitting under the shade of a striped canopy, surrounded by courtiers, slaves and guards. The emperor looked around the great amphitheatre, trying to gauge the crowd's preference. From the senators in their marble seats in the front rows, through the equites behind them, up through the packed ranks of the plebs and, finally, up to where the women and slaves stood in the dizzying heights of the top tiers, Brude saw the waving of white handkerchiefs and the signals of thumbs thrust upwards. The emperor eventually gave the signal for life. Brude lifted his foot from the man's chest and stalked out of the arena, his back sticky with blood.

He spent a week in the infirmary. The physician, a Greek called Tygaeus, told Curtius that the wound was quite bad and he wanted to keep an eye on it. In fact, Brude could have left after a day but Tygaeus knew he would go back to training too soon and possibly re-open the wound, so he insisted Brude stay. Brude did not mind for the beds were comfortable and he was able to watch Tygaeus working. He asked about his remedies, even helping him to reset a broken arm that one young novice suffered.

"I don't know why I bother," Tygaeus grumbled. "He'll be back sooner or later with some other injury."

Brude certainly returned a few times over the next couple of years. By the time he was twenty-four years old, he had fought thirteen times and won twelve of his fights, surviving his one defeat because he had given as good as he got against a Murmillo and only lost because he slipped at a vital moment. The crowd had let him live but the feeling of lying on the sand, helpless and waiting for the decision, was one he would never forget. Sprawled there, at the mercy of the mob's whim, he saw death and closed his eyes, picturing Mairead in his mind's eye. Then he heard Curtius telling him to stand up and his opponent was gone. He had been allowed to live but his legs were shaking so much he barely made it out of the arena.

Against that one defeat, though, his victories brought him some fame. Success brought other benefits too. As well as the small sums of money Curtius would give him from the winnings, he soon discovered that there were many wealthy women who were willing to pay for a night alone with a successful gladiator, provided he was discreet and handsome. Brude qualified on both counts. He had little respect for the women who cheated on their absent husbands this way but he was a young man and his life was likely to be short, so he always complied whenever Curtius told him a woman had asked for him. Being in the homes of the upper class was a revelation for him, so luxurious were they compared to what he was used to, even though he rarely saw more than the bedroom.

He was one of the veterans now. Of the twenty-six gladiators who had been at the school when he first arrived four years previously, fourteen were still alive although several who had joined later had died during the same period. Survival, it seemed, was a matter of experience; if you survived your first half dozen fights, you had a good chance of surviving for quite a long time. And if you survived long enough, you might earn your freedom and retire. The problem with that was that few people wanted much to do with a retired gladiator. While they were young and fought well they were heroes to the people who watched them, idolised by the crowd, who bought small statuettes and even decorated their homes with paintings and mosaics of gladiators. But once they retired, they were just ex-slaves who were trained in violence. Most retired gladiators ended up, like Curtius, training other men to become gladiators.

A quicker way out was to get an injury serious enough to stop them fighting but not so bad as to leave them permanently disabled. Getting old and slow only meant that you had more chance of dying in the arena before you could honourably retire. The only other hope that Brude clung to was that he would earn the rudis, be presented with a wooden sword by the emperor to signify that he was free and need never fight again. But as Curtius kept telling him, that did not happen often. Brude had already fought in front of the emperor several times, fought well and beaten more experienced men yet he was still a slave, just as he had been for the last eight years.

In the eleventh year of the reign of Lucius Septimius Severus, emperor of Rome, the Secular Games were to be celebrated. For the Romans, a saeculum of one hundred and ten years was regarded as the longest possible span of a human life and was celebrated to mark the dawning of a new era. Septimius Severus announced a grand festival of theatre performances and chariot racing, culminating in three days of gladiatorial combat, all to be provided at his own expense to mark this new dawn for his dynasty.

Brude thought the Romans' arithmetic must be faulty as he had never known anyone live beyond eighty years old, let alone one hundred and ten. Most of the Boresti thought sixty was a long life. Josephus claimed he had met a man who was one hundred and two. He even said that the Jews' holy men talked of a man who had lived for nearly a thousand years. Nobody believed him; they all knew Josephus was mad.

One man who was happy about the Secular Games was Lentulus. The school was to provide eight gladiators for the final day of the games as well as six men for earlier bouts and he anticipated a significant income. The news even brought the mysterious Trimalchio, the owner of the school, out to pay a visit to watch the men training. Brude saw him from a distance, a short man but very fat, his body virtually round and his face chubby with a double chin. He wore a toga and talked animatedly to Lentulus and Curtius for a while before going off, a dozen slaves scurrying after him. "Pompous ass," Brude heard Curtius say to Kallikrates afterwards. "He's got a covered litter and it takes eight men to carry him in it, all the way out here from Rome." Kallikrates said nothing and Curtius went on, "That's not all. He's got a slave boy going ahead blowing a trumpet to announce his presence. The man's a bloody disgrace."

"He's very rich," Kallikrates said diplomatically, remembering that Trimalchio was technically his owner. "I expect he can do what he likes."

"He says he'll be at the games to watch his boys fight," Curtius grumbled disgustedly. "Lentulus will need to sit with him to point them out to him because he won't bloody recognise them."

Brude watched Curtius wander off, kicking out at the sand as he went. "What's wrong with him?" he asked Kallikrates.

"Fourteen men from the school all going to the same munera. He's worried a lot of you will not come back."

The training intensified as Curtius strove to ensure as many of them survived the games as possible. He drove them hard, cursing and lashing out with his whip, spurring them on until they dropped with exhaustion and their muscles ached. "I wish he didn't care so much about us," Josephus gasped after one particularly harsh session which left them lying on the ground panting for air. Curtius heard him and made him run fifty circuits of the courtyard carrying a heavy lead weight in a back pack. Brude had to do the same for laughing at Josephus' joke.

Four days before they were due to fight, they were allowed to rest, with only light training sessions. Curtius also allowed them access to some female slaves for the night. Two of the novices and four of the less experienced men were marched away on the night before the first day of the games. Four of them returned the next evening although one of them had a nasty gash on his head, which Tygaeus clucked over anxiously.

Two days later, as the sun was setting, Curtius assembled the eight men he had chosen to fight on the final day, had them coffled together then marched them up the Appian Way to Rome. Gladiators always entered the city after dark so that nobody would see them. Brude and Josephus were there but Pollio, the school's most experienced fighter, would miss the games. He had taken a stab wound from a trident in his previous fight and it was not healing well. Tygaeus thought some of the muscles were so badly damaged they might not heal properly, a prospect that pleased Pollio. Lentulus was not so happy and pestered Tygaeus to make sure he did everything in his power to bring about a full recovery.

"I always do," the Greek physician muttered, much to Pollio's annoyance.

Led by Curtius and flanked by armed guards, the eight gladiators made their way through the narrow streets of Rome to the amphitheatre. Its dark bulk loomed above them and Brude realised that he had never seen the outside of the enormous structure in daylight. Perhaps he never would.

They were led through one of the many arches and down into the bowels of the amphitheatre, under the very floor of the arena where it was perpetually dark. Down here the air was filled with the sounds and smells of wild animals and sweating men. They were released from their coffle and put into small cells, four men to each tiny room with barely enough room for them to lie on the floor and try to snatch some sleep. All night they heard others arriving and Brude realised this was something special. The Colosseum was always busy but this time it was crammed with men and animals, full of noise and the smell of fear.

Breakfast was a thin, barley gruel and a piece of freshly baked bread. They sat, talking in a desultory way about nothing of any consequence. Brude and Josephus were roomed with two relatively new men who seemed in awe of them and hardly spoke a word.

Just after midday, Lentulus took his seat beside Trimalchio. They were good seats with an excellent view of the arena, but Lentulus felt a little awkward there. He was not a knight and, according to the law, he should have been seated further back but Trimalchio had insisted he join him in the lower tiers for this special occasion, so Lentulus donned his toga and wore a gold finger ring, as the Romans of status did, and pretended that he was in his rightful place. Trimalchio was rich and well known so nobody asked any questions. Only senators sat in front of the knights and the two men arrived early enough to get seats only a few rows from the front. The seats were marble, spacious, with soft cushions for comfort and they were rapidly filling up, as were the upper tiers where Lentulus normally had to sit.

"It promises to be a fine day," Trimalchio said jovially, his chubby face looking almost childlike as he smiled. "We have eight men in the final show, you say?"

"That's right," Lentulus said. "Curtius is not happy, though."

"He is not paid to be happy," Trimalchio responded irritably, his good humour clouded by the reminder of his employee's discontent. "He is paid to train the gladiators."

"And he does it very well," Lentulus said hurriedly. "Very well indeed. But he does tend to become rather protective of them. He was not happy when he learned about the arrangements."

"The arrangements were made at the request of the imperial palace," Trimalchio pointed out. "The emperor wishes to put on a show that will be memorable. And we have been well paid for them."

You mean that you have been well paid for them, Lentulus thought sourly. Aloud, he said, "Yes indeed. But gladiators are expensive to train and to lose so many at one games means a significant loss of future revenue."

Trimalchio's brow furrowed. The phrase *loss of revenue* was always guaranteed to vex him. "Perhaps, but there is nothing we can do about it." A thought came to him. "And perhaps one of our men will win. That will bring extra gold as well as extra fame for the school."

"Perhaps." Lentulus did not sound convinced. He was not an expert on the finer points of gladiatorial combat but he knew Curtius was and the old lanista had not been confident of his men's chances. "Josephus is very good," he had admitted. "And Brutus has something special. But you need a lot of luck to win this type of fight." So Lentulus had offered up some prayers to Fortuna, goddess of luck. There was nothing more he could do.

The great canvas awning, hauled into position by a thousand sailors from the imperial Roman navy using a mass of ropes and ingenious block and tackle devices, was pulled over the top of the arena, providing shade for the spectators but leaving the arena itself open to the sun. Even under the shade of the massive cover, the temperature inside the amphitheatre was oppressively hot. They fanned themselves constantly while Trimalchio ordered cold drinks and fruits from the vendors who patrolled the stadium.

There was a fanfare of trumpets as the emperor and his family took their seats in the imperial box. The emperor, smiling broadly, gave a wave to the crowd who cheered and applauded him. He sat beside his wife and two sons and the show began.

The sounds of the games sometimes filtered down to the cells beneath the floor of the arena but mostly Brude and the other gladiators sat in the gloom, the small oil lamps casting more shadows than light, while they tried to estimate the passing of time. From time to time they heard the sounds of men or animals being taken out and led up to the arena. The Roman mob liked to see strange and exotic animals from far away places.

First of all the criminals would be taken up, either to play the part of novelty acts, fighting blindfolded, or simply to be fed to the wild beasts. Brude was thankful that, as a gladiator, he at least had a chance of escaping the arena alive. For the criminals there was no escape. The Romans were constantly thinking up new and ingenious ways to both humiliate and terrorise the victims before they were killed in as brutal a fashion as possible. Curtius had told him once how one woman, an adulteress and murderess, had been tied naked to a wooden frame then covered in a cow's hide to be raped by a bull. Brude wasn't sure whether the story was true or not, but it was certainly something the Romans were capable of. After the animals had done their work, came the men who specialised in fighting these animals, the bestiarii, dedicated to showing that Rome was powerful enough to pacify far flung lands and bring their wild animals back to be slaughtered for entertainment. Brude did not envy the bestiarii. Men were usually predictable in a fight but animals were not. The thought of facing a lion or a bear was not one that appealed to him. He smiled as he realised that what he was about to do did not appeal to him either.

The dark maze beneath the arena floor echoed with the sounds of men and animals, hundreds of slaves constantly at work, under threat of the overseers' lashes, to keep the show moving for the crowd. Always there was the constant grinding of wooden winches and levers as trapdoors were opened and cages winched up to release the animals into the arena. It was a dark hell of noise and fear.

After a while a slave brought them a lunch of dried figs and cheese. One of the young men could not face eating so Brude and Josephus split his share. "It could be your last meal," Josephus said brightly.

"Yours too," Brude pointed out.

"Not me," Josephus laughed. "I told you, the Lord is protecting me, keeping me alive to kill more Romans."

Brude just shook his head. He knew there was little point in arguing with Josephus when he started talking about his god.

The show must have been in full swing because they could sometimes hear the roar of the crowd and there were few animals left below ground now to judge by the sounds. Then Curtius appeared at the iron grille that formed the cell's door, his face like thunder.

Brude saw at once that the old lanista was worried and angry about something. "What's wrong?" he asked.

"Bloody Lentulus!" Curtius snapped angrily. "The last show is to be sixteen pairs all fighting at the same time, with winners pairing up in rounds."

Brude and Josephus exchanged glances. "Last man standing?" Josephus asked.

Curtius nodded, his eyes blazing with anger. "I didn't know," he said. "But listen to me, all of you. Unless you can win every fight, there are only two ways to survive this. You either do enough to be reprieved or get yourself wounded badly enough so you can't continue."

"That's a dangerous plan," said Brude.

"Then win every round!" Curtius snapped. He looked at Brude and Josephus. "I'm sorry," he said. "I didn't know about this." He paused then said. "I probably shouldn't tell you this but the word is that the winner will be given his freedom." And then he was gone, off to tell the other gladiators the news.

"Sixteen pairs," Josephus said, doing a mental calculation. "That's five fights you have to win."

Brude nodded. "Not easy." But his mind was racing, dreaming of other things. Freedom for the winner.

"Let's try to make sure we don't meet before the final pair," said Josephus. "By that time we can probably make them believe we're too tired to fight well. You can go down when I cut you the first time."

Despite his preoccupation, Brude laughed at Josephus' confidence. "Let's make sure we get to the final pair," he said. "Then we can worry about who goes down." Whatever Josephus said, he was determined it would not be him. Freedom for the winner. The prize he had sought for eight years was within his reach.

All he had to do was win five consecutive fights against the best Rome's gladiator schools had to offer. It was a daunting prospect. He knew he was good, but he did not know whether he was good enough. Josephus normally beat him nine times out of ten in their training sessions. And Josephus, as Curtius had warned him, could soon be his enemy.

He looked at the little Jew. Josephus knew what he was thinking because he was thinking the same thing himself. Josephus grinned maniacally while the two novices looked as pale as any men Brude had ever seen.

In the small room they began warming up their muscles, bending and stretching, leaning against the wall with their arms taut and pressing hard. There was little room but none of them wanted to lose a fight because they were not prepared. All too soon, the door was unlocked and they were led out. They walked along a dark corridor, lit by flickering oil lamps, to join a queue of men waiting to be given their armour and weapons under the watchful eye of the lanistas. Brude was able to shut out all distractions by now and waited patiently. They were all hot and sweating in the stifling heat of the underground labyrinth but he knew he had to conserve his energy to get through even one fight, let alone five. He stood still while his greave, belly guard and arm protection were fastened, took his shield, sword and helmet then forcibly slowed his breathing and tried to relax his muscles.

There was a barked command and the file moved forwards, the lanistas ensuring there was plenty of space between them to prevent any man trying to gain an early advantage by injuring one of his potential opponents. The atmosphere was tense and nervous but Brude, a veteran now, managed to remain calm.

They marched up a ramp then on to a flight of steps and up through one of the amphitheatre's many trap doors into the arena. The sunlight dazzled them as they climbed the steps to be welcomed by a huge roar from the crowd. Flanked by the lanistas, watched by the guards and archers, they strode across the freshly raked sand to stand beneath the imperial box where they would give the traditional salute. In the full glare of the sun, the arena was hot, bakingly hot, and already the heat was sapping the gladiators' strength. The familiar smell of blood, human sweat, death and the scent of saffron, which had been sprinkled on the sand to sweeten the air, filled Brude's nostrils with the sickly concoction of odours that were only ever found in the amphitheatre. He thought it strange that the Romans should worry about trying to perfume the air with saffron so as not to offend the olfactory senses of the spectators when their eyes and ears were about to be filled with the sights and sounds of violent death.

The gladiators stood together to give the salute to the emperor who sat with his wife and two teenage sons, close enough, thought Brude, that he could hit him from there if he had a spear. It would be the last thing that he would ever do, of course, but at that moment he wondered whether it might not be preferable to get a quick, certain death. But he did not have a spear and trying to climb the wall was pointless; even if he could jump that high there were great wooden rollers around the top of the arena wall which would simply spin to drop him back to the ground.

The emperor was close enough that Brude could see his bearded face clearly, a face he recognised from statues and busts which were found all over the empire. The emperor studied them all eagerly before waving for them to continue. There was the customary fanfare of trumpets as the lanistas paired them up at random, spreading them out around the arena.

Brude was at the narrow end of the oval furthest from the imperial box. The arena was crowded with thirty-two men pairing off. To the onlookers it may have seemed they had plenty of room but for fighting men who needed to keep moving, the confined space was dangerous. Brude did not want to collide with a neighbouring pair while he was trying to avoid his immediate opponent, and the restricted view from his helmet made that a distinct possibility. He stood with his back to the wall, where he could see along the length of the arena but he turned his eyes on his opponent, a young man who fought as a Thracian.

Brude fastened his helmet on his head, then studied the young man. He reckoned he was a novice, for his body had no scars, which either meant he had not fought much or he was very good indeed. He looked scarcely more than a boy, so Brude reckoned he was a beginner. He felt a pang of pity for him to be thrown into an event like this but soon dismissed the thought. Only one of them would walk away from this and Brude was determined it would be him.

The boy was good, potentially very good, but his lanista had probably been fooled, like Curtius, into thinking he would face only one bout. Brude was a veteran who had practised against Thracians with the speed of Josephus. Any novice needed time to gain experience and develop their speed. After only a few tentative moves to test each other out, Brude moved his shield to leave a tempting gap which the Thracian saw and leaped for, his long curved blade arcing towards Brude's exposed belly while his small round shield lifted as he used his left arm as a counterbalance to help the thrust of his right. Brude moved too quickly for him, bringing his shield in to close the gap and thrusting with his sword to catch the boy's exposed side. The Thracian screamed and staggered back. Brude let him go. The tip of his blade had only gone in to the depth of his index finger but he knew it would be enough. The boy's face was stricken with pain and fear as the blood flowed from his side. He looked helplessly at Brude who simply watched him begin to bleed to death. Brude watched him carefully but took deep breaths, relaxing his muscles, for he knew this fight was won and he wanted to conserve his energy. The Thracian took a faltering step then stumbled and sank to his knees on the bloodied sand, his sword and shield lowered.

Brude looked to the imperial box. He already knew the boy's fate for he could see the downward thrusting of thumbs in the crowd. The fight had been finished too quickly for the boy to have had any chance of pleasing the crowd. The emperor confirmed it. Brude carefully walked round behind the kneeling Thracian, steadied his shield arm on the boy's shoulder and rammed his sword down into his spine, just below the neck, severing the spinal column and bringing instant death. "I'm sorry, lad," he whispered.

He waited, conserving energy, feeling the strength-sapping heat beating down on him from the afternoon sun, making him desperate for a drink. He saw Curtius, whip in hand, acknowledging his victory and he turned to watch the others. Josephus' opponent was down too, his throat cut by a vicious slash from the Jew's sica. That was a difficult blow to make, Brude knew, because the helmet of Josephus' Samnite opponent covered the whole head, leaving little room for striking at the neck and throat.

Things were not going so well for the other six men of Lentulus' school. One of the novices who had shared the cell with Brude and Josephus was down, the other was still battling hard but losing to a Retiarius. If he kept fighting, and was lucky, the crowd might let him live. Of the other four, two had won, one had lost and been finished off while the last was still fighting, Curtius urging him on. It was in vain for he was struck down only a moment later. The crowd bayed for his blood and he was quickly despatched.

Brude was horrified, for none of the losers seemed to be receiving mercy. Perhaps it was the sight of so many men fighting at once but whatever it was, it did not bode well. He saw the novice go down at last, blood pouring from several cuts but the lad had done well and his opponent was scarcely in better shape. The crowd signalled and called for him to live so the emperor granted him his life. Brude was relieved. It meant there was at least some hope for the losers.

Slaves rushed in to clear away the fallen, dragging them to the death door, tossing them down the dark tunnel after a man dressed as Charon, god of the underworld, ritually struck each one on the temple to ensure they were dead.

The remaining men were paired off, although two of the victors from the first round were too badly hurt to continue so there were only fourteen men left, fighting in seven pairs.

Curtius skilfully managed to keep his men from fighting each other, somehow managing to match them against men from other schools. This time, Brude was up against another Samnite, a man wearing the same armour and with the same weapons as himself. There was no advantage to either man here; whoever was faster or stronger would survive.

This opponent was experienced and he was strong. They sparred for a few moments, testing each other, trying to gauge each other's strength and speed. Brude heard people in the crowd yelling for them to get on with it. He ignored them as he ignored the gasps and cheers as other fighters entertained the crowd when they came to blows. In this heat he knew he could not afford for the fight to take too long; the physical effort of maintaining concentration, as well as holding the heavy shield and wearing the helmet, would soon wear him down.

He made a half-hearted attack, backing off when the other man blocked and thrust back. Then Brude used a trick Josephus had once used on him in training and which had caught him out badly. He moved his right foot as if he had slipped, and he crouched, letting his shield and sword fall slightly. His opponent moved as quick as lightning, shield held forwards to batter Brude to the ground. The crowd gasped as they saw Brude stumble.

His left foot, though, was firmly planted and he jumped forwards, moving slightly to his right. The two shields crashed together with a force that jarred both men's shoulders but Brude was in the air, both feet off the ground and swinging his gladius in a wide arc as he jumped past his opponent. It was a move no Samnite would normally ever try, a move more suited to a Thracian who had less weight to carry, but Brude put everything into the leap and the swing. The tip of his blade, usually used for short thrusts, slashed across the back of his opponent's left shoulder, drawing a gush of red blood. The man moved to avoid the pain but, because it was on his left, he moved to his right. It was a fatal mistake for his back was to Brude and it would take him time to turn. Too much time. Landing lightly, Brude did not hesitate. He powered forwards, ducking low as he blocked the wide reverse swing of the man's sword with his shield then jabbing upwards with his own sword, feeling it bite into the man's side. He stabbed, twisted the blade and pulled it out, then battered the man with his shield. He went down, collapsing face-down on the sand.

The crowd had recognised Brude despite his face being masked by the helmet, perhaps because they had seen him fight before and recognised him or perhaps because some of them heard Curtius yelling at him. They chanted his name, clapping him loudly. "Brutus! Brutus!" He was breathing heavily now and he glanced at the imperial box, seeing the signal to finish his fallen opponent. He dutifully slammed his sword into the back of his fallen opponent's neck, although he was fairly sure the man was dead already.

Curtius came up to him. "Are you all right?"

"So far. Who else is left?"

Curtius looked heartbroken. "Josephus is through but he took a nick. He was paired against a Retiarius." Brude looked for the little Jew and saw him binding a piece of cloth around his thigh. It did not look too bad but in a battle like this even a fractional slowing could be bad. "You're the only two left from our school now. Atticus will live, thank the gods." Atticus, a Murmillo, was one of the more experienced men. He would have put up a good show, Brude knew.

Then he saw that there were only six men left standing. Curtius quickly pointed them out. "There's a Murmillo, two Thracians and a Retiarius. One of the Thracians is good and so's the Retiarius. They're both from Propertius' school. I'll try to get you paired with the smaller Thracian. I think Josephus can take the Samnite." He stalked off, making his way across the sand to check on Josephus, while Brude tried to recover his strength. He looked into the crowd to see whether he could make out Lentulus and Trimalchio but the amphitheatre was a sea of faces and he gave up. He wondered whether Trimalchio thought he was getting a good return on his investment.

The arena was cleared, the men paired off and Brude found himself up against the Retiarius, the one opponent he had not wanted. Curtius gave him a look of resignation as if to say he had tried.

"Fight!" shouted the lanistas.

The Retiarius was good. Brude knew instantly that he had a fight on his hands. In his favour, the man had obviously had a hard fight before and he was breathing heavily. Brude did the same, making sure the man could hear the great gasps of air he was taking in and could see his chest heaving. He made his movements look sluggish, hoping the Retiarius would think he was more tired than he was.

It did not work.

The net came looping for him and he dodged, then had to block a thrust of the trident with his shield and immediately dodge again as the net came lashing low for his legs. He jumped and it missed but the Retiarius danced away from his attempt to close the gap between them.

Again the net came for him, its lead weights rattling off his shield. He thrust, trying to hit the man's arm but the Retiarius was too quick and the chance was gone. They circled each other. Brude had to stifle a momentary panic as he tried to figure out how to beat this man. Everyone had a weakness, a part of their technique that was less good than their favoured moves, but he could not spot this man's weakness at all.

More circling, more thrusts, feints and dodges. The Retiarius danced around, moving swiftly with fluid grace, jabbing his trident to wear Brude down, probing and waiting for Brude to tire first.

There was a roar from the crowd and Brude knew that one of the other gladiators had scored a good hit, which meant that one of the other fights was probably over. Whoever had won that would have time to rest. Brude's momentary distraction nearly killed him and he only just avoided the next thrust of the trident. He began to grow anxious because realisation was dawning that this man was better than him. Just as Curtius and

136

Kallikrates had said would happen one day, he had met his match. He decided that he would have to try something desperate, something the man would not expect. Victory or death, he told himself.

Curtius was behind him, shouting encouragement, telling him to get in close but Brude knew that his opponent was too good to allow that to happen. He crouched, saw the flick of the left wrist and saw the net looping to settle over his head. He moved forwards, suddenly thrusting his sword high in the air, pointing skywards. The net caught it as it began to fall. In the space of a heartbeat, it would have fallen over his crested helmet and he would be doomed but, as soon as the sword struck the net, he jerked it with all his might. At the same time, he threw his shield arm forwards, ducking as low as he could. It was an awkward, muscle-popping, spine-wrenching move but it was totally unexpected. The net draped itself across his shoulders, catching on his helmet but he had used his sword, already tangled in the net, to pull the Retiarius so hard that they were now close together. The man had no room to move his long trident because Brude was inside its reach. He used his shield to block the pronged weapon as he smashed his head forwards, hitting the Retiarius full in the face with the iron visor of his helmet, shattering the man's nose. The Retiarius staggered back, pulling Brude with him. Entangled in the net, Brude let go of his sword, pushed hard and fell on top of his opponent, fighting viciously to make sure that he stayed on top. They hit the sand hard, the air driven from the Retiarius' lungs with the force of his landing. Brude smashed his helmet onto the man's face again. Awkward with the shield twisting his left arm, Brude pushed down hard, battered the man's face again, then used his right arm, still caught in the net, to raise himself slightly. He slipped his left arm free of the huge shield, punched the Retiarius across the jaw then grabbed the trident which was lying limply in the man's hand. Brude knelt up, reversed the trident in his left hand and plunged it down into the man's chest, driving it home as hard as he could.

Curtius ran to him, grabbed the Retiarius' knife and began to cut away the net. "Stay on your knees," he hissed. "Take your time to get up. By Jove, you're a mad one. What made you try that stupid move?"

"Couldn't think of anything else," Brude gasped.

Curtius sawed at the net, slowly releasing Brude from its clutches. "Well it's got the crowd on your side. They loved it. As well as that Thracian leap you did earlier."

Brude's head was spinning from the force of the blows he had inflicted on the dead man. "Who's left?" His eyes were blurred, bright lights flashing across his vision.

"Josephus. The other pair are still fighting but I think Propertius' Thracian will get through. You and Josephus should work together, take him out and then one of you had better make a convincing job of going down badly wounded. I guess they'll let the loser live."

"You don't know that."

"No," Curtius admitted, "I don't."

"Josephus won't go down."

"Then you'd better do it. Let him nick you. Lots of blood, no real damage. I'll tell him."

"No! I need to win this." Brude was more determined than ever. With thirty-two men in the arena, his chance had seemed slim, but soon there would be only three of them left and he would have as good a chance as any. Freedom for the winner.

Curtius rested a hand on his shoulder. "No friends in the arena, eh?" he said sadly. "Good luck to you. You'll need it."

Brude hauled himself to his feet. He gathered up his shield and sword, taking his time and making sure he was ready before striding towards the other end of the arena where Propertius' Thracian was just despatching his opponent. Now there were only three men left.

Brude saw Josephus give him a broad grin and a wave of his sica as if inviting him to take on the Thracian first. Brude gestured with his own sword, returning the invitation. Josephus laughed and made for the Thracian, a dark-haired man with deep blue eyes. Brude made for him as well, circling to the man's left while Josephus went to his right.

The Thracian backed away slowly, trying to get his back to the perimeter wall so that he could see both opponents but Brude moved quickly to block that. Josephus yelled a strange war cry and leaped at the Thracian. Arms flashed, swords and shields clashed then the two men were past each other and circling again. Brude feinted an attack, saw the Thracian skip easily away and circled right, trying to keep the man between him and Josephus.

A sound made him move, spinning quickly to his left, instinctively blocking with his shield. Josephus' curved blade rang on its iron rim as he tried to deliver a killing blow. Brude thrust with his own sword, reactions working in spite of his shock at Josephus' attempt to kill him. No friends in the arena, Curtius had said and Brude had forgotten it so quickly. Josephus jumped back to avoid Brude's thrust and he was now between Brude and the Thracian who saw his chance. He swung his curved blade in a blindingly fast backhanded arc to strike Josephus in the neck. The little Jew's eyes opened wide and blood sprayed from the awful wound as he toppled.

Brude had one chance, a chance Josephus had given him and he was already moving, almost before the Thracian's blade had stuck the little man. The Thracian had swung quickly, putting everything into the blow to make sure it struck home. Brude was past his friend and on the man before he could recover his balance. A sweep of Brude's shield knocked the Thracian's own small shield aside, then a back-handed shove to block the sica and a powerful thrust of his sword took the man in the belly.

Brude stood alone as the two fighters hit the ground almost at the same time. He dropped his shield and sword, turning to kneel beside Josephus whose life was ebbing away as the blood pumped from the artery in his neck. "You got him?" Josephus asked.

"Yes."

Josephus smiled. "Good plan, eh?"

Then he lay still.

Curtius pulled Brude to his feet and unstrapped his helmet while the crowd roared his name wildly. Numb, Brude gulped in the air when the helmet came off. At Curtius' prompting, he looked up to see the bearded face of the emperor smiling down at him. One of his freedmen passed him something which he tossed down to Brude, who was too tired to catch it. He bent to pick it up from the blood-soaked sand. It was a wooden training sword, a rudis. The symbol that said he need never fight again. The symbol of his freedom.

A.D. 209

Brude's first year back in Broch Tava was a hard one in many ways. Fothair, though, recovered well from his injuries and was up and around in a few weeks. "Thank you for what you did for me," he said to Brude as he stamped his leg, testing for a reaction from his wound. "I'm as good as new."

"Are you going to run now?" Brude asked him with a smile.

"That depends."

"On what?"

"On what you are planning to do."

They were standing outside Seoras' home, enjoying the summer breeze from the sea. Brude pointed eastwards along the foot of the hill. "I thought I'd build a house over there," he said.

"You're not going to live here?" Fothair was surprised.

"With my mother watching my every move? No. I had years of people watching me and I'd prefer some space for myself."

"And what then?"

Brude shrugged. "I'm not sure. I have some knowledge of healing. I might do that. Travel around the local villages, that sort of thing."

"Your magic herbs won't last forever," Fothair pointed out.

"I can always get more from the Romans. They have infirmaries at every fort on the Wall."

"That's a long way."

"There are always merchants who will get things, if you pay them enough. Maybe that's what I'll do as well. Travel around, do some trading."

Fothair nodded. "It doesn't sound very exciting."

"I don't want exciting," Brude told him. He sensed the tall man was working up to asking a question. "What do you want to do?"

"I'm a slave," Fothair said amiably. "Does it matter what I want?"

"Well I can't free you. Colm would not stand for that, but as long as you act as if you're a slave, I don't really mind what you do. I could do with some help building a house, but I thought you were going to run."

"I might." He thought for a moment then said, "If I stay, would you teach me how to fight?"

Brude saw from his face that Fothair was serious. "It takes a long time and I told you I've had enough of fighting." He idly picked up a small pebble and threw it, striking the trunk of a tree some twenty paces away.

Fothair said, "Not bad." He bent to pick up a pebble, threw and missed by a wide margin. "But if you do decide to travel you'll need someone to watch your back. What use would I be if I didn't know how to fight? Someone might attack you while you were sleeping."

Brude laughed. "You could just wake me up and let me do the fighting," he said.

"Maybe I'll just run away after all," Fothair muttered, although his tone suggested he was not really serious.

"All right," Brude conceded. "If you help me build my house, that will build your strength and I'll show you how to improve your speed. That's the first part of the training and it takes a long time. As for fighting, let's see how you get on with the first bit."

Fothair grinned hugely. "When do we start?"

"Right now. Can you catch a fly?"

"What?"

Brude held up a hand for silence. It was early summer and the air was full of insects. He did not have long to wait before a fly came close. His hand flashed out and he clenched a fist.

Holding it in front of Fothair's face he slowly opened his hand to set the fly free. "Like that," he said. "You have to catch it, not kill it."

Fothair was dumbfounded. "How did you learn to do that?"

"Lots of practice," Brude told him. "You should start now. You can do it while you're walking up to the broch. Go and speak to the smith, Caroc, and ask him what he wants for four axes, two for felling trees and two smaller ones for the trimming."

"Coin or kind?" Fothair asked.

"Either."

"Anything else while I'm up there?"

"Maybe, but climbing the hill a few times will help build the strength in your legs. Run, don't walk."

"You've got a mean streak, do you know that?" Fothair smiled happily.

"I learned from the best," Brude replied. "And you're supposed to call me Master."

"Am I?" Still grinning, Fothair set off up the hill towards the broch. "You might have to keep reminding me about that," he called back over his shoulder. Laughing, Brude watched him go. He saw the tall man fling his hand out a few times as he went, vainly trying to catch a passing insect.

They got their axes in exchange for some silver coins Brude had safely tucked away in a money belt. Then they set about planning the house. Brude had been toying with the notion of making a Roman style house but he had no idea how to make bricks or tiles and he knew nobody in the village would have the skills either, so he decided on a traditional roundhouse. In any event, he wanted to fit in, not to stand out as someone different.

Brude asked around the village to make sure nobody had any objections to his chosen site, a flat piece of rather stony land near the foot of one of the steepest parts of the hill. It was unused land and nobody minded except his mother, who did not understand why he wanted to build a house of his own. "You can stay here," she said. "There's only Seoras and me. Some families have ten people in one house. There's plenty of room for all of us."

He made excuses, which didn't satisfy her, but she eventually realised that his mind was made up and only occasionally mentioned that a new house was an unnecessary luxury. Seoras offered to help with the building but Brude told him he wanted to try to do this by himself, which made Seoras and Fothair burst out laughing. "Have you ever made a roundhouse?" Seoras asked him.

"No," Brude admitted sheepishly.

"It will take more than the two of you," Seoras told him. "Unless you want it to take all year to build."

"I'm not doing anything else," said Brude. "And Fothair wants to build up his muscles."

"Do you know how to thatch a roof?" Seoras persisted, his eyes gleaming with amusement.

"I remember seeing it done years ago," Brude said. "We'll figure it out."

"You're game, lad, I'll say that for you," laughed Seoras.

Seoras helped anyway and so did a few other villagers when they learned what Brude was planning. Castatin came down from the broch most days with some of the other boys so Seoras organised them to clearing the site, lifting all the stones and levelling the surface off as much as possible while Brude and Fothair went off to find suitable trees; oak for the rafters and door, and hazel wands for the walls. Even with the axes Caroc had provided, it took them days to fell the trees, then cut and trim the stakes. They used Brude's mule to haul the wood back to the site. Brude felt pleased with himself but Seoras told him he did not have enough wood so they had to go and find more. After two weeks of chopping, trimming and shaping the wood, Brude began to realise it was going to take a very long time to build his house.

Mairead came to see them one afternoon, laughing as she saw them struggling to haul another load of timber to Seoras, who was patiently scraping and polishing some of the beams. "You're mad!" she laughed when she saw Brude.

"And you're very beautiful," he told her.

She made a face but he saw that she was pleased by the compliment. "Why don't you ask Colm to send some of his men down to help? They spend most of their time lazing around pretending to be warriors."

"Do you think he would do that?" Brude asked doubtfully.

"Probably not, but if you offered him something valuable enough he might do it."

"I thought he was rich enough already," Brude said.

Mairead frowned. "He'll never be rich enough to satisfy him."

"That's not the way to live a happy life," Brude said. "He needs to learn to be content with what he has."

"Like you?" Mairead asked, raising an eyebrow quizzically.

"I've got everything I need," Brude nodded. Mairead was about to speak but bit back the words when he held up his hand. He knew what she was going to say. "And I learned from a very wise man in Rome that there is no point in dreaming about things I can't have. That would only make me unhappy."

Mairead's blue eyes stared into his. He saw her lips tremble, then she pulled herself together and snapped, "Well I am glad you can be so happy, Brude. Not everyone is as lucky as you." She turned, stamping her way back to the track that led up the hill. Brude followed her with his eyes and saw the giant warrior Cruithne waiting for her at the foot of the hill. The big man glared at him, then followed Mairead as she climbed the track.

Brude gave himself a mental kick. He turned to see Seoras and Fothair watching him. "Let's get back to work," he told them.

Castatin appeared the following day, approaching cautiously and staying at the edge of the trees at the foot of the hill. When Brude saw him, he waved him over but the boy shook his head, signalling to Brude to come to him. Putting down his axe, Brude wandered over to say hello.

"I shouldn't be here," Castatin told him, his eyes constantly moving, looking for anyone who might see him. "My father says I'm not to come here any more and neither is my mother."

"Then you'd best be off," Brude told him. "I don't want you to get into any trouble."

"Mother was crying yesterday," said Castatin. "She was upset when father started shouting at her, but she told me to come and tell you why we wouldn't be down any more."

"I understand. Thank you for telling me. Now you'd better get back before anyone sees you."

Castatin scampered back into the trees and began clambering up the rocky slope. Thoughtfully, Brude returned to the pile of wood he and Fothair had gathered. He picked up his axe, returning to the never-ending task of trimming the beams. He tried to banish all thoughts of Mairead and Castatin from his mind, losing himself in the monotony of the work.

"Lost another helper?" Fothair asked.

"Apparently. It seems I am not popular with Colm. And you're supposed to call me Master."

Fothair ignored the last comment, just as Brude knew he would. It had become more of a joke between them than anything else. Instead he said, "Well, it's your own fault."

Using the axe to lop off another small branch, Brude asked, "What do you mean? I've barely spoken to him since that first day."

Fothair laughed. "Keeping out of his way won't help you. You've done a much worse thing than that. You came back when he thought you were dead and gone. And his woman wants you instead of him."

"No she doesn't!" Brude protested.

Fothair laughed. "If you say so. I expect you'll tell me next that you don't want her either."

"Why don't you go and chop down another tree," Brude suggested. "Build up your arm muscles."

"Ha! I was right. I knew you wanted her."

"I never said that," said Brude, growing annoyed at Fothair's intrusion into his privacy.

146

"You didn't have to," said Fothair. "Well, I'll go and find another tree, shall I, Master?"

By the time of the Lughnasa festival they had still barely started on the house. It had taken weeks to find, gather and shape the wood. Brude realised that, without some help, they would never finish in time for winter even if the fine weather held. Still, they rested for Lughnasa and enjoyed the feast, which Colm arranged for the whole village. It was harvest time so food was plentiful and there was music and dancing. Mairead danced with everyone, even Brude, but they were barely able to exchange more than a handful of words because Colm was watching them closely and Mairead soon moved on to dance with someone else.

The fires were lit and everyone daubed their faces with the ash, blackening their features in symbolic attempts to conceal their identities. Some, especially the children, played pranks on each other and on unsuspecting adults. The adults themselves grew more and more uninhibited as the drink flowed and Brude knew that the village would have a few more babies in the springtime. There were more men than young women in the village, though, and he suspected the drink might cause some arguments or fights among the young warriors, so he slipped away, returning to Seoras' house as the sun was setting.

Most people rose late the following morning but Brude and Fothair were back at the new house early, gouging a circular perimeter line using a wooden peg hammered into the ground where the centre of the house would be. A long piece of twine was tied to the peg and attached to a sharp piece of antler, which they used to mark a line in the ground where the walls of the house would be built. Then they began hacking at the turf with more antlers, digging a narrow circular trench. It was hard work. Brude was tempted to ask Caroc the smith to make some metal picks and shovels but he knew they would take time to make and, by the time they were ready, they could have the trench dug using the traditional tools.

Seoras came over to watch them working. "I've organised some help," he told them. "It will take you a year to build at this rate. Lulach the thatcher and his son will gather reeds and dry them out. Seoc's sisters will start making the twine and rope. Seoc will help, when he can, and I've asked Gruoch to help with the wood. He's supposed to be building ships for Colm but that work won't be starting until after the harvest is all in, so he says he'll help out with making the beams."

Brude felt a mixture of relief and concern. "Why would they do that for me?" he asked.

"Because," Seoras replied, "you're one of us, even if you do seem a bit odd to some folk. Mind you, you'll be expected to return the favours in kind." He laughed at Brude's puzzled expression. "Lulach could do with some meat and some clothes. Gruoch needs wood and Seoc needs a husband for his sister."

Fothair laughed aloud as Brude held up a hand in shock. "Hold on! I don't mind cutting more wood or doing some hunting but I'm not looking for a wife. Whose idea was that?"

Seoras gave him a gap-toothed grin. "Your mother's keen on it. Barabal will be sixteen by next year." Barabal was the elder of Seoc's sisters, Brude knew. She was a pretty girl who seemed shy and hardworking, but he barely knew her and he had not even considered taking a wife. Apparently his mother had other ideas. "A man your age needs a wife," Seoras told him. "It would mean fewer problems with Colm," he added pointedly.

Brude ignored the advice.

Seoc turned up the next day, helping them to knock oak pillars into the trench they had dug, each pole as long as Fothair was tall. They hammered them in to the trench so that about two thirds of their length remained above ground, the distance between the stakes carefully measured by Gruoch, the carpenter, who had also come to help. Brude, Fothair and Seoc started weaving hazel rods, some horizontally between the oak stakes and others vertically to form an interlocking wall, the wattle as it was known. While they were doing this, Gruoch and Seoras began to work on the longer stakes they would need for the roof.

Gruoch had a fine selection of metal tools which he used to cut and shape the ends of some of the shorter stakes Seoras had told them to chop.

As they worked the flexible hazel between the stakes, Brude said to Seoc, "I hear my mother has been trying her hand at match-making."

Seoc looked embarrassed. "I thought you knew. Do you mind?"

"I prefer to sort out my own life," said Brude. "Don't get me wrong, your sister is a pretty girl, but I'm almost twice her age and I don't even know her."

Seoc nodded. "She's a bit afraid of you," he said. "But she'll need a husband next year and I'd rather she didn't end up with one of the lads from the broch."

"Plenty men to choose from up there," Brude commented dryly.

"Oh, I suppose some of them are all right but most of them look up to Colm and are too impressed with themselves for my liking."

"So why do you serve him?"

"It was either that or be a fisherman and I don't like being on the water," Seoc said with a grin. "I'm no good as a farmer either."

"Are you any good as a warrior?" Brude asked him, smiling to let him see the question was intended to be light-hearted.

"Not really," Seoc admitted cheerfully. "I can just about hold my own with most of them. Mind you, the way things are going, we might all find out soon just how good we are."

Brude's ears pricked up. "Why? What's happened?"

"Haven't you heard? Colm has refused Gartnait's latest offer to buy back his son. That's three times now."

Brude glanced at Fothair. He saw that the tall man was listening intently as he worked on the hazel wall. "I expect Colm won't ever release him unless Gartnait offers him everything he owns," he observed.

Seoc nodded. "It's worse than that," he said. "Caroc sent for some high grade iron ore from the Damnonii but Gartnait has stopped the wagons and seized the ore. His messenger arrived this morning with the news that no ore will come through unless his son is released."

Brude stopped work on the wattles and stood up straight, stretching his back muscles. "How did Colm take that?" he asked.

"Not well. I think he's planning a raid to get his iron."

"Well if he does, you take my advice and volunteer to stay behind to guard the village," Brude told him. "It would be daft to get yourself killed over such a stupid argument."

"I don't expect that will be a problem," Seoc replied. "There are plenty of them up there who are dying to have a go at fighting someone. I never wanted to be a hero, not after my dad left and never came back."

"He never wanted to be a hero either," said Brude. "But he was one, in his own way. He was a good friend to me for the short time I knew him."

Seoc nodded grimly. "I never forgave him for leaving us like that." He sniffed and wiped his eye. "Damn wind. Making my eyes water."

"Mine too," said Brude.

Later that day, as they sat in Seoras' house and Brude's mother dished up their evening meal of fish stew with wild mushrooms and pulses, Fothair said to Brude, "I think I might have to run soon."

Seoras shot him a startled look but Brude knew what was troubling the tall man. "You want to warn Gartnait?"

"Peart is my home," said Fothair. "What do you expect me to do? Wait for Colm to attack and slaughter my people?"

"Gartnait is no fool," Brude told him. "He'll be expecting Colm to do something rash. Anyway, unless you grow wings you'll not get there before Colm's horsemen, even if you start now."

"I can't sit here and do nothing!" Fothair protested in helpless rage.

"You can't stop the wind blowing off the sea either," Brude pointed out. "And if there's nothing you can do about things, you might as well forget them."

They argued long into the night but none of them could come up with any plan for getting word to Gartnait. Fothair fretted and cursed but, when Brude awoke the next morning, he was still there, a look of thunder on his face, but clearly having decided not to run. He looked at Brude and said, "I know you would do something if you could. I just don't like feeling so helpless. But I'll stay and hope that nothing too bad happens."

They went back to work on the house, resuming the weaving of the wattle while Gruoch carved and smoothed more wood in preparation for building the roof. Seoc's two sisters, Barabal and her younger sister, Seasaidh, arrived bringing great lengths of hemp rope they had twisted. Brude thanked them. Barabal, the older girl, dark-haired and with shy, dark eyes, blushed in embarrassment but her younger sister, who was nearly fourteen years old, precociously piped up, "Seoc says you're going to marry Barabal. Is that true?"

Brude looked at the older girl who was now blushing a bright red and nudging her sister in an effort to shut her up. He looked at Seasaidh and replied, "I honestly didn't know anything about that until yesterday. I think some people have been trying to make a match without asking the people involved."

Seasaidh looked at him with eyes that were older then her years. He had seen that look before on young girls, and it disconcerted him as much now as it had before. Seasaidh, he thought, would be a handful for whoever married her. She ran her gaze over his chest and arms. He was stripped to the waist because the day was warm but now he was starting to regret it. "You've got a lot of muscles," Seasaidh said boldly, "and a lot of scars. If you don't want to marry her, I'll marry you instead. I think you would give me strong sons."

Brude didn't know what to say. Fothair burst out laughing while Barabal tried in vain to hush her sister. Brude was annoyed with himself for feeling so disconcerted by a thirteen-year-old girl but he felt that anything he said would only land him in deeper water, so he just smiled, thanked them for the rope and told them he had to get back to work. The girls stayed a short while then went off, Seasaidh promising they would be back with more rope the next day. "I'll look forward to that," laughed Fothair.

Gruoch chuckled as the girls walked away. "She's a vixen, that Seasaidh. Needs a damn good thrashing but she's never had one because her father died before she was born."

"It looks like you've got them waiting in line for you," Fothair told Brude.

Brude threw a clod of earth at him, hitting him unerringly on the chest. "Get back to work, Slave," he ordered.

Fothair grinned, bobbing his head. "Yes, Master."

In the afternoon a young warrior, wearing a sullen expression on his beardless face, arrived with a summons for Brude. "Lord Colm wants to see you."

"What for?" asked Brude.

The young man shrugged. "How would I know? He just said to fetch you. Now."

Brude picked up his shirt and pulled it on over his head. With a word to Fothair to keep working, he followed the warrior to the track and up the hill. Neither of them spoke. They went through the south gate, past the buildings and straight to the broch. The two guards stood aside, allowing the warrior to duck inside. Brude followed.

It was the first time he had been inside the broch since his return home more than four months previously. This place had once been his home where his father had held court and his mother had lived. He felt he knew it intimately. The doorway was small and the entrance tunnel, stone on all sides, dark and low. They reached a passageway running left and right, a circle formed by the massively thick inner and outer walls of the great broch. Each wall was three paces thick, filled with rubble and faced with smoother stones. By the standards of the Boresti it was an impressive building but again Brude, when he considered it against the wonders of Rome, had a feeling of disappointment at its crude construction. He wondered whether he was perhaps more Roman than he cared to admit.

Stone steps climbed the passageway to the left. He followed the warrior up them, round the circle of the building to the right until they reached another low doorway. They went inside to stand on the wooden floor of the upper level. Here were Colm's private quarters, partitioned off by hanging curtains. A bearskin rug lay on the wooden floor, blazing torches flickered from brackets round the walls and Colm sat in a great wooden chair like a king on a throne. High above, a circular hole in the upper walkway admitted a little daylight to ease the gloom. At one side of the chamber, to Brude's left, Mairead sat on a smaller, plain chair, beside a wooden table where plates held the remains of a meal. She looked anxiously at Brude and he saw the fear in her eyes. He could not tell what she was afraid of but he stayed on his guard. Behind Colm, standing like a great bear, was Cruithne, dressed in his usual leather armour with his chain mail overcoat and a long sword hanging at his waist. He was studying Brude carefully, his eyes alert. Brude ignored him. There was another warrior beside Cruithne, a bearded man with many painted designs swirling across his cheeks and forehead. He was leaning casually against the stone wall of the broch, looking bored with everything around him. Brude had seen him around the village from time to time but all that he knew was that the man was called Lutrin and that he was supposed to be one of Colm's closest advisors. He was often away from the village, doing Colm's bidding.

Colm waved away the young warrior who had brought Brude up from the village. "You may go," he said imperiously. Colm was dressed in fine clothes, deerskin, Brude guessed, with strong leather boots. He still wore rings on each finger and had a long blue cloak, fastened with a large golden brooch. He smiled a wolfish welcome as he said in honeyed tones, "Brude. Welcome. We have not seen you for a long time. You've been busy I hear."

Brude nodded. "That's right."

"Not too busy to spend some time with your old friends, I trust?"

"I always have time for my friends," Brude replied carefully.

"Good. Have some uisge." Colm snapped his fingers. Mairead jumped up, reaching for a small flagon. She poured some of the golden liquid into two small beakers. She brought one to Colm, passing it to him, with her eyes lowered, then did the same to Brude, her gaze never meeting his.

"Thank you," whispered Brude. She did not acknowledge him but quickly returned to her seat.

Brude knew that Colm was aware he did not drink uisge so he drained the beaker in one go, forcing himself not to react as the drink burned his throat with its fierce heat. Colm sipped his own, watching Brude with an appraising stare. "Have you heard what Gartnait has done?" he asked. "Have you heard what he has stolen from me?"

"I heard something about some iron ore," Brude admitted. "I don't know the details."

"Details?" Colm almost shrieked. "The details are that he has stolen my iron ore. What more is there to know?"

"You could always trade his son for it," Brude suggested, deliberately keeping his voice calm and even.

"No!" Colm smashed his left fist down on the arm of his chair, almost spilling his uisge. "Shall I tell you what I am going to do?" He paused, but Brude made no comments so he went on, "I am going to get it back. Tomorrow, I am leading my men to Peart. We will take the wagons back by force." He glared a challenge at Brude, who realised that Colm was more than half drunk. "What do you think of that?"

Brude kept his eyes on Colm, studying him as he would study an opponent in the arena. Colm was just as dangerous, he thought. Not as an individual, but as a man who commanded over seventy warriors. "I think you are the head man. You don't need my advice."

"You are the great warrior," Colm scoffed. "I hear it from my son all the time. Yet you have no advice on how to fight a battle against my enemies?" He drained his beaker then threw it to the floor where it smashed into a dozen pieces. "Perhaps you are not such a great warrior after all? Perhaps my men have been avoiding you for no reason, scared to annoy you in case you beat them as you did the men from Peart? Is that it?"

"I have no skill in battles like the one you intend to fight," said Brude, "but if you want my advice, then I would say do not fight at all. Gartnait has probably used the ore already in his own smithies, so you would fight for nothing."

Colm's lips twisted in a sneer. He turned to look at Lutrin and Cruithne. "You hear that? Not fight? Not fight a man who has stolen from me? Shall I tell you what I think, Brude? I think you are afraid. Am I right? Are you afraid?" Behind him Cruithne grinned a savage grin and drummed his fingers on the hilt of his massive sword. Brude saw, though, that his eyes did not match his expression. Brude had seen men like that before. Once again he suspected that Cruithne was far more than the oaf he made himself out to be. Such men were dangerous.

"I have seen men die," Brude said, holding Colm's gaze. "It is not pleasant. Why should I not be afraid?"

"Hah! I knew it!" Colm gripped the arms of his chair, leaning forwards to stare at Brude. Then he turned his head to look at Mairead. "Do you see, wife, how fortunate you are that you did not marry this coward? He was a slave so long he has forgotten how to be a man." He turned back to Brude. "I will not ask you to come with us for I expect you will want to stay behind with the women and children."

Brude licked his suddenly dry lips. He saw Lutrin grinning at him, mocking him. Looking Colm in the eyes, he said calmly, "That would be my choice."

Colm shook his head then twisted his neck in a move to relieve some tension. "Cruithne will be in charge while I am away. He will have ten men here and you will do as he says. You can stay with the women and children but you obey Cruithne as if his words were mine. Do you understand?"

Brude looked at Cruithne. He saw a feral grin on the man's face. He wondered whether Colm had seen past the giant's mask. If he had not, it was hardly believable that such a man would be left in charge. But whatever Colm's reasoning, there was nothing to be gained by arguing. "I understand," he said.

Colm looked at him triumphantly. "And tell your slave, the man from Peart, that I have hunting dogs. If he decides he wants to try to warn Gartnait, I will set them loose on him. Do you hear me?"

"I understand," Brude repeated.

"Good. You may go," said Colm with a wave of his hand.

Brude nodded. He turned to Mairead to give her a nod of farewell. "My lady," he said. She returned the nod with one of her own. At the same time, with her arms clasped across her chest, he saw her very deliberately push up the right sleeve of her dress with her left arm, revealing a dark bruise. It was the side facing away from Colm so nobody but Brude could see it. He hesitated but she quickly dropped the sleeve back, covering the mark. He nodded again, turned on his heels and got out as quickly as he could.

"He's mad," Brude announced to Fothair. "He has no idea what he's doing."

"Is there no way to stop him?" Fothair asked desperately.

"Not unless you want to fight seventy warriors to get to him, or try to outrun his dogs."

"That might be tricky," conceded Fothair. "We could steal a boat or a couple of coracles."

"To travel upriver? You'd be almost as fast walking. And who mentioned 'we'?"

So Fothair did nothing except worry, and the following day Colm led sixty men off towards Peart. Brude and Fothair went back to building the roundhouse because there was nothing else for them to do. Barabal and Seasaidh turned up again, bringing their hemp twines with them. They sat down to twist them together into ropes while they watched the men working. Gruoch worked on the oak stakes then showed Brude, Fothair and Seoras how to fit them over the upright stakes round the wall. He had carved them so that they fitted neatly on the top and also slotted into each other. When it was done, the wattle wall had an oak ledge along its top. Then they took some of the ropes the girls had brought the day before and tied them to the great centre pole which was formed from a solid piece of oak the height of four men. Gruoch had cut notches in it for most of the way up its length. They placed one end of the huge log in the centre of the house and Gruoch helped them raise the pole upright. It required a lot of effort but Seoc arrived as they were starting. He dropped his spear, grabbed a rope and helped them haul the pole into position. They quickly pegged the ropes to the ground to keep the pole standing upright. Seasaidh applauded their efforts happily.

"We need to get the other beams attached before it blows down," Gruoch told them. Using the notches he had cut, he climbed the pole. When he signalled that he was ready, the others hoisted another long beam up. Quickly, and with the ease of someone with years of experience, he lashed it to the top of the centre pole while the others tied it to the ledge on the top of the wattle wall, leaving a length, about the same as a man's forearm, hanging down over the ledge. With Gruoch urging them to hurry, they hoisted a second beam on the opposite side of the house, lashing that in position, too. By the time they got the third beam up, the centre pole was more stable so Gruoch took his time with the next ones. It took all afternoon but they eventually had nine long beams tied to the centre pole, forming a peak. Even though the roof was open to the sky, Brude thought the framework of the house was at last starting to take shape.

Brude's mother came along with some freshly baked bread and a flagon of small beer. A few other villagers arrived as well, to view their handiwork. Brude had a suspicion that he had more of an audience because Colm was away, but he chided himself that he was being uncharitable. He was feeling good about the house although Seoras told him there was a long way to go yet. "That's enough for today, though," the old man said. "There's clouds coming. Looks like rain."

Then another cloud arrived in the shape of Cruithne.

He had four men with him, all of them carrying spears. Cruithne was, as ever, wearing his long tunic of chain mail, his sword swinging at his side. Mairead, her face a mask of fear, followed him, with Castatin walking nervously beside her. Cruithne marched up to Brude, villagers moving quickly out of his way as he approached. Brude put down his beaker and waited for him, knowing there was no way to avoid a confrontation this time. The way Cruithne was stalking towards him made his intentions plain for all to see.

A hush fell over the crowd as Cruithne, towering over everyone, spoke in a loud voice. "I want you to tell them all what you said yesterday," he boomed. "I want you to tell them you are afraid to fight." He stared pugnaciously, his face thrust forwards to within a hand's breadth of Brude.

Brude took a deep breath. "Yes, I said that." There were gasps of surprise from the crowd. He heard Seasaidh blurt, "No!" A public admission of fear from a man of the Boresti was shameful.

Cruithne grinned. He scanned the assembled villagers and his eyes fell on Barabal, trying to hide behind Seoc. Cruithne pushed the young man out of the way and grabbed the girl's arm, jerking her back to shove her in front of Brude. "I hear you intend to marry this one. Pretty little thing, isn't she?"

"Leave her alone," said Brude, keeping his voice calm but firm, his eyes never leaving Cruithne's face.

"Why? Are you frightened I'll hurt your precious wife to be? Or have you already been there?"

"Leave her out of this," said Brude. "I have no intention of marrying her so you are hurting her for no reason."

Cruithne leered at him. "Then if you don't want her, I'll have her." He pulled the girl close, wrapping his huge arm around her, holding her pinned against his body.

Seoc shouted "No!" He jumped forwards but Brude flung up his arm to block his path. Barabal screamed, bringing muttered protests from the villagers. Cruithne smiled a challenge at Brude.

"What is it you really want?" Brude asked him.

"You know," Cruithne growled. "I hear all the time from the boy about your fighting. I hear your stories of fighting in Rome. I think you are a liar as well as a coward and I want everyone to see that I am the best fighter here, the strongest."

Aware that all eyes were on him, Brude said, "I won't argue that you are the strongest, so will you let her go?"

"Not until you fight me," Cruithne said, his eyes blazing a challenge.

Brude knew in his heart that Colm had set Cruithne up to this. Why else was Mairead there to witness it? Colm wanted Brude humiliated in front of everyone and Cruithne was the ideal man for the task. Brude had thought there was something more than brutishness to the giant Cruithne, but what was certain was that the man was Colm's creature. "You don't have to do this, you know," he said, keeping his voice low so that only those closest to him could hear. "If I judge you right, there is more to you than being Colm's bully. Why should you do his dirty work for him?"

Cruithne's eyes showed that he understood what Brude was trying to do. "Lord Colm took me in when others cast me out," he growled. "Why should I not do his bidding? He is a great man."

"A great man who goes off to fight a war but leaves his strongest warrior behind to beat up one of his own tribesmen?" Brude was scornful. "That doesn't sound so great to me. I say again, that you do not need to prove anything to anyone here. So let the girl go and you can tell Colm that I admitted my fear in front of the whole village."

Cruithne, his arm still clamped like a vice around Barabal, shook his head. "I cannot do that. Lord Colm was very specific."

Brude raised an eyebrow. "Really? He wants me dead, then?"

"No. He wants you nearly dead," said Cruithne. "But if you happen to die, he won't be too upset."

"Well that is something, I suppose," said Brude, frantically try-ing to think of a way to avoid a fight but realising that there was no real option. Speaking so that everyone could hear, Brude said, "You know I don't want to fight you. I've already admitted you are stronger than me, so how about some other sort of contest?"

Cruithne's brow furrowed. "What sort of contest?"

"What about spear throwing?"

Cruithne suspected a trick. "What will that prove?"

"It will prove who is the most skilful," Brude said. "You are stronger than me, but I am faster than you. To contest such things proves nothing, so why not have a test of skill? You can throw a spear, can't you?"

"Of course I can!" Cruithne was becoming riled by Brude's tone but he still kept a firm hold on Barabal.

"Then you already have an advantage, because I have not thrown a spear for thirteen years," Brude told him. He looked around, seeking suitable targets. "I'll make it even easier for you," he said. "You see that small tree stump over there?" He pointed to an old stump some fifty paces away jutting just above the grass, barely three hand widths high. Cruithne nodded. "That will be my target," Brude told him. "I will stand over here beside my house and you will stand near the stump. Your target will be the wall of the house anywhere between the doorway and the first beam."

Cruithne looked doubtful. He could sense that Brude was trying to outwit him in some way but could not figure out how. His target was at least twenty times larger than Brude's. Having been publicly challenged, he did not want to lose face by turn-ing down such an easy contest. "And if I win?" he asked.

"Then I will acknowledge that you are the better man. I will leave the village and find a home somewhere else." There were gasps from the villagers and Brude heard his mother protesting. He went on, "But if I win then you will be as a dead man when we meet. You will walk away and have nothing to do with me. If you cannot walk away, you will sit silently, never speaking in my presence. Is that agreed?"

160

Cruithne thought for a moment, aware that Brude had somehow forced him into a corner but unwilling to back down. He nodded. "Agreed." He released Barabal from his grip, shoving her roughly back to Seoc. Lowering his voice to little more than a whisper, he said to Brude, "Farewell, little man. The best you can hope for is that you'll be leaving soon. Spears can be dangerous, you know." He stalked off towards the tree stump, his warriors following in his wake, leaving Brude in no doubt that Cruithne's spear throw would be aimed at him, not at the designated target.

Brude turned to Seoc. "Can I borrow your spear?" he asked. The young warrior handed it to him while he wrapped his left arm around his terrified sister.

Fothair tapped Brude's arm. "Are you crazy?" he asked. "I know you're good, but he's an animal. It's all very well catching flies but this is something different."

"I need to sort this one way or the other," Brude told him. "Anyway, you'll be all right even if I lose. We can go to live in Peart."

Fothair just grunted in answer to that suggestion.

Mairead pushed her way towards Brude. She grabbed his other arm. "What are you doing?" she demanded. "This is what Colm wants. Don't you realise that? You can't beat Cruithne. That's why Colm left him here."

"That's what I've been trying to tell him," Fothair grumbled.

Brude took off his shirt and handed it to Fothair, saying, "I suggest you keep everyone back out of the way." He saw Castatin watching him, his young face glowing with eager anticipation. He winked at the boy who grinned. *At least one person thinks I've got a chance*, he thought. He turned to Mairead. "Colm wants Cruithne to beat me up. This way, I am hoping that we can resolve things without anyone getting hurt."

"Don't do this," she pleaded.

"What's the alternative? Try to fight him single-handed?"

She looked at him, her eyes showing her hurt, her lips slightly parted as if she was about to say something more. Before she could speak, he smiled at her, took Seoc's spear then strode out to face Cruithne.

It was like being back in the arena, only this time the audience was small and most of them were not looking forward to it. Brude felt the heightened awareness of his senses that came with the danger. The summer breeze from the sea felt cool on his bare skin, the grass under his feet seemed soft and he could smell it even over the usual riotous assortment of smells from the village. He looked to where Cruithne was flexing his muscles near the tree stump, his four young warriors admiring him. Unlike the villagers, they were looking forward to this.

Brude had his usual moment of doubt. He was reasonably sure that Cruithne, no matter how strong he was, would be no match for a trained gladiator in a one-on-one fight but he could not take that for granted. Turning this into a contest of skill rather than a fight would, he hoped, give him an even greater advantage. But there was always a doubt. *Don't mess this up*, he told himself. He walked to stand in front of the partially built roundhouse and stabbed the blade of his spear down into the ground so that the shaft stood upright a few paces from the wall. Cruithne stared at him and called, "You are standing in front of my target, little man." He did not sound disappointed by that fact.

Outwardly, showing a calmness he did not feel, Brude called back, "This is probably the safest place. I don't think you'll come close to hitting the wall." He heard murmurs of concern and even a few nervous laughs from the villagers standing away to his left but he kept his attention on Cruithne.

The big man grinned. He still wore his heavy mail shirt and his sword was still strapped round his waist. If Brude's plan worked, this would be to his advantage for the added weight would slow Cruithne down. Cruithne, though, did not seem bothered by the weight. Few men wore mail armour, unless they actually expected a fight, for it was heavy and made hot work of any exertions but Cruithne was so strong it barely seemed to bother him. He hefted the long ash spear with its sharp iron blade and prepared to throw. Brude saw the giant smile. He had obviously decided that if Brude got in the way of his spear then that was Brude's fault. Cruithne slowly advanced to within thirty paces of where Brude stood, drew his right arm back, took a few running paces and, with a grunt of effort, hurled the spear as hard as he could.

He threw it with incredible force. It sped through the air faster than Brude would have thought possible, aiming almost straight for him. It was as good a throw as Cruithne could ever hope to make and both of them knew it.

Brude moved. No matter how fast the spear was, for a man trained to fight in the arena, it was an easy target. He took a half step to his right, swivelled his body so that he was side-on to the approaching spear and snapped his right hand out, catching the shaft just behind the blade as it went past him. Without pausing, only dimly aware of the shouts of astonishment from the watching villagers, he grabbed the spear in both hands and started running towards Cruithne.

The giant warrior stood with his mouth open, a look of utter disbelief on his face as Brude swiftly covered the ground between them. As he approached, Brude made to dodge round him but Cruithne, realising what Brude was attempting, moved to intercept, bellowing a roar of anger as he tried to grab him and wrestle him to the ground.

Brude swerved, avoiding Cruithne's first lunge but the big man was still between him and the tree stump and coming for him again, faster than Brude had expected him to move. Brude had to adjust his plan. He stopped, swinging the spear low, catching Cruithne hard on his right shin but had to jump back, spinning away as the giant warrior ignored the blow and reached to grab the spear. Cruithne charged again, intent on simply flattening Brude to the ground. Brude had to leap back again, swinging the spear as he did so and this time landing a powerful smack on Cruithne's left hand. That blow must have hurt because Cruithne instinctively pulled his hand back. In doing so he left an opening, which Brude pounced on, driving the butt end of the spear forwards to stab Cruithne in the belly. Even with his mail shirt with its leather undercoat and a woollen jerkin beneath that, the blow struck home so hard that Cruithne gasped in pain and doubled over. Despite this, he tried to grab the spear with his right hand. Brude quickly drew it back, whirled it in his hands then brought it down with a crashing blow which hit home on Cruithne's head just behind his left ear. The big man staggered then fell face down, unmoving, on the grass.

Brude exhaled deeply then walked to the tree stump and rammed the point of the spear into the hard wood. He shot a warning glance at the four warriors who stood nearby, nervously looking at each other, unsure of what to do. The other villagers were watching him, their faces displaying a mixture of awe and delight. Castatin pushed free and came running over to meet him, carrying Brude's shirt, which he had snatched from Fothair. "That was amazing!" he said, as he handed the shirt over.

Cruithne groaned as he pushed himself up, his long hair hanging down around his head. He struggled to his knees, looked at Brude with unfocussed eyes and then saw the spear standing proud on the tree stump. He groaned. "Kill me," he said.

"Don't be silly," Brude told him. "In fact, I think we should forget our wager. I'd prefer it if we could just get along without fighting. What do you think?"

Cruithne looked at him blankly. "What?"

"Never mind," laughed Brude. "Come over to Seoras' house and we'll have a look at your head. That must hurt." He held out his hand. Cruithne stared at it for a moment. Brude thought he was going to refuse but then the giant reached out, allowing Brude to help him to his feet. Brude wrapped Cruithne's arm around his shoulders and helped him walk slowly towards the village. "Go and fetch his spear," Brude told Castatin.

Practically everyone in the lower village gathered round Seoras' house while Brude sat Cruithne down on a stool at the doorway and carefully examined his head. Castatin stood, proudly on guard, holding Cruithne's spear upright. The four warriors hovered nervously nearby, uncertain and confused but at least doing nothing more than watching. Brude gingerly pulled Cruithne's straggled and greasy hair aside so that he could examine him. There was a nasty bruise, purple and yellow, and a rising lump but the skin was not broken. He applied a cold cloth, telling Cruithne to hold it firmly in place while he mixed a potion for him to drink.

Brude told the crowd, "He'll be fine. Just a sore head. You know how tough he is." He acted as if Cruithne was an old friend who had simply had an accident.

Some of the villagers started to wander off, chatting animatedly about what they had seen. A few who had missed the fight but had come to see what was going on, expressed doubts but the evidence of Cruithne's defeat was there for all to see.

Mairead and Fothair stood nearby, not sure what to say. Mairead watched Cruithne nervously but Brude calmly made the big man drink his potion. "It will help with the pain, but it might make you sleepy," he told him. "Probably best to rest here for a while before going back up the hill." He shot his mother a warning glance to stifle any protest she might make.

Seasaidh came up to Brude and said, "If you're not marrying Barabal, you should marry me. I like a man who is a good warrior."

Brude raised his eyebrows. He saw Fothair stifling a laugh. "At the moment," he told the girl, "I have no plans to marry anyone. But I'll certainly remember what you've said."

"Don't wait too long to make up your mind," she pouted. "I won't wait forever, no matter how strong you are." She blew him a kiss before going back to Seoc and Barabal. The three of them headed for their own house. Brude saw that Seoc was giving Seasaidh a talking to. Fothair was laughing aloud.

Brude turned back to Cruithne whose eyes were now more focussed. "Are you all right?" he asked.

Cruithne winced as he withdrew the cold compress from his head. "Where did you learn to fight like that?" he asked in his throaty growl.

"Rome. I told you, they like to watch slaves fighting. They have special schools where they train men so that they can offer better entertainment."

"Maybe I should go there and learn," Cruithne rumbled. "Did you have to make it look so easy?"

"Believe me, it wasn't easy. You're strong and you're fast. You nearly caught me a couple of times. If you were trained as a gladiator you'd probably be unbeatable. But I would say it is better to be a free man who fights his own battles than to be a slave who fights for other people's pleasure. Or because other people tell them to."

Cruithne nodded slowly, understanding what Brude was saying to him. His great hairy face looked up at Brude. "Why don't you just kill Colm and take over as head man?" he asked.

There was an expectant silence. Brude was careful not to look at anyone else. He wasn't sure what he would say if he looked at Mairead and saw the same question on her face. Instead he stared at Cruithne, pursing his lips thoughtfully. "Why don't you?" he responded. "You are strong enough."

From Cruithne's expression, Brude saw that the thought had never crossed the big man's mind. Cruithne answered, "Because he is my lord and I owe him everything I have."

"And why should I be any different?" Brude said. "He is an old friend of mine from our boyhood. His wife is an old friend and his son is my friend as well. It would be a strange friendship if I betrayed that, wouldn't it?"

"He's not your friend," Cruithne said. "I told you that. He really does not like you."

Brude shrugged. "Then he will have to learn to live with his dislike for I have family and friends here and I do not intend to leave." He squatted down so that his face was level with Cruithne's. "I would like it if we could be friends as well. Or, at least, not enemies. What do you say?"

Cruithne's brow wrinkled in thought. "Will you teach me how to fight like that?" he asked.

Brude chuckled. "You don't need much help from me," he said. "You are good enough to beat just about anyone. Anyway, there are better ways to live your life than going around frightening people just because you are stronger than they are. Perhaps I should teach you those things instead for I'm afraid I don't think you will learn them from Colm. It saddens me, but I think he is in danger of losing his sense of honour. You need to make sure you don't lose yours."

Cruithne was uncertain. "He will not be happy if we are friends," he said pensively.

"What can he do to you? If he throws you out, you can come and live down here. But I don't think it will come to that. Mairead will tell him what happened and he will see that no blame can come to you."

Cruithne lumbered to his feet. "I can see why he doesn't like you," he said softly. "You undermine his authority."

Brude knew then that he had been right about Cruithne. For an apparently simple man he was more shrewd than anyone gave him credit for. Clasping the big man's hand, he said, "Then I rely on you to convince him that I am harmless. I'll keep out of his way as much as I can and do nothing to upset him. Can you persuade him of that?"

"I will try," said Cruithne. He clasped Brude's hand firmly. "I think it would be good to be your friend." He took his spear from Castatin then slowly set off towards the trackway, his four bemused young warriors trailing wordlessly after him.

Seoras, standing in the doorway of his house, watched them go. He said to Brude, "You should have killed him."

Mairead, her whole body radiating confusion, agreed. "At the very least you should have stuck to your first plan and made him act like a dead man around you. You can't trust him. He's an animal. That's why Colm keeps him." Brude remembered the bruise on her arm and wondered whether it was Cruithne who had put it there and not Colm as he had thought. Now was not the time to ask, he knew.

"Brude can beat him any time," Castatin chirped confidently.

"Not if he brings a gang with him or sets fire to his house at night, or stabs him in the back," Fothair pointed out gloomily. Castatin's face fell.

Brude, watching Cruithne slowly climb the track up the steep hill, said, "That's exactly why I don't want him as an enemy. I think I can trust him. He has some honour and he's not as stupid as he makes out."

"Honour?" Mairead was scathing. "What makes you think he has honour?"

"He could have drawn his sword when he tried to grab me. I'd have been in trouble then, but he didn't. He could have ordered his four men to attack me, but he didn't. I think I can trust him. I'd rather have him on my side than against me, that's for sure."

Fothair wasn't convinced. "You're crazy," he announced cheerfully. "But life certainly isn't dull while you're around."

"That's the trouble," said Brude. "I'd be happy with a dull life."

"You won't get one if you marry Seasaidh," Mairead observed. He heard an unspoken question in her voice.

"She's more Castatin's age than mine," Brude told her. "Like I said, I have no intention of marrying anyone just now."

Castatin looked alarmed, plainly terrified by the very mention of Seasaidh. Fothair laughed at his consternation. Mairead stepped close to Brude, looking into his eyes, studying his face as if she were looking for something. "You've changed a lot, Brude," she said softly. "I think you are more Roman than you like to pretend."

He wasn't sure whether that was a criticism or not. "We all change as we grow older," he replied. "The Romans always thought I was more like a Pritani than I let on. I used to think I was neither one nor the other, but then I met a man who taught me that I can only be myself, whatever others may think of me. He told me that, instead of being worried about not fitting in either place, I should take the best from everyone I know and everything I see and use these things to make myself a better person."

"He sounds very clever, this man," Mairead said. "Was he a fighter too?"

Brude laughed. "Cleon? No. He was a book-keeper."

A.D. 204

Curtius didn't know whether to laugh or cry. "Twenty-six men dead and five badly wounded. The school's lost six men but you walk out without a scratch. I don't know how you did it, boy. If it wasn't for the bruise on your head from where you nutted that Retiarius, I would swear you hadn't fought today."

Brude didn't know how to react either. He sat in the underground darkness below the arena, stripped of his weapons and armour. He had a loincloth, an old, dirty tunic, sandals and a wooden sword. He had some money back at the school, a few coins but hardly a fortune. Apart from that, he owned nothing. He was free and he should have been overjoyed but all he could think about was Josephus, lying dead in his arms, his neck ravaged by the fatal wound. Brude may have been free but he still felt trapped.

"Come on," Curtius told him. "We'd best get you cleaned up. You'll need to look your best for the celebration." He tugged Brude's arm and led him to the main corridor, which ran the length of the arena. Brude followed, his mind still numb. They climbed the stairs and the guards unlocked the gates, letting them out into the open air.

It was daylight. Brude had always come and gone from the great amphitheatre at night. Now he walked out through its massive arches and into the heat of the late afternoon. The place was crowded as the last of the spectators made their way home, still talking excitedly about the day's spectacle. None of them paid any attention to Brude or Curtius except perhaps to give them a passing glance. Brude stood still, looking around him in wonder. The walkway beneath the arches was filled with small merchant booths selling all sorts of food, drink and trinkets. He saw one displaying an array of statuettes in the shapes of assorted gladiators. He was amazed that people could actually buy such things. Outside in the bright, sweltering sunlight the houses crowded round the amphitheatre and there, on the Palatine hill, was the palace of the emperor himself, a massive sprawling building of arches, columns and white marble splendour. It was the heart of the empire. Brude felt almost overwhelmed.

Curtius nudged him into motion. Looking back over his shoulder, Brude saw the outside of the Flavian amphitheatre for the first time. He stopped again, staggered by its size and grandeur. Its successive rows of arches rose skywards, gleaming in the sun, dwarfing everyone and everything around them. The sheer scale of it amazed him. He had known it was large, of course. He had sensed its bulk when they came in darkness, sometimes seen its silhouette against a lightening sky and he had seen it from the inside many times. In the arena, though, he was more aware of the crowd than the stadium; more concerned about his opponent than where they were fighting. Seeing it now he felt he was being reminded of just how unimportant and small he was, how vast, impressive and powerful the empire was. He could not even begin to understand how anyone could conceive of such a building, let alone actually build it. Josephus had always insisted that it had been built by thousands of Jewish slaves, brought from Jerusalem when the emperor Titus had stormed the city after yet another of the revolts that the Jews were famous for. The little gladiator had also claimed that the walls contained the bodies of the slaves who had died building it. But then, Josephus had claimed a lot of things. The thought of his dead friend made Brude shudder. Curtius, misunderstanding, clapped him on the shoulder. "It gets you the first time, doesn't it? It's some place."

Curtius led Brude eastwards, through a maze of narrow, busy streets. One or two people saw the wooden rudis in Brude's hand

and a cry went up that the gladiator who had won the games was there. A crowd quickly gathered, mobbing him, cheering him and trying to touch him. He was too numb to fend them off but Curtius snarled at them, shoved and pushed then dragged Brude into a small public bathhouse, asking the attendants to keep the crowd at bay.

"You get cleaned up," Curtius told Brude. "Give me your rudis and I'll look after it for you. These places are full of thieves, so you don't want to leave it lying around here. I'll go and get you something better to wear."

A young woman, wearing a plain grey tunic, approached. Curtius handed her some coins. "My friend is new here. Show him the baths and give him a massage. Make him presentable for a dinner with someone important, will you?" The woman nodded, tucking the coins away into a small pouch. "By the way," Curtius added, "he's a gladiator, just been freed by the emperor himself, so perhaps a little extra something would be nice."

The woman smiled a humourless smile, which never touched her eyes. "If he wants sex, he pays for it like everyone else," she said.

Curtius grunted. "Never mind then. Just a bath and a massage. I'm sure he'll get plenty of free offers later on."

The woman showed Brude to a changing room where she told him to strip. He left his clothes with a slave who assured him they would be safe. Brude didn't care; they were old, dirty and ragged and Curtius had said he would get new ones. The slave passed him some wooden sandals, telling him to put them on. Then the woman led him through a door, to a room with a cold pool, which they walked round. They passed through some more doors to a warmer room where several men were sitting relaxing, some of them talking in easy tones. There was no pool here but around the room were several niches with stone benches, giving it a pleasant and relaxing atmosphere. All the men were naked but if that bothered the young woman, she certainly didn't show it. She walked on, Brude following her obediently, his mind still too overwhelmed to have any thoughts that might lead to an embarrassing reaction. He was more interested in his surroundings anyway. The gladiator school had a bathhouse but it was little more than a small pool of warm water where the slaves could wash off the sweat of the day's training. This place, although small by Roman standards, was far more impressive, with its painted, tiled walls and floors, and its statues of goddesses and nymphs decorating the small niches in every room.

The third room they went into was stifling. They walked through the wooden doors into a wall of steamy heat. Brude quickly realised why he had the sandals on, for the tiled floor was incredibly hot. The walls were decorated with paintings of trees, flowers and birds but they, too, were hot to the touch. In the centre of the room was a pool of steaming water. There were a couple of men already in the pool and the woman indicated to Brude that he should join them, pointing out the steps. "When you're ready, come to one of the couches at the far end," she told him.

He slipped off the sandals, making his way cautiously down the steps. The water was hot and felt wonderful. Trying not to be self-conscious, nor to betray his inexperience in places like this, he stepped in until the water came up to his waist. He found that there were stone benches around the edge of the pool, under the water at a convenient height so that he could sit with his head above the surface. He closed his eyes and relaxed. He had never felt anything quite like it. No wonder the Romans were always going on about the baths, he thought.

He idly listened to the two other men talking. With everyone naked it was impossible to tell what their social status was. The Romans, Brude knew, were very class conscious but here everyone was apparently equal. Until they started to talk, he suddenly realised. The two men were discussing some poem a friend of theirs had composed and they may as well have been speaking Persian for all Brude could make out of their conversation. He ducked his head under the water, letting it wash away the grime and sweat of the arena. *Am I really free*, he thought;

am I really here? It seemed like a dream, but he could feel the luxuriously hot water, hear the voices of the other bathers and the hiss of the steam that swirled through the room. He knew he could not have dreamed this because it was like nothing he had ever experienced.

He thought again of Josephus. Had the little man really intended to kill him with that sudden attack or had it been a ploy to distract the other gladiator? Perhaps Josephus had meant for him to dodge and so fall victim to the other man, giving Josephus a chance to win. Brude supposed he would never know. All that he knew was that he was here and Josephus was dead. There were no friends in the arena.

He decided he had had enough of the hot water, for his skin was hot and the room was stifling. He walked up the steps, water dripping from his naked body, found his slippers and went in search of the woman. She saw him approaching and waved him to a long slab of a table draped with towels. At her instruction, he lay down on his belly. She began to rub warm oil across his back and shoulders, then all over his body, kneading his muscles, forcing the tension from them. Then she scraped the oil off, cleaning his skin, making it feel fresh and alive. She took her time, working patiently. Brude relaxed and enjoyed the sensation. When she made him turn over, she threw a warm towel across his crotch. "Just the massage and clean, your friend said," she told him, her voice quite matter-of-fact. Brude had felt a stirring when her hands had begun to rub his chest, and he was more alert now, conscious of the shape of her body under the tight tunic, but he knew that if he had paid the extra she would have performed the sex in the same detached, dispassionate way as she was cleaning him. For her it was just a job. She was not all that pretty anyway, he decided, and his passion quickly died.

When she was finished, she told him to return to the pool for a few minutes, then go back to the frigidarium, the cold room, and use the pool there. She walked away, leaving him to suppose that the treatment Curtius had paid for was over. He went back into the warm pool, busier now as three more men had arrived. They were talking animatedly about the climax to the games and Brude listened as they discussed what they had seen. They began arguing about the move the Samnite had made to defeat the tall Retiarius, deliberately getting caught in the net so as to get close to the man with the trident. One of them insisted it was an accident, the second thought it was deliberate while the third man wasn't sure because he had been watching another pair fighting and had missed it. They talked as if the men who had fought and died were unimportant. Brude knew that was because, to them, they *were* unimportant. Gladiators were merely slaves who fought to please the people of Rome; they had no other purpose and were not regarded as real people at all.

One of the men saw Brude was listening. He smiled across at him. "Were you at the games, friend?" he asked.

"I was there," Brude acknowledged.

"Did you see the Samnite getting stuck in the net? Was it deliberate, do you think?"

Brude felt he should have been angry. Twenty-six men had died, his friend among them, and these men were sitting arguing about the niceties of one fight. Yet the warm bath and the oil seemed to have washed his anger away along with the dirt. He looked at the three of them and, though they had been part of the crowd baying for blood, he knew they were just men, men with lives of their own who could not possibly understand what he had been through. They were not worthy of his anger, he decided.

It was then that he made a silent promise to himself. He had had enough of killing. The promise started as a vague notion but quickly grew into a conviction, becoming firmer and more solid as he thought about it. He would not fight again unless there was no alternative and, if he did ever have to fight, he would not kill unless there was no other way. He smiled, the promise having lifted a cloud from his mind the way the oil and water had lifted the dirt from his skin, a cloud he had scarcely realised was there.

The men watched him, waiting for an answer, seeing him smile. "I had a very good view," he told them. "It was deliberate."

One of the men grinned, saying loudly to his friend, "I told you so!"

"That's just an opinion," the second man countered. "Only a crazy man would do something like that." He turned to Brude, appealing to him. "I think you're wrong, my friend."

Brude pointed to his forehead where he knew there was a small bruise. "I'm right, friend," he said pleasantly. "I got that when I hit his head with my helmet, just before I took his trident from him." The man's jaw dropped in astonishment when he realised what Brude was saying. Brude nodded politely to the three of them then climbed out of the pool, hearing the laughter of the first man and the mutters of "It's him!" as he made his way back to the room with the cold pool. He felt good. The hot bath, the massage, the joy of putting the innocent spectator in his place, all combined to free his spirits. Free. He really was free. He had spoken to a Roman and had not had to call him 'Master'.

He began shivering as the colder air in the frigidarium passed over his warm skin. He knew that to climb into the cold pool would be an agony so he jumped straight in, gasping for breath and feeling the exhilaration of the sudden change of temperature. He splashed about in the small pool, which he had to himself, swimming quickly from one side to the other. He had learned to swim as a boy in the cold waters of the Tava but this was infinitely more fun, even if he could cross the pool in only five strokes.

Refreshed, he climbed out, accepted a towel from an attendant and went back to the changing room where Curtius was waiting for him with some new, clean clothes; fresh undergarments, a white tunic and leather sandals. "Feel better?" the old lanista asked him.

"Wonderful," Brude replied as he pulled on his clothes and smoothed his damp hair.

"This is just a small bathhouse. You should try the Neronian baths some time. Now, though, we need to get a move on. We are expected for dinner."

"Dinner? Where?"

"At the house of Trimalchio, your former master. The man's an ass, but he throws a good dinner party and you're guest of honour. Here, you'd better take this." He handed Brude the wooden sword. "It would probably be easier if you wrap it up to keep it out of sight while we're going through the streets, though."

Brude was inclined to agree with Curtius' assessment of Trimalchio. Brude's former owner was gross in many senses of the word. His huge round belly and chubby features were exceeded only by his ostentatious wealth and the delight he had in showing it off. There were around twenty guests at the table, reclining on couches in the way of upper-class Romans. Brude could tell that, apart from one or two individuals who looked as though they found Trimalchio rather vulgar and would prefer to be somewhere else – but were either too well mannered, or perhaps too hungry, to leave – the guests seemed to be in a similar mould to their host, laughing too loudly at his jokes and fawning over his every word. Brude wasn't quite sure how upper-class Romans were supposed to behave but he had a feeling that this was not it. They ate and drank to excess, laughed and occasionally tossed food at each other while servants and slaves brought dish after dish, each one more exotic and fabulous than the one before.

Curtius sat in a foul humour all evening but Brude was enjoying himself. He was the centre of attention, especially from the women who seemed to grow more attractive the more wine he drank. Lentulus sat at the head of the table alongside Trimalchio, both of them exuberant over Brude's success at the games. Brude tried the various dishes that were presented, drank copious amounts of expensive Alban wine and said as little as possible. These people may not be the elite of Roman society but they were still his social superiors. Curtius had warned him that, once the glamour of his victory had worn off, they would want little to do with him. "Everyone loves a successful gladiator," Curtius had told him, "but nobody loves an ex-gladiator. Enjoy it while you can, lad."

Brude intended to. He drank some more wine and tasted some lark eggs. Then he realised that Trimalchio was speaking to him. "A name!" the fat man said loudly, clapping his hands together to get everyone's attention. "Our friend Brutus needs a proper name."

Brude was puzzled. He had a name, even though they never called him by it. To the Romans he was simply Brutus, if they bothered with a name at all. *Slave* or *Boy* was usually good enough. But he saw that Lentulus, who had never even spoken to him directly, was nodding sagely. "Yes indeed, he must have a proper name. Brutus is all very well as a name for the amphi-theatre but he is a citizen now, after all."

"Well, the *nomen* is easy," Trimalchio said. "He was freed by the emperor so he must take the emperor's family name." There were choruses of agreement from around the table. Brude looked across at Curtius for help but the old gladiator just shrugged. It was decided that Brude's family name was to be Septimius and the conversation moved to his *praenomen*. It seemed he had to pick from a fairly short list of names, one of which every Roman man used. He had no idea whether he wanted to be a Gaius or a Lucius and there was much drunken debate around the room. Curtius sourly suggested that he did not need a *praenomen* as it was usually only family who called people by this name and Brude had no family. Trimalchio dismissed this objection. "We are his family now!" he boomed.

"In that case, call him Marcus," Curtius said. "It's supposed to be the name of those who follow Mars, the god of war, and he's a warrior if I ever saw one."

Brude could think of no objections and Trimalchio was happy at the suggestion so Brude was now Marcus Septimius Brutus. Most people would call him by his third name, the *cognomen*, of Brutus, the name that would mark him out from the hundreds of other Romans scattered around the empire who also happened to be called Marcus Septimius. The woman sitting next to Brude, a brown-eyed, brown-haired woman who he guessed was older than she was trying to appear, told him that a *cognomen* was usually given for a distinctive feature or trait. She suggested in a rather lewd way that he take the name Maximus because he was very large. She smiled suggestively at him and he smiled back, not discouraging her.

"Excellent," Trimalchio gurgled over his wine. "Our friend has a proper name. So what are your plans now, Marcus?"

Brude wondered who Trimalchio was talking to when the woman beside him nudged him, reminding him that he was now Marcus. Plans? He had no plans, did he? "I thought I would go home," he said, without thinking.

"Home?" Trimalchio was intrigued. "And where is home?"

"The land of the Boresti, north of the Wall of Hadrian."

"North? You are from Caledonia?" Trimalchio was surprised but Brude sensed a renewed interest from the woman reclining alongside him. "Whatever do you want to go there for?" Trimalchio asked him. "No! No! Tomorrow you can go back to the school to collect your things and then you must return here. I have plenty of work for a former gladiator." Brude was about to argue but Curtius threw a small piece of bread at him and shook his head.

After the meal there was some entertainment as jugglers and clowns tumbled around the room. As the evening wore on, some guests made their excuses and left. Trimalchio invited those who remained to join him in his private bathhouse. Brude, more than a little drunk by now, thought the chance of a second bath in one day was too good to pass up so he went along. He was surprised to find that the men and women all shared the same hot pool. Trimalchio's bathhouse was large, tiled with yellow-streaked marble while the pool itself was lined with blue painted tiles, making it seem like a warm part of the sea. Slaves stood around the edge of the pool, with trays of iced drinks and small pieces of cut fruit, while Trimalchio and his guests threw off their clothes and clambered into the warm water. The woman who had been next to Brude stayed close to him. He could not help but look at her naked body. She sat beside him, their arms and legs touching. Then she leaned over and whispered, "I was right, we should have called you Maximus." She leaned into him and kissed him full on the lips, her breasts, warmer than the warm water around them, brushing his chest as one hand clamped round the back of his neck, pulling him to her hungry lips. He was startled, wondering what the others would think, but when she eventually pulled away, he saw that other couples were already entwined in each other's arms. The woman, who told him her name was Poppaea, took his hand and led him out of the pool, both of them naked and dripping wet. They passed through a maze of corridors with tiled floors and garishly painted red and yellow walls which eventually led to a bedroom. She pushed the door shut behind them then kissed him again. They did not go back to join the others.

Curtius woke him early the next morning. Brude's head was sore from the wine and he cursed Curtius for waking him on the first day in eight years that he had had the chance to sleep late. Poppaea mumbled and stirred on the bed but did not wake. Curtius threw Brude's clothes at him and told him to get dressed. "We have six funerals to attend," he snapped.

As well as Brude's discarded clothes, Curtius had found Brude's wooden sword, which he had left lying in the dining room, still wrapped in a piece of cloth. Brude could not face breakfast so Curtius led him through the still sleeping household, out through the atrium, the small courtyard open to the skies at the front of the house, and into the streets of Rome.

It was the second hour but the summer sun was already hot. Curtius apparently knew where he was going so Brude tagged along, his stomach churning and his head thumping. They had only gone a short distance when he had to stop to throw up in the gutter. Passers-by moved to avoid the unpleasantness but

Curtius, who seemed to be happiest when he had something to complain about, laughed. "Too much wine and too much rich food, lad," he chuckled. "I expect you'll feel better now, though." He hauled Brude upright, forcing him to walk on, heading towards the centre of the city. Brude could make out the top of the Flavian amphitheatre occasionally peeking over the roofs of the high tenement blocks that housed most of Rome's inhabitants. Curtius asked him, "So what do you think of Trimalchio?"

Brude smiled weakly. "He's an ass, but he throws a good dinner party."

"Glad you've been paying attention," Curtius said grimly. "You'll be well fed at his house and have your pick of the women. For a while at least, until they get bored of you. Just watch you don't overdo the good eating or you'll end up as fat as Trimalchio."

Brude didn't want that to happen. He had never seen anyone as fat as Trimalchio and said so to Curtius. "That's because he has nothing to do except make money and spend it on food," the old lanista told him. "Whatever else he is, the man's got a fine business brain. He's richer than most people in the city, including some senators. That's why he has all those hangers-on and whores at his house every evening."

"Poppaea's not a whore," said Brude sharply.

Curtius grunted. "Not the way the street girls are, maybe. Her husband's a merchant. He's away a lot, working for Trimalchio. She has to eat so she either buys her own food from what money her husband leaves her while he's away or, like a lot of Romans do, she gets herself invited to other people's houses for dinner. She gets invited there a lot. In fact she gets invitations to lots of homes because people know she's free and easy with who she sleeps with."

Brude did not reply. Poppaea had certainly seemed very keen on him but he wondered now whether Curtius was right. He decided to reserve judgement. Curtius saw his expression and laughed his grim laugh again. "Don't worry, lad. Take advantage of it while you can. Just don't expect her undying love, that's all."

Brude decided to change the subject. "Where are we going?"

"The forum," answered Curtius. "We need to get your manumission papers drawn up and signed. It might take a while."

Brude discovered that Rome had more than one forum. The original forum lay between the Capitoline and the Palatine hills, near the amphitheatre, but it was too small to cater for all of Rome's commercial and legal business so various emperors had built other fora nearby. There were smaller ones devoted to market trade in cattle and vegetables but the imperial fora were great, rectangular open spaces, dotted with statues and ringed by covered porticoes which were supported by extravagantly carved columns. The fora, surrounded by temples and basilicas, were the heart of Rome in a way that no palace could ever be. Around the edge, market stalls and shops clustered under the shade of the porticoes. People thronged there to meet and talk, to conduct business or to show off their wealth. Brude was amazed at the noise, the bustle, the colour and the astounding variety of goods for sale; food and trinkets from all over the empire, brought to Rome and on offer to anyone who could afford them.

Curtius took Brude through the forum of Augustus where he marvelled at the high colonnades, each niche with a statue representing a hero of Rome, some of the columns carved in the shape of beautiful women. He saw the great temple of Mars the Avenger, with its huge statue of the god and dramatic carved reliefs. He wondered again at the power of Rome, which seemed full of incredible buildings at every turn. There, in the centre, was a great stone block, its sides carved smooth and regular, surmounted by a bronze statue of a man in a chariot drawn by four galloping horses. Augustus himself. The first emperor, the man who had made Rome what it was today.

The two of them edged through the crowd, making their way to the forum of Trajan, even larger than the forum of Augustus and surrounded by enormous buildings. There was a great column of shining stone, its sides decorated with carvings of

Roman soldiers in action, the picture story spiralling upwards, so high that the images at the top could not be made out. On top of the column stood a statue of a Roman, shining gold in the morning sunlight. "What is that?" Brude asked Curtius, his breath taken away.

"Trajan's column," Curtius replied sourly. "Bastard!"

"What?" Brude was surprised at the feeling in Curtius' tone.

"It commemorates the victory of Rome over Dacia. That's where my family are from. My grandfather was brought here as a slave when Trajan killed our king and stole our land."

Brude was surprised. He had always viewed Curtius as a Roman. Which he was, he supposed, but the old gladiator obviously still remembered his roots. Brude said, "That's what the Romans do, isn't it? They've built an empire by conquering other people. Even I know that."

Curtius nodded. "I know, and there's no beating the power of Rome. Dacia was an independent kingdom for centuries until the Romans needed some hard cash and discovered we had gold mines. There's only ever one end to a story like that. You should just be grateful that your homeland has nothing but mud and rain. If you had anything the Romans needed, you'd find yourselves part of the empire before long."

Brude was shocked. Back in Broch Tava, he had been brought up to believe that the Romans had been forced to abandon the lands north of the Wall because of the power of the assembled tribes. He had sometimes wondered how that could be true when every story he ever heard of battles were Roman victories. He knew from bitter experience how good the Roman army was. Now, contradicting everything Brude had been taught as a boy, Curtius was telling him the only reason the Romans had left was because the lands of the Pritani had nothing of value to offer the empire. It was a disappointing revelation but one Brude realised could well be true. Any nation that could build the things he could see all around him, and conquer tribes all over the world, would surely not be afraid of the Pritani.

Curtius took him into the shade of the portico and inside the great basilica. The place was crowded and noisy with people, many wearing togas, jostling and shouting, while others sat behind wooden tables covered with scrolls; quills and ink near at hand. It was all incredibly confusing to Brude but Curtius barged his way through, asked directions and eventually led Brude to join a queue at one of the tables. They waited nearly an hour before they had their turn at speaking to the scribe. When Curtius explained that Brude had been awarded the rudis by the emperor himself at the games, the scribe gave Brude a look of mixed admiration and suspicion. After Curtius showed him the rudis, the clerk selected a scroll, which already had a lot of writing on it. He carefully filled in some blank spaces. Brude had to give his new Roman name, which still sounded to him like it belonged to someone else, then the scribe handed him the scroll. "You need to get it signed and sealed by the praetor," he said, waving the quill in his hand vaguely towards one end of the basilica.

Another queue and this time they waited until it was nearly midday before Curtius presented Brude and his scroll to the praetor, one of Rome's senior magistrates. There were normally eight praetors elected each year, though in practice those who were elected were usually approved by the emperor, or at least were men he did not disapprove of. The praetors were responsible for the smooth operation of the law so they were extremely busy men. Brude's audience lasted no more than a few heartbeats before he came away with his papers. He looked at the documents, admiring the red seal and the flourish of the signature. Curtius laughed at him. "Stop pretending you can read. Come on, we need to leave one copy here as a record. You keep the other copy safe. It's your proof of manumission."

Manumission. Freedom from slavery. Today, at last, Brude was living life as a free man. "Can I go home now?" he asked Curtius.

"Home? You mean that nonsense about going back to Britannia was serious?"

Brude nodded. "It wasn't nonsense. I want to go home."

"What for?" Curtius seemed genuinely puzzled.

"I have family there. Friends." He wanted to say he had Mairead waiting for him but he had been away for eight years and he knew she would probably be married to someone else by now.

Curtius dragged him over to a small stall selling sweet-meats and cold drinks where he handed over a few coins to the stallholder. Then he led Brude to a shady part of the portico where they sat on a stone bench as the crowd passed by on all sides. While they ate, Curtius spoke to him earnestly, his face etched with concern. "Listen lad, you've been away a long time. Things in your homeland won't be the same as when you left. Going back is never a good idea, believe me. Anyway, how would you get there? It's a long way and you have no money to pay for food. You can't afford to go by sea and it would take you months to walk there. A man alone can run into all sorts of trouble on a journey like that."

Brude had travelled enough to know how to get round that problem. "I could work for a merchant. Bodyguard! That way I'd be fed and paid while I work my way home."

Curtius looked at him long and hard. "You really mean it, don't you?"

"Yes."

With a sigh, Curtius said, "Well I think you're mad, but then you've done your share of crazy things so I shouldn't be sur-prised. But, if you take my advice, you'll stay here a bit longer. Earn yourself some money before you start off on such a long journey on your own. Don't leave Rome until you are sure of what you'll be leaving behind."

Brude wasn't sure why Curtius was so insistent that he stayed, but he respected the old man enough to at least give his words some thought. It was only later that he realised Curtius led a lonely life that meant he had few friends and probably didn't want to lose someone he had known for so long. Now, though, they left the forum, making their way back to the amphitheatre where they found the guards from the gladiator school waiting with two wagons already loaded with the familiar cheap, rectangular boxes which acted as coffins for the dead gladiators. Brude wondered which one held the body of Josephus. Curtius acted as though he did not much care but he was silent for most of the journey back through the busy streets which led out of the city to the school.

Lentulus was not there, probably still sleeping at Trimalchio's house, but Curtius gathered the remaining gladiators and told them what had happened. They were pleased for Brude but saddened at the loss of so many of their companions. Pollio, still limping badly, clasped Brude's hand warmly. "Well done, boy," he said with feeling. "I know how hard that must have been."

Brude nodded but could think of nothing to say. He was free while Pollio, vastly more experienced, was still a slave and would go back to the arena once his leg was healed. Brude had toyed with the idea of asking Curtius for a job as a trainer at the school but he knew now that he could not do that. He had been one of them but now he was raised above them, a free man, and he could not go back to being one of them again.

The funeral was short but well attended. Every gladiator in the school was there, the guards as well, along with the slave girls who helped to run the school. Even Tygaeus the physician came. All six coffins were placed in one grave, an old ram was sacrificed by an even older priest and Curtius sent for a stone mason to carve an inscription on a simple headstone.

Afterwards Kallikrates and Curtius said their farewells to Brude, laughing together over Trimalchio's instructions for him to collect his things from the school. "What have you got?" Kallikrates joked. "Sixteen sesterces and the clothes you're wearing?"

"And he owes me four for them," said Curtius glumly. Then he tried to pretend he was only joking when Brude insisted on paying him. They clasped hands again and, with a lump in his throat, Brude walked out of the main entrance of the school, carrying his wooden sword, his manumission papers and twelve sesterces.

He had nothing, but he had everything, for he was a free man.

Brude soon discovered that freedom was a relative term. Trimalchio was incredibly rich and loved to show off his wealth but, although he provided free food and lodgings for his retainers, he did not pay them very well. Brude was constantly at his beck and call, for everywhere Trimalchio went, whether in his carriage or in the small covered chair carried by eight slaves, he insisted on being accompanied by a retinue of guards. Most of the men he employed were old soldiers, veterans with grey hair and tired limbs who had taken money instead of land when they left the army and had managed to lose most of it through bad luck or bad judgement. But they were tough and uncompromising men who served Trimalchio well. They hated Brude.

They were not allowed to carry swords in the city but each of them usually had a short wooden cudgel, which could be deadly if used properly. Brude got one for himself and eventually had to threaten to beat one of the old soldiers to death to keep them from constantly antagonising him. He had quickly learned that Curtius had been right. Gladiators were popular as long as they were slaves who fought to entertain the crowd but, once out of the arena, they were despised almost as much as actors. He tried hard to keep to his promise of not fighting, but his patience was tested frequently. He assured the other guards that he intended to stay only until he had enough money to allow him to travel home in comfort but his life was full of tension. He was fairly certain that the only reason the men did not jump him as a gang was because they knew Trimalchio favoured him.

There were compensations, of course. He enjoyed visiting the baths, whether accompanying Trimalchio or on his own. And there was usually a woman available if he wanted one but, again, as Curtius had predicted, Poppaea, although she slept with him from time to time, soon moved on to other men.

Summer slowly turned to autumn and gradually the winter rains arrived. There was even some snow one day. Trimalchio

187

did not venture far when the days were wet and cold. Brude realised that, after so many years of living in the heat, even he was feeling the weather cold when he knew it was nothing like the chill winters of the north. He decided he would go home in the springtime, for there was nothing to keep him in Rome. He had no time for the sycophants who flocked round Trimalchio and he was starting to despise himself for growing used to the luxury. In particular, he hated it when Trimalchio forced him to go to the amphitheatre so that he could give the fat man the benefit of his expertise as they watched the gladiators fight. On one occasion, Pollio was in the arena and Brude could hardly watch the combat. Pollio won, but was wounded again, this time on the arm. Brude felt helpless and angry watching Curtius lead the veteran gladiator from the arena. Trimalchio, of course, thought it was splendid entertainment.

Then, one dull day not long after the midwinter festival of Saturnalia, Trimalchio summoned Brude to his private room. "Marcus, my dear friend," said Trimalchio, with a sad expression on his chubby face. "I have a great favour to ask of you."

Brude wondered what was coming next. "What is it?" He could not bring himself to call Trimalchio by his *praenomen* of Publius. He did not feel close to the man at all and had no wish to seem too familiar.

"My former master, Gnaeus Vipsanius Aquila, the man who freed me years ago as a reward for my services, has asked a favour of me. I am, of course, duty bound to assist him." Brude nodded. He had learned that slaves who were freed were still obliged to support their former masters. He felt no such compunction about being loyal to Trimalchio, although the fat man seemed to take it for granted that he did, for such was the Roman way. Roman society depended on patronage, even if there was no formal master/slave relationship. Wealthy men looked after the interests of their clients while, in return, the clients acted to support their patrons in their political ambitions. When a slave was freed, the obligations were even stronger, although Brude reasoned that, technically, it was the emperor who had freed him so he owed nothing to Trimalchio.

The fat man blinked as he tried to explain his predicament. "Aquila has a son, a young man who will be seeking a military post within two years. Aquila has requested that I allow you to work for him to train his son in the art of combat before he joins the army." He went on, "Aquila's first son was killed while with the army in Judaea and he wants to give his one remaining heir every chance of survival that he can." Trimalchio clasped his hands together, almost pleading. "It is a most unusual request, I must say, but it is one I really cannot refuse. Would you do this for me, Marcus? Would you be prepared to leave my humble home to help my patron Aquila?"

Brude managed to stop himself from smiling. He had no idea who Aquila was, and he was still determined to leave for home in a few months, when the weather was easier for travelling, but even a few months away from Trimalchio's house would be a bonus. "Yes, I will go to Aquila," he said.

Trimalchio's eyes filled with tears. In an uncharacteristic display of gratitude, he gave Brude two silver denarii as a farewell gift.

Two hours later Brude had found the home of Gnaeus Vipsanius Aquila, a large two-storey house near the Capitoline hill. A slave admitted him to the atrium. In the centre of the atrium was the impluvium, the small pool used to collect rainwater, and in the centre of the impluvium was a small bronze statue of an eagle with outstretched wings. Around the walls of the atrium were small niches in which stood carved busts. Brude recognised one of them as the emperor Septimius Severus with his curly hair and beard. The emperor's image was everywhere in the city, of course. Nobody was allowed to forget who was responsible for maintaining the safety and security of the empire. The other statues were distinguished-looking men but he had no idea who they were. Above them, on the bare white wall, hung face masks of yet more men. These, Brude knew, must be the death masks of Aquila's ancestors, kept so that they and their deeds could be remembered down through the generations.

Through a wide, open doorway, beyond the eagle statue, Brude could see the peristyle, a square garden courtyard, surrounded by columns. Beyond that, he saw the doors which led to the private rooms of the large house. Household slaves scurried silently about their duties and he saw immediately that this house was owned by somebody of more refined tastes than Trimalchio. It was elegant, yet functional at the same time, merely hinting subtly at wealth rather than screaming opulence as Trimalchio's home did.

The slave showed him to one of the large public rooms off the atrium, and there he met Aquila. Trimalchio's former master was a tall man with thinning grey hair, piercing blue eyes and a hawked beak of a nose, which Brude guessed had been the inspiration for the man's *cognomen* Aquila, or eagle. He was seated in a finely carved wooden chair but rose to greet Brude, his manner rather stiff and formal but very polite. He was wearing a toga of white linen with a thin purple stripe running down it and around its edges. There were two other people in the room. Aquila introduced them. "This is my son, Lucius," he said, indicating a young boy of around sixteen years of age, with a mop of dark hair and the same eyes as his father. He was dressed in a white tunic of fine linen. Brude noticed that he was not wearing his bulla, the good luck amulet worn by all Roman children, indicating that Lucius had now come of age and was a citizen in his own right. "And this is Cleon, who keeps my business affairs in order," said Aquila in a tone which suggested some affection for the man. Cleon, short and running to fat, with a balding head and a pock-marked face, nodded with a welcoming smile. He stood beside a wooden table which was covered in neatly stacked papyrus scrolls and vellum parchments.

Aquila offered Brude a drink of watered wine, which he accepted. Cleon poured the drink into a fine silver goblet for him. Brude took the opportunity to look around the room, admiring the wall paintings, depicting mythical heroes and a fine mosaic on the floor showing Neptune, god of the sea, blowing a favourable wind into the sails of a large sailing ship. He took the wine from Cleon and, while he sipped it, Aquila studied him with an appraising look. "I take it Trimalchio has explained why I asked you here?"

Brude felt nervous being so close to the first really refined Roman he had met at close quarters but he managed to answer, "Yes, sir. He said you were looking for someone to train your son how to fight."

Aquila gave a slight nod. "That is correct. I am sure you understand that this is rather an unusual arrangement. Gladiators are not normally welcomed in polite society, as I am sure you have learned."

Brude gave a rueful smile. "Yes, sir." He interpreted Aquila's words to mean that the nobleman did not regard his former slave, Trimalchio, as belonging to polite society.

"My son is destined for the military and then, hopefully, to a senatorial career. I have already lost one son and I wish to give Lucius the best possible chance of surviving whatever dangers he may face in the army, so that he returns home, a hero of Rome, able to begin his way through the career of honour." The career of honour was the political path for the elite in Roman society. If selected, a Roman would hold a succession of magisterial posts, each one with more responsibility, culminating in the position of consul, the highest position a Roman could have, short of being emperor. Before he could start his political career, though, Lucius would need to demonstrate his capability as a soldier. Aquila went on, "Trimalchio speaks very highly of you but, more importantly, so does Lollius Curtius. He claims you are more than just a simple gladiator. What were his words, Cleon?"

"He said that Marcus Septimius Brutus is a thinker, sir," said Cleon. "A man who tends to make the right choices."

Brude was surprised that Aquila had spoken to Curtius. The old lanista was hardly the sort to frequent the same social circles. Then again, Aquila seemed like a man who would check things before making any decision. Probably, Brude thought, it was the freedman Cleon who had actually spoken to Curtius. Aquila nodded. "A thinker. He also says you are from Caledonia?"

"Yes, sir." Brude knew that Romans had only a vague idea of places outside their empire. The Caledonii were just one of the tribes of the Pritani who lived north of the Wall but few Romans had ever heard of the Boresti, so Brude let the distinction pass.

"And your father was an important man?"

"He was the head man of our village," said Brude, impressed at how much checking Aquila had done. "One of the leading men of our tribe." And even if Broch Tava was only a small village, thought Brude, he was still important to me.

"So, a noble background," said Aquila, his bright eyes still examining Brude. "And now a Roman citizen, freed by the emperor himself. I was at the Secular Games that day. You were rather lucky to win, were you not?"

Brude hesitated before answering. He saw Cleon watching him intently, waiting to see how he would answer. Aquila stared at him as well. He sensed that his answer to this question would decide what would happen next. "Everyone needs a bit of luck," he agreed, "and yes, I had my share that day. But a man who relies on luck will not survive long in the arena. Hard work, and a lot of practice, helps outweigh bad luck. I took some risks and they paid off, for Fortune smiled on me."

Aquila nodded thoughtfully. He turned to Cleon, raising a questioning eyebrow. The balding man nodded and Aquila said to Brude, "You will have your own room and will become part of my family. I will pay you fifty sesterces a month over and above your food and board. You will train my son every day for at least two hours. I may have other duties for you, such as accompanying members of the family when they leave the house. Other than that, your time will be your own." He looked hard at Brude. "Are these terms acceptable?"

Brude did not have to think about it very long. He still intended to leave for Britannia in a couple of months but there was no point in telling Aquila that. This was a way to escape Trimalchio's suffocating clutches. Becoming a member of Aquila's family was only a technical issue. All members of the household were members of the family, including the slaves, and the master of the house controlled their lives. Under Roman law he had the power of life and death over each and every one of them, although few men ever actually exercised that power in practice. It was a strange concept for Brude to understand but it did not affect his decision. "Thank you, sir. I agree."

Aquila's thin lips twitched in what might have been a smile. "Excellent. Cleon has the contract already drawn up, so let us sign it. Then I will let Cleon show you around. You can begin training Lucius tomorrow."

Cleon unwrapped a scroll, passing it to Aquila who carefully scratched his name with an ink-tipped, goose-feather quill. He passed the quill to Brude, who took it clumsily, making his mark beside, and just beneath, Aquila's signature.

"You cannot read or write?" Aquila asked him.

"No, sir."

"Yet you sign it anyway?" He seemed amused.

Brude looked him in the eyes. "I trust you, sir. Among my people, the spoken word is as binding as anything written in Rome."

"Then welcome to the house of Vipsanius Aquila."

Brude had intended to stay for two months but, somehow, he never quite managed to make the break and the two months stretched into two years.

He had his own room with a small window overlooking the street; the work he had to do was relatively easy, the food was good and Cleon quickly became his guide, mentor and friend. It was the happiest time he had experienced since leaving Broch Tava.

Cleon was a Greek, retained by Aquila as a tutor for his two sons but who had also acted as a personal secretary and book-keeper to Aquila since Trimalchio's departure. Brude learned more about Rome from Cleon in six months than he had learned in eight years of slavery. As a Greek, Cleon had a healthy disdain for Roman culture, yet at the same time he revelled in life in the imperial city. He would often walk through the streets with Brude, showing him the sights, explaining what the various buildings were and which emperor or other important person had built them.

Brude loved strolling through the forum of Augustus or the Campus Martius, outside the city walls on the banks of the Tiber. There, Augustus, the first emperor, had his magnificent mausoleum. He had also erected a huge Egyptian obelisk which acted as a sundial, casting its shadow on marks carved into the paved square around it. It was a simple concept yet, like so many things in Rome, the scale of it was stunning. Brude also spent hours walking round the gleaming white marble of the Ara Pacis, the Altar of Peace, another monument erected by Augustus. "He must have been a great man, this Augustus," he said to Cleon one day.

"The Romans hold him up as the exemplar of what a good emperor should be," Cleon agreed. Then, in his mocking way, he added, "Mind you, he only became emperor in the first place after he had slaughtered or murdered anyone who opposed him."

Brude shrugged. Such was the way in Rome, as he was rapidly learning. The empire was at peace but the threat of violence was always there for anyone who stepped out of line. Emperors often came to power through violence and had no qualms about using more violence to hold on to that power once they had achieved it. Cleon told him that, years before, there had been one year when the empire had had no fewer than four emperors, three of whom had met violent deaths.

Brude also began to understand more about how Rome operated and why Aquila had hired him. Aquila was an *eques*, a knight, wealthy enough to become a senator but barred from doing so because he had made his money through commerce, and still did. He owned several ships which plied the sea between the port at Ostia and various parts of the empire around the Mediterranean Sea, carrying pottery and iron tools on the outward trip and bringing back olive oil or other, more exotic, foodstuffs on the return journey. Rome's demand for olive oil was insatiable and while the imperial fleet carried huge quantities of it, there was always room for private enterprise to bring more. Aquila would have liked to have become involved in the transport of the grain that Rome needed to feed its citizens, but the imperial fleet had the monopoly on that; the emperor would take no chances that someone else could control the food supply for the citizens of Rome. Aquila also traded in precious goods throughout Italy and owned country estates in the hills of Latium where his family usually spent the hot summer months. He had high hopes for his son, Lucius, whose full name was Lucius Vipsanius Festus because he had been born on the day of the Saturnalia festival. Lucius, Aquila hoped, would one day become a senator, the first in the family to reach the rank. After a successful spell in the military, he would progress through the career of honour, perhaps even becoming a consul, after which fame and wealth beckoned if he could be appointed as governor of an imperial province. Under Cleon's instruction, Lucius was being taught oratory as well as studying the works of Rome's famous poets, and learning Greek, the second language of the empire, so that he could read Homer's classic tales in their native tongue. These were all essential skills for a Roman senator. All he had to do was survive to inherit his father's wealth, which was why Aquila wanted Brude to teach him how to fight.

Brude liked Lucius. He was a serious boy, of average build but with a quick mind. He spoke well and Cleon always praised his oratorical skills. He reckoned the boy had the makings of a fine senator. As a fighter, though, he was no better than average although he tried hard and listened carefully to Brude's advice, doing his best to put the tips into practice.

Brude went back to Lentulus' school to buy some wooden swords from Curtius. The old lanista was pleased to see him, as was Kallikrates, but something in the relationship had changed so Brude did not stay long. While he was there, though, he learned that Pollio had been killed. His leg had never properly healed and had slowed him enough to allow a Retiarius to snare him. "The crowd were in a bloody mood that day," Curtius complained, "and the emperor's son, who was hosting the games, wanted to please them, so he let Pollio die. Bastard!"

Before leaving, Brude went to see Tygaeus. He obtained the name of a pharmacist who imported the various herbs and oils that the physician used. Brude found the man in a narrow side street in the city and spent a portion of his wages stocking up on some basics. He wasn't sure why he did that but his time working with Tygaeus had sparked an interest in healing and he felt a strange impulse to keep a supply of medicines handy.

Lucius was delighted with the wooden swords. He trained hard with Brude, using the peristyle garden as their training ground. Brude could not use the brutal training methods of the gladiatorial school and he rarely worked with Lucius for more than two hours each day, but the boy was slowly improving his speed and anticipation and was working at building up his muscles. They practised every day, often with Aquila looking on, as well as other family members who would lean out of the windows from the rooms overlooking the garden. The slave who tended the garden was not pleased at the treatment it suffered but did not complain at the occasional damage done to his plants, at least not out loud.

The other family members Brude came to know were Agrippina, Aquila's second wife, and Vipsania, his youngest child. He had two daughters, and both, in the Roman fashion, were called Vipsania. Being female, they did not warrant proper names themselves. To tell them apart, they were simply called Vipsania Prima and Vipsania Secunda; the first and second daughters of the family of Vipsanius. Brude thought that incredibly odd. For such a civilised race, the Romans treated their women like second-class citizens, a point of view quite alien to one of the Pritani. To Romans, of course, the fact that the Pritani traced their lineage through the female line, and even sometimes had women rulers, was simply a sign of their barbarism. Even Cleon struggled to follow Brude's explanations. "You mean your kings are not the sons of kings, but the sons of the sisters of kings? How strange!"

"At least our women are not treated like breeding cows," Brude retorted. "They are equals to men in most things."

"Equals to men?" Cleon was aghast. "My dear Brutus, women can never be the equal of men. As well as being physically weaker, their brains are smaller so they cannot possibly have the same mental capacity as men. This is a well known scientific fact."

Brude knew better than to argue with Cleon when he got onto science. Cleon was very proud of the Greek traditions of science and mathematics. "The Romans may be great engineers," he would frequently say, "but their philosophy is entirely borrowed from Greece and there is not a single Roman mathematician to match Pythagoras, let alone Archimedes. The Greeks are unmatched when it comes to science."

Now that Cleon had pronounced his verdict on women, Brude knew he would never win an argument about it. He supposed his friend must be right, but he could not help wondering whether Cleon would dare voice his opinion of women's abilities in front of some of the women of the Boresti that Brude had known. His mother, for one, would have had a few words to say about it.

As for the women of Aquila's family, Vipsania Prima was a year older than Lucius and had been married to the second son of a senator, only two months before Brude had joined the household. It was a good marriage and Aquila was delighted at the match, even though he had had to pay a large dowry.

Vipsania Secunda was only thirteen years old. She was quiet and pretty, saying little but with eyes that suggested a quick and alert mind, whatever Cleon thought about the limitations of the female brain. Brude learned that Aquila's wife had died when Vipsania Secunda was born. He had remarried several years later, his new wife Agrippina being more than twenty years younger than him, and still only in her early thirties. A strikingly attractive woman, she was a typically demure Roman wife who ran the household with quiet efficiency and who obeyed her husband's every word. Brude soon learned that Vipsania Secunda hated her.

"One day my father will find out what she's really like," the young girl said to Brude as she brought him a drink, after he and Lucius had finished a hard workout which had brought gushing praise from the boy's step-mother. Brude had looked at Vipsania questioningly but she would say no more so he did not pursue the matter. Family squabbles were best avoided.

Cleon decided that Brude should learn to read and write, so he set out to teach him. Brude was delighted when he could start to make out what the various signs and engravings on statues and buildings actually meant, not to mention the graffiti scrawled on walls. He mastered the basics quickly and Cleon soon had him reading Virgil's great work, the Aeneid. This was harder going but Brude's mastery of the skill improved, as did his Latin vocabulary. He was forever asking Cleon what a particular word meant and Cleon always explained patiently and with good humour. It took Brude nearly four months to finish the book but Cleon was impressed. "For a beginner, that was quick and you understood it well. If only you could read Greek, then you'd be able to read Homer."

"You could teach me," suggested Brude enthusiastically. Cleon laughed, saying he would see, which meant that he would. Greek was the second official language of the empire anyway and was often heard, even in Rome. At first Brude thought he would never master the tongue for the alphabet the Greeks used was entirely different from that of the Romans, but he was determined to try so he spent hours each day learning the sounds and the grammar. In many ways the language was similar to Latin in its structure and the more he learned the more Cleon urged him on. "It will take you a few years to learn it all," Cleon told him, but when they were together, they often spoke in Greek to help Brude learn and he picked it up quickly. "You have a better ear for languages than most Romans I've taught," Cleon told him. Brude was delighted at the praise but Cleon then grinned and said, "Of course, you should learn it more quickly because you are a lot older than the boys I usually teach." His eyes twinkled with good humour as he spoke.

Brude laughed. "Maybe I should teach you my native tongue," he suggested.

"What on earth for?" Cleon said in mock horror. "I have no intention of ever going anywhere near your homeland with its mists and rain and savage tribes. It's bad enough putting up with the Romans, who are at least partially civilised."

Brude had to admit that he enjoyed life in Rome, at least in the circles Aquila moved in. Visits to the baths were virtually a daily occurrence and Aquila usually took Lucius, Cleon and Brude along with him, as well as several slaves. Brude learned that there were nearly two hundred bathhouses in the city, ranging from the small ones, like the one Curtius had first taken him to, up to enormous complexes with huge pools, glass windows, libraries, gardens and spaces for playing ball or exercising. Brude never tired of visiting the baths but he quickly found that they were more than just places where every Roman could mingle in apparent equality. Aquila usually had several clients with him, men who worked for him or whose interests he looked after. They were obliged to him for assistance, either through him mentioning them to other friends, who might need something done, or through donations of cash to support them. In turn, these clients were expected to support Aquila when he asked them to. Aquila's house was always busy as his clients paid him daily visits, meeting every morning in one of the rooms off his atrium to discuss business. Trimalchio, as one of Aquila's former slaves, was, technically, his client but Brude noticed that the two men rarely met. When they did, there was a coolness from Aquila, which Trimalchio seemed oblivious to, but which was all too obvious to everyone else. Aquila was always polite, of course, but never friendly towards his erstwhile slave.

The complex web of patronage worked the other way as well, for Aquila himself had a wealthy patron, a senator named Gaius Ampulius Varro. Sometimes Aquila would meet with Varro at the baths, leaving Cleon and Brude to their own devices. "Rome is built on patronage," Cleon told Brude one day as they relaxed in the hot steam of the Neronian baths. "It's not just about how rich you are. It's about who you know. Of course, if you back the wrong man, it can all go horribly wrong for you if he falls from favour, but Aquila wants Lucius to get a good, safe posting in the army and he's keeping in with Varro because he thinks he can put in a good word with those who are close to the emperor."

The other great benefit of living in the home of a wealthy man was that food was never a problem. Aquila dined with friends most evenings, either at his own house or at the homes of other knights. As a member of his family, Brude was naturally invited. Brude was surprised that Aquila played up his noble lineage, referring to his father as a tribal chieftain, but Cleon explained afterwards that Aquila was concerned that having a gladiator in the house, even a retired one, was not really socially acceptable. "Gladiators are like prostitutes or actors," Cleon explained. "They sell themselves for the entertainment of others. Not at all what polite Romans do."

"It's not as if I had a choice," Brude protested.

"I know that. So does Aquila, but it's still better if he plays that down and emphasises the fact that you are descended from kings."

"I never said my father was a king!" said Brude. "Anyway, I've told you that we reckon descent through our mothers, not our fathers."

"A detail which will offend most Romans so is best kept quiet," Cleon warned him. "The truth has very little to do with how you are presented to others in Rome. You should know that by now. Who is ever going to know about your strange barbarian customs unless you tell them? There are plenty of people in Rome who go around pretending to be of higher social rank than they really are, even if it is just to get better seats at the theatre. Anyway, Appius Claudius Longinus was invited along this evening and he wouldn't say too much about social niceties. His wife used to be his slave until he freed her so he could marry her."

Cleon was always full of such gossip. But whatever others may have thought in private, Brude was generally accepted and partook in all of Aquila's leisurely pursuits. He enjoyed the theatre, where the actors, despised though they were in social circles, were usually funny and entertaining in a very crude way. He also enjoyed the circus where Aquila often went to see the chariot racing. Aquila was a devotee of the Whites, so naturally Brude had to cheer for them as well. He admired the skill of the drivers who steered their flimsy vehicles round the tight curves at the ends of the long elliptical course and galloped along the straights at incredible speed. It was exhilarating to watch and he loved being part of the crowd, listening to the shouts and the banter. If the Whites had a good day it also meant that Aquila would tend to be generous with bonuses to his freedmen and put on a more lavish spread at meal time.

The evening meals were nothing like the ostentatious affairs that Trimalchio had overseen. They never ended in orgies, but were quiet affairs where the men discussed politics or business, or listened to a reading from the works of Virgil, Horace or some other famous poet, while the women sat patiently, only speaking if they were spoken to.

One evening Aquila was invited to dine with the senator Varro, along with Lucius, Cleon and Brude. The freedmen sat at the foot of the long table but Brude was close enough to overhear much of the conversation from the top end. There were two or three senators present and Brude soon gathered they were discussing more than just their usual complaints about the debasement of the silver coins the emperor was minting. This evening they were talking about the death of Plautianus, the Praetorian prefect, which had caused a stir amongst the senatorial class in Rome. As commander of the Praetorian Guard, Plautianus had been close to the emperor. His daughter was even married to the emperor's elder son, Marcus Aurelius Antoninus, universally known as Caracalla because of his habit of wearing a Gaulish style cloak over his tunic. From what Brude could hear, as he was straining his ears to catch the conversation, Caracalla had summoned Plautianus to the palace, accused him of plotting against the emperor and had him killed on the spot without trial or even giving Plautianus any chance to refute the allegations. The senators were anxious because Caracalla, who was destined to be the next emperor, was already showing signs of having a temper combined with a vicious streak, not attributes that senators looked for in an emperor. Life could become precarious with such a man in charge. The emperor's younger son, Geta, was clearly more popular with the senators although Brude noticed that nobody actually said anything about Caracalla that could be interpreted as detrimental or derogatory. There was, though, an unspoken fear, which was plain to see. Brude recalled Curtius telling him about Pollio's death in the arena, which Caracalla had ordered, pandering to the crowd's blood lust. He was glad that, as a simple freedman, he would never be in a position to be close to the imperial family. Proximity to power seemed a dangerous luxury.

Things soon died down though. The emperor and his sons went off to the east, to fight the Parthians and bring more glory, wealth and slaves to Rome, leaving life in the city to continue as it had done for centuries. Aquila ran his business affairs with Cleon's help, while Brude trained Lucius and spent most of his spare time reading, learning Greek, wandering the streets or visiting the baths where he often paid the extra coin required by the proprietors to have sex with the female slaves. All things considered, it was an easy life and, although the memories of Broch Tava and Mairead never quite left him, he could understand why so many people who came to Rome, whether as free men or slaves who later gained their freedom, decided to stay in the city rather than return to their homelands. He told himself that he would go home one day but realised that he had already spent two years in Aquila's home and he did not want to leave.

He confided his worries to Cleon who clucked his tongue thoughtfully. "Well if you think this woman of yours is still waiting for you, you could always go and bring her back here," he suggested after a few moments' consideration.

Brude had to admit that it was doubtful Mairead would be unmarried after all these years. "She probably thinks I'm dead," he conceded glumly.

"If I was a religious man," Cleon said, "I'd suggest going to an augur to seek a prophecy but, in truth, I doubt that would do any good."

"You don't believe in the gods?" Brude was surprised. The Romans were generally scrupulous in their attention to the gods. Every home had its own household gods and there was a daily ritual of pouring libations and offering prayers to them, in addition to the public prayers and sacrifices at the major temples, which many people attended. Brude realised that Cleon, though he observed the rituals, never discussed the gods nor gave any offerings. For his own part he had stopped offering any prayers to the gods of the Pritani because they seemed to have deserted him. He suspected they had no power so far from his home. For the Pritani, virtually every river and woodland had its own local god, and he was surprised the Romans had so few. But he knew from bitter experience that the Roman deities rarely answered the prayers of gladiators who were wounded or killed, no matter how generous their offerings were. Josephus had been sure his god, who he claimed was the only true god, had been looking after him, but even he had failed the little man in the end. Brude did not know which gods Cleon worshipped but he suspected it was not the pantheon of the Romans.

"I am a follower of Epicurus," Cleon told him when he asked.

"Who?"

"A very famous philosopher who lived a long time ago. His credo is the pursuit of happiness."

"That sounds good," said Brude, smiling. "Most gods demand sacrifices and prayers, not happiness."

"I said happiness, not material wealth," Cleon frowned.

"Aren't they the same thing?"

"Don't be foolish, Marcus. A happy man is one who is content with what he has and who does not seek to make himself unhappy by thinking about things he does not have. That is why Epicurus has few followers among the Romans. They are always hankering after more."

"And this fellow Epicurus says there are no gods?"

"Of course not!" Cleon protested quickly. "That would be atheism. Anyone professing that would be a criminal. No, he simply says that the gods have no interest in what mortals do so there is no point in worshipping them for they do not listen."

"But I have seen you join the prayers to the household gods and to the emperor," Brude challenged.

Cleon shrugged. "It is expected. I confess I am a coward and it is easier to conform than to be seen to be different. The Romans take a dim view of people who do not worship their gods. It is mostly just following a ritual and if the gods don't listen anyway, then it does no harm, except waste a bit of my time."

Brude nodded. "My own gods stopped listening to me years ago."

Cleon sensed he had a potential new convert. He tried to explain Epicureanism to Brude although he warned him to keep it a secret between themselves. Brude discovered why, when Cleon told him the famous riddle of Epicurus. "If you let people know too much about this," Cleon cautioned in hushed tones, "they will accuse you of atheism and you will be a social outcast, at the very least."

Brude slowly read the Greek writing, translating it with some help from Cleon.

> Are the Gods willing to prevent evil, but not able?
> Then they are not omnipotent.
>
> Are they able but not willing?
> Then they are malevolent.
>
> Are they both able and willing?
> Then whence cometh evil?
>
> Are they neither able nor willing?
> Then why call them Gods?

Brude looked at Cleon with a studied gaze. "This sounds like atheism to me," he said quietly.

"Rather call it a belief that a man should make his own way in life and be prepared to take responsibility for his own decisions without seeking to blame some invisible higher beings."

Brude liked that interpretation. It was a philosophy he could relate to.

A.D. 209

Colm had been in a good humour when he returned from his sortie against Peart. Brude stayed away from the upper village but he heard about it from Seoc, who told him that there had been a brief battle outside Peart, with three of Gartnait's men being killed as well as one warrior from Broch Tava. Several of the Broch Tava men had returned with minor injuries but the fight had, apparently, been over quickly, for the men of Peart were badly outnumbered and Gartnait did not really want to fight. The old chieftain agreed to hand over the wagons of iron ore and to pay some compensation in the form of cattle. Colm had been overjoyed, celebrating by burning a few outlying farmsteads and seizing yet more livestock. The men returned to Broch Tava in good spirits with a whole train of cattle, goats, pigs and sheep in tow.

To Brude, the affair sounded more like a minor skirmish than a battle but, still, four men had died to satisfy Colm's ego and Brude was glad that he had decided to live in the lower village where Colm rarely visited. Seoc told him that Colm had been in such a good mood that he had remained fairly calm, even when he heard how Cruithne had failed to intimidate Brude. "Cruithne told him he reckoned you used magic but he had managed to persuade you to take an oath not to do anything against Colm's wishes. Mairead backed him up and Colm seemed satisfied."

Brude wasn't convinced Colm would be satisfied by that explanation for long but Seoras said, "He'll believe it because he wants to believe it. The only other choice he has is to call you out himself. He knows that he would not win a fight with you, not if you've already beaten Cruithne."

"Maybe, but he could send a whole gang of his men to get rid of me."

Seoc said, "Don't worry. I doubt many of them would relish a job like that. Not if they think you can use magic against them. I think you're safe enough."

Brude was annoyed and disappointed. He had waited for so many years to return home, it was galling to find that the village could prove just as dangerous as the arena. More so, perhaps, as in the arena he at least knew exactly when and who he was fighting. Here, there was a threat of sudden attack whenever Colm felt like it. It was not a pleasant feeling and he found the constant need to stay alert wearing on his nerves. He decided not to take any unnecessary chances so he hardly ever climbed the hill to the upper village. Instead, he went back to building his house.

He was pleasantly surprised to find that he had a lot of help. Several villagers came to lend a hand, none of them asking anything in return. "They saw what you did to Cruithne," Seoras told him, "and they're grateful."

"Or scared of you," Fothair said under his breath, although loud enough for Brude to hear. The tall man grinned, adding, "Master." Brude slapped him on the head for his impertinence but Fothair just laughed.

The work on the house went quickly with so many hands to help. Gruoch the carpenter fashioned small beams, which were laid around the roof beams in horizontal circles or ring beams. More oak rafters were joined to the centre pole from the ring beams then, when it was well and truly attached to the roof frame, Gruoch took his prized saw to the centre pole, cutting it away just below where the rafters joined it. There was a cheer from the villagers as the lower part of the pole came down, carefully guided with ropes so that it hit the ground in the doorway. Brude told Gruoch he could keep the remnant of the pole because oak was not prized as firewood, being too hard to burn well.

The next job was to thatch the roof. Here Lulach and his son took over. They carefully fitted hazel wands across the roof beams, fastening them with twine and small wooden pegs. Then they wove the bundles of reeds they had been gathering, hundreds upon hundreds of them, fastening them down with more hazel and twine. Brude asked Lulach to show him how to do the thatching and the man obliged, only to have to repair Brude's clumsy attempts, so Brude was relegated to passing the bundles of reeds up to Lulach to fit.

The roof took three days to complete and then they got to work on the walls. They made a mixture of clay, cow dung, straw and water, plastering it onto the wattle walls, both inside and outside. The overhanging roof gave some protection from the weather so they were able to finish the work in only two days, despite some light showers of rain. It was smelly, disgusting work but the finished result was impressive as the daub dried into place.

Brude helped Gruoch shape and fit a proper wooden door to the entrance while Fothair found a flat slab of stone, which, with the help of several others, he laid as a threshold. Most roundhouses had two doors on opposite edges of the circular wall, but Brude decided he only wanted one door.

The door was hung and the house was finished.

Brude had no furniture, not even a stool, but the villagers rallied round and everyone brought something for his new home. He felt touched by their generosity, telling them that he would go out hunting to try to bring back enough meat for them to have a celebration.

He was as good as his word, although he had to borrow a couple of bows and some arrows from Seoc and after two days of trailing through the deep woodlands inland from the village it was Fothair who eventually brought down a small deer, Brude's shot having missed by some way. "I'm better with stones," he said. He was able to prove it on the way home by stunning a couple of hares with deftly thrown pebbles.

The feast was the happiest night he had spent since returning to the village. Mairead and Castatin had heard about it, surprising him by coming down from the broch. "Colm is away on a hunting trip," Mairead explained. She had brought a finely woven blanket as a gift for him. He thanked her and she smiled. He was glad to see her happy at last, even if it was for only a short time.

His mother had made a fine fish soup and baked some bread and oatmeal pancakes. Someone else had brought some honey while there were always plenty of fish to go around. Gruoch even produced a small cask of uisge. They all crammed in to Brude's new home, crowding round the newly lit hearth fire to help themselves to the food and drink and to wish him well.

Castatin sat beside Brude, begging him to tell them again of the things he had seen in Rome. Brude refused at first but others asked to hear the stories as well and Mairead told him he should reward their hard work in building his house with tales of his adventures. Conceding defeat, he told them about the city of Rome and the mighty buildings made of stone and gleaming with marble. He told them of the statues, carved and painted to make them look like real people. He told them of the strange creatures he had seen in the amphitheatre, the panthers, lions, giraffes, ostriches and elephants. He saw their rapt faces, drinking in every word and the scepticism when he tried to describe an elephant. The scepticism turned to utter disbelief when he told them about the bathhouses with hot floors, hot walls and steaming water to bathe in every day. "That's what I miss the most," he said with a smile. "The hot water and always being clean."

"Well, now that you've built this place, perhaps you should build a bathhouse next," Fothair suggested. They all laughed, telling him that if he wanted to be clean, he should use a rain barrel like everyone else.

"You make it sound so wonderful," said Mairead. "It makes me wonder why you ever wanted to leave."

He looked at her, her face shining in the reflected glow of the fire. He could not tell her the real reason because he was still ashamed of it, even after nearly three years, so he said, "It wasn't all good. I was lucky in the last couple of years because

I stayed with a wealthy family. Life was easy and food was plentiful. But in Rome, the rich are very rich and the poor are so poor they have to rely on the emperor handing out grain and money to keep them alive. Even a free man can live in fear because he has to do as his betters say. They are a mighty race, the Romans, but they live in fear all the time, even if they don't realise it."

"What are they afraid of?" Castatin asked him. "I thought you said their armies ruled the whole world?"

Brude remembered a conversation he had had with Cleon one balmy summer evening in Aquila's summer home overlooking the sea. Recalling Cleon's words, he said to Castatin, "They are afraid of anyone who is not a Roman. That is why they try to conquer the world. They want everyone to be like them and they would rather destroy a whole nation than have it corrupt their people with un-Roman ways."

"Are they afraid of us, then?" asked Castatin, puzzled.

"We are a long way from Rome and we are lucky because we have nothing that they want, so they leave us alone. There are not many of us compared to Rome and we are scattered so we pose no real threat. If we raid them, or steal from them, we are like a fly trying to eat a horse. Sometimes the horse gets annoyed and flicks its tail, catching the fly."

"Like this!" shouted Fothair. He lashed out his hand, trying to catch a passing insect, but he was drunk and missed, nearly falling into the fire. Seoc caught him just in time, pulling him upright to gales of laughter.

Castatin grabbed for the fly next as it buzzed past him but it was too quick for him. He laughed as he missed it by a long way, only to gasp in amazement as Brude caught it effortlessly, snapping his hand around it. There was a sudden silence. Brude opened his fist, releasing the insect which flew off with a buzz of consternation. He realised that he had done something they considered almost magical so he laughed and said, "It's not a very useful trick. You can't live on them." There was more drunken laughter and the awkward moment passed.

It was well after dark when his guests began to leave, a few of them needing help from their friends and families to get them on their feet and out into the night. Mairead was one of the last to go. He offered to walk up the hill with her, to make sure she found her way in the dark. It was a poor excuse for someone who had lived there all her life but she did not object, so he took a burning torch to light their way as they walked up the hill together. Castatin, yawning and slow, tagged along behind them.

It was the first real chance they had had to talk in relative privacy since he had returned nearly six months before. "Why did you really come back?" Mairead asked him as they began the steep walk, treading carefully in the dark. Even though the track had white stones placed every few paces along its edge to mark the way, the well-worn path could be treacherous underfoot. "You make Rome sound like such a wonderful place. Something must have happened to make you give up that life and come back to this."

He wondered what to say. Aquila had thought he was a man who made the right choices but Brude knew that was not always true. He didn't want to make another mistake now. "Lots of reasons," he said eventually. "There is clean air here and my family and friends are here. In Rome I was free but not free. I just wanted to come home." He hesitated. "I wanted to see you again. I used to think about you all the time. It was what kept me alive."

She was silent, making him wonder whether he had said the wrong thing after all, wonder whether she would be upset. With remorse dripping from every word, she said, "It is too late for you and me now, Brude. I used to wish it was you who had come home a rich man, instead of Colm, but you didn't. I wish you had. But we all thought you were dead because Colm said he had seen you fall. What was I supposed to do?"

"You did what you had to," he told her. As he spoke he reached for her hand, clasping and holding it tightly as they walked. "I just didn't want to spend my whole life wondering what had happened to you."

"You're a fool, Brude," she said, but she was happy and almost in tears at the same time as she spoke. "You should have stayed in Rome with your hot baths and your houses of stone. I expect you had a lot of women after you as well, didn't you?"

She had hit near the mark, but still he could not tell her everything. "None of them like you, though, Mairead."

She laughed, wiping a trace of a tear from her cheek. "Liar!"

As they reached the stockade, she slipped her hand free, thanking him loudly so that the sentries would hear how formal and polite she was being. Lowering her voice, she said, "Do not do anything stupid to upset Colm. He is not a bad man, really. He just dreams of greatness. I am his wife and I have my son to consider as well."

"He is a good boy," Brude agreed as he tousled Castatin's hair. The boy was exhausted, barely awake.

"He is a constant reminder to me of happier times," Mairead said enigmatically. "Promise me you will do nothing to upset Colm."

"I promise. Not intentionally anyway. I suspect I annoy him enough just being here."

He saw her eyes, tinged with tears, reflecting the flickering torchlight. Then she nodded, took Castatin's hand and turned towards the gate, leaving Brude standing alone on the track in the darkness.

He picked his way carefully down the path to his new home where Fothair was lying sprawled on the floor, a blanket over him. His mother was tidying away the scraps of food while Seoras was banking the fire. They were both more than a little tipsy and his mother was in a talkative mood, which was the last thing Brude wanted after the long evening. "You would have made a good couple, you and Mairead," she said to him. "She always loved you, you know."

"That was a long time ago, Mother. It is too late now to turn back time. She's married and she has a son."

"And a good boy he is, too, as you would expect."

Brude agreed. "I like him."

"Well of course you do. It would be sad if you didn't, considering."

"Considering what?" Brude knew that the drink had loosened his mother's tongue. He could tell that she was skirting round something.

Seoras hissed, "Mor! I think it's time we went home." He reached to take her arm but Brude was intrigued now. He felt that there had been an undercurrent ever since he had got back to the village, as if everyone knew a secret that he didn't. A growing suspicion filled his mind. "What is going on?" he asked.

His mother looked him straight in the eyes. She reached out to take his hands in hers, holding them firmly. "The girl's a damn fool not to have told you when nearly everyone else knows it, or thinks it whether they know or not." Seoras tried to tell her to be quiet but she glared at him and said, "I will not be hushed, Seoras. He has a right to know." She looked back at Brude. "Castatin is not Colm's son. He is yours."

"What will you do?" Fothair asked him when Brude told him the following day.

"Nothing. She made me promise."

"Clever woman. It does explain why the boy looks like you, though."

"No he doesn't," Brude retorted.

Fothair grunted. "If you say so."

"I do say so."

"Fine. So what will you do?"

"I told you. Nothing."

"You're a bloody fool," Fothair said with feeling. "Master."

But fool or not, Brude kept his promise to Mairead. He puzzled over why she had not told him and he quizzed his mother mercilessly until she grudgingly revealed the whole story. Colm had returned from the raid with only a handful of other men, but wealthy, having brought home a great deal of cattle, gold and silver. Somehow the other men looked to him even though he was still barely more than a boy. He had told them that Brude, his father and all the others were dead. Then he had asked Mairead to marry him and she had agreed immediately, so Colm became head man through marriage to a daughter of the line of Beathag. The child had been born in the springtime, less than eight months after the wedding and Mor had known, as the other village women had known, that a child born that early must be small and weak. Yet the boy was strong, well developed and healthy so Mor had gone to speak to Mairead and asked her outright. "She cried and cried and she wouldn't say, but I knew the child was yours," Brude's mother told him.

"Does Colm know?"

"He's a man. What would he know of children?"

"I know," old Seoras pointed out.

"Only because I told you," Mor replied, waspishly. "I doubt many of the young folk suspect it, but all of the older women know." She glanced meaningfully at Seoras. "And a few of the old men."

"What will you do?" Seoras asked Brude.

Brude gave him the same answer he had given Fothair. "Nothing. I made her a promise."

Seoras agreed with Fothair. "You're a damn fool, boy."

The Samhain festival came as the days grew shorter and the longer, dark nights began. Food was still plentiful following the harvest but everyone knew that Samhain was the night when evil spirits roamed the earth. They all made sure to blacken their faces with ash and cinders from the fires to disguise themselves so that the spirits would pass them by, not knowing who they were.

Brude sat quietly at the feast, drinking little as usual and try-ing to enjoy the atmosphere. On this occasion, though, he spent a lot of his time looking at young Castatin and at Mairead. He chatted to the boy, who was always pleased to see him, sitting beside him and asking question upon question about life beyond the confines of the village. Brude answered as truthfully as he

214

could, telling Castatin about the Selgovae and the Damnonii who lived to the south and west, and of the Brigantes who lived restlessly under Roman rule beyond the Wall. But all the time he just wanted to throw his arms around the boy and hold him close, to tell him that he was his father. Yet he could not do that because he knew that it would only bring trouble. He wanted to speak to Mairead but there were always other people around and the chance never came.

He did speak to Cruithne. The big warrior was friendly, although not talkative. Brude was glad that he had decided to trust him. They were not what he would call close friends but they shared a mutual respect which was good enough for Brude.

The nights grew longer and the weather turned colder. Broch Tava, lying on the eastern coast of the lands of the Pritani, was relatively lucky in winter time. Snow rarely fell on the village, even when it covered the hills to the north, but this winter was a hard one with severe frosts and twice the snow did fall, to the delight of the children and the annoyance of the adults. Winter time was a time for staying indoors, for keeping warm, for using up the food stored from the previous year while the storms lashed at the village and made life outdoors miserable.

Some things did continue. The fishermen still went out to cast their nets so that Broch Tava was never as short of food as many inland villages were, but fishing in the winter was dangerous so the tiny boats never went far out to sea for fear of a sudden storm.

Colm occasionally came down to the lower village to talk to Gruoch about the ships he wanted built but work was slow because Gruoch had few skilled men to assist him and Colm would not let many of his warriors help. When the weather was mild, Colm and the warriors would often go hunting. They brought back meat for the whole village, although the best cuts usually stayed in the broch. It seemed as if Colm had decided to deal with Brude by ignoring him, which suited Brude perfectly.

Sometimes Brude and Fothair would go off hunting on their own, but never far and their results were modest at best.

The villagers also replenished their supply of salt by evaporating sea water in great, flat, iron pans heated gently over small fires. In the forests beyond the upper village, the slaves – Gartnait's son, Oengus, among them – watched the charcoal pits, which was a long and tedious job in the bitter cold of winter, but provided essential fuel for Caroc's smithy. Caroc's work never stopped, winter or summer. The smithy swallowed charcoal and iron ore at an alarming rate as he turned out the tools, implements and weapons that the villagers needed. He was skilled but was so busy that he rarely had the time to produce items of great artistry, concentrating instead on functional tools. He made a spearhead for Brude who fixed it to a long pole of ash, which he shaped and smoothed himself. Brude also persuaded him to make a pick and shovel of iron to help with digging. The work took a couple of weeks and Caroc was sceptical of the result but Brude used the tools to dig a well at the back of his house. The metal tools hacked into the hard earth far more easily than the antler and wooden implements usually used for such tasks. Soon Caroc was busy making more picks and shovels for other villagers.

Brude also dug a hole inside his house. Taking care that nobody saw, he took his Roman gladius, his wooden rudis and his manumission papers, carefully wrapped them in leather, then inside sealskin and finally placed them inside a large clay jar. He also put in most of the gold and silver coins he had left, all carefully wrapped in a leather bag inside sealskin. It was a tidy sum, several thousand sesterces in all. Not enough to make him rich, the way the wealthiest Romans were, but enough to live on for a year or two if he ever did return to Rome. With the jar almost full, he sealed it with a sealskin cover then placed it into the hole in the floor. He filled in the hole, patted down the earth and placed his sleeping mat over it. He hoped he would never need to dig the jar up again but it was always good to know he had some valuables hidden away in case of need.

Brude found that his skills as a healer were also in demand. He soon became the first person anyone called on when they were ill. In truth, he often felt helpless for his dwindling supply of herbs could not cure many things and he could do nothing to ease some ailments, but he remembered Tygaeus the physician telling him that the greater part of healing came from the patient themselves. "It's all in the mind," Tygaeus had told him. "If a patient wants to get better, they will, more often than not. Half the skill of healing is persuading them that what you are doing for them is making them feel better. Once they believe that, they cure themselves."

So Brude would set bones broken in accidents, tend to cuts and grazes and do his best to alleviate the symptoms of colds and chills. He could do nothing about more serious illnesses or fevers except try to ease people's pain. He was powerless to save a new baby, born prematurely to one of the fishwives. The child was sickly beyond his skill. He was more used to treating wounded men than newborn children and the baby died, which, although he knew it was a common occurrence, upset him. And all he could do for one elderly grandmother was to make her comfortable before she slipped away in the middle of one cold winter's night. Still, his efforts were enough to give him a reputation for healing, however little he thought he deserved it.

One day he was called to tend young Seasaidh, who said she had a bellyache, although Seoc spoke to him on the way to his home, suggesting that his sister was only claiming to be ill to get Brude to come to examine her. "She heard you examined Eilidh the other day," Seoc told him, "I think she's jealous."

Seasaidh was lying on her low bed, moaning softly and complaining that her belly and head were sore. Brude knew that it could be genuine but when he felt her forehead, he was satisfied that there was no fever. After a cursory examination during which the girl watched him carefully with her big, dark eyes while he placed his hands on her bare belly, he mixed a bitter-tasting potion which he forced her to drink. It made her feel sick, as he had known it would and she threw up. "That'll be you sorted now," he told her cheerily. She wailed that he was cruel but she did not complain of any other illnesses after that.

In the dark nights of the early months after midwinter, they celebrated Imbolc and still Brude had not been able to speak to Mairead about Castatin. In winter time, when people tried to shun the outdoors unless they had to go out, life was often divided between those who lived near the shore in the lower village and those who lived in the upper village around the broch and farmed the land cleared from the forests. Brude was torn between wanting to speak to Mairead and knowing he had to try to avoid Colm. He considered asking Fothair to find Mairead and speak to her but decided it was his problem, not Fothair's, so he stayed away from the broch and fretted.

Gradually, the days grew longer once more and the first signs of spring began to appear. It brought new buds, green leaves and also a trader, who came to the village accompanied by a train of pack ponies and three armed guards.

He was of the Votadini but travelled all the lands of the Pritani, both north and south of the Wall, buying and selling items wherever he went. Brude, like most of the villagers, made the trip up the hill to meet him and to see what he had. There was nothing much that Brude wanted but he spoke to the man, asking him if he could get supplies of herbs and medicines from the Romans. The trader was at first surprised, then astonished when Brude wrote out the names of what he needed on a small piece of faded parchment using a burnt stick as a pen. "You can write Latin?" the man asked him.

"Not very well, but they should understand this. If you can get them I'll be grateful. I can pay in Roman coins."

The trader gave him a quizzical look but did not ask any more questions. A customer was a customer after all. "I probably won't be back this way for another year," he said.

Brude shrugged. "Then I'll wait."

"And even that is doubtful," the trader said. "Things are happening down south that make life tricky for travelling merchants."

"What sort of things?"

"You haven't heard? The emperor has come over from Rome. He's brought a whole army with him. The Brigantes are crushed, the Wall has been repaired and he is marching north. The Novantae have been defeated and the Damnonii too. The Votadini submitted without a fight. Well, they never fight the Romans anyway, I suppose. The Romans reached the Wall of Antoninus, just before winter, so I dare say they'll be heading this way soon." Brude felt a shiver run through him. The Wall of Antoninus was, he knew now, the turf rampart that the Romans had built across the whole island, cutting through the land of the Damnonii. If the emperor had reached the northern wall already, then his army could easily reach Broch Tava in a matter of days. The trader did not seem too concerned for his own safety. "I have papers from the Romans which let me pass the Wall. All the same, I intend heading north for a few weeks yet, just to get well clear of any trouble." Brude didn't blame him.

He was troubled by the news and considered going to speak to Colm. He eventually decided against it because he already knew how Colm would react. Instead, he asked Seoc to get Cruithne to visit his home. The two of them arrived that evening and Brude invited them in. His mother, Seoras and Fothair were already there. He told them what he had heard from the trader. Cruithne nodded. "He told Colm as well."

"What did Colm say?" Brude asked, relieved that the trader had passed on the news.

"He said he is not concerned. He says the Romans want friendship with him. They have sent him gifts before. If they have come to fight, this time, he thinks we are strong enough to see them off." Cruithne sounded as if he, too, was confident of that.

"He has no idea what he is up against," Brude cursed, exasperated at Colm's attitude. "I doubt very much that they will come in peace this time."

"They are only men," Cruithne said. "They can die as easily as other men."

Brude knew that Cruithne had no experience of Romans. He also knew that he needed to get them all to understand the seriousness of the situation. "Yes, that is true, but it is not that easy to kill them. Every Roman soldier wears armour and they practise fighting every day, for the soldiers have no other jobs except to train as a team, so you do not fight one Roman, you fight many of them, all of them working together."

"We can do that as well," Seoc said, trying to support Cruithne. "We practise with our spears and swords. Colm sees to that."

"I know," said Brude. "If it was a fight between the men of Broch Tava and any other village in the whole of the islands of the Pritani, I would back you to win. But tell me this, how many warriors does Broch Tava have?"

Cruithne and Seoc looked at one another. They began naming warriors, counting them on their fingers. After a while, they came up with a figure of seventy-three, although that included some men who lived in outlying farmsteads.

"A Roman legion has over five thousand soldiers," Brude told them. "They have cavalry as well. And the emperor would not come with only one legion. He will bring at least two, possibly more. On top of all that, the legions have auxiliary troops who fight for them but who are not Roman citizens. The emperor will bring at least the same number of them. If they attack, it won't matter a damn that they are not Roman citizens, because they fight like Romans and they can kill you just the same. So you and your seventy-three men would face perhaps twenty thousand soldiers. I don't care how good you are, Cruithne, even you couldn't beat that many."

Cruithne's brow furrowed. Brude could tell he was having trouble visualising just how many men made up twenty thousand. "That is a lot," the big man conceded. "So what do you suggest we do if they come?"

Brude took a deep breath. Cruithne had got quickly to the heart of the matter. If they could not fight and win, what choices did they have?

"If they come by land, you do not fight them. You send most people to hide in the woods and you welcome them. Offer them friendship and submit to whatever they want, without resisting. That won't be pleasant, for the Romans usually want pretty much everything, but if they think you are friendly they may leave you alone. That is how the Votadini have survived for generations."

"And if they come by sea?" Cruithne asked. "What then?"

"Take shelter in the broch. They won't have any weapons capable of knocking it down if they come by sea. Either way, though, don't fight them! Fortunately I'll be able to speak to them. Perhaps I'll be able to persuade them we are prepared to surrender to them. They will take some tribute and then they will hopefully leave us alone."

"That is not how a warrior should behave," Cruithne said with some feeling. "To submit without a fight is not in our nature."

"I know," Brude agreed. "But if you resist they will simply kill everyone or take them as slaves. We cannot beat them in a straight fight. There is no shame in this. If you met a bear in the woods you would not fight it, you would let it have its way." He remembered Cruithne's drunken boast from the year before and added, with a laugh, "Well, you might try to fight it, my large friend, but most of us wouldn't."

Cruithne nodded. "I hear what you say, Brude. I will think on it, for you have experience of these Romans and you have shown yourself to be a man of your word. There is, though, one big problem with your plan."

"I know. Colm."

"He will never agree. He thinks we can beat anyone."

"Then you have to think of a way of making sure I speak to the Romans before he starts a fight with them."

"That won't be easy," said Cruithne. "I don't like going behind his back. He is our lord."

"I know. Perhaps I should leave here and go to find the Romans first."

Fothair spoke for the first time. "That would really get Colm to like you, wouldn't it? Going to the Romans to represent his village. He'd probably start a fight with them, just to spite you."

In the end they all knew that there was not much they could do except try to persuade Colm not to fight and somehow get Brude to speak to the Romans, if they ever did reach Broch Tava. As plans went, it was pretty poor, Brude knew, but he could not think of any alternative.

As things turned out, his fears seemed to be unfounded. Spring came, the Beltane festival passed and he counted himself thirty years old and still there was no sign of the Romans. Colm let it be known that he thought the Romans were afraid of the power of Broch Tava, which was either stupid bravado or an attempt to undermine Brude and make him appear afraid.

The villagers went about their daily lives, ploughing their fields, sowing seeds, grinding corn, fishing and tending their livestock; the never-ending work of getting food in their bellies, while others made pots or spun their yarn and wove clothes and blankets. While daily life continued, Colm flexed his muscles by leading another strong war band to Peart to extort some tribute from Gartnait, who paid without a fight. Brude began to think the Romans had decided to stop when they reached the Wall of Antoninus Pius and that his fears were indeed groundless. He hoped they were.

Gruoch needed timber for the boats he was supposed to build for Colm, so Brude and Fothair would walk the woods, chopping down trees, using Brude's mule to drag the wood back to the village. It was hard work but Brude enjoyed it and it was something he could do that kept him in shape.

For an hour or so each day he sparred with Fothair, helping the tall Peart man to slowly improve his fighting ability. They always did this out of sight of the village in case anyone saw them because Brude thought he would have a difficult task explaining why he was teaching a slave how to fight. Like his sessions with young Lucius in Rome, though, they were not enough to make a huge difference to Fothair and served more to keep Brude sharp than anything else. He sometimes questioned himself as to why he wanted to keep his skills honed when he had vowed not to fight or kill, unless he had no choice. He persuaded himself it was because it kept him fit and because it was the only real skill he had.

They hauled the wood back for Gruoch, also bringing firewood for others in the village. Most things were done by barter rather than coin and the firewood they chopped and stacked was exchanged for bread or fish. Gruoch told Brude he would have a job for life chopping wood because Colm's grandiose plans for a fleet of ships to raid the lands south of the Wall were coming along only slowly. Gruoch knew how to build a small boat for fishing but Colm wanted larger ships and Gruoch admitted he was struggling. "I need more men, more nails, more tools, and more rope," he complained to Brude. "Just about the only thing I've got enough of is wood, thanks to you. It will take all year to build this damn thing and Colm wants six of them."

"You can only do what you can do," Brude told him.

"Very profound," Gruoch said. "Doesn't help a lot, though."

The next day, while Brude and Fothair were helping Gruoch saw planks, Colm himself came down to the riverside, half a dozen of his warriors following dutifully behind. He inspected the skeleton of the ship, nodding appreciatively as he ran his hands over the joints. He did not seem at all perturbed by the slow progress, congratulating Gruoch on what he had achieved and telling him he was sure it would be a fine vessel.

Then Colm wandered over to Brude, a happy, relaxed smile on his face. "I'm glad you are here," he said amiably. "It saves me having to come to look for you."

Brude wasn't sure what this change in Colm's demeanour meant so he simply gave a non-committal nod of welcome. Whatever was pleasing Colm so much would no doubt become clear, sooner or later. What worried Brude was that if something had happened that was good for Colm, the chances were that it was bad for someone else. Probably for him.

"We really don't see enough of you up at the broch," Colm said. "But I hear you have been busy."

"Yes. There always seems to be plenty to keep me occupied," Brude agreed.

"Good. I am glad that you have settled in. I am sorry that things between us have not been as good as they should have been. I'm sure you understand that having you come back from the dead was a bit of a shock."

Brude wasn't at all sure where this was leading. Colm's words were full of reconciliation and his tone was easy and relaxed but Brude thought he detected something else, something unspoken, that Colm was keeping from him. Still, if Colm was genuinely trying to make amends, then he had to go along with it. "I understand. It has been difficult for everyone."

"Exactly so," Colm agreed. "I also hear that you have not yet taken a wife even though you seem to have had a few offers?"

Brude knew that there were few secrets in a place as small as Broch Tava but it still annoyed him that his marital position seemed to concern the whole village. "Not yet," he replied, not wanting to say too much.

Colm grinned happily. "Well, there is plenty of time, I suppose. Now, to business. There is something I need you to do for me."

Here it comes, thought Brude. "What is that, Colm?"

"I am going to visit Nechtan and I would like you to come with me."

The unexpected request caught Brude by surprise. "Me? What for?"

Brude wondered if he had made a mistake. Colm was used to people obeying his every whim, without question, but Colm merely smiled conspiratorially and said, "Well, Nechtan has a druid. Veleda her name is. She is said to be rather formidable in the magic arts. I would like to take along our very own magician."

Brude almost laughed aloud. From behind him, he thought he heard Fothair trying to stifle his own laughter. "I'm sorry, Colm. I'm no magician."

Colm was unperturbed. "That's not what I hear. You can catch insects on the wing, you can catch spears thrown at you,

you are invulnerable to weapons and you heal the sick. Are these things not magic?"

Brude shook his head. "No, Colm, they are just skills I have learned. Anyway, I wasn't able to heal everyone. I am very limited when it comes to healing."

"You still know more than anyone else in the village," said Colm. "And all of these things you do appear magical to everyone else, whatever you may say. Above all, you have returned from the dead. What greater magic is there?"

"You don't really believe that, do you?" Brude asked him.

"What I believe is neither here nor there," Colm replied evenly. "What is important is what other people believe. If Nechtan believes you can control powerful magic then it enhances the position of our village."

"It enhances your standing with Nechtan, you mean?"

"If you like to put it that way. Now, will you come with me? Believe me, it will be to your advantage, for there are great plans already in motion."

Brude raised his eyebrows questioningly. "What great plans?"

Colm laughed. "Always questions, Brude. You always asked questions, even when you were a boy, and still you do it. You will learn soon enough. As I say, it will be to your advantage. So will you come with me?"

Brude could not think of any excuse that would sound at all plausible. He also recognised that Colm could simply have ordered him to accompany him, so he said, "Yes, I will go with you."

"Excellent! We leave tomorrow morning. Be at the broch just after sunrise."

With a friendly word of farewell to Gruoch, Colm and his retinue made their way back through the village towards the fort hill. Brude exchanged glances with Gruoch, who just shrugged, and with Fothair who said, "He's up to something."

"Just because he was nice to me, you think he's up to something?"

"Yes. A man like Colm does not change his character. He has a plan that involves you. He probably means to murder you in the woods and claim you were killed by bandits or by a bear. You shouldn't go."

"I have said I would go," Brude told him. "But you are right. He is up to something. It's just as well I have you to watch my back, isn't it?"

They climbed the hill at dawn, each of them with a small pack containing food and water. They also carried long staffs, which could serve as walking aids or as weapons, depending on circumstances. Colm was there, wearing fine clothes which were topped by a cloak of green and blue fastened by a large golden brooch. With him, in the open space of the stockade, were nearly thirty warriors, each with a spear, helmet and shield. Some also carried swords. Lutrin, Colm's mysterious bearded advisor, was there as well, wearing a sword but with his head bare. Many of the warriors held horses, ready to mount for the journey. Brude saw Mairead and Castatin among the assembled villagers who had gathered to see them off. The giant Cruithne stood outside the broch. He raised a hand in salute when he saw Brude approach.

Fothair whispered under his breath, "Well if he wants you dead, you've had it. Not even you can beat this lot."

"It would be difficult," Brude admitted. "Even with your help."

Fothair laughed but not in humour. "Hah! First sign of trouble and I'm off. I told you I would run one day."

"Perhaps you should have run last night then," said Brude. "I think you may have left it too late."

Colm greeted them with an amused smile. Those men who had horses mounted up with a jingle of harnesses and whinnied protests from the horses. Colm waved his arm and they set off, following in a long line, riding or walking two abreast. Brude and Fothair joined the procession rather nervously but the warriors around them seemed in good humour and if they had murder in mind, they were better actors than Brude gave them credit for.

The column made its way northwards, past the fields the villagers had hacked from the encroaching trees, into the woodland then on towards the hills. Colm set a good pace for it was a long walk to Dun Nechtan, the hill fortress where Nechtan, acknowledged overlord of the Boresti, had his seat. There was a trackway of sorts for much of the way but the woodland was always growing, ever changing and sometimes the path vanished though they still made good time.

Colm rode at the head of the column, chatting to Lutrin in a light-hearted mood. The mounted warriors followed, eight of them, riding side by side, in pairs when the path was wide enough or in single file when it wasn't. Two men had been sent on ahead to bring word of Colm's coming. Brude and Fothair walked behind the mounted men with the rest of the group, who were on foot, following them. There was a lot of banter among the warriors, who talked of inconsequential things and joked at each other's expense. Brude thought the march had the feel of a pleasant day's outing. Around midday, they stopped briefly for a light meal before pushing on. After a long but uneventful afternoon, they reached Dun Nechtan as the sun was heading towards the western horizon, turning the sky a glorious shade of orange. Nechtan's home was situated on a long narrow oval of a hill, surrounded near the top by a wall of stones covered with turf. There was only one path to the top where a massive wooden gate was guarded night and day. Inside the wall, crammed all along the top of the hill, were roundhouses and the great rectangular hall where Nechtan held his court.

Colm ordered his men to make camp at the foot of the hill, near a huddle of peasant houses that formed a small village. There was a stream nearby for water and the ground was flat enough to make a good camp site. Fothair set about building a fire for himself and Brude but Colm walked over to them, speaking to Brude for the first time that day. He was not pleased. "Nechtan is showing off his power," he said angrily. "He has sent word that he has no room for so many men in his fortress so we must camp outside. You, though, can come with me."

Leaving his pack and his staff with a forlorn Fothair, Brude went with Colm. They made their way to the wide pathway which led up the side of the hill. Colm's man, Lutrin, followed them a discreet distance behind. The path ran along one side of the long hill, gradually climbing to the main gate. Above them, the Dun wall was on their right so that, if they had been hostile, their unshielded right sides would be exposed to men on the wall. Now, the sentries simply looked down on them with idle curiosity. "This is not seemly," spat Colm. "Nechtan dishonours me, especially when I come on such important business."

"What important business is that?" asked Brude, knowing Colm had given him the opening for the question.

Colm gave him an amused smile. He answered his question with one of his own. "What do you want most in the world, Brude?"

Brude was so surprised by the question that he almost mentioned Mairead's name, without thinking. Fortunately, he remembered his promise to her and caught himself in time. "Ever since I was captured, I only ever wanted to get back home. I have done that. I am content with what I have."

"I think you are lying," said Colm. "You are very good at keeping your face expressionless but I know you want something more."

"I do miss the Roman baths," Brude admitted with a smile.

Colm was not to be put off. "Don't take me for a fool, Brude. I have seen the way you look at Mairead. I know you have kept your word and stayed away from her but every feast night you sit there with your eyes always following her. I know what you want."

To Brude's surprise, Colm did not seem angry. If anything, he seemed amused. Brude said to him, "She is still the best looking woman in the village, Colm. Lots of men look at her. But everyone knows she is your wife."

"Not for much longer," said Colm with a triumphant gleam in his eye. "That is why we are here." Brude was so astonished that he stopped dead in his tracks. Colm laughed at him. "Do you know Mairead's main fault?" he asked.

"You know her better than I do," said Brude, moving again to keep up.

Colm ignored that remark. He explained, "Her problem is that she is barren. Since she gave birth to my son, there have been no other children. And I need a daughter if my line is to continue."

Brude suddenly understood. Colm was trying to establish a dynasty. Castatin would become head man because he was Mairead's son, not because he was Colm's son. But if Mairead had no daughters, Colm's line would come to an end. "You want a daughter so that your grandson can become a tribal leader after Castatin?" he asked.

"That's right. Mairead cannot give me one, so I will divorce her. I am going to marry one of Nechtan's daughters. He has one who has just turned fifteen and who is of the line of Beathag. It is all arranged. Lutrin has been negotiating on my behalf for some time."

Brude could not help thinking, once again, that Colm would have made a good Roman. The Romans valued sons above daughters because sons would continue the family line. Among the Pritani, the female line was more important when it came to inheritance, yet Colm still wanted his descendants to be the leaders of the village. Brude thought it was a bizarre desire.

Nechtan's daughter was of no concern to Brude. "What about Mairead?" he demanded. "Does she know about this?"

"Not yet," Colm admitted. "She'll find out when we get back with my new bride."

"And what happens to her then?"

Colm grinned a wide grin. "Isn't it obvious? You can have her."

Brude's mind was a whirl of confusion. Colm was simply discarding Mairead and he should have been happy that, at last, he had the opportunity to be with her, a chance to recover what had been taken from both of them by his captivity. Yet the callous way Colm was getting rid of her astonished him. He did not know what to say.

"Aren't you happy?" Colm enquired. "I thought you would be happy. There is, though, one condition."

"What is that?" Brude managed to ask through his confusion.

"You must both leave Broch Tava and never return. I do not want your presence to cause any discontent."

A year ago Brude would have jumped at that offer but now things had changed. "What about Castatin?" he asked. "Mairead will not want to leave him."

"The boy stays," Colm said flatly. "He is my son."

Brude wanted to tell him the truth, to tell him that Castatin was not his son, but he bottled up his emotions, holding his tongue because he knew that it could only lead to more trouble for Mairead and Castatin, as well as for himself. He was in turmoil as thoughts and dreams raced through his mind. He had a vision of seeing Cleon again, taking Mairead with him all the way to Rome to meet his friend. He could see Cleon's smile of joy and the welcome he would give them both. Then the dream shattered and faded because he knew that Mairead would not leave Castatin, just as he knew that Agrippina and Vipsania were in Rome. They both knew how Brude had betrayed Aquila. He could not go back there again.

He scarcely paid attention as they were admitted through the huge gates of Dun Nechtan and led to the great rectangular, wooden-framed hall where Nechtan held his court. It was only when they went inside, strode down the length of the hall, under the watching eyes of Nechtan's household, his warriors and their women, that Brude forced himself to cast the dream aside and concentrate on what was happening around him. Colm rarely did anything without some purpose and Brude suspected that springing his surprise news on Brude, just before they met Nechtan, was designed to distract him. For what reason, only Colm knew, but Brude relaxed his mind, focussing his attention as if he was entering the arena again, concentrating on his surroundings.

Nechtan was seated on a raised platform at one end of the hall. A great fire burned behind him, both heating the room and making him appear large and powerful as he basked in its light. There were other men seated on the dais: one of a similar age to Nechtan, on his right and two young men to his left. Standing behind Nechtan, just to his right, was a woman with long silver-white hair that hung down over the shoulders of her long, grey robe. Her skin was wrinkled and weather-worn but her blue eyes sparkled with intelligence and keenness.

Colm strode down the hall, his left hand resting on the hilt of his sword, looking as regal as he could. Brude followed, keeping to Colm's right while Lutrin was on the left. To either side, by the walls, Nechtan's people stood watching them. The three men stopped a few paces from the dais. In a loud voice, Colm greeted Nechtan. "Hail, Nechtan, son of Feartal, lord of the Boresti. I come to your hall as arranged." To the others he said, "Hail Talorc, son of Feartal, hail Eairsidh, son of Nechtan, hail Danaidh, son of Oengus." He did not acknowledge the old woman.

Brude recognised Nechtan, but the warrior chief who had led the Boresti on their disastrous raid nearly fourteen years before, was now an old man, his belly fat, his hair completely grey and his body tired. *The man to his right must be his brother*, thought Brude. Talorc would be the next leader of the Boresti when Nechtan died. The two younger men were Nechtan's son and nephew, his sister's son. Nechtan, thought Brude, already had the dynasty that Colm craved.

Colm continued his greeting. "I bring with me my man, Lutrin, whom you know well. I also bring Brude, son of Anndra, who has returned from the dead and is a master of dark magic."

All eyes looked at Brude. He wanted to curse Colm for the introduction. In particular, he saw the old silver-haired woman give him a sharp look as if she were trying to see inside his soul with her blue eyes, which reminded him of Aquila's searching gaze. Over the murmurs of the watching men and women, Nechtan spoke to him. "You are Anndra's son?"

"I am." Brude made sure he spoke clearly enough for the assembled men and women around the hall to hear him. "I marched with you to the Wall thirteen summers past. I was the first of the Boresti to climb the Wall and I stood in the battle line beside my father when we met the Romans."

Another wave of low whispering sped round the hall. Nechtan shook his head sadly. "That day is not a happy memory for me," he said. "We thought you lost, along with all the others."

"Some survived to be taken captive," Brude explained. "My father was not among them, but I remember a man called Drugh, who was one of your warriors."

A swell of voices showed that some of the people remembered Drugh. Nechtan's eyes filled with tears. "Drugh lives?" he asked.

"I am sorry. I do not know. He lived at least through that summer but we were all sold as slaves, to different owners, and I never saw him again. I do not know whether he is alive or dead."

"If you have returned, then there is hope that one day Drugh will do the same," Talorc said, bringing much nodding of agreement from everyone round the hall. Brude doubted that Drugh would ever return home, but he said nothing. The big warrior had obviously been well thought of in Dun Nechtan.

Nechtan nodded thankfully to Brude. "You are welcome in my hall, Brude, son of Anndra. Your father was an honourable man and a good friend to me. And I thank you for news of our kinsman, Drugh." Then his face grew hard as he turned to look at Colm. His old hands gripped the carved arms of his chair as he leaned slightly forwards. "But you, Colm, son of Lachlann, are not welcome here."

Brude saw Colm stiffen at Nechtan's words. He felt the tense expectation in the hall. There must have been around forty or fifty people present, the elite among Nechtan's people, and they were all waiting to see how Colm would react to the inhospitable welcome.

Colm gripped the hilt of his sword tightly with his left hand. "Your hospitality is rather lacking, Nechtan. I have come, as arranged, to collect my new bride so that I can take her back to Broch Tava." He kept his voice firm and even but Brude could sense the anger and confusion in him.

"There will be no wedding," said Nechtan, holding Colm's gaze as he tried to stare him down. "The arrangements we made these weeks past are no longer of interest to me."

Colm's face was dark with anger but he fought to keep his temper under control. Brude, watching him, was reminded of how Colm would react to failure when they were boys. He realised that he was holding his breath, waiting for Colm to explode. The Broch Tava head man, though, somehow managed to keep his raging emotions in check. Still, there was venom in his voice when he spoke. "What has changed then, Nechtan? What is so different now that you treat me like this? We had a bargain!"

Nechtan was not perturbed by Colm's tone. He remained calm but firm. "What has changed? You pretend you do not know? My friend Gartnait has sent messengers to me, telling me of what you have done to his village."

"He stole from me!" Colm shouted, his voice filling the hall. "Am I to sit back and let him cheat me?"

"And do you have nothing of his? A son, I am told." Nechtan waved his hand dismissively. "But petty cattle raids and arguments over goods do not concern me. These things are between you and Gartnait. What does concern me is that you are now demanding tribute from Gartnait under threat of attack."

Colm had overstepped the mark, Brude realised. Nechtan was overlord of the Boresti. If anyone was going to gather tribute from other villages, it would be him. By demanding tribute from Gartnait of Peart, Colm was setting himself up as a rival to Nechtan, and the old chieftain was clearly not prepared to put up with that. The tribal leader jabbed a gnarled finger towards Colm. "War between our villages is the last thing we need just now. Already Gartnait has received emissaries from the emperor of Rome who is marching north towards our lands with an army the like of which no man of the Pritani, now living, has ever seen."

That stunned Colm and Brude alike. The rumours were more than just talk then. The Romans really were coming north. Brude felt a shiver of doom run through his body at the news. Nechtan's voice lowered to little more than a harsh whisper but the hall was so quiet now that there was no difficulty in hearing what he said. "Gartnait has no choice but to submit to the Romans but he has told them that you are his enemy. Soon your tiny village will be wiped from the face of the earth and your people will be killed or taken into slavery. So tell me, what am I to do?" His eyes were fixed on Colm as he spoke. "I am leader of the Boresti yet my own people are fighting among themselves. If I fight against the Romans, we will surely perish yet, if I do nothing, one of the villages of the Boresti will be destroyed. You, Colm of Broch Tava, are the cause of this dilemma so I say to you that you are not welcome here."

Colm was silent for only a moment. If Nechtan had expected him to be cowed by the accusation he had thrown at him he was soon disappointed. "You may be the leader of the Boresti," spat Colm, "but you are more like an old woman than an old man. You and Gartnait are alike in that. Spineless and afraid. We have fought the Romans before and we returned home rich men. Or do you not remember that?"

Nechtan's eyes were suddenly sad. He lowered his gaze for the first time. "I remember all too well, Colm, son of Lachlann. That day still shames my memories. We lost too many warriors to call anything we did afterwards a victory. We may have returned richer in wealth, but ever since that day we have been poorer in spirit. I fear the time has clouded your memories. We cannot defeat the Romans. You are only fooling yourself if you think otherwise."

Colm's right hand moved to his sword. He began to scrape it free of its scabbard until Brude reached out to grip his arm, stopping the dangerous gesture even as many of Nechtan's men had reached for their own swords. The threat of violence hung heavy in the air. Colm glared at Nechtan and his brother, his body tense. He shrugged off Brude's hand, pushed his sword back into its scabbard and sneered at the old men who sat on the raised platform. "I will not stay here any longer to listen to your fears. You are not worthy to lead the Boresti. If Gartnait is too afraid to stand up to the Romans, I am not. When I have defeated them and sent them back south of the Wall, I will return here and we will speak again." The dire promise in his words was unmistakeable. Brude was tense, his eyes darting round the room, watching for any signs of immediate danger. If Nechtan ordered them to be cut down now, they would have no chance of escape.

Nechtan nodded sadly once more. He waved a hand, gesturing for his men to stand down. "You are not welcome here, Colm of Broch Tava, but neither will I see the blood of any Boresti spilled in my own hall. Go now. Return to your village and think on what I have said. I hope you reconsider. You should send emissaries to the emperor and seek terms with him. If you do that, perhaps you will indeed live to return here again."

Colm glared at Nechtan then span on his heel, striding towards the door, his head held high. Lutrin turned and followed him but Brude looked at Nechtan, his brother, son and nephew. He gave them a bow. As he made to turn, the old woman, who had remained silent throughout the confrontation, pointed a bony finger at him and said in a loud voice, "Brude, son of Anndra! Stay! I must speak with you."

Brude looked at her, glanced at Nechtan and saw the old man nod. He twisted his head to see Colm and Lutrin going out of the doors. They must have heard the woman's words telling him to stay behind but neither of them looked back. Warriors pushed the doors closed behind them, leaving Brude alone in the centre of Nechtan's hall.

Fothair was already anxious but when he saw Colm and Lutrin walking hurriedly back down the path from Dun Nechtan without Brude, he grew even more concerned. The sky was growing darker now but it was still light enough for him to see the silhouettes of warriors lining the ramparts of the hill fort. But where before there had been a couple of sentries, now there was a line of some forty or fifty men looking out over the wooden wall. To Fothair, that could only mean trouble.

He cursed himself for a fool for coming on this trip but the truth was that Brude was the only real friend he had. Their nominal relationship of master and slave was a facade that Fothair knew Brude was maintaining only because of Colm. Brude was more like the older brother he had never had than anything else. Fothair did not really have anyone else to look to, nor anywhere else to go. His father had never returned from that fateful raid, which had been the cause of so many deaths among the Boresti and which had marked the start of Brude's captivity. His mother had died of a fever four winters after his father had vanished and both of his brothers who had survived infancy had also died, one breaking his neck when he fell off a horse and the other drowning in the Tava when his small coracle had overturned. Fothair had been left to bring himself up from the age of eleven. He had attached himself to Oengus, Gartnait's son, becoming one of his followers even though he did not really like the chieftain's son. Living with Brude, despite being nominally a slave, had been a year of more freedom and happiness than he could ever remember.

Now Brude was still inside Dun Nechtan while Colm and Lutrin were back. The warriors were rising to their feet, leaving the comfort of the fires they had lit, to greet their leader. Fothair quietly joined the throng in an attempt to discover what had happened.

Colm was in a furious temper, kicking out at small stones and twigs, his face contorted with rage. "We should storm the place!" he yelled. "Drag that old man out and slit his worthless throat. That would show him who is the real man among the Boresti."

Lutrin tried to agree while also providing the voice of reason. "You are quite right, Lord. But they have armed men watching us to thwart just such an attempt. It would be better to return home to gather more men before trying such a thing."

"Do you think I am afraid of them?" Colm rounded on Lutrin.

"Of course not, Lord," Lutrin replied, holding his hands up to calm Colm down, "but I suspect that Nechtan wants you to try something now. Far better to wait until he has let down his guard and then pounce."

Colm stared at Lutrin, then up at the Dun. He nodded and some of the fire went out of his mood. "You are right, as always, Lutrin. Let him think he is safe and has scared me away. We will strike when he least expects it. Then I will have my new bride and see him and all his brood with their heads on spikes on the walls of their fort."

Lutrin gestured for the men to back off, telling them all to get some sleep. Colm made his way to the fire that had been prepared for him, and one of the men took him a plate of roasted meat. Fothair, not really understanding what had caused the problem, and confused over Colm's reference to a new bride, decided it would be more sensible to speak to Lutrin than to try to approach the manic chieftain. He sidled up to the bearded man and caught his attention. "Excuse me, Lord," he said in a low voice. "What has happened to Brude? Why did he not return with you?"

Lutrin gave him a look of surprise, as if he had not expected anyone to ask after Brude, but he nodded his head towards the Dun. "Nechtan's witch woman has him," he said.

"What for?" Fothair was really alarmed now. Then he saw the look on Lutrin's face and hastily added, "Lord."

Lutrin shrugged. "Who knows? We do not question the desires of Veleda."

"Forgive me, Lord, but will he be coming back?"

"I neither know nor care," said Lutrin angrily. "Now be gone, Slave." He turned his back to Fothair and went to speak to some of the warriors, posting sentries and organising the changes of watch. He may have persuaded Colm not to attack Dun Nechtan but there was no saying Nechtan would not try to attack them. It was too dark to set off for home, so they would have to stay where they were.

Fothair returned to the small fire he had made, picked up his pack and looped the strap over his head, then did the same with Brude's pack, hanging it down over his other shoulder. Retrieving both of their staffs, he slipped away from the camp site, heading towards the Dun.

The guards on the gate watched him as he climbed the path. He had half expected Lutrin to send some men after him but the men of Broch Tava were too busy to worry about one slave. It was almost fully dark by the time he reached the gate where a group of warriors waited, spears and shields at the ready. "What do you want?" one of them challenged.

"I am looking for Brude, son of Anndra."

"And who are you?"

"His slave," Fothair said, managing not to choke on the words. The men laughed but they opened the gate. One of them took the staffs away from him while two others grabbed his arms and marched him inside. The great gates were swung shut behind him. At least he had managed to get inside, he thought ruefully. Whether he would get out again was another matter. He was taken, unprotesting, round the side wall, followed a path between some roundhouses, past the edge of the great hall towards the rear where they approached another hut. One of the men knocked on the door frame. A woman's voice called out for him to enter. The man pushed aside the leather curtain, which served as a door, and went inside. He came back out again after only a few moments. He nodded to Fothair. "You can go in." To the other warriors he said, "Give him back his staffs."

Gathering the wooden poles with as much dignity as he could muster, Fothair ducked through the thick curtain. He found himself in a small house with a blazing fire in the central hearth. An iron cauldron sat over the fire with a glorious smell of food coming from its steaming contents. He suddenly realised that he was hungry. More important, though, were the two occupants of the hut who sat cross-legged by the fire. One was an elderly woman with long, silver-grey hair. The other one was Brude.

Brude waved him in with a long wooden spoon he was using

to sup some broth. "Glad you could join us," he said with a smile. "How is Colm?"

"I've rarely seen a man so angry," Fothair replied. "But I see I shouldn't have worried about you. Quite comfortable are you? Not too worried about me?"

"This is your slave?" the old woman asked. "You need to teach him some manners."

"He is my friend," Brude said. "Which is why he has come here, despite the danger."

"What danger is there here?" Veleda asked, her eyes sparkling mischievously.

"Well, there is said to be a witch woman in here somewhere," said Brude.

Veleda smiled a thin smile. "Well, what is in a name? Witch or druid? Slave or friend?"

"He's my friend," Brude repeated firmly.

"Not that you'd know it from him leaving me out there with thirty angry warriors," grumbled Fothair. He dumped down the staffs and packs then sat beside Brude. "Cold and hungry, with no idea what had happened to you."

"There was not a lot I could do about it," Brude told him. "But I reckoned that someone as resourceful as you would either get in here or would lie low until morning."

"I should have run away," said Fothair, accepting a bowl of steaming broth from the old woman with a nod of thanks.

"I wouldn't blame you," Brude said.

The old woman waved them to silence. "Enough!" She looked at them both sternly. "I am Veleda, last of the druids in these parts. I have heard of you, Brude, son of Anndra. Stories reach me from all over the lands of the Pritani. I know you returned last year from the lands of the Romans. Many things I know, but much of it I learned only from tales told to me long ago by those who taught me. They in turn learned it from those before them. Nechtan looks to me for advice and guidance but to give this, I must know as much as I can." She fixed him with a piercing gaze. "So now you must tell me about the Romans and their army."

A.D. 207

Lucius was to join the army in Germania as a military tribune on the staff of Quintus Aemilius Tertius, the imperial legate who commanded three legions stationed on the banks of the Rhenus, the great river which divided Gaul from Germania, flowing from the hills and forests of southern Germania to the northern sea. Despite the best efforts of the empire to expand beyond it, the Rhenus marked a natural boundary between the civilised land of Rome and the barbarians of the forests. Aquila was delighted with the posting, for this was the first step for his son in his path to glory.

To cap off Aquila's delight, he had also arranged a marriage for Vipsania Secunda. She was now fifteen years old and would be married later that year to the son of another knight who lived in Ostia and who Aquila knew from his shipping business. Vipsania herself, though, had caught a winter chill, which had turned to fever, so she was confined to bed by the doctors. Brude was not impressed with the prescribed treatment, which seemed to comprise applying warm poultices and praying to Aesculapius and various other gods. He mixed a potion from the collection of herbs he had been accumulating and took the girl a warm drink, which she accepted gratefully. "Will you be leaving us soon?" she asked him as she cupped the warm beaker in her hands.

"I don't know," he answered truthfully. If Lucius was leaving then there was no reason for Brude to stay, except that he liked the family and had found a true friend in Cleon.

Aquila broached the subject too, summoning Brude to the room with the Neptune mosaic, where they had first met. Aquila, ever formal and business-like, got straight to the point. "My wife and my daughter, as well as Cleon, have asked that I find some other position for you within the family," he told Brude. Brude was surprised that Agrippina had said anything for even though he had been living in the house for two years, their paths rarely crossed. She had hardly ever spoken to him, except to ask questions about Lucius' training or to discuss some domestic issues. Even when Brude acted as an escort to Agrippina and Vipsania when they visited the forum or went to the baths at the appointed time for women and children to bathe, Agrippina did not often speak to him directly. She was always very formal, always very correct and rather aloof in her behaviour.

Aquila continued, "For my own part I had hoped that you would accompany Lucius in some capacity. Tribunes are allowed some attendants and even though they are usually slaves, that is not always the case. Freedmen are permitted to act as servants and I know Lucius values you as a companion." He paused to let that sink in, his piercing blue eyes studying Brude carefully. "I will let you think on it," he said after a few moments. "I am going to Ostia tomorrow and will be away for two or three days. Let me know your preference when I return. Lucius does not leave until the end of the week so there is plenty of time for you to make up your mind."

"Thank you, sir. I will give the matter careful considera- tion." Which he would have to. Aquila had let him know what his preference was. Brude knew that he could have ordered him to accompany Lucius, for the head of the family had the final say in all things. Aquila, though, always listened to advice and if Cleon, Agrippina and Vipsania were all asking for Brude to stay, then he knew that Aquila would not object, even if it was not what he wanted himself. Still, to go against the head of the family's choice would be a bold move, even if his own inclina- tion was to stay.

He discussed it with Cleon who urged him to stay, though Brude had known that the old Greek would say that. Cleon was always telling him that he was like the son he had never had.

Cleon was a friend, a teacher and a confidant, but he was hardly impartial.

The following day Aquila left for Ostia, taking Cleon and Lucius with him. Brude, left with no duties, visited Vipsania in her room. The elderly slave woman who acted as her nurse sat disapprovingly in the corner, watching his every move while Brude checked the girl's temperature. She was still hot, so he mixed her another drink, telling the slave to cool her down by washing her in tepid water. "The doctors say we need to pray to Aesculapius," the woman told him, with a reproachful frown.

"You could try that as well," Brude agreed. "But wash her first. She needs to keep cool."

He left the girl, telling her to rest and sleep as much as she could. He thought the fever was abating but he did not really know what was wrong with her so it was hard to tell. The doctors didn't know either, which was more worrying.

Downstairs, in the shady peristyle garden with its columns and covered walkways, he found Agrippina waiting for him. Aquila's wife was dressed in a long gown of white linen. Her hair was neatly curled and piled on her head in the fashionable style and she was wearing a golden necklace with matching long, gold earrings studded with emeralds. She was dressed as if she was attending a dinner party. One of the household slaves, a young girl called Marcella, was standing patiently beside her, eyes downcast. A large wicker basket lay at her feet.

Agrippina smiled when she saw Brude coming into the garden. "There you are, Brutus. I need to go to the forum. Will you accompany me, please?"

"Of course, my lady," he answered. He followed, a discreet pace behind her as she led the way out into the street, the slave girl, Marcella, trailing behind him, carrying the basket as befitted her station.

The day was warm and the streets of the city were crowded and dusty. Agrippina, as usual, barely spoke to Brude although she occasionally turned her head to make sure he was still with her. She wandered through the forum, paying little attention to anyone else and seemingly in no hurry. Brude and Marcella followed her as she eventually made her way to the vegetable market, where she spent a long time picking a selection of fruit and vegetables which she piled into Marcella's basket. Once the basket was full, she sent the girl home. Then she said to Brude, "I wish to go to the temple of Aesculapius to offer prayers for Vipsania's recovery."

Brude nodded, acknowledging the unspoken command that he would accompany her.

The temple of Aesculapius lay outside the walls of the city in one of the wealthy suburbs to the north, at the foot of the hill the Romans called the Hortulorum, the Hill of Gardens, because each villa in the district had extensive and well-maintained grounds. The temple of the god of healing nestled there, not far from the Campus Martius where Augustus had his mausoleum, but it was a long walk from the forum and the day was growing very hot. Brude waited while Agrippina paid some silver denarii to the priest to offer a sacrifice to the god, seeking a swift recovery for Vipsania. Brude, despite having listened to Cleon's tales of Epicurus' teachings regarding the gods' utter lack of interest in human affairs, decided it would do no harm to seek some extra help for the young girl so he offered up a silent prayer of his own.

It seemed an even longer and hotter walk back through the city. They sought the shade of the narrow streets as much as they could but Agrippina appeared to be content to wander. To Brude's surprise, she took a circuitous route back, heading round the northern side of the city. He began to grow concerned. They were in the Subura, near the Viminal hill, one of the poorer parts of the city. The Subura was home to a large Jewish population and had a bad reputation among most Romans, who were generally apprehensive about the Jews. Brude, having often listened to Josephus talking about the traditions and beliefs of his people, was not bothered by the Jewish customs that shocked the Romans so much. He thought them strange but, apart from circumcision, which he had never understood, he at least had some understanding of why the Jews followed the traditions that they did. He remembered Josephus asking why the Pritani painted themselves with the blue war paint, laughing when Brude could not explain it except by referring to tradition. Brude thrust aside his reminiscences because at that moment the Jews were the least of his problems. The Subura was also home to many of Rome's poor and more violent citizens. A beautiful, high-class lady, dressed in fine clothes and displaying valuable jewellery, was a worryingly easy target. He was about to say something when Agrippina said to him, "Come, Brutus, it is hot. There is a bathhouse nearby where we can freshen up and get something to eat." Not waiting for any response, simply assuming he would do as she commanded, she turned down a side street which led to a small square where a noisy crowd of children were laughing and playing beside a small fountain. In one corner of the square was a small bathhouse, alive and boisterous with people playing ball in its outer court.

Agrippina strode to the door, ignoring the looks from the locals as they saw her fine clothes and jewellery, but Brude hesitated. He saw the statue outside the bathhouse, a naked goddess standing in a provocative pose. He could read well enough now to understand the writing above the doorway, which proclaimed the name, The Baths of Venus.

He hurried to catch up with Agrippina, gently touching her arm. "My lady, you should not go in here. It is a rough place."

She turned to look at him, an amused smile playing round her lips. "Are you afraid, Brutus?" she teased. All of a sudden she was no longer the aloof Roman mistress of the household and Brude's concern for her safety was replaced by an unexpected desire.

He looked down, not meeting her gaze. "I am not afraid for myself, my lady. But for you."

"Nonsense!" She dismissed the idea of danger. "I have nothing to fear when you are with me."

"But I will have to wait outside," he told her. "I cannot escort you inside."

"Of course you can, Brutus. That is why we are here. The Baths of Venus allow mixed bathing at all times. Now come in with me." She reached for his hand. He saw the look on her face, recognised the expression in her eyes and he knew he should not go in with her. Her lips were slightly parted and flushed, her tongue rubbing the edges of her white teeth. He was certain that he would be making a terrible mistake if he went inside with her. She leaned close to him, whispering, "People are watching us, Brutus. I insist you come with me now."

Resisting the temptation she was offering, he hissed, "My lady, I cannot. Your husband…"

"Is far away," she said. "But if you do not come in with me I will make sure that he hears how you abandoned me in such a dangerous part of the city, first forcing your unwanted attentions on me then running away when I spurned your advances. Do I make myself clear?" Her voice was low and soft, the words quiet but with iron behind them. He was in no doubt that she meant what she said.

He did not know what to say. She laughed at him. "Am I so ugly that you do not desire me?" she asked him. He shook his head, aware of her beauty, unable to resist her any longer. She pulled his arm and led him inside.

The bathhouse was crowded, men and women sharing the pools, all entirely naked. Agrippina did not remove her jewellery, saying it would be safer than leaving it to be stolen by the slaves who were supposed to watch the patrons' belongings.

Brude was astonished at how beautiful she was. He had lived in Aquila's house for two years but, although he knew she was attractive, he had seen her as a passive figure who stayed in the background, always quiet and undemanding. He had certainly never guessed the perfection of the figure she kept demurely hidden beneath her gowns. She took him to the cold pool, cooling off after the heat of the sun. She laughed, swimming to him. She had let down her long hair and it lay, wet from the water, plastered about her shoulders. She giggled girlishly as she put her arms around him so that he could feel every contour of her body. "You have no idea how long I have wanted to do this," she told him. "Come! Let us use one of the small rooms. I can tell you are ready for me."

All around the pool were small, private rooms, where couples could retire in privacy, each room with a wooden door. She took his hand. Quite unashamed at being naked and in full view of the other bathers, she led him into a room that was free. She closed the door and fastened the bolt. The room contained nothing except a small couch. Agrippina threw her arms around him, kissing him passionately and now he could not help himself. She was no longer Aquila's wife, she was a gorgeous woman with the body of a goddess, a woman who wanted him. He kissed her back, marvelling that she could have been so close to him for so long without him guessing at the passion in her. The change in her was incredible, intoxicating, and irresistible. He picked her up and carried her to the couch. She lay back, wrapped her legs around him and urged him on to ecstasy.

Vipsania knew almost straight away. She was feeling much better and sitting up in bed, propped up by a horde of coloured cushions. She sent the nurse away while Brude sat beside her bed, checking her forehead, which was much cooler. He looked into her eyes and saw they were clear, not heavy, the way they had been. He smiled at her and told her he thought she was well on the way to recovery.

She thanked him but did not seem happy. Studying his face with her large, blue eyes she frowned and said, "You have been with my stepmother."

Brude tried to cover his consternation. "Yes, we went to the forum and then to the temple of Aesculapius to offer prayers for your recovery. I see they worked."

"You don't believe in the gods any more than Cleon does," she told him with certainty. "And you know that is not what I meant. You have been with my stepmother..." she searched for a word, "intimately."

Brude could think of nothing to say in answer. He lowered his eyes so that he did not have to look at her but she reached out her hand, lifting his chin. Instead of accusation, he saw sympathy in her expression. "You are a very clever young woman," he managed to whisper. "I don't know what to say. I had no choice."

"Of course you did," she said. Despite her youth, she seemed to be the one in charge. "There is always a choice. You could have told her you have the pox. That would have stopped her."

Brude gave her a weak smile. "I never thought of that."

"Of course not. You're a man." Vipsania spoke with all the self-assured authority of a fifteen-year-old girl. "I don't think any of you actually use your brains when a pretty woman throws herself at you. And she is very beautiful, isn't she?"

"Yes she is."

"Not on the inside, though. She acts all quiet and shy when my father is around; the perfect wife. Well, you have seen that side of her, of course. She plays it very well. But my father's the same as the rest of you. He won't see what is right in front of his face. All she has to do is take her clothes off and he believes everything she tells him."

"How did you know?" Brude asked her.

"You are hard to read, Brutus," Vipsania told him. "But when you came into the room just now there was something different about you. It wasn't hard to guess what it was when I heard she had sent Marcella home alone. I thought she would try something with you eventually. I have seen her looking at you."

"Then you are more observant than I am," Brude told her. "I didn't think she had even noticed me that much."

"She's a sly one, my stepmother. She is very patient. She never takes many risks. But now that she has got you, you will not escape her easily. I expect she has told you to go to her room tonight?"

Brude nodded. "She has. But I think now that I will stay away."

Vipsania was horrified. "You must not do that now! The time for excuses is past. If you refuse her now you will find yourself accused of rape. My father will never take your word against hers. You will be sent back to the arena to face the wild beasts without any weapons to save you."

"Your father would believe you, though," Brude said, urgently, trying to think of a way out of his predicament.

Vipsania scoffed at that, too. "I am a girl, still wearing my bulla. She is a free born Roman citizen and you are a freedman. Her word carries more weight than either of ours and you know it. She will always convince my father of whatever she wants him to think." She softened her tone as she took his hand, stroking the back of it gently. "My dear friend, Brutus, you are trapped. There is only one thing you can do now though it breaks my heart to tell you."

Brude could hardly believe that he was taking advice from a girl as young as Vipsania but she was his friend and she was clever, so he asked her, "What should I do?"

"Go to her room tonight and do what you have to do. After that you can either stay here until she gets bored with you and discards you as she has done with her other lovers or you can leave. I will miss you terribly if you go, but I think that is what you should do for the best. She once had one of the slaves executed after she forced him to become her lover. She grew tired of him when he began to act above his station. She accused him of trying to rape her so the poor man was taken away and thrown to the lions. I do not want that to happen to you."

"You are a better friend than I deserve," Brude told her. "You are right. I don't think I could stay in your father's house knowing how I have betrayed his trust."

"You are not the first and you will not be the last," said Vipsania sadly. "But you are the only one I have wished could have escaped her clutches."

Just then the door opened. Vipsania hastily let go of Brude's hand as the nurse came back in. They said farewell formally, under the scathing look of the nurse, who did not approve of him being alone in Vipsania's room.

248

That night he went to Agrippina's bedchamber where he learned that Vipsania was right about her stepmother's beauty being all on the outside, for even while he was making love to her, Agrippina was whispering warnings of what she could order done to him if he did not please her. To Brude, beautiful as she was, she was less honest than the cheap whores who thronged around the amphitheatre.

"I have decided I would like to accompany your son to Germania, sir."

Aquila was delighted, thanking Brude enthusiastically. "My wife and daughter will be upset, I expect, but I am pleased you have decided to do this. I know Lucius will be pleased too."

Brude managed not to react when Aquila mentioned his wife. He felt like a traitor, for he had spent the last two nights in the man's marriage bed doing things with Agrippina, which, she had claimed, Aquila had neither the energy nor the imagination for. Brude made his excuses and left the old Roman as quickly as he could.

Cleon was heartbroken when he heard Brude was leaving. He tried to persuade him to stay but Brude's mind was made up, although he could not tell his friend why. Eventually, Cleon brought out an old map and showed Brude where Germania was. He was surprised when he saw how close it was to Britannia. Then he remembered how long it had taken him to walk from Broch Tava to the Wall. When he saw how tiny a distance that was on the map, he realised that Germania was still a long way from his home. But, for the first time in months, the thought of home had more appeal than the luxuries of Rome.

They left three days later. Lucius was dressed in a breast-plate of bronze which portrayed a carving of an eagle across his chest. He wore a red cloak fastened round his shoulders and a helmet with a red horsehair plume. A gladius hung at his right side. He looked every inch the young soldier. Brude wore a tunic and leggings. He, too, had a cloak, a plain one, and a gladius looped over his shoulder to hang at his side, a gift from Aquila.

Aquila had also purchased four horses. Lucius' belongings were packed onto two of the animals while they had one horse each to carry them the long miles to Germania. Brude had only a sleeping blanket and a small pack containing the wooden rudis, his manumission papers and what few coins he had saved, carefully sealed in a waterproof case.

After a brief halt at the temple of Capitoline Jupiter, to offer a sacrifice for a safe journey, the family came to the gates of the city to see them off. Brude was astonished to see old Curtius and one-armed Kallikrates from the gladiator school there as well. They hugged him and Curtius had a tear in his eye as he said farewell. Cleon was crying, tears rolling down his cheeks, his old, lined face wrinkled even more than usual. He gave Brude some scrolls. "It's Homer. Lucius will be able to help you with any words you cannot make out. I think you will enjoy it."

"I will read every word, my friend," Brude promised him.

Vipsania kissed both of them on the cheeks. Brude whispered his thanks to her. "I will not forget you," he told her.

"Nor I you," she answered softly.

Then Agrippina embraced Lucius, kissing his forehead. She turned to Brude and embraced him as well, pressing herself against him. "I will miss you," she whispered.

"And I you, my lady." He had been afraid she would denounce him to Aquila but, when he had told her of his plan to accompany Lucius, she had simply smiled and said, "I know, my love. Why do you think I let you into my bed? It is best that you go now before things become difficult." He knew that he meant nothing to her. Vipsania was right about her and he guessed that someone else would soon take his place. For the moment, though, Agrippina was once again the chaste Roman lady he had known before. Now, feeling the hidden promise beneath her gown, he was glad that he was leaving. Life would become far too complicated if he stayed.

Aquila shook his hands warmly, thanking him for his service as he handed him a small pouch of coins. "A little something extra for you," the old Roman said, making Brude feel even worse about his betrayal of the man. It was as if he was being paid for sleeping with Aquila's wife.

He climbed onto his horse then clumsily followed Lucius away from the city, along the Via Aurelia, heading north. They turned to wave farewell to the tiny figures at the city gates, then they crested the hill, leaving Rome behind them.

The journey north took them over a month. Brude had never ridden a horse before and he was in agony after the first day. While he slowly got used to being on horseback, he never felt comfortable at any pace faster than a slow trot, so they made poor time. Aquila had given Lucius several letters, carefully scratched onto clay tablets, to deliver to friends and acquaintances, with whom they would sometimes stay overnight. Most nights they stopped at an imperial staging post where, because Lucius was on military duty, they were able to get a bed for the night and where their horses could be stabled alongside the mounts used by the imperial messengers.

Lucius was talkative on the journey and Brude realised that the young man was nervous. He was only a couple of years older than Brude had been when he had first gone to war and, despite his training and education, this was a daunting step for the young Roman. He called Brude by his *praenomen* of Marcus, insisting that Brude call him Lucius, at least when they were in private. He also helped Brude decipher some of the unfamiliar Greek words in the scrolls Cleon had given him. Despite Cleon's teaching, Brude still struggled to read the strange-looking Greek script but he slowly learned of the adventures of the Greek hero, Achilles, in the famous war against Troy, a story every Roman seemed to know by heart.

They took the road through Cisalpine Gaul, rather than cross the mighty mountain range of the Alps because the coastal route was easier for an inexperienced rider like Brude, even though it added several days to the journey. From the coast, though, he could see the sheer sides of the immense mountains, huge slabs of grey rock rising from the plains, their peaks often shrouded by clouds and always tipped white with snow, despite the summer heat. He had crossed the mountains into Hispania and they had been impressive enough but the Alps were simply stunning, dwarfing even the magnificent buildings of the Roman towns and cities that lay at their feet. Lucius told him a story about a famous soldier called Hannibal, who came from Carthage, once an enemy of Rome. Hannibal had crossed the Alps in midwinter to bring war to the very doors of Rome itself. "He even brought some elephants with him," said Lucius.

Brude could scarcely believe that. He would not have liked to try crossing the mountains in the summer, let alone in the middle of winter. "He must have been quite a man," he said wonderingly.

"He was. Three times he annihilated the armies Rome sent against him. He stayed in Italy for nearly twenty years."

"What happened to him?" Brude asked.

Lucius said, "The same thing that happens to all enemies of Rome. He was defeated eventually and Carthage was destroyed. Now it has been rebuilt as a Roman city."

That part of the story rang true. The Romans believed, with a conviction as strong as any Brude had ever seen, that they were destined to rule. No matter that they might suffer a setback in war, they knew, as they knew the sun would rise each morning, that they would always win in the end. Rome had few enemies left.

Following the military roads, the two riders headed northwards, circling round the edge of the huge mountain range until they eventually reached the Rhenus. The mighty river, broad, deep and fast-flowing, surged through the hills on its way northwards, carving its own valley as it went. They crossed after a few days of following it northwards, using a wide wooden bridge, then headed eastwards, through the hills and forests until they reached the camp where Quintus Aemilius Tertius, imperial legate, commander of the legions of Germania Superior, had his headquarters.

Military life was another new experience for Brude. The camp was a permanent one, with buildings built of stone, brick and tiles rather than wood. It was laid out in a rectangle with two main roads, one heading north to south, the other east to west, although the intersection was not in the centre because the north-south road was nearer the western side of the camp. The headquarters building was at the intersection and the whole encampment was laid out in a regular pattern. Brude soon learned that Roman army camps were always laid out the same way so that it was easy for the soldiers to find their way around. Lucius, as a tribune, had a large room to himself in one of the barrack blocks, while Brude had to share a dormitory at one end of the officers' quarters with the other freedmen and slaves.

In practice, his duties were light. He simply had to be available to attend to Lucius when called upon. He polished the young man's breastplate and helmet, tended the horses, although he usually left that to the camp's experts, and sometimes fetched light meals from the kitchens when Lucius was not dining with the legate.

The camp housed around three thousand men, although it was capable of holding an entire legion. Some men were permanently out on detachment, others might be building roads, bridges or new buildings while those based in the camp could be out on patrol. The legion was never up to full strength anyway due to illness or to men who died or retired not being replaced straight away.

Brude, as a freedman servant to an officer, was in an unusual position of being one of the few civilians allowed inside the legionary fort. He was, though, subject to military discipline so he was careful not to infringe any rules for he quickly learned that the discipline in the army was extremely harsh. Men were flogged or beaten for even relatively minor misdemeanours.

As legionaries, the soldiers were Roman citizens, although not all were from Italy. There were men from all over the empire: Hispania, Africa, Syria and even a handful from Britannia. They served for twenty years plus another five as veterans on light duties. At the end of their service they could expect either a plot of land of their own or, more likely, a cash sum. The soldiers were well paid because the emperor, whose authority relied on the power of the legions to keep him in his exalted position, knew that he had to keep them happy. For the soldiers, though, the life was hard. They trained most days, not the brutal training of the gladiatorial schools that Brude was used to, but almost as hard none the less. These men were professional soldiers. Alone among the nations of the world, Rome kept a permanent standing army. While other people would raise an army of conscripts from their farmers in time of need, Rome always had thousands of soldiers available. While the warrior elite of German tribes, or even the Pritani of Brude's homeland, spent their days hunting and feasting, the Roman soldiers trained for war. They were drilled daily by the centurions, not as individuals the way Brude had learned to fight in the arena but as a unit, each man protecting his neighbours, all moving forward at the same time, supporting each other. It was the difference, Brude realised, between being a warrior and being a soldier. The Romans did not play at war. Their tactics were scarcely subtle but they were deadly and effective. "You know what they say," Lucius told him, one evening after a particularly harsh battle drill. "Our exercises are bloodless battles so that our battles are bloody exercises."

In addition to the legionaries, the Romans used auxiliaries, men from allied or subject states who were not Roman citizens. In equipment and weapons, they were almost indistinguishable from the legionaries and they were commanded by experienced Roman centurions. The reward for an auxiliary who survived to retirement was full Roman citizenship, so there was rarely a shortage of recruits, even though their pay was not as good as that of the legionaries. The auxiliaries also provided the Roman army with cavalry. There were few of them in the headquarters camp but, in total, Tertius commanded as many auxiliary troops as legionaries.

Brude spent a lot of his time at the infirmary. The Romans had some soldiers who were trained in ways of helping wounded colleagues, and who could give first aid, which might allow the soldiers to survive long enough to be taken to where the surgeons could operate on them. Some of the medical orderlies were veterans who had served their twenty years and were working out their final five years of service before their discharge. But even in times of relative quiet, the infirmary was understaffed, so the surgeons were grateful for Brude's help, quietly turning a blind eye to his non-military status. He was also able to use the camp's bathhouse, although only at specific times of the day. It was fairly basic but still enjoyable.

Inevitably, a small town had sprung up around the fort, where the soldiers could find all sorts of goods and services which the camp did not supply. Many of them also had families there. Technically, soldiers were not allowed to marry while in service but unofficial marriages and children could not be stopped so the Romans tended to pay no attention, as long as it did not affect discipline. The children, if they were boys, might very well grow up to become soldiers themselves as they rarely knew any other life. For the Romans, a supply of potential recruits was always worthwhile.

Brude was surprised to find that he enjoyed life with the army. The soldiers were hard men who could be difficult to get along with but once they accepted him, he could sense the camaraderie among them. His time in the infirmary made sure that he did get along with them as he always made a point of treating the patients well and sneaking in some extra rations for them when he could.

Lucius, on the contrary, had a hard time at first. Tertius was a tough old man who drove his tribunes hard. Lucius was usually exhausted by the time evening came as he struggled to get to grips with the demands of military life. Still, he soon began to get the hang of things and, thanks to the months of training with Brude, he impressed both his fellow officers and the men with his stamina and his skill with a sword. Now he was learning tactics, logistics and the basics of engineering. Brude learned with him, for the young man would stay awake at nights going over things, using Brude as a sounding board to test his own knowledge. They both learned some new words as well, picking up the odd word or phrase from the native Germans who lived in the town.

They discovered that Tertius was an African, a friend of the emperor from the city of Lepcis Magna. The legate often lapsed into his native Punic when he was annoyed, which was quite often. The emperor, being from Africa himself, had placed many of his friends and countrymen in positions of authority, because no emperor wanted men he could not trust in charge of large armed forces. Too many emperors had lost their thrones that way in the past.

The province was generally quiet, which suited most of the soldiers. They drilled, they patrolled and they built or repaired buildings and roads but they rarely had any need to fight. Lucius had all summer to learn the ways of the camp and, after a few months, he had grown used to the life. Brude was still trying to read the scrolls Cleon had given him, although he often had to ask Lucius for help with some of the more obscure words. He eventually finished the Iliad and argued with Lucius over who was the better man, Achilles or Hector.

"Achilles was the greatest warrior," Lucius insisted. "I thought you, as a gladiator, would relate to that." Like many Romans, he firmly believed that gladiators were fortunate to be able to prove themselves in battle or meet a glorious end trying to win in the arena.

"I can admire the man's skill," Brude agreed, "but Hector had a family and was simply trying to protect his home. He still faced Achilles even though he knew he could not win. Achilles never had to be brave because he knew he was invincible. It takes a real man to do a brave thing even though he is afraid."

Lucius, though, was imbued with the invulnerability of youth. It made Brude feel old in comparison when Lucius hankered after some real action, wanting to emulate Achilles. Brude hoped the young man would live long enough to appreciate the old soldiers' desire for a quiet life.

The winter brought snow such as Brude had never seen. It piled against the buildings in deep drifts, blanketing the earth in white, which soon turned to a dirty brown and degenerated into a horribly wet slush as the men tramped through it. Lucius had never seen snow at all, except on high mountain peaks. He was at first amazed and delighted with it, then cold and miserable like everyone else, as the winter frosts took a grip.

Tertius, though, drilled the troops whatever the weather. Brude was kept busy as the infirmary filled with men coughing and sneezing, requesting cures the surgeons were unable to provide because nobody could cure a winter chill. Brude caught a cold himself but recovered after a few days in bed, getting up and about just in time to tend Lucius who also succumbed.

The rest gave Brude time to do some more reading. He started on the second batch of scrolls Cleon had given him, the story of the hero Odysseus and his twenty-year journey to return home after the Trojan War. Again Lucius helped him with the reading, as he so often did but, sitting there in the small room with winter gripping the outside world as he read of Odysseus' homecoming, Brude felt the call of home growing inside him again. Lucius saw that something was bothering him and asked him what it was. "I want to go home," Brude told him.

"You miss Rome so much?" Lucius asked through a sniffle.

"That's your home," Brude told him. "I mean my own home in Broch Tava."

Lucius was amused and alarmed at the same time. "Whatever for? What does your home village have to offer that life in the empire does not have?"

"Friends. Family." It was the same conversation he had had with Curtius the day after he had won the rudis. Brude could not explain but there was an ache in his belly, the more he thought of Broch Tava. He had been away for so long that it hurt him to think of it. He recalled Curtius' warnings about going back but the thought was there and it would not go away.

Lucius was not receptive and refused to discuss it any more. He could not conceive of anyone giving up the luxuries of Roman life for the barbarous lands beyond the empire, so Brude was forced to tuck the idea away though he decided to make plans for the journey anyway. He was not sure when he would get the chance to go, but he felt he should be ready if the opportunity arose.

Letters arrived from Rome when the first thaw came. Small clay tablets with the characters carefully picked out by small, sharp writing sticks. Lucius read them avidly. "Vipsania is married now," he told Brude. "She asks for you and so does my stepmother. She says she misses your company when she visits the forum or the baths now."

Brude had to look away. The last thing he wanted was to get involved in a discussion about Agrippina. "How is Cleon?" he asked, changing the subject as quickly as he could.

"The same as ever. He urges us to keep studying our Homer."

"That's no problem," said Brude, gesturing towards the scrolls.

"I shall write back and tell him how well you are doing," said Lucius. "Then we shall read some more."

The winter passed slowly but, in the first months of the new year, while the frosts were still hard and the rain was still threatening to turn to snow, Tertius marshalled his troops and led the better part of two legions eastwards, deep into the forests. Lucius was delighted, excitedly telling Brude, "There's talk of some tribes raising rebellion. We are off to crush them. We shall show them what it means to defy Rome."

The Romans were organised with an astonishing efficiency. The baggage train was packed, the sacrifices made and auspices taken. When the officiating priests announced that the signs were propitious, the legions were on the march a mere two days after Tertius told his officers what he intended. Lucius, mounted on his finest horse, joined the legate's staff while Brude tagged along with the medical detachment, helping to load their small wagons with supplies. He wasn't sure whether he should go with them but he had promised Aquila that he would look after Lucius and nobody told him he couldn't go, so he looped his gladius over his shoulder and followed the Roman army into war, only too aware of the irony that raised.

Eight thousand legionaries, five thousand auxiliaries and a thousand auxiliary cavalry made the march into the dark forests of Germania, accompanied by a horde of supply wagons and a contingent of artillery. There was also a rag-tag group of camp followers, prostitutes and traders, the permanent accompaniment to every army on the march, no matter how much the officers tried to stop them. The army crossed the *Limes*, the frontier line of forts they used to keep watch on the German hinterland, and kept going eastwards, the long column stretching for miles along the narrow forest paths. Brude had heard the legionaries tell stories of how three Roman legions had been destroyed by the Germans, two hundred years before, caught strung out on just such a march through the deep, dark woodland, but Tertius was too canny to be caught in a similar trap. They sent out scouts and used their cavalry to screen their infantry and supply column.

Memories of his long march from Broch Tava came to Brude but this march involved many more men and was far better organised. The Romans, he grudgingly accepted, knew how to wage a war.

Against his expectations, the Germans tried to fight. He was too far to the rear to know much about how it happened but he soon found that the army had deployed along a low ridge overlooking a lightly wooded valley where there was a fortified town. The Germans had mustered several thousand warriors, who were grouped in front of the town. One of the older men in the medical detachment grunted to Brude, "Poor fools. They've not caused trouble for near a generation so they don't know what to expect." Brude, who had personally experienced the might of Rome from the receiving end, felt a pang of sympathy for the Germans.

It was past midday. He wondered whether the Romans would delay until the following morning. For the moment, the soldiers took a light meal, waiting in their ranks. Brude thought they might try to simply hold the ridge, inviting the Germans to come up the slope to them. Lucius, riding along the ridge, came over when he saw him and said, "We are just waiting for the scouts to return. Tertius wants to make sure there are no others hidden in the woods, where we can't see them." If Lucius was surprised to see Brude there, he did not say anything. "Isn't this grand?" he asked cheerfully.

"Just try to stay out of trouble," Brude warned, knowing Lucius would pay no attention to his words.

The scouts must have given Tertius the news he wanted because the Roman artillery soon began firing. The ballistas and onagers flung long wooden bolts and large rocks, smashing into the German warriors, disrupting their cohesion and spreading confusion. Then there was a blast of a trumpet. The Roman infantry marched forwards, leaving the high ground and heading straight for the enemy.

Brude knew what it was like to face an attack like this. Yet the line of troops he had faced twelve years previously had scarcely been two hundred men strong. This army comprised over fourteen thousand men.

The Germans cheered and yelled their war cries but the Romans advanced steadily, silently, an ominous tidal wave of armour and steel. They threw their javelins, the dreaded *pila*, which bent on impact to disable their opponents' shields, causing more confusion and panic in the German ranks. A second volley, then each soldier drew his gladius, hefted his shield and marched forwards.

The Germans died in their hundreds. If a man fell, the Romans trampled over him, allowing the men in the second rank to stab down with their swords to make sure he was dead. The Germans who still stood slashed with their long swords and axes but the Romans, fighting as a unit as they had been trained, could get in between the warriors who needed room to wield their huge weapons. And still the Germans died. They were outnumbered and outclassed, and they had no chance to do anything except run or die.

It was, as Lucius had said, a bloody exercise. This was where the Roman training paid dividends. It was all over in under half an hour. The Germans were either dead, wounded, captured or fled. While the auxiliary horsemen pursued the fleeing warriors, the Roman infantry stormed into the town in search of women and loot. For Brude, it was like watching the slaughter of the Boresti once again. The battle had followed precisely the same awful pattern he remembered so vividly, although this time he was thankful that he was on the winning side.

Now he had a job to do. He and the other medical troops ran down the slope, carrying their small bags of bandages and ointments. There were not many Romans who actually needed treatment, a few score at most, but Brude was busy for an hour or so, patching men up or organising stretchers for those who could not walk. Beyond where the dead and wounded lay, the town was starting to burn as the looting continued. He could hear the screams of the women as the Romans killed the ones they considered too old or too young to rape. The price of defeat, Brude knew, was high.

The wounded men who were unable to move from where they had fallen were moaning in pain. Having attended to the Roman soldiers first, Brude now went to see whether he could help any of the German warriors. He heard one young man calling out, the pain clear in his tortured cries. Brude knelt beside him. The man was very young, hardly more than a boy, with long, fair hair now dirty and matted around his head. He had an awful wound in his belly and it was obvious there was no chance of him surviving. The boy clutched at him, gasping with pain, his eyes beseeching Brude for help. Brude gave him a drink of water from his canteen. The man muttered, "Danke," before his face contorted with pain. Brude held him until he died, which did not take long, and he continued to hold him, looking into the boy's sightless eyes as he cursed the folly of men who sought glory in war.

A shadow fell over him and he looked up to see Farinus, one of the medical orderlies, a veteran legionary, looking down at him. "Poor kid," Farinus said. "Has he got much on him?"

Brude had not even checked the young German's body for loot. Farinus laughed. "You'd better be quick, that's a small town and the legions will be back soon enough to search the bodies."

Farinus began expertly patting down a nearby corpse, rummaging for hidden valuables. He clucked disappointingly when he found only a silver ring and necklace. "They usually have more than that," he cursed. He moved on.

Brude was well enough used to death not to be sickened by the looting. What upset him was how pointless and futile the battle had been. He saw some legionaries streaming back out of the gates in the town's wooden wall and heading straight for the fallen. Soon every corpse would be stripped of any valuables and any man who was not quite dead would be despatched by the sharp swords of the Romans. He moved quickly, searching the dead boy but finding only a small gold ring. He moved to another body nearby, a large man with a long coat of mail which would have been worth something but which he discounted as too cumbersome and heavy to take. Still, the man was obviously someone of high status so Brude checked him over. And found the means of going home a rich man.

The warrior wore two golden armbands and had a torc of twisted gold around his neck. In a pouch tucked under his mail shirt Brude found several gold and silver Roman coins, more money than he had ever seen before in one place. The man also had a silver belt buckle fastening a wide, ornately decorated, leather belt which Brude unfastened. He tugged it off before rolling it up and shoving it into his medical case. Three gold rings completed his haul. He had time to quickly check two more bodies, adding a few more silver coins and a handful of rings and brooches before he decided the legionaries were getting too close. He did not want to end up in an argument over loot, especially with men who were fired up and excitable after a battle, so he picked up his bag and made his way back up the ridge to where the walking wounded were gathering.

It took the army several days to return to camp. Tertius sent out some detachments, particularly the cavalry, to harass the defeated Germans. Another couple of villages were destroyed as the main force made its way back by a different route. Brude saw Lucius several times. The young man was ecstatic about the army's success. "That will teach them a lesson they won't forget in a hurry," he declared. Brude could not argue with that.

Back at the fort, Brude carefully hid his new-found wealth in several caches, usually buried in pots in the woods just out of sight of the fort. The town's merchants were awash with wealth as many soldiers had managed to get hold of some loot, so Brude waited for a few months for the glut of gold and silver to diminish. Then he began slowly selling small pieces in exchange for coins, most of which he hid behind a brick that he levered out of the wall behind Lucius bed. He could easily retrieve it from there and, as he and Lucius were the only two who ever used the room, there was little chance of accidental discovery by anyone else.

By the end of summer he felt ready to leave but he wasn't sure how to raise the subject with Lucius. As a freedman, he had the right to go but he also had a conflicting duty to Aquila. Lucius did not really need him although he knew the young man would still object.

His chance eventually came as the leaves were turning brown and beginning to cover the grass in the golden carpet of autumn. A messenger arrived from Rome, bringing Lucius the news that his father had died quite suddenly one evening. It was a shock for both of them but Lucius showed the stoic reaction of a true Roman and, at least outwardly, gave no display of emotion. The messenger had brought a short note from Agrippina, urging him to return to Rome to attend to his father's affairs, so Lucius obtained Tertius' permission to return home.

"We shall leave tomorrow," Lucius said to Brude that evening.

"With respect, Master Lucius, I will not be coming with you. It is time for me to return to my own home."

Lucius sat on his bed, hands clasped together. He looked at Brude with some concern. "You do not wish to return to

Rome?" He shook his head in wonder. "My dear Marcus, why ever not?"

They had had this discussion before. Brude had rehearsed his response many times in his head. He could hardly say that he did not want to return to Rome because he wanted to avoid the temptations of Lucius' stepmother. He had thought up some other reasons but now that the time was right to put them into words, he felt awkward and clumsy. "What is there in Rome for me now?" he asked. "Apart from Cleon, who I loved like a father, the home will not be the same. Your father is dead, your sister is married and, the truth is, you do not need me any more. Any slave could do for you what I have done these past months. I am closer now to my home than I have been for many years, so I think the time is right for me to return. I want to find out whether I still have friends and family there."

"It will not be easy for you," said Lucius. "You know that Rome does not approve of citizens travelling beyond the borders of the empire."

"I will go as a trader," said Brude. "Who knows, if there is nothing for me when I get back home, perhaps I will trade some goods and return to Rome." That was the other temptation. Brude, who had seen what the empire could offer if a citizen was wealthy enough, had a worry that Broch Tava would disappoint him when he did eventually get there, just as Curtius had warned him it would.

"You have thought this all out, haven't you?" Lucius asked him. "But to travel as a trader you will need some goods. Do you have money to buy some stock to maintain your pretence?"

"A little," Brude replied, knowing he had more than enough for what he needed.

Lucius reached into his pack and withdrew a small pouch, which he tossed to Brude. Brude caught it easily, his reactions still sharp. The small bag was heavy with coins. "Use that," Lucius told him. "If you do return, I will expect a share in whatever profit you make on your journey."

Brude felt embarrassed by the young Roman's generosity but it was impossible to change his story now so he could do nothing except thank Lucius profusely.

Lucius left the following day. Brude, having recovered his stash of coins, said farewell to him at the gate of the fort, under the eyes of the Roman sentries. Lucius took with him Cleon's scrolls containing the Homeric poems along with a clay tablet bearing a short note from Brude, the words clumsily carved out in large, awkward letters. Lucius had offered to write it but Brude felt he at least owed Cleon a farewell note in his own hand. Now, all he carried was his gladius, his pack with a sleeping blanket, his manumission papers, his rudis and a small piece of flint for lighting fires. And, hidden away at the bottom of the pack, his hoard of gold and silver coins. Lucius insisted on giving him one of his horses to make his journey swifter. "I am your patron now," Lucius told him. "I want to make you a gift of this horse." He would take no argument about it.

Lucius clasped Brude's hands, thanking him for his help and advice over the past three years. Then he mounted his own horse, waved farewell and, accompanied by Agrippina's messenger, set off on the long road south to Rome.

After a backward glance at the legionary fort, Brude rode as far as the nearest main town before selling his horse. He knew he would travel faster with it but he was never comfortable in the saddle and a man alone on horseback was often a target for thieves and bandits. He decided it would be safer to hide under a guise of poverty so the horse was sold and his supply of coin was increased.

He followed the road north, trying to stay in sight of other travellers when he could, finding somewhere to sleep in towns where possible, but outdoors if he had to. After five days he felt fitter and leaner than he had for some time, although his feet were protesting at so much walking. He reached the city of Augusta Treverorum and was stopped in his tracks when he suddenly recognised the great black stone of the gate tower. This was the town where he had been brought with the other slaves to be bought by Marcus Arminius, who had taken him away to work the farmland of Sextus Arminius Rufus. In a kind of daze, he wandered slowly through the massive gateway. Inside, he found the slave pens. Even after so many years, the memories flooded back as he gazed around at the crowds of people and the high wooden walls of the slave pens with their iron gates. There were slaves in there now, waiting their turn to be sold to the highest bidder who would soon have them working for the continuing glory of the empire. He looked back out through the open gates, realising that he must have passed the estate that had formerly belonged to Arminius Rufus without recognising it. He had a fleeting temptation to go back to see it again but he quickly dismissed the notion. Even if Batix was still alive and still there, what could Brude, now free, say to him? And if Julia, his one-time lover, was still there, she would have another man by now and children as well. Even if one of the children was his, he had no right to see them for they belonged to whoever their master was now. The weight of his coins at the bottom of his pack hinted that he might be able to buy their freedom but then what would he do? With his conscience mocking him, he turned away from the east gate and headed northwards through the city.

A week later he reached the coast where he bought passage on a merchant ship, which was heading to Londinium with a cargo of wine and the ubiquitous red Samian pottery that Gaul produced in such quantities. The ship's captain was a cheery soul, who chatted away harmlessly, even though Brude gave him few answers to his questions. Brude felt sick again crossing the strait between Gaul and Britannia. This time over, though, he was able to stay on deck where he could feel the sea breeze in his hair and smell the salt of the sea. Gulls screeched overhead as the ship slowly ploughed its way past sheer, white cliffs, following the coast until they reached the broad estuary of the Tamesis. Here they turned westwards, sailing on until they reached the bustling city of Londinium. There, Brude spent several days using a good portion of his money to buy some stock to provide a cover for his story of travelling as a merchant. He bought a mule which he loaded with bolts of cloth, some pots of clay, a large number of jewellery trinkets, which were small and easy to transport, and some other odd bits and pieces which took his fancy, including a dagger with a finely carved ivory handle and a matching razor. By chance, he found a merchant who had a fine stock of medicinal herbs so he took the opportunity to top up his supplies.

After four days in the city he had no more excuses for putting off the journey. The news he had gathered suggested that the north of the province was a dangerous place for travellers. The Brigantes were, if not in open revolt, causing enough trouble to make the Governor concerned. Brude decided he would avoid the main roads once he got near Eboracum and travel across country.

Early the next morning, leading the mule by its halter rope, he set off for the north and the regions beyond the edge of the empire.

A.D. 210

"So how can we defeat the Romans?" Veleda asked. "It seems to me, you think we are defeated already."

"We cannot fight them and win, at least not in open battle," Brude responded, aware of how easily his Roman citizenship had slipped away from him. He was once again Brude of the Boresti, trying to figure out how to defeat the Romans, no longer Marcus Septimius Brutus who had marched with the legions of Germania. "If we do fight them, the best we can hope for is to hide from them in the forests and hills. We should carry out small raids, attacking their supply lines until they decide to leave again."

"You think they will leave?" Veleda was surprised. "I thought they wanted conquest and tribute?"

"They do. But what do we have that they need? We grow barely enough to feed ourselves. Our land offers nothing they cannot get elsewhere. To hold down a conquered land needs a lot of soldiers. They have had trouble with the Brigantes for years." The more he spoke, the more confident he was that he was right. "The Romans are coming to make a show of force. They may well march all the way to the lands of the Caledonii but I don't think they will stay for long. The problem for our people is that they are likely to kill or destroy anyone and everything in their way as they pass. That is the Roman way; you either submit to them or they crush you completely."

"You said the Brigantes still cause them trouble," Fothair pointed out, looking for some inspiration as to how to defeat the might of Rome.

"Pinpricks," Brude said dismissively. "The Brigantes never fight in open battle; they simply carry out the occasional raid, steal cattle or rob merchants. They act more like brigands than warriors, but that is the only way they can fight against such odds. I expect they are suffering for it now. There will be villages and farms burnt to the ground whether they were involved in rebellion or not." He stared hard at Veleda. "I have seen it before. I do not wish to see it again, not here among the Boresti."

Veleda considered his words thoughtfully. They had talked long into the night and the more she heard, the less hope she saw. "Then I must tell Nechtan to submit to Rome, to send tribute and hostages. He must sue for peace."

"I can't see any other way," said Brude, sadly. "Rome has conquered mightier people than the Pritani before now."

"And they have conquered us before, as the stories tell," agreed Veleda. "The remains of their camps and watchtowers are still to be found everywhere across the land of the Boresti, all the way beyond Peart." She fixed Brude with her steely gaze, challenging him once more. "So why did they leave the last time?"

"Trouble elsewhere," Brude told her. "The empire has many enemies and often there are fights among the powerful men of Rome to see who will be the next emperor. The soldiers must have been needed in some other part of the empire. And, as I said, why keep men here to pacify a land which is so poor it would cost more to control it than they could take from it?"

"So there is some hope for us?"

"A small hope. The emperor is a powerful man. There are few who would dare oppose him. But if trouble breaks out somewhere else, the emperor will be forced to go. If he does, he will take his armies with him."

"Then I will offer prayers to all the gods that some other people, far away, try to throw off the Roman yoke so that we may be saved. It is clear that even Belatucadros, god of war, cannot match the power of the Roman gods. If we oppose them then Babdah the Raven, who haunts the battlefield, feeding on the corpses and blood of the dead, will feast so much that his wings will not raise him from the earth. The coming of the emperor is dire news for the Boresti, Brude, son of Anndra. Up until now, the Romans have sent envoys bearing gifts of silver and other trinkets to the powerful tribes of the Caledonii and the Maeatae, seeking to buy peace. Now they come with war, not peace, in their minds and I fear for the Pritani."

There seemed nothing more to say. The three of them sat, gazing into the flickering remnants of the hearth fire while all around, outside, was quiet with the still of night. Brude saw Veleda staring at him, as if she was trying to see inside his mind. "Is there no other way?" she asked, her voice low, yet insistent.

Brude knew that there was, but it was a desperate way, a way that meant death for whoever tried it. He hesitated, recognising that he was afraid. He had faced and escaped death so often in the arena that life was now sweet. He did not want to throw it away. Veleda saw in his eyes that he had an idea. He whispered, "If the emperor dies, they will probably leave, for there will be a fight to gain control of the empire."

"So how can we kill the emperor?" Veleda asked calmly.

Brude looked down, staring into the dying fire. "I don't think we can. He has many guards around him, night and day."

There was a short silence, then Veleda spoke the words he knew she would say. "But you could get close to him, could you not? You speak their tongue. You could approach him on some pretext and you could kill him."

Brude nodded. "Perhaps. But nobody is allowed to approach the emperor bearing a weapon."

"A man like you could find a way. But you would die. And you fear to die, is that not so?"

"I have faced death before," Brude told her. "But always with a chance to escape. In this, there would be no escape. I would be dead within a heartbeat of striking a blow."

Veleda spread her hands in a conciliatory gesture. "I do not ask you to do this, Brude, son of Anndra. I merely ask if it could be done. Perhaps there will be no need. Perhaps the emperor will accept our surrender. But if not...." She left her words hanging, planting a seed in Brude's mind which he knew would stay there. Trying to shake off the feeling of doom, which threatened to overwhelm him, he said to Veleda, "It is late. Where can we sleep for the night?"

"You can sleep here," she replied, content not to press the matter. "But we are not done yet, Brude, son of Anndra. You have told me what you know. Now I must tell you what I know."

Brude was intrigued. Tired as he was, the words of a druid were always important, even if sometimes, as on this night, the druid said things a man did not want to hear. "I am listening," he said.

"There is bad blood between you and Colm, son of Lachlann. Over the woman, Mairead, no doubt?"

"There is no bad blood on my part," Brude said. "Neither of them are to blame for what has happened to me and I cannot blame them for how they react to my return."

Veleda's eyes twinkled. "You have learned more from the Romans than you care to admit, I think." She held up a hand to stifle any protest as she went on, "I think your words say one thing while your heart says another. But I also say to you that there should be bad blood between you and Colm."

"What do you mean?"

"I mean that I know that Castatin, son of Colm, is in truth your son. I was in Broch Tava just after he was born. I know what I know."

Brude clenched his teeth then took a deep breath. It seemed everyone he met knew about Castatin's true parentage. "I have heard this from my mother, Mor. But I have not heard it from Mairead."

"That does not mean it is not true."

"I know. But Colm could say that I was not here when the boy was born and that he has been his father for the past thirteen years. What claim do I have on the boy apart from blood ties?"

"Blood should be enough," Veleda told him. "But there is more you need to know. Colm has not only taken your son, he has taken the whole village from its people, based on a lie."

"What lie?"

"The same lie that haunts Nechtan, night and day, causing him to pray to all the gods, to give alms to the poor and to build his people into a peaceful nation instead of a warlike one. The same lie that has turned Gartnait into an old man fearful of vengeance. The lie of where their wealth came from."

Brude watched the old woman closely. He found he was holding his breath. He had to force himself to relax, just as he used to do when entering the arena. This moment was possibly just as dangerous. "I heard it came from the Romans. They went back across the Wall, after our defeat. They found some wealthy Romans."

Veleda laughed scornfully. "That is not what happened. Nechtan has told me of that day, the tears of shame rolling down his cheeks as he spoke the words. He would not lie to me." There was no argument from either man. Nobody would lie to a druid. "He told me they ran like terrified children, abandoning their men who could not cross the great wall as they ran for their lives to escape the wrath of Rome. There were scarcely forty men of the Boresti who escaped and they had nothing left but what they wore or carried.

"So they decided to return home but, to avoid pursuit, they went by a long route, winding their way through the lands of the Selgovae. They were tired, afraid and hungry. Then they came to a village of the Selgovae where they asked for shelter, which the Selgovae willingly gave them, for many of their own men had also gone on that raid and had not yet returned. They took pity on the Boresti and gave them hospitality, as the Pritani should."

Brude had a sense of foreboding about what Veleda was about to tell them. This was turning into a night of dark tales and forbidding thoughts. "What happened?" he asked.

"One Selgovae warrior mocked the Boresti for their cowardice. Colm, who had drunk more than he should to quell his fear, jumped up and killed the man. Then others of the Selgovae threatened him so he called to his tribesmen to help. To their shame, the Boresti joined him, killing the few Selgovae warriors who guarded the village. Then they put everyone to the sword so that there would be none who could bear witness against what they had done. The cattle, horses, goats, pigs and sheep they brought home, along with any other valuables they could find, enough to make all of them wealthy."

"And Colm married Mairead so he would be the head man of Broch Tava." Brude was shocked by Veleda's tale but he knew no druid would lie about something as serious as this. Warfare between the tribes was endemic among the Pritani but to turn on people who had offered hospitality was something no true warrior would ever dream of.

"Gartnait too?" Fothair asked.

"And the others who came back," Veleda confirmed. "In Peart and Dun Nechtan, the survivors of that raid are all important men now, sworn to secrecy, a vow they keep to hide their shame. But the pain of the memory haunts Nechtan to this day."

"What about Broch Tava?" Brude asked her. "Who are the other men who came back home rich?"

Veleda bared her teeth in a humourless grin. "Only five men, apart from Colm, returned alive to Broch Tava, for the men of your village bore the brunt of the fight against the Romans. So twenty-eight men left and six returned. Yet now, only one survives apart from you, Brude."

Brude's eyes widened in surprise. "Colm is the only one left? What happened to the others?"

"They died," Veleda shot back. "Mostly in accidents. It seems Broch Tava is a dangerous place to live."

"Colm," breathed Fothair. "He killed them. But why?"

"I did not say he killed them," said Veleda. "I said they died. Perhaps they were all accidents. The sea, the woods and the hills can be dangerous. But Broch Tava was not lucky after the men marched away on that raid." She studied Brude, looking for a clue to what he was thinking. "What will you do now that you know all this?"

Brude stared back at her. He knew she must have a purpose in telling him this but he did not want to play her games. "Nothing. I made a promise. I have to keep it."

"It is dangerous to break oaths," Veleda agreed. "To whom did you give your word?"

"To Mairead. And to myself."

"To yourself? The hardest kind of oath to keep. And the hardest to bear if you break them." Brude thought she would try to persuade him to take some action but instead the old woman sighed, "You must do as your heart tells you. Just beware of Colm."

"I think he has enough troubles of his own without worrying about me," said Brude.

"Probably so," Veleda agreed. "Colm's problem is that he thinks he has big dreams but, in truth, they are the dreams of a small man. Nechtan, for all his faults, has a wider vision as well as greater cares."

"What do you mean?" asked Brude.

"I mean that there are changes afoot in the lands of the Pritani. Already the Caledonii have absorbed the Creones who live in the far lands by the western sea. The Damnonii are scarcely independent of them either. The Caledonii are building a nation, not a scattering of people where every village names itself a different tribe. To the north of us, the Vacomagi and the Taexali now call themselves the Maeatae and are united. They make war on Rome, sailing south in their ships while, at the same time, they take Roman silver as the Romans attempt to buy peace. The Boresti are a small tribe, as you know, stuck between the might of the Maeatae and the greater might of Rome. Nechtan fears being trapped between the Caledonii and the Maeatae, on the one hand, and crushed by the Romans on the other. Colm thinks only of himself. He makes war on his own people, thinking himself a man the Romans consider a friend when, in truth, he is of little consequence in the great scheme of things. That is why Nechtan wanted an excuse to marry his daughter off to someone else."

"To a nobleman of the Caledonii or the Maeatae, I presume?" said Brude.

"To the Maeatae," Veleda confirmed. "It is all arranged. Perhaps some day her son will rule over the Maeatae and the Boresti. Perhaps we will become part of a larger nation, speaking with one voice, powerful enough to withstand even the Romans."

"It's a nice dream," said Brude. "One day it may become real."

They slept after that, even though Brude's mind was full of dark thoughts and troubled dreams. They woke late and the sun was high in the sky when they rose. Veleda gave them a breakfast of porridge and bread then walked with them to the gate, which the guards opened for them without a word of protest. Veleda wished them well, then surprised them by sending for two horses for them to ride home. "It will be dark before you get back, if you try to walk," she told them.

"We cannot accept such gifts," Brude protested. "We have done nothing to deserve such kindness."

"Then look on it as a loan. You can return them when you are able," Veleda told him. "But Nechtan will not miss them. He has more than he needs anyway."

Two warriors arrived, each leading a small Pritani horse. Brude and Fothair mounted the uncomfortable wooden saddles, wishing Veleda good health. She nodded in farewell and her look showed Brude that she did not need to speak to remind him of the things they had talked about the previous night.

They set off down the hillside trackway. Brude still felt uncomfortable on a horse but Fothair loved it, although there was more than just the joy of being on horseback to bring a smile to his face. "We got out alive," he said with feeling. "Yesterday I didn't think we would have managed that."

"So now all we have to do is get home and survive whatever Colm has in store for us," Brude told him. "If we survive that,

I have to think of a way to kill the emperor and escape with my life."

"If anyone can do it, you can," Fothair told him airily.

"Trust me. Nobody can do it. If I do get close enough to strike him, I am a dead man."

"Then let's hope the Romans are in a mood to let us all live," Fothair replied.

Brude just grunted.

Down below, the camp site where the men of Broch Tava had stayed overnight was now deserted, Colm and his men having long gone. Even on horseback Brude doubted whether they would catch up with them much before they reached home. What would happen when they did reach home was more uncertain than ever.

Appius Flaminius Philo stood on the deck of the war galley savouring the tang of the sea spray and the rhythmic splash of the oars. He checked that the three other ships under his command were all maintaining position. Satisfied, he turned back to survey the land. He had looked over the maps the evening before when they had beached the ships in a wide, shallow bay and he knew that they should be reaching a broad estuary when they rounded the next headland. They were now north of the emperor's army so, as he had told his men that morning as they boarded the ships, anyone they came across was to be considered hostile.

They reached the estuary where he saw the narrow plain and the line of low, steep hills that ran down to the shore. He also saw what he was looking for. There was a huddle of roundhouses near the shore at the foot of one of the hills. There were even the bare spars of a small boat under construction. He turned to his assistant Decimus. "Tell the ship masters to pick up the pace. All marines to don armour and prepare for action." Decimus ran lightly back to the stern to relay the message. Soon, Philo heard the beat of the hortator's drum pick up, the slaves manning the oars reacting to the increased rhythm and pushing the galley on faster. Signals would be flying to the other galleys, he knew. He could trust his men to obey his commands, so he turned back to examine the northern shore of the wide river. He thought he could make out people moving around in the village and there were even a couple of the ludicrous oval-shaped, leather-skinned vessels the barbarians used for fishing, sitting out in the river. Nobody had yet seen the approaching ships, he thought, though he knew they would soon enough. Decimus scampered back. "All done, sir," he said in his young, eager voice.

"Very good. Fetch my armour." Wearing armour aboard ship was only countenanced when the men were about to go into action. Falling overboard was bad enough if you could swim and were wearing ordinary clothes. In full armour a man would sink like a stone. Philo was experienced enough to know not to take any unnecessary chances, even when the seas were calm, as now.

He looked again at the village. A quick in and out raid with little opposition was what this called for, he thought. He saw the small shapes of three people running along the grassland towards the village. They, at least, had seen the galleys but he was not concerned about that. At best all they could do was warn people to run.

According to the maps he had studied, there was a fortress tower on the hill above the village. He searched for it, eventually spotting the tip of a bony finger of stone appearing beyond the wooded ridge at the top of the long hill that towered over the village. He clucked his tongue. A fortified tower meant warriors but all the reports said there were not many people living here and the tower was a fair way from the village. He knew he would not be able to storm a fortified position because his marines had no siege weapons, but they were more than capable of taking on anyone who came out of the tower to challenge them.

Dismissing the tower as inconsequential, his eyes scoured the shoreline for a landing point. There was a long, sandy beach ahead of him, lying to the east of the village. It looked open and inviting but he thought he could make out swirling patterns in the waves near the north shore, which suggested there might be shallow shoals or rocks. Where the sand stopped, there was a small piece of land jutting into the estuary. Beyond that, where the houses and the boat were, the shore was pebbles and stones rather than sand. The sand would be easier, he thought, but the houses were near the stony beach so that meant there were probably no hidden rocks or sandbanks for his galleys to founder on. Even barbarians were not stupid enough to sail out from a beach that had hidden dangers. He would go straight for the village, he decided.

With the eyes of experience, he made his plans as the ships surged towards their target, the oars biting into the waves to the beat of the drums. A line of sixty men would suffice to stop anyone coming down from the tower, he decided. The rest of his men could get in to the village, take whatever they could find by way of loot or prisoners, burn the houses and especially the half built boat, then be back on board in less than half an hour. Simple and efficient, the way Philo liked it. The Roman way.

With many of the men away, Castatin had been bored so he had gone down to the lower village where he had met Seoc's sisters. Barabal was nice, he thought, but a couple of years older than he was. Still, her figure was developing and he was starting to take an interest in such things so he offered to go with the girls to the rock pools out on the sandy beach. The tide would be heading out soon so they would be able to collect small crabs and shellfish which would be trapped in the pools. Seasaidh, who normally scared him with her forthright manner and teasing words, seemed friendlier than usual, even speaking politely without the mocking laugh she usually used when she spoke to any boy. For Castatin, it seemed a morning full of promise.

The tide was just starting to turn so the rocks were not visible yet. They would probably have at least an hour or so to wait so they climbed down the grass bank on to the sand. They quickly found a sheltered spot under the edge of the grass where they could pass the time. Seasaidh asked Castatin if he knew why his father and all the men had gone away to Dun Nechtan. Castatin was busy explaining that he had no idea when Barabal suddenly pointed out to sea. "Look!" she said. "There are some ships."

There were four galleys, their square white sails catching the thin breeze, ranks of oars splashing in rhythm. Castatin thought he heard the distant sound of a drum beat rolling over the water. Eyes painted on the prows gave the ships a demonic look. When Castatin saw the men standing on the flat decks, the sunlight reflecting from their armour, he knew who they were.

"Romans!" he shouted. "Come on, we have to get back to the broch." Seoc had told him about Brude's warning. If the Romans came by sea, they were to take shelter in the broch.

They scrambled up the bank onto the flat grassland strip, where the village's sheep and goats were allowed to wander and graze. It was a fairly long walk back to the village from here, but they set off at a run. Castatin knew that the safest path to get to the broch would be to cut inland, between the low, lumpy hills so that they could approach the broch from the north east. But he also knew that the watchmen on the broch would not be able to see the ships because of the narrow wooded ridge which blocked the view to the south east. If they ran along the shore, he thought, they would get back in time to warn everyone.

They dashed along the rough, tussocky flatland, arms pumping, their breath rasping in their throats. Castatin had to slow to allow the girls to keep up with him. Anxiously, he watched the ships as they entered the broad estuary. He half hoped that they would head for the apparently smooth landing on the sandy beach, which he knew would probably mean they would either run into one of the sandbanks that lurked just below the surface of the receding tide or they would grind onto the rock shoals which lay just off the beach. He cursed in frustration when he saw that the Romans were heading further west, straight for the village.

Seasaidh suddenly fell with a scream of pain. Castatin ran back to help her. He tried to lift her up. "My ankle!" she sobbed, tears of pain and fright streaming down her cheeks. "I hurt my ankle!" She tried to put some weight on it but she could not stand. Castatin looked anxiously out at the ships. They were moving far faster than he thought possible, the banks of oars powering them through the waves with incredible speed. Seasaidh was crying, both from her ankle and from the fear of the Romans while Barabal was biting her lips nervously, watching the ships' inexorable approach to the village. The steady beat of the drums was clearly audible now and they could easily make out the individual men standing on the flat deck. Castatin could hardly believe how many oars the ships had. The galleys were so big they made Gruoch's half-built vessel look puny and insignificant. He looked towards the village where people were now streaming up towards the hill, heading for the sanctuary of the broch. Then he realised the warning horn was blowing from the top of the tall tower of the broch where the watchmen had, at last, seen the Roman galleys. Watchmen had stood atop the great tower for many years without ever having to sound the horn, but it was blowing now, urging the villagers to safety. Castatin and the girls were still several hundred paces from the nearest roundhouse and the boy, with a terrible feeling of despair, knew he had made the wrong choice of where to go. To get to the broch now, they either had to head towards the village and up the track, try to climb the hill at its steepest, most densely wooded slope or turn back eastwards, retracing their steps before circling round the hill to approach the broch from the other side.

He had to make a decision. Seasaidh could hardly walk so climbing the steep slope was out of the question. Going back was a long walk and she would slow them down. It would take them away from the Romans but, if chased, they would be out in the open with no chance of escape. Which left the shortest and most dangerous route. The Roman ships were perilously close now so they would have to hurry. He turned to Seasaidh, ordering her to climb onto his back. "I'll carry you," he told her. To Barabal he said, "You run for it. Go up the hill through the trees, if you can. It will be safer if you keep out of sight."

Barabal, her face strained and pale with fear, shook her head. "We should stay together."

He did not have time to argue. With Seasaidh clinging to his back, her arms wrapped around him, almost throttling him, he set off in a lurching run for the trackway. The ground was relatively flat but the grass was long, with many tussocks and dips, lumps and bumps to impede him. Without the weight of Seasaidh on his back, he would have thought nothing of covering the short distance to the village but, slowed down by his burden, his breath was soon coming in great gasps and his legs and arms were growing incredibly tired.

The Roman ships crunched onto the gentle slope of the beach, the prows grinding on to the pebbles. Men leapt from the decks, splashing into the water and running ashore, shields and swords at the ready. As he saw them fanning out quickly in small groups, Castatin knew with a dreadful certainty that he was not going to reach the trackway before the Romans cut them off. He had almost reached Brude's new roundhouse, the nearest home to the foot of the hill, but the trackway was still two hundred paces away and the armoured soldiers were far closer. "Into the trees," he gasped. He swerved, almost falling as his legs betrayed him. Seasaidh squealed in fright and he heard Barabal almost sobbing as she ran for the nearby trees. Behind them he heard a shout but he kept running. He staggered to the trees, twigs scraping at his face as he ducked into the shade but he soon had to stop for the hill was steep and impossible to climb unless he let Seasaidh go. Barabal turned, her face ashen and her eyes wide with fear. There was a crash of someone charging into the trees behind them. Castatin turned to see three heavily armed Roman soldiers burst into the wood. The first one shouted, triumphantly as he ran straight at Castatin. He saw the deadly sharp blade of the man's gladius, just like the sword Brude used to carry. He tried to step away but he was hemmed in by the trees and Seasaidh was screaming in his ear, weighing him down. He tried to dodge the sword but, instead of thrusting, the soldier suddenly rammed his large shield forwards. The metal rim hit him hard, knocking him to the ground. He twisted in a desperate effort to save falling on top of Seasaidh. He felt her release her grip on him, but in doing so he crashed into the trunk of a tree, hitting it hard with his head. Everything went black.

Cruithne saved the villagers that day. At the first sound of the warning horn, he was calling up to the watchmen to find out what was wrong. When he heard that four Roman war galleys were approaching, he did not hesitate. He wore his heavy mail coat all day, which at first had been an affectation, a device to show everyone how strong he was, but now he was glad of it. He strapped on his sword, grabbing his shield and spear as he yelled for the warriors to assemble outside the broch. He saw Seoc running to join them. Urgently, he pointed, jabbing his spear towards the man. He knew he could rely on Seoc to follow orders. "Get everyone up here inside the broch. Everyone! Have five men hold the door and you hold the stockade gates with ten more. You do not come down. If the rest of us have to retreat, you hold the gates to cover us. If the Romans get here first, get inside the broch and hold it. Understand?"

Seoc nodded. Without wasting time, he counted off fifteen warriors, sending them to their posts while Cruithne gathered the remaining men around him. "We're going down the hill," he told them. "I don't know how many of them there are, so we stick together. All we need to do is hold the path long enough for everyone from the lower village to get up here." He saw their faces, tense and excited at the same time. Some, he knew, had been involved in the fight against Gartnait's men the previous year but, if what Brude had told him about the Romans was true, this promised to be a different affair.

Mairead ran up to him. "Castatin is down there!" she told him. "Please! You must get him back."

Cruithne nodded. "I'm on my way." A year ago, he knew, Mairead would not have sought his help. A year ago he was just Colm's enforcer, a man everybody feared. But things had changed a lot for Cruithne since then. He had been born into the tribe of the Caledonii but he had been thrown out by his father for his constant fighting. He had wandered the lands of the Pritani, seeking employment as a mercenary wherever he could find it. But in the close-knit tribal groups of the Pritani, a mercenary was an outsider, a man not to be wholly trusted. When he had heard how Colm of Broch Tava was seeking men who could fight, he had come to the village where the young chieftain had given him a position in his warrior band. Cruithne was not a clever man. He knew that. But he did have a talent for fighting. Because he was so big, people were naturally wary around him and Colm had encouraged him to use his strength to bully people into doing what Colm wanted. Cruithne, for so long an outsider, had felt wanted at last, at least by Colm. He had been happy.

Then Brude had arrived. Colm had made it clear that he did not like the man and even Cruithne could sense there was an old rivalry there over Mairead. But when Brude had beaten him so easily and then, to Cruithne's astonishment, had treated his injuries and spoken to him like a friend, Cruithne had lain awake at nights re-evaluating his life. He watched Brude, saw how he acted among the villagers and saw how they responded to him. Cruithne compared that with how people reacted to Colm. He realised that people obeyed Colm because they were afraid of what he might do to them. But they did as Brude told them, or more usually what Brude merely suggested to them, because they respected him, because they liked him and because what he said usually made sense. It was hard for Cruithne to change who he was, but he decided that he would try to be more like Brude. Now Mairead had turned to him for help.

He would have helped anyway. His task was to protect the village and the village was under attack. This was what he was good at. For a moment he wondered whether to fetch Colm's hunting dogs but he dismissed the idea; the hounds were trained to attack deer, not men. So he gave the command; fifteen of the warriors of Broch Tava followed him as he hurried out of the gate where Seoc stood with the men who would defend the stockade. Seoc's home was in the lower village as well, Cruithne remembered, and he had those two pretty sisters. He could see the anxiety on the young man's face but Seoc, he knew, was better here, where a cool head was needed, rather than down in the village where things could get nasty. Cruithne had grown to like Seoc and he knew that there was a chance that any of them going down to face the Romans might not survive. Better to let the young man have a chance of life, he thought.

Cruithne led his men down the hill, running in a crazy, dangerous charge where the slightest slip would lead to a horrible fall. Already the first villagers were passing them, making for the broch. Cruithne shouted at them to move as fast as they could. He saw Lulach and his son carrying old Caitlin, the oldest woman in the village. She was berating Lulach for a fool because she could manage well enough without his help. Lulach ignored her and trudged on.

By the time the warriors reached the foot of the hill, most of the villagers had passed them on their way up. Brude's mother and old Seoras were there, moving slowly but at least on the way. Gruoch the carpenter followed, carrying his precious tools even though they slowed him down. But Cruithne had seen no sign of Castatin or Seoc's sisters.

Their headlong charge carried them further than Cruithne intended, bringing them almost to the houses by the time he pulled them into battle line. He forced them back to form a wall of shields at the foot of the hill. He barely had time to get them organised when he saw that the Romans were prepared for them. He had been watching as he ran down the hill, seeing the armoured men scurrying all through the village, entering houses and ransacking them before setting light to the thatch. He had hoped to catch them spread out but someone down there knew what they were doing for the Romans had stopped their running around and withdrawn to form up. Now they marched out in good order through the houses to meet the Pritani.

Cruithne heard one of the warriors muttering a prayer to Belatucadros. He felt a sudden, unfamiliar pang of uncertainty. Even though he was still only twenty-three years old, he had fought many times before, but mostly in one-on-one combat. This was warfare and he had heard Brude speak of the Romans' deadly prowess in battle. He wanted to charge at them, screaming like a devil and swinging his mighty sword but he knew he had to buy time for the villagers to climb the long road to the broch. "Hold the line," he shouted, surprised at how calm his voice sounded. "We need to give people time to reach the broch. Hold the line."

The Romans advanced. There were around sixty of them, in two ranks, each of which was longer than his own small, single rank. They could easily outflank his small force. He wished he knew what to do to change the inevitable. He thought of Brude, wondering what the gladiator would do. An idea born of desperation came to him. He turned to his men. "Hold your position. We just need to delay them as long as we can. There are too many for us to beat them here, so we delay them, then we go back up the hill as slowly as we can without being cut off." He looked at Iomhar, one of the men he could trust, and said, "You are next in charge if anything happens to me." Iomhar nodded nervously. Cruithne looked along the line of warriors and said aloud, "Now I'm going to see what these Romans are made of. Watch and learn."

It was an act of bravado, he knew. He had once boasted that he would fight a bear to prove how strong he was but he knew this was a far greater test. He turned to face the Romans, then advanced towards them.

Castatin groaned as he came to his senses. He did not know how long he had been unconscious but it did not seem like very long. He was lying awkwardly on his side, his neck twisted, his head up against the thick trunk of a tree. He sat up, feeling his skull thump in protest. He blinked against the pain. His vision cleared and sound rushed back into his ears, making him suddenly aware of what was going on.

Seasaidh lay a few paces from him. She was on her back, her clothes ripped and half stripped from her but she was quite still because, where her throat had been, was a mass of red blood already swarming with flies. One Roman soldier was standing, watching Castatin with an amused expression while another was lying on top of Barabal, his undergarments round his ankles, his buttocks rising and falling rhythmically. The third soldier was kneeling, pinning Barabal's arms to the ground so that she could not resist. Castatin could see that she was sobbing, her eyes clenched tightly shut. He attempted to jump to his feet to help her but he collapsed with dizziness and pain. The Roman who was standing near him stepped towards him, his sword pointed meaningfully at the boy. He said something that Castatin did not understand but he got the message when the soldier pushed him down and stood over him.

After a while the rape was over. The Roman soldiers laughed as they hurriedly dressed themselves. One of them threw Barabal's dress at her. He shouted at her but she did not respond, so he slapped her, then grabbed her dress, throwing it at her again, clearly meaning for her to put it on. He pulled her roughly to her feet and this time she obeyed, but her eyes were blank, staring at the body of her younger sister. Castatin saw blood on the inside of Barabal's thighs. Sickened, he looked away. Then he, too, was yanked to his feet. He moaned at the sudden pain in his head. The Romans laughed again. Then they shoved the two captives out of the trees, towards the village.

They rounded Brude's house. One of the Romans went inside but soon came out, obviously disappointed at the poor fare he had found. They headed towards the village. Then Castatin saw Cruithne.

The giant warrior was walking towards a line of Roman soldiers, spear in hand, shield held low as if he was out for a walk and not expecting danger. The Romans, so many of them that Castatin could not count them all, stopped, waiting to see what the big warrior would do. The soldier holding Castatin said something which made his two companions laugh.

Cruithne stopped. In a loud voice, he began speaking to the Romans. They obviously couldn't understand him but Castatin was able to pick out a few words, even from a distance. It was a boastful challenge Cruithne was issuing, telling his foes they were women, cowards who were not fit to wipe his arse. Then he raised his spear and hurled it towards the Roman line. Shields were hurriedly raised. The spear struck with a bang and was diverted high over the heads of the soldiers. Then Cruithne drew his great sword. Slowly, he dragged the point across the earth in front of him, marking a line that he was daring them to cross.

Castatin expected the Romans to throw their javelins, the *pila* that Brude had told him about, but these soldiers from the sea did not seem to have any. Instead, two archers stepped forwards, drawing their bows. Cruithne sneered at them but when they fired he had to move quickly. One arrow lodged in his shield, the other narrowly skimmed past his head. Standing where he was could only end in his death so, with a bellow of rage, Cruithne charged at the archers who immediately turned to run, ducking behind their comrades.

Castatin could not believe it. One man was charging at a small army.

There was a crash as Cruithne hit the Roman line. Castatin expected a quick end for the giant Pritani but the Romans were standing still, not moving forwards as they usually did, probably because they did not expect this lone madman to attack them. Cruithne's hammer of a blow with his shield knocked one soldier back, a mighty swing of his sword hacked into the sword arm of the man to his right and he had carved a gap in the line. He hewed left and right. Incredibly, the Romans began falling back to escape him.

Castatin shouted encouragement, which earned him a box on the ears. He heard one of the soldiers muttering what was clearly a coarse oath. Cruithne was in the gap, fighting like a demon. Then there was a yell from the Pritani shield wall as fifteen more warriors charged into the attack.

Cruithne heard them. He turned to yell at them to remain where they were but they had seen him force the Romans back and they were committed, eager to join his fight. His distraction gave a Roman a chance. A gladius stabbed forwards, the blow blunted by Cruithne's mail coat. He turned, swinging at the man, his heavy sword crashing onto the soldier's shield but then another Roman was behind him, and another was to his right. The blows were landing and his mail coat did not cover all his body. Cruithne was wounded in several places on his arms and legs. Bleeding, roaring defiance, he killed two more Romans, the bodies piling up around him. Then an arrow caught him in the neck and he swayed. He made one more desperate lunge, which plunged his sword deep into the thigh of a Roman, then he fell to his knees.

Shouted commands sent the ends of the long Roman line wheeling round the other Pritani warriors who were quickly surrounded. The fighting was brutal and savage but over all too quickly. With Cruithne's fall, the Romans regained their composure and their superior numbers soon told. Castatin saw a Roman who was wearing a long red cloak. The man was pointing and shouting commands as he re-ordered the lines of soldiers. After what seemed only a few moments, there were no Pritani left standing. Castatin heard himself softly calling Cruithne's name as tears rolled down his cheeks.

The three soldiers with him shoved him and Barabal forwards, heading for the shoreline before turning back towards the Roman ships. They were dragged into the shallows and hoisted up onto the deck of one of the galleys, where they were ordered to sit while more soldiers stood watch over them. There was a lot of talking but Castatin could understand none of it. He nudged Barabal. "Are you all right?" *What a stupid question*, he thought.

She did not look at him. Her eyes just gazed blankly at the wooden deck of the galley. "They killed her because she tried to fight them," she whispered. "I didn't want that to happen to me so I didn't fight them." Her words came through more tears. He put his arm around her shoulders but she shrugged it off. "Don't touch me!"

Castatin sat on the wooden deck, not knowing what to do. The thought that haunted him was that Seasaidh would still be alive and he and Barabal would be safe if he had not decided to run along the shore towards the village. If they had run inland they would have escaped harm altogether. But he had made the wrong choice. Seasaidh was dead because of him and now he and Barabal were destined for a life of slavery. It was all his fault.

Appius Flaminius Philo was annoyed. The attack on the village had not gone well at all. The villagers had fled to the tower on the top of the hill, allowed time to escape by the fanatical giant who had opposed his men single-handed. He had sent some marines up the hill to scout out the chances of storming the place but he knew before they returned that it would be pointless trying to take a fortified tower without some siege weapons. His men confirmed that there were more warriors up there and that the tower also had a high wooden stockade round it. He posted some sentries to watch for another attack then turned to concentrate on the village. The pickings were slim. They found some supplies of grain, some salted meat and fish, and they caught a few goats and pigs, which were taken back on board the galleys. They had slaughtered a mule and two dogs because they were no good for eating. They had also caught two slaves, a boy and a teenage girl. He was certain his men had raped the girl, which was against orders, but he did not want to punish his men any more after the day they had suffered so he pretended not to know what they had done. Two slaves was a poor return, though.

He had lost five men dead and another seven wounded, two of them badly. That one solitary madman had accounted for six of the casualties on his own. Philo would not have believed it if he had not seen it himself. Romans were used to victories on land. Centuries before, he knew, Rome had lost thousands of men and hundreds of ships in their wars against their great rival city, Carthage, the world's great naval power whose ships controlled the sea that the Romans now called *Mare Nostrum*, Our Sea. Time and again the superior seamanship of the Carthaginians had outwitted and outfought the Roman navy, even when the Romans had overwhelming numbers on their side. So Rome, a land power, had turned the naval battles into land battles by fitting their ships with huge wooden ramps, which they raised vertically on their decks. It made the Roman ships unstable and unwieldy but when a Carthaginian ship came close, they would swivel the ramp, releasing the ropes holding it in place. The ramp would crash down onto the deck of the enemy ship, a huge iron spike on its underside driving into the wooden decking to hold it firmly in place. The Romans would storm across the ready-made bridge, fighting as if they were on land. The *corvus*, they called it; the Crow. It turned the tide of the war, which was won by the soldiers of Rome, not the sailors. Romans rarely lost battles on land but now one giant warrior had almost turned that on its head. Philo knew the chances of the tower holding another man of that sort were low but he recognised that his men were shaken by the experience so it was time to pull out.

He rattled out orders. Every house was set alight. The half-built boat on the shore was burned, too. Then the animals they could catch easily were driven aboard ship. The dead and wounded Romans were carried on board while Philo, watching his men destroy the village, began mentally composing his report. Sixteen enemy warriors killed in a tough battle for the loss of only five dead; many houses destroyed, grain and livestock captured, along with two slaves. And a boat destroyed. It didn't sound too bad when you put it that way, he thought, though in his heart he already considered the raid a failure.

Satisfied that they had done all they could, he climbed the wooden ramp onto his galley. Men in the water heaved the ships back out to sea. They struggled because the tide was going out, leaving the ships in much shallower water than when they had landed. They were heavier with booty too, but they edged slowly free, backed oars, and were soon heading south again, leaving the village to burn. Philo congratulated himself on his choice of landing spot because he saw that his earlier suspicions had been correct; if he had aimed for the softer landfall of the sandy beach, the receding tide would have left his galleys high and dry. Where they had landed the river was more in sway than the sea, so the tidal effect was less. Just a short distance eastwards, the difference between high and low tide was far more significant. He could already see the rocks and sand shoals which would have trapped him. He was pleased and relieved that he had had the experience to make the right call. The Mediterranean Sea had no tides to speak of, with barely two feet of a difference between high and low tides. Many an inexperienced Roman had been caught out when coming to these northern waters by the great distances the sea would retreat from the land.

Feeling more pleased than he had a short time before, Philo glanced at the two slaves. The girl was quite pretty and had a decent figure but her face was blotched by her tears. The boy was a couple of years younger but looked quite alert. He might be intelligent enough to make a decent slave for someone, Philo thought. A look back at the burning village showed him that a group of spearmen had come down the hill to watch the Roman galleys depart. He ordered the two captives to be lifted to their feet so that the barbarians could see that some of their people had been taken. Then, because they were only slaves, he ordered them to be taken below and put in chains.

A.D. 210

Lutrin was an ambitious man. The youngest of four of the eight children his mother had borne who survived infancy, he had grown up on a farm some three days' walk north east of Broch Tava, near the coast overlooking a wide tidal bay. Life had been hard and Lutrin had always been hungry. Being the youngest, he felt he was constantly overlooked and though his two older brothers and his sister always complained that he was the one who was spoiled by their mother, Lutrin felt they were forever picking on him. As he grew older, he learned how to manipulate his parents to cause dissension between his brothers and sister. By watching carefully, biding his time and seizing opportunities when they arose, he was often able to steal scraps of food or even small trinkets, which he would hide away. Sometimes not even he knew why he had taken them except that they belonged to someone else and he wanted them for himself. Taking things was easier than working for them.

When he was eleven years old, his eldest brother marched away to join the great raid that Nechtan was leading against the Romans. Lutrin had no idea who the Romans were, nor why his brother was leaving to fight them. In fact he had only the vaguest idea who Nechtan was, but with one of his brothers gone it meant he had to do a greater share of the work around the farm, so he was not happy. Nechtan, he decided, was his enemy, taking his brother away and causing hardship for him.

His brother never returned.

By the time Lutrin was thirteen, his sister was married and living on another farm several miles away, resulting in even more work for Lutrin. Five years later his mother died, which meant he was left to work the farm alongside his ageing father and his one remaining brother. This was not the life Lutrin wanted. He thought his father and brother were dull, stupid men who had no ambitions beyond surviving the next winter. Lutrin wanted more. Above all, he wanted things without having to work all the hours of the day to get them.

Then one day, in his nineteenth year, some warriors arrived, riding on sturdy war ponies, telling Lutrin's father about Colm of Broch Tava, a mighty warrior who was turning the tiny village into a power to be reckoned with, a rival even to Nechtan. The men demanded tribute to help pay for the protection Colm would give him. When Lutrin's father wanted to know who he needed protection from, one of the warriors leaned down in his saddle, giving him a grin full of menace. "Us," he said meaningfully.

Lutrin's father had little enough to give but he handed over some grain and some salted meat. The warriors seemed satisfied and rode off. Lutrin thought his father a coward and told him so. He expected an argument but the old man just closed his eyes and sighed. The next morning, Lutrin left home, taking as many of the few valuables his father possessed as he could carry. He headed for Broch Tava.

He joined Colm's growing band of warriors but he soon found the opportunity to tell Colm that his main talent was in thinking, not fighting. Within a few months he was the first man Colm of Broch Tava looked to for advice. Lutrin quickly learned to manipulate Colm as easily as he had once controlled his parents. Colm was not stupid, but he was blinded by his desire for power. Lutrin was happy to plant seeds of ideas, to make subtle suggestions and to let Colm take the credit for the resulting idea. At Lutrin's subtle prompting. the tribute gathered from the coastal farms was increased, a stockade was erected around the upper village, a smithy was built and Caroc the smith recruited to make the iron tools and weapons the village needed. Lutrin had plans for gold and silver working, too, along with a fleet of ships so that Broch Tava could extend its influence south across the river more easily and contend with the tribes from the north.

As Broch Tava grew in power and influence, so Lutrin grew rich, little by little, willingly taking gifts that Colm gave him. Whenever the fancy took him, he simply helped himself to coins or small items of jewellery from Colm's growing wealth. He was, at last, a man of wealth and power. Yet he dreamed of more.

Colm had everything that Lutrin wanted so Lutrin worked to make himself indispensable to the head man. Colm's enemies had a habit of having accidents, often arranged by Lutrin. But he was careful and never obvious. Sometimes his plans took months, or even years, to come to fruition, but all the time he had his eyes on the main prize. One day, he had promised himself, he would be head man of Broch Tava. Which would give him power and wealth. And Mairead.

She was a few years older than Lutrin, but she was still beautiful. Lutrin encouraged Colm to treat her harshly, but only so that she would be more receptive to his own advances when he did decide to take the final, fatal step on his path to power. It was Lutrin who planted the idea with Colm that Mairead was not capable of producing a daughter and that without a daughter, none of Colm's descendants would ever hold positions of power after Castatin was gone. It was an argument even Lutrin thought was facile, going against everything in the culture of the Pritani, but he planted the idea and Colm remembered it. The thought grew and festered in his mind until he told Lutrin to visit Nechtan to make overtures about arranging a marriage between Colm and Nechtan's daughter. Colm would divorce Mairead and Lutrin would be free to take her for himself. Then Colm would have an unfortunate accident. When that happened, Lutrin, already married to a woman of the line of Beathag, would be the obvious choice for the new head man. It was a good plan, he thought. All he had to do was wait for Nechtan's daughter to come of age.

Then the man Brude had arrived, throwing Lutrin's plot into confusion. He suggested to Colm that they would all be better off if Brude was dead, but Colm, usually quite happy to let Lutrin dispose of his enemies, was reluctant to take such overt action against his childhood friend. Lutrin thought Colm was afraid of the man. He realised that he would have to find a new plan but had still not managed to formulate one by the time Colm was ready to divorce Mairead and marry Nechtan's daughter. Now, though, Colm was seriously considering letting Mairead marry Brude. Lutrin was forced to think quickly. He managed to persuade Colm that allowing Brude to stay in the village, married to Colm's former wife, would be dangerous, a focus for any malcontents among the villagers. It would be better, he suggested, to banish them both. Colm liked the idea. Lutrin, though, was counting on Mairead not wanting to leave her son. If she refused to go, Lutrin would insist that he marry her. But if she did leave with the man Brude, he had enough warriors loyal to him personally to waylay Brude and kill him. Lutrin had visions of arriving in time to drive off the assailants and rescue Mairead. He had not figured out all of the details, but he knew there would be a way to achieve what he wanted. There always was.

Now things had turned out better than he could have hoped. Colm was in disgrace with Nechtan and the witch woman, Veleda, had taken Brude for her own purposes. Lutrin had no idea what the old druid wanted with Brude but he did not really care; all he knew was that men who got into the clutches of the old crone were usually never seen again. All he needed now was a way to dispose of Colm.

Still, Lutrin was wary of taking the final step. He had arranged that the men loyal to him were those who were mounted on horses but that was just the sort of precaution Lutrin always took. He toyed with the idea of simply drawing his sword as he rode alongside Colm on the journey home, killing him without warning, trusting to his men to either overpower or simply escape from the foot soldiers. There was a great temptation to do this but Lutrin preferred more subtle means if he could achieve his ends without direct action. If direct action was called for, he knew he still had Cruithne to deal with. The giant warrior was a potential problem, even though the big man's attitude towards Colm seemed to have changed since Brude had beaten him in what the villagers were calling the spear challenge. Lutrin would have liked to have seen that because he had not believed that anyone could beat Cruithne in a straightforward fight. It would have been instructive to see how Brude had managed it. The stories he had heard from the likes of Seoc and young Castatin were hard to believe, even though everyone told more or less the same tale, even Cruithne himself.

Lutrin resolved to bide his time. Colm was still in a rage at the affront given to him by Nechtan and Brude was out of the picture, at least for the time being and, possibly, permanently. Lutrin decided he would have to dispose of Cruithne somehow before he could act against Colm. He was a patient man. He could wait a little longer.

The journey back to Broch Tava was not a happy one. Colm seethed and railed against Nechtan, threatening revenge and calling on every god he could think of to bring ruin on Nechtan and all his people. Lutrin stayed mostly silent though the few words he spoke were designed to encourage Colm's anger.

They rode slowly out of the trees to the north of Broch Tava and saw the familiar sight of the great tower with its huddle of buildings clustered around it. The fields and pastures were lush and green with the ripeness of early summer but Lutrin saw immediately that the fields were empty. No workers, no slaves, and precious little livestock were to be seen. Something was wrong.

Above the tree line, on the ridge of the hills above the coast, he could make out faint wisps of smoke, indistinct yet visible, far more than he would normally expect to see from the village's cooking fires.

Colm, his mind full of thoughts of vengeance, had not noticed so Lutrin, mindful of his role as trusted advisor, tapped

Colm's arm, pointing out the lack of field workers and the unusual smoke.

Colm swore. He jabbed his heels into the flanks of his horse, urging it forwards. Lutrin followed, calling to the other riders to stay close. In a thunder of hoof beats, they sped along the edges of the fields, heading for the main gate in the stockade.

Armed men opened the gates to let them in. "What has happened?" Colm demanded.

"The Romans came," one of the men answered. "The village is destroyed and many men are dead."

Lutrin saw the shock on Colm's face, watched the colour drain from him and felt an inner exultation. Colm's world was disappearing before his very eyes.

Leaving their horses, they hurried down to the lower village where they found every house burned to the ground, the ashes still hot and smoking, charred timber beams lying in blackened heaps. The bodies of the dead were being gathered and laid out. Lutrin saw Cruithne among them and his heart began to beat faster for fate had removed another obstacle from his path to power.

Mairead ran up to Colm, calling his name. "Castatin is gone!" she blurted, her fear evident on her face. "They took him and Barabal."

Colm stared at her as if she were a stranger to him. "What?"

"The Romans came. They took Castatin away on their ship. Barabal too. And they killed little Seasaidh."

Lutrin looked again at the row of bodies. He saw Seoc kneeling at the far end where one corpse, smaller than the others, lay. The young warrior's long hair tumbled down around his face, hiding his grief from the other villagers though Lutrin could see that everyone was in a state of shock and would have paid no heed to Seoc's tears had they seen them.

Colm was especially affected. He shook his head as if to deny Mairead's words and the evidence before his own eyes. "The Romans would not do that. They are our friends."

Mairead gaped at him. Angrily, she gestured around at the devastation. "Is this the work of friends?" she demanded. "Seoc saw Castatin and Barabal being taken onto their ships. We found Seasaidh just a short while ago. Colm, my son is gone! Do you not understand?"

Lutrin intervened. "My lord Colm, we have much to do. Can I suggest that you and your lady wife come with me to the broch. I will have men organise a funeral pyre. Then we must find shelter in the upper village for those who have lost their homes."

Colm nodded blankly but Mairead said, "I need to stay here to help."

"Please come up to the broch first, my lady," Lutrin said. He looked meaningfully at Colm. "Your husband needs your support just now and we must plan what to do next. It will not take long. I promise."

Mairead looked as though she would argue but she nodded. Taking Colm's arm, she led him back to the track that climbed the hill to the broch. Lutrin hastily signalled to Irb, one of the warriors he knew he could trust. Irb was a burly man with a cruel streak, which Lutrin admired. "It is time," Lutrin told him. "Get our men together. Once I am in the broch, make sure that those who might oppose me are dealt with. Permanently." He named nine men, telling Irb to repeat the names back to him. All were warriors Lutrin knew would be loyal to Colm. "Get them to the upper village and send all the other men down here. Tell them to help get a funeral pyre built. That will keep them busy while we go about our business."

Irb grinned. "It is about time."

The warriors who had been on foot on the march from Dun Nechtan had now arrived so, while Lutrin set off after Mairead and Colm, Irb began shouting orders, directing men where Lutrin wanted them.

As Lutrin climbed the hill, he started humming to himself. All of his dreams were about to come true and he wanted to relish the moment. He trudged up the track, admiring the way

Mairead walked as she led Colm towards the upper village some way ahead of him. What a fine woman she was, he thought. She was upset at the destruction of the village, appalled at the loss of her son, yet she was still strong, not giving in to the crushing despair the way Colm was. Lutrin knew she was unhappy in her marriage. He looked forward to freeing her from that burden, to offering her a new opportunity for a better life at his side.

He became aware of someone else walking up the slope behind him. He glanced back to see Caroc, the taciturn smith. Caroc's eyes met his and the big man said, "Going to get some more axes," by way of explanation.

Lutrin nodded. "Good idea." He really didn't care.

Looking back down the hill he saw Irb leading a group up the slope, some of them Lutrin's men, some of them his intended victims. It was all coming together perfectly.

Apart from a few warriors, the upper village was nearly empty. Only the old, the very young and a handful of slaves were left while the others were down in the ruins of the lower village. Lutrin saw Brude's old mother, Mor, approach Mairead and Colm. She began to harangue them. Then Mairead was asking Colm questions. Lutrin hurried over because he knew what this would be about and Colm was in such a state of shock that he would not know what to answer.

Mairead rounded on Lutrin as he approached. "What has happened to Brude?" she demanded.

"Nechtan's witch woman, Veleda, has him." The pain in her expression annoyed Lutrin. Brude meant too much to her, he thought.

"The druid! What does she want with him?"

Lutrin shrugged. "She had heard of his magic. Perhaps she wants him dead. Perhaps she wants him as a pupil. Either way, I'm afraid we won't see him for a very long time, if at all." He gave her a look meant to convey sympathy. "I'm sorry. There was nothing we could do. One does not refuse a druid when demands are made."

Mor, her lined old face crumpled in tears, buried her head in her hands at the thought of losing her only son for a second time. Old Seoras came over to comfort her, gently putting his arm around her. Mairead glared at Lutrin, obviously wanting to argue, but he ushered her towards the broch, leading the unresisting Colm by the arm. "Come inside. I will explain as much as I can," he told her insistently.

He closed and barred the low door, sealing them inside. The three of them climbed the stone steps to the living quarters. The light was poor inside, the wooden floor of the upper level blocking most of the daylight coming through the small circular gap, which normally let the smoke from the hearth escape. There was no fire now, no warmth, just gloom and shadows. In here, Lutrin knew, even the watchmen in the very top of the circular tower could not see or hear them. He led Colm to his throne-like chair, another of Lutrin's innovations, where he sat him down, helping him to unstrap his sword belt. Lutrin placed the sword and dagger on a nearby table. Colm sat there, staring into space, seemingly oblivious to his surroundings. "The Romans are my friends," he said in a flat monotone. "They brought me gifts."

"The Romans have my son!" Mairead retorted. She knelt in front of Colm, grasping his hands and trying to break through the barrier his mind had built to protect him from the collapse of his dreams. He barely noticed she was there. "We have to do something!" she said urgently.

"Indeed we do, my lady," Lutrin agreed. He carefully drew Colm's dagger from its leather scabbard, testing the tip of the blade against his finger, drawing a pinprick of blood. Still with his back to the others he went on, "But I'm afraid the lord Colm has had more than one nasty surprise in the past couple of days. Perhaps you could pour him some wine. That might help." He half turned to watch her. She climbed to her feet and moved away from Colm. The head man of Broch Tava was sitting in his chair, hands gripping the carved wooden arms, head down as he gazed blankly at the floor. Committed to his plan, Lutrin span on his heel, driving the dagger into Colm's chest as hard as he could, aiming for the heart, feeling the blade grind against the ribs. Colm gave a single gasp of pain, jerked upright, eyes staring, then slowly slumped forwards. Lutrin stepped back, letting the body fall to the floor while Mairead turned, staring at him in horror, one hand held to her open mouth. She backed away from him. "What have you done?" Her voice was hoarse but he saw again how strong she was, a true warrior woman of the Boresti. No screaming or fainting from her, he was pleased to see.

"I have done what you wanted," he told her calmly. "Now you are free of him." He gave her a smile. "Do not deny that you wanted him dead."

She shook her head but no words came. He was certain that she had dreamed of this, of being free from Colm and he, Lutrin, had made her dreams come true. He knew she would love him for it.

Instead, she looked at him, aghast, and whispered, "Not like this. Never like this." Her eyes blazed accusation even in the shadowy gloom of the unlit broch. "You have murdered your lord."

Lutrin spread his arms out from his sides, palms towards her. "Nonsense! Lord Colm killed himself with his own dagger. He was overwhelmed by grief at being humiliated by Nechtan, then finding his village destroyed by people he thought were his friends. When he learned that his son had been taken captive, it was too much for him."

Mairead looked at Colm's corpse lying crumpled in a grotesque heap on the wooden floor, a small pool of blood seeping from under his chest. Her eyes narrowed as she turned her gaze on Lutrin. "You want to be the new head man, is that it?"

"Naturally."

"That will not happen. There are men who are loyal to Colm. They will oppose you."

"No, they will not. Cruithne is already dead and the others you speak of, Cailean, perhaps? Or Gordan? Murchadh? They will be dead very soon, if not already. And a few others besides." He lifted his hand, pointing at her. "And when you show that you are happy to be my wife, the others will accept me, for you are a descendant of Beathag, mother of kings."

She stood there, proud and erect and he thought she was very beautiful with her long dark hair and sparkling blue eyes. It was hard to tell in the dim light, but he thought that the look she gave him almost resembled one of hatred. "You think I will marry you?" she asked scornfully. "I would rather die."

His patience snapped. He drew his own dagger. "That can be arranged, my lady. But I think you will change your mind when you hear how I have saved you from Colm's plans for you."

She spat at him. "I will hear none of your lies!" She turned to run for the door, charging down the stairs more quickly than he would have guessed she could move. With a yell of outrage, he set off in pursuit. He took the wide, shallow steps at a run, almost slipping a couple of times but she had a good head start. She reached the door first, threw aside the bar and yanked it open, letting in a stream of late afternoon sunlight which dazzled him with its sudden glare. He lunged for her but she was gone, out into the light. He hit the door hard with his shoulder. Cursing, he pulled the door back furiously and ran outside, barely two paces behind her now. His eyes were struggling to see in the bright daylight but he saw her shadow. He grabbed for her, catching her arm and pulling her back. She staggered, almost falling as she whirled in a circle around him. Then he had her properly. He clamped his left arm round her chest as his right hand held the dagger to her throat. "Do you still want to die, my lady?" he whispered venomously in her ear. "What do you have to say now?"

She stiffened. He heard her whisper, "Brude."

Brude and Fothair knew something had happened as soon as they saw the fields were deserted. They approached the stockade cautiously but, as they grew nearer, they heard the sounds of screaming. Brude pursed his lips. "Something is very wrong," he said.

"We should leave," suggested Fothair, though he knew they would not.

Brude spurred his mount towards the gates. They were wide open and though there were a few warriors at the entrance, they were all looking inside the stockade, not out. They turned when they heard the horses approach and Brude could see the alarm on their faces. "What's going on?" he demanded as he reined in his horse.

The men looked confused and anxious. "Some men have been killed. Murdered." Confusion radiated from the young man who spoke.

"Where is everyone?" Brude asked.

"Some Roman ships came. They burned the village," another sentry said. "Most folk are down the hill."

At that moment, a villager, middle-aged and with his hair flying in disorder as he ran, charged round the corner of a house, hotly pursued by two warriors who quickly caught him. They cut him down before their eyes. Brude stared at the killers. He recognised Irb, one of the men who had been on the trip to Dun Nechtan. Irb saw him at the same time. His jaw fell open in surprise, then he turned and ran towards the broch, still holding his sword with its bloody blade. His companion ran after him.

Brude leapt from his horse. "Give me your spear," he snapped to the warrior at the gate, taking the weapon from the young man's hand. He strode after the running men. Behind him, Fothair grabbed a spear from another warrior and followed, offering up silent prayers to Belatucadros and Camulos to protect him from what was about to happen. Whatever was going on, it was going to be bloody work, he was sure.

More people were cautiously coming out of the houses, peering nervously round the sides of the buildings and edging closer to the open space in front of the broch. Irb and his companion were running towards the low wooden door when it suddenly burst open. Mairead staggered out, trying to run but blinded by the bright sunlight. Then Lutrin was after her, grabbing at her. Brude saw her spin round, saw Lutrin hold her close and saw, too, the knife at her throat. He stopped dead in his tracks as her eyes, blinking in the sunlight, saw him. Her lips moved and though he could not hear what she said, he knew she was speaking his name.

Lutrin saw him too. He stiffened, the knife blade pressing close to Mairead's neck. Slowly, Brude walked forwards, keeping the spear low. There was an audience now, he knew, as people gathered at the edges of the green. Some warriors were pushing their way through to take up a position beside Irb. He counted ten of them and thought they had the look of men who knew they had done a terrible thing.

"Is it done?" Lutrin demanded, his voice loud and clear.

Irb replied, "As you ordered." But his eyes kept flickering towards Brude. He and his men kept their distance from Lutrin, obviously waiting to see what was going to happen next, not willing to declare their allegiance so fully as to oppose Brude.

Brude knew Fothair was with him, a pace or two behind, but he also knew that they could not hope to defeat ten armed warriors. He had to rely on more than his fighting skill to save Mairead. Slowly, he edged to his left, circling towards the broch. In response, Lutrin turned, stepping backwards, dragging Mairead with him. The tip of his blade never left her throat. Brude stopped when he was satisfied that he was closer to the door of the broch than Lutrin was. He did not dare let the man get inside with Mairead. If that happened, nobody would be able to reach them. Lutrin backed away, towards the roundhouses where the warriors lived. The small crowd of onlookers retreated a few paces from him while Irb and his men also shuffled back, keeping their distance from both men, their nervous eyes constantly moving from one to the other.

Brude decided he had to keep the warriors out of this. He looked directly at Irb. "You have seen and heard what I can do," he said. "What I learned from the Romans. Now the druid, Veleda, has taught me many more things. It would be best for you and your men if you never found out what those things are." He saw Irb lick his lips, nod nervously and take another pace backwards. Brude stared at him, trying to ensure that the man's imagination would feed his fears of magic and keep him out of the fight. Because a fight seemed inevitable. Satisfied he had done all he could to keep Irb out of it, he turned back to Lutrin and Mairead. "Let her go, Lutrin."

"She is mine!" Lutrin told him. "Not yours."

"She is Colm's wife," Brude reminded him, keeping his voice calm.

"Colm is dead," Lutrin snarled. "He killed himself, while wallowing in grief. Isn't that so, my love?" He jerked Mairead though the dagger stayed near her exposed neck.

"*You* killed him," she exclaimed accusingly, her voice tinged with fear but clear for all to hear.

"You lie! He killed himself and you will be my wife now."

Mairead looked at Brude, her eyes pleading with him but he could not take a chance with Lutrin's knife so close to her throat. He could see the mad desperation in Lutrin's eyes. He said, "If Colm is dead, then Mairead is free to choose her own husband."

"You want her for yourself," Lutrin snarled at him. "I have seen how you look at her. But you cannot have her. Put down your spear or I will make sure that nobody has her." He raised the knife a fraction, indicating his intention if Brude did not obey.

Brude crouched, laying his spear on the grass. He slowly backed away from it. He stood looking helplessly at Mairead. He did not know what to do and he feared she would try something foolish, for he saw the look in her eyes. He gave a tiny shake of his head, trying to warn her. He was too far away to reach Lutrin before the man could harm her.

Lutrin waved his knife hand towards Irb. "He is unarmed now. Kill him!"

Irb hesitated. He looked at Brude, glanced back at Lutrin and then at Brude again. Deciding that Lutrin had the upper hand, he gripped his sword and took a step forwards, growling at his men to follow him.

"Do you have a plan?" Fothair whispered from behind Brude.

"Not a good one."

"I thought not. I'll take the five on the right if you take the five on the left."

"Maybe you should run now," Brude told him.

"I think it's a bit late for that," Fothair answered. He stood beside Brude, spear clenched in his hands, watching Irb and his men slowly cross the green towards them.

Brude suddenly jumped into a fighting stance. The movement made Irb and his warriors stop their advance to watch him, wondering what he was about to do. All eyes were on him as he began to move his arms and neck, exercising his muscles. Then he laughed aloud, and said, "Come on, then, if you really want to die. I warned you."

"You're mad!" hissed Fothair.

"Keep them looking at us," Brude whispered through clenched teeth. He began to weave his arms and legs in a bizarre, half dance. Irb and his warriors watched him, fascinated and bemused. He should have been terrified, fleeing for his life, yet he was waiting for them, daring them to attack him. Uncertainty and fear of magic held them still.

But Brude had seen what they could not, so he kept up his weird movements to keep their attention on him. When he saw Lutrin wave his hand to urge Irb to attack, he called out, "Belatucadros! Strike down my enemies!"

And Lutrin was struck down.

Caroc the smith had crept out of the shadows between the houses, an axe in his hands. Seeing Brude facing Irb and his warriors, he had nodded to him, gesturing towards Lutrin. While Brude kept everyone watching him with his bizarre movements, Caroc had silently moved up behind Lutrin. He paused, holding his breath, not wanting to strike while the knife blade was so close to Mairead's throat but then Lutrin had waved towards Irb, urging him to attack Brude. Caroc seized the opportunity. With one blow he buried his axe in Lutrin's head, smashing through the man's skull with all the power his massively muscled arms could muster. Mairead screamed as the knife tumbled from Lutrin's lifeless hand, then she staggered away from him while Caroc tugged the axe from the bloody mess of Lutrin's skull.

From across the open grass, Brude nodded his thanks to Caroc. He walked towards Irb, still unarmed. He stopped a few paces from him. "There has been enough killing, I think," he told the warrior. "It should stop now. If Colm and Lutrin are both dead, you really have no reason to kill anyone else, do you?"

Irb, even with his men around him, felt isolated, confronted by Brude. He had heard how the former gladiator had beaten Cruithne. He had no wish to suffer the same fate. The expression in Brude's eyes told him that if any of his men made a threatening move, Irb would be the first to die. He took his sword, reversed it and handed it to Brude in a gesture of surrender. Brude accepted it, hefted it admiringly then, to Irb's amazement, handed it back. "You cannot stay here, though," said Brude. "You have killed men of the village and there would be too much ill feeling."

"So what do we do?" Irb asked, relieved to discover that he was to be allowed to live.

"Gather your things, take a horse each and go to join Nechtan. I hear he has need of warriors. If he does not want you, you should go north, because the Maeatae will certainly welcome you. But don't come back here or I will surely kill you myself."

Irb stared at him, saw the iron in his eyes and nodded. "As you wish." He turned and his men followed him, sheathing their swords.

Brude let out a deep breath of relief. Then Mairead ran to him, throwing herself at him, kissing him on the lips and hugging him so hard that he could scarcely breathe. Then his mother was there, calling his name, as Seoras, Fothair and Caroc the smith came to him as well.

"Thank you for your help," Brude said to Caroc when he had untangled himself from Mairead's arms. "I was in a bit of trouble there."

"My pleasure," said Caroc. "I never did like that sneaky bastard."

"Do me one more favour. Keep an eye on Irb and his men. Make sure they leave."

Caroc nodded. Taking Fothair and Seoras with him, he went off with some other men, including the young guards who had left their post at the gate, to make sure Irb and his gang caused no more trouble.

Mairead held on to Brude tightly while his mother grabbed his free arm so that he was imprisoned by the two of them. "I thought you were going to fight them all," Mairead said.

"I would have if I thought I could have saved you by doing it," he told her. Despite the promise he had made to himself, he knew that he meant it. He saw that she knew it as well, and that she was pleased. He also realised that there was something else troubling her. "What's wrong? Is Colm really dead?"

She nodded. "He's in the broch. Lutrin killed him. But there's more than that. The Romans took Castatin." She looked into his eyes. "They took my son."

Mairead glanced at Mor, who nodded. "He knows."

"Brude, they took our son."

Brude found himself as the new head man of Broch Tava. There was no debate, no formal choosing, but everyone looked to him for advice and instructions. Mairead stayed close to him, so everyone took it for granted that she had chosen him, which was good enough for the villagers.

It was a painful beginning for him. They went to the lower village where he learned how Cruithne had saved the people by holding up the Romans almost single-handedly until he had eventually fallen, as had the other warriors with him. He heard how they had found Seasaidh's ravaged body in the trees at the foot of the hill. Seoc had organised a huge funeral pyre, for there were far too many bodies to bury. They brought Colm's body down from the broch, together with those of the eight men Lutrin had had killed. They also brought the corpse of Lutrin himself, although his body was buried in a shallow grave out on the small headland so that he would not sully the funeral of the others.

Broch Tava had lost almost half of its men in a single day. With Irb and his followers gone, there were barely thirty warriors left and there were so many widows and fatherless children that the village felt as if its heart had been torn out. Not since the great raid that had taken so many men had they known anything like it.

Brude ordered all the slaves to be freed. There were not many of them, and most were grateful and told him so. He dismissed their thanks. He knew all too well what it was to be a slave so he felt a warm glow of satisfaction at freeing them, even if Oengus, Gartnait's son, was among them, surly as ever.

Down near the sea front, as evening drew on, Brude lit the funeral pyre. The flames rose, crackling and writhing into the evening sky as the villagers gathered round, watching in grim silence, comforting each other. It took a long time for the flames to devour so many bodies and the smell was horrible but at last it was done. They all made their way up the hill to the stockade in darkness, their path lit by the moon. Those who had lost their homes moved in to the roundhouses and barrack halls where the warriors had lived, grouping together to help one another.

Once she was satisfied that everyone had shelter for the night, Mairead led Brude into the broch. Although she was tired, frightened, and worried about Castatin and had seen Colm murdered, she wanted to be with Brude so she took him to her bed. They made love, then lay awake talking for most of the night, cradled in each other's arms, together at last and taking comfort in that. They had lost much, but they had also found what they had both been dreaming of for so many years.

"How long have you known?" she asked him. "About Castatin, I mean?"

"My mother told me a few months ago."

"And you never said anything?"

"I didn't think there was much I could do about it. It would have meant fighting Colm. I did not want that."

There was a short silence before she said, "I'm glad. He was not all bad, you know. He just loved power too much. The more he got, the more he wanted."

"I know. He was my friend once. I would have liked it if he had been my friend when I got back."

"He was scared of you," Mairead said. "We all thought you were dead. Then you came back with all those riches and you fight like nobody we have ever seen. It's no wonder he was afraid of you."

"You weren't afraid of me," he pointed out.

"You never threatened my position."

He was glad of the inky blackness inside the broch now for he did not know whether he could say what he wanted to say if she could see his face. "I meant what I said before, that night on the path. It was thinking about you that kept me going while I was a slave," he said, pulling her close. "I didn't know whether I would ever manage to get home but I always wanted to, and it was because of you."

He felt her hand gently stroking his cheek. "That is a nice thought, Brude. I often thought of you too, especially when I looked at Castatin. But are you trying to tell me there have been no other women in your life?"

"Nobody special," he said, after a moment's pause.

Mairead laughed. She pressed her hand on to his bare chest. "Liar! Who was she?"

Now he was really glad it was dark. "Who?"

"The woman you are thinking of right now."

"I'm only thinking about you," he lied, dismissing a vision of Agrippina from his mind.

"If you say so." She lay still then nudged him with her elbow and asked, "Was she pretty?"

He had to laugh. He could not keep a secret from Mairead. "Only on the outside. She was very beautiful but she was selfish and spoiled and not a nice person. And she was married."

"Did her husband find out?"

"No. If he had, I wouldn't be here to talk about it. Anyway, it is in the past. I am here now and so are you. That is what is important." He reached over to kiss her on the lips. "I have always loved you, Mairead."

She returned his kiss. "And I have always loved you, Brude."

Neither of them slept much that night, because they were hungry for each other after so many years of separation, and because they had so much to tell each other but mostly because Mairead kept thinking about her son and where he might be.

"I will get Castatin back," Brude told her as the first grey hint of the pre-dawn began to lighten the upper reaches of the broch.

"How?"

"I don't know yet. But I will get him back. And Barabal, too." He made the promise, not knowing how he would be able to keep it.

A.D. 210

Castatin had thought the ships would take them all the way to Rome, but instead, they made landfall before dusk. He and Barabal were marched ashore to a small fortified camp where there were more Roman soldiers guarding other captives. The two of them were shoved into a corner of the camp where they had shackles placed round their legs while armed guards stood watch over them. Then they were left alone.

There were nine other prisoners, five men and four women. Castatin learned they were from a small coastal village of the Venicones, which had been destroyed because they had tried to oppose the Romans. "We killed a couple of the first ones and stole their horses," one man explained. "Then a whole army of them came. We had no chance."

They were given some food and water. The Romans even brought them a few blankets so they huddled down for the night. Barabal began to cry, her whole body trembling. She cuddled in to Castatin. Because he was still only a boy, he felt uncomfortable and awkward but he put his arms around her, holding her and telling her they would be all right. The truth was that he felt like crying himself. He had been a captive before but that was just as a prisoner of the men of Peart. Even though they had hit him and treated him quite roughly, he had always known that his father was not far away and would come to rescue him eventually. This time, he did not think there was much chance of being rescued. He recalled how Brude had said the Romans made some captives fight each other for their entertainment and how most died without ever having a chance at freedom. Or they were made to work in the fields all day long until they were worn out. He wished Brude were here now. He would save them. Castatin had a mental image of the gladiator smashing his way through the camp, throwing Roman soldiers aside as if they were mere dolls, snapping the leg irons with his bare hands and setting them all free.

But there was nobody except the two of them and the miserable wretches from the Venicones, and the leg irons were solid and unbreakable.

The next day they were marched inland. They were taken to another, much larger camp where there were hundreds of Roman soldiers and yet more prisoners. The captives were coffled together and led south while most of the Romans headed north.

Castatin's biggest fear was being separated from Barabal. Not for himself but for her sake. She barely spoke at all and only ate or drank because he told her to. He still blamed himself for what had happened to her so he felt it was his responsibility to look after her, even though she was three years older than him. If they were separated, he was confident he could survive, but he was not at all sure about Barabal. Once or twice he saw some of the soldiers looking at her. He could not understand what they said but he could understand the look in their eyes, so he got her to do what most of the other women prisoners were doing, which was to make themselves look unattractive and dirty. That way, he hoped, she would not be raped again.

The weary trek southwards went on for day after day. One day, they passed the great Roman Wall that Brude had spoken of. Castatin was amazed at how strong it was. No wonder Brude had talked about it. He had little time to admire it, though. They were marched through the gates and onwards with no rest.

On the other side of the Wall was the cobbled Roman road that Brude had told him about. He wondered whether he was now marching along the same part of the road the former gladiator had walked on when he had first been captured.

By now there were over a hundred captives, all chained together in coffles, all hungry and exhausted by the long marches, dirty and grimed with sweat, all heading ever southwards towards the heart of the empire. Then the weather, which had remained fine for several weeks, turned. The sky grew dark with heavy, grey clouds, which gathered ominously, blanketing the sky. The rain began as heavy drops which splattered on the road and on their faces, but the few drops turned to many as the downpour began. They were soon soaked, their clothes heavy with water, weighing them down and sticking clammily to their skin. The deluge continued all day. They had no shelter that night, so were forced to sleep in the open. The soldiers escorting them tried to light fires but with little success, the sodden wood producing more smoke than flames. The captives huddled together under some trees, trying to stay as warm as they could but it was a miserable night and they got little sleep.

The next day brought more rain in scattered showers, interspersed with bouts of warm sunshine. The same pattern continued for the next few days. Many of the prisoners began coughing, sneezing and feeling unwell. Castatin was one of those who was affected. His head felt hot and his body was wracked with shivers. He wanted to stop, to lie down and rest, but he saw the guards beating anyone who did that, forcing them to stand and press on, so he held on to Barabal and she helped him trudge on for mile after mile, his bones aching and his head throbbing. Yet, in one way he was almost happy because Barabal began speaking to him again. He thought she was, at last, coming out of the depression that had gripped her for so many days. Even if it was only because he was now unwell, he was pleased to hear her encourage him, to see her eyes free of the numb blankness that had engulfed her. There was hope for her yet.

They lost count of the days but eventually they reached a great city with massive walls, large buildings of brick and stone, temples with columns and brightly painted statues, and wide open spaces surrounded by colonnades. The place was crowded with people who stopped to point and stare at them. They were taken to a large wooden structure, which Castatin, even through his fever, recognised when they went inside. It was an amphitheatre. He had listened to Brude's tales of what went on in the arena and he felt his legs turn weak when the soldiers marched them in at spear point before releasing them from the coffles. Castatin thought they were going to be made to fight each other or, worse, be eaten by wild animals. He clung to Barabal's hand, waiting for the end, feeling the tears spring to his eyes. He was in no condition to fight anyone and felt too ill even to walk any further, let alone run from wild beasts.

The soldiers finished unshackling them then left through the same gateway, closing the huge doors behind them.

And nothing happened.

Castatin looked around. He saw that the rows of seats around the amphitheatre were empty except for a handful of soldiers who were slowly patrolling the tiers, watching the slaves in the arena. There were other captives already in the arena. They were sitting or lying down on the earth floor with no danger threatening them. Relief washed over him and he almost laughed aloud.

"What is it?" Barabal asked.

"This is the place where they make people fight, but I think they are just using it to hold us here because there are so many of us."

"Is that good?" Barabal asked, puzzled.

"Well it means we are still alive, so I think that's pretty good."

"We should try to escape," she said.

He smiled weakly when he saw the spirit in her eyes once more. He was glad, but his thumping headache and the hot flushes coursing through his body meant that he could muster little enthusiasm. "You are right, but I need to rest. I feel awful." He slumped to the ground and lay down. The earth was hard-packed and damp but he did not care. The afternoon sun was warm and all he wanted to do was sleep. From far away he heard Barabal calling his name but he was too tired to answer.

In the early morning, Brude climbed to the top of the broch with Mairead. The view from the narrow parapet was incredible. They could see for miles inland, as well as southwards and westwards along the river. The sky was clear, with only light clouds, bringing the promise of another fine day.

Down below, people were already stirring but Brude's eyes were fixed westwards, surveying the river valley. The low hills and the volcanic plug of the Law blocked a lot of the view but away in the distance, where the river faded to the horizon, he saw what he had feared.

Thin tendrils of smoke were rising skywards, twisting and dissipating in the light breeze. They were a long way away, over twenty miles, but they were clearly visible, grey streaks against the blue sky.

He pointed them out to Mairead. "What is it?" she asked.

"I think it is Peart. The Romans are coming."

Brude called the villagers together. They gathered on the green outside the broch, where he had confronted Lutrin and his men the day before. They stood or sat on the grass as he faced them, Mairead at his side. Fothair gave them a knowing look and grinned.

Brude felt uncertain. All of them were watching him, nearly two hundred men, women and children waiting for him to speak but he had no words of encouragement to give them. He felt Mairead's hand gently resting on his arm, offering support. He coughed before saying what he had to say. "We do not have much time, because I believe the Romans are coming. There is smoke from the direction of Peart. Homes are burning. They will be here soon."

There were murmurs of concern from the crowd. Caroc asked, "What will they do when they get here?"

"They seem to be coming intent on conquest. I cannot say for sure, but I expect they intend to kill or enslave anyone they find." This was his greatest fear, a fear he now saw reflected in the faces of the villagers. The raid from the sea had shown what the Romans were like. He held up a hand to quieten them. "I am happy to listen to whatever plan anyone else can offer, but my

316

belief is that we have only one chance. We need to make them think we are already defeated. I will have to talk to them, to try to persuade them there is nothing here for them. We must show them we are beaten already."

"And how do we do that," asked old Seoras.

"We knock down the gates to the stockade, burn a couple more houses near the main gate, and empty the broch. They will certainly want it destroyed."

There were cries of protest at this. He let them talk for a while but it soon became clear that nobody had any other suggestions. Brude went on. "It would be best if the young men and women were able to hide somewhere out of sight in the woodlands. In fact, it would be best if everyone could hide until I can learn what the Romans intend. So you should gather up what you can carry and head into the woods."

"Why don't we go to Dun Nechtan?" Seoras asked.

Brude shook his head sadly. "Because that is where the Romans will go next. If they are intent on destruction, Dun Nechtan will not save us."

"So you are saying we should hide in the forests until they are gone, or just sit here hoping that they think we aren't worth killing or taking as slaves?" It was Oengus, Gartnait's son, freed from his shackles only the previous evening yet already challenging Brude's authority. Brude had an insight into how Colm must have felt when he himself had returned to the village so unexpectedly.

Staring back at Oengus, he replied, "That is exactly what I am saying. You are free to do what you want. Anyone who wants to try to get to Dun Nechtan should go now, for the Romans could be here in a few hours. Those who want to stay have two choices. Either to gather as much as they can and head inland, to hide in the forests, or to wait here and hope I can persuade the Romans that the village is harmless. I will assure them that there will be no resistance. If they want the broch and the rest of the village burned, we will not protest. When they have gone everyone can come back and try to rebuild, or build somewhere else. But as soon as I can, I must go to try to find Castatin and Barabal."

Seoc nodded. That last part was what he wanted to hear. Oengus, though, was not satisfied. "But you will be safe because you are a Roman yourself. You can just walk away and leave us here to suffer whatever the Romans want to do to us." Whatever else a year in slavery had done to Oengus, it had not made him any less hostile to Brude. The young man spat on the ground. "If Peart is truly destroyed then I am going to Dun Nechtan. There are warriors there who will fight, not cowards who want to run and hide."

"Do as you wish, and take anyone else who wants to go," Brude told him bluntly. He did not think it was worth telling Oengus that Nechtan intended to submit to Rome if he could. The young man would discover that soon enough.

There was more discussion, more questions but there was nothing else Brude could tell them. In the end, Oengus, who clearly had no intention of going back to Peart to see what had become of his family, decided to go north to Dun Nechtan. Many of the warriors, together with some of their women and children, went with him. Fothair urged Brude to stop them but Brude said that everyone should make their own decision about what they wanted to do. "I don't know what is for the best," he admitted. "Perhaps they are right."

Caroc was appointed to lead the bulk of the remaining villagers into the woodland to the east. He began organising work parties to gather as many supplies as they could. They ransacked the broch where they found a great store of Roman coins, which Caroc gave to Brude. "You should have these," the burly smith told him. "We won't need them."

Seoras announced that he would stay in the village. Quite a few of the older men and women said they would stay, too. "We're too old to go traipsing around in the forests," Seoras said. "And I doubt the Romans will want us as slaves."

"Perhaps not," agreed Brude, "but that is not all they can do."

"You mean they might kill us? Well, we will take that chance. You can use your magic on them and persuade them to leave us in peace."

Brude was appalled at the faith the villagers had in him. He was not at all sure that he would be able to persuade the Romans to leave the villagers unharmed. "I have no real rank among the Romans," he told Seoras. "I was a slave. Even after I was freed, I was still at the bottom of their society. They are just as likely to kill me as to listen to me."

"You underestimate yourself," Seoras told him, which made Brude feel simultaneously better and yet more worried.

Brude turned to Fothair. "Could you go and look for a horse for me, before Oengus and his men take them all? I have a couple of things to do but then I'd better go and try to find out where the Romans are."

"I'll get two," said Fothair. "I thought I'd tag along with you for a while. I'd like to see Rome."

Brude was relieved. He had wanted to ask Fothair to come with him but he was reluctant to, in case the tall man took it as an order. Better that he came of his own accord. "Thank you. But I have no intention of going all the way to Rome. Come to think of it, we'll need three horses, one each plus a spare to carry food and act as a replacement if one should go lame. If we can get past the army, we will be pushing our mounts hard."

"I'll see to it," Fothair said with a decisive nod.

"We'll not have many horses left at this rate," Caroc pointed out.

"And we'll need four," said Mairead.

Brude stiffened. He twisted his head to look at her. "Why?"

"If you think I'm letting you go away without me, after I've only just found you, you have another think coming. We will find our son together."

Fothair laughed. He looked at Brude questioningly.

Seoras laughed too. "Don't bother arguing, boy. You'll never win."

"Four horses then," said Brude. He decided it would be best to argue with Mairead later, when they were alone. Seoc and Caroc had obviously picked up on Mairead's comment about who Castatin's parents were, but they said nothing. Seoras would explain it to them or, more likely, his mother would. She had probably told everyone else by now anyway.

While Fothair was fetching the horses and gathering supplies, Brude asked Mairead to cut his hair short. He sat patiently while she trimmed away the growth of the past year. She was far from expert but he looked at himself in a small mirror and reckoned the shorter hair made him look less like a Pritani. Fothair was back by the time Mairead had finished. The two men went down to the lower village. The carcass of Brude's mule had been carted away to be butchered and skinned. It was no good for feeding people but the dogs would eat it and the skin and bones could serve a whole range of uses.

With Fothair's help, Brude cleared away the blackened timbers of the ruins of his house. He found the spot where his bed had been and began digging with an antler pick. "What's down there?" Fothair asked him.

"Some things I hoped I'd never need."

The earth was hard, baked by the flames, but he soon reached the clay jar which was undamaged. He tugged off the sealskin cover and retrieved the contents. He looped the sword over his shoulder then shoved the money and his papers into a pack, which he slung on his back. Fothair raised an eyebrow. "You're a rich man what with that buried treasure and the stuff from the broch."

"Where we are going, we may need a lot of money," Brude replied. "And it's not much use here, is it? It's only important men who use Roman coins."

"You are intending to buy back Castatin and Barabal?"

"Better than trying to fight the whole empire on our own."

"Aye, you have a point there."

Brude lost his argument with Mairead. She was ready and waiting for him, wearing riding breeches and a leather shirt with a woollen jerkin, her hair tied back and her expression full of determination. Fothair beamed when he saw her, complimenting her on how lovely she was. Brude shot him a look that spoke volumes.

Fothair had found four horses, three saddled with Roman-style saddles, high at the front and back, with four pommels, providing a solid seat that allowed the riders to move their arms freely while still being able to stay on the horse. The fourth horse had bundles of baggage strapped to it.

Fothair had also found a long sword from somewhere and had strapped it at his side. Brude told him to get rid of it. "You can't wear that," he told him irritably.

Fothair, who realised Brude's bad temper was because Mairead was coming with them, smiled innocently. "Why not?" he asked. "You've got a sword."

"I am a Roman citizen and I can prove it. The two of you are never going to convince anyone you are citizens. You'll have to be my slaves. Slaves don't carry swords, especially not bloody great things like that."

Fothair pulled a face. "As Erecura is my witness, you are a hard man to follow. You only freed me yesterday but now you want me to be a slave again." Mairead laughed. Fothair grinned at her. "What about you, my lady? Are you his slave too?"

"Only when I want to be, Fothair," she smiled. "Apparently you are my brother if anyone asks."

"Well I'm glad to hear it, my lady. Why?"

Brude said, "It will explain why she sleeps with me and not you."

Fothair had the good grace to look embarrassed. "Master's privilege?"

"That's right. And just you thank the gods I am not a Greek or you'd find yourself on the receiving end of the same privilege."

Fothair got the message and shut up, unstrapping his sword. Reluctantly, he handed it to Caroc who, with Seoras, Mor and Seoc, had come to see them off. Brude helped Mairead climb onto her horse, then he and Fothair mounted as well. He looked down at his friends. "Good luck to you all."

"And to you," nodded Seoras.

To Caroc, Brude said, "Keep the people safe if you can."

Caroc nodded. He had already sent most of the villagers on the march eastwards, following the shoreline but cutting inland, keeping to the shelter of the woodlands. They had some cattle, sheep and goats and as much as they could carry. "We'll keep out of sight," the burly smith assured him. Neither of them mentioned what would happen if they could not return before the harvest time. They could scrape a living in the forests during the summer but the winter would be hard without supplies of wheat, oats and barley. There was no need to talk about that, for they all understood the danger of going hungry.

With a nod to Seoc, his promise to find Barabal already made, Brude nudged his horse into motion and the three of them set off, out through the broken gates of the stockade, which had fallen to Caroc's axe. They rode westwards to find the Romans.

They skirted the volcanic plug of the Law, riding at a slow trot, Brude's eyes constantly searching ahead. When possible, he kept to the high ground to get the best views of the river valley and the broad plain. Much of the land was forested but, here and there, were gaps where small farms carved a living from the land. Most of the inhabitants of these farms sent their surplus produce to Broch Tava as tribute in return for Colm's protection. There was no protection to be offered now.

They did not have long to wait before they saw what they had been looking for. Barely two hours out from Broch Tava, as they reached the edge of a low ridge and looked west, a line of horsemen appeared, still a few miles away but heading slowly and steadily eastwards. They were in a long column but with outriders on either side, keeping a watchful eye as they rode. The early afternoon sun glinted off armour, letting Brude know who they were. "Scouting party," he said.

"There are a lot of them," Fothair pointed out nervously.

"I guess around thirty. Probably one *Turma*. Come on, let's go and meet them."

They went down into a dip, then up another low rise. When they crested it, they could see the Roman horsemen cantering up the other side. The leader wore a red cloak, which hung across his horse's rump. Brude stopped at the crest of the ridge where he waited, telling the others to be sure to make no threatening move. He nudged his horse forwards so that he was a few paces ahead of his companions, then held his arms out wide to either side, showing he was not holding a weapon.

The Romans slowed as they approached then stopped a few hundred paces from him. The leader gestured with his hands and the column split, riders moving to left and right in a practised manoeuvre to form a line facing the ridge. The man in the cloak, with six others, rode on. He came up the slope to meet Brude who called out in Latin, "Hail, Caesar!" He thumped his fist against his chest then lifted his arm in salute.

The Romans reached him in an extended line, the leader stopping close to him. He was a middle-aged, veteran soldier, with cynical eyes that surveyed Brude and his companions warily. The man next to him was not in uniform but wore a plain tunic and breeches and a thick leather jerkin. He spoke to Brude, talking in his own tongue but Brude stopped him. "I speak Latin," he said, looking at the officer rather than his interpreter. "I am Marcus Septimius Brutus, citizen of Rome."

The Romans were surprised and the officer's eyebrows shot up questioningly. "What are you doing here?"

"I'm a travelling merchant," said Brude. "I have sold my goods and am on my way back. And you are?"

The officer growled. "Tiberius Servilius Cato, Decurion Speculatorum." That confirmed Brude's guess. A Decurion was normally in charge of one Turma, a cavalry unit with a nominal strength of thirty-two men. The *Speculatores* were scouts, the eyes of the army. Each man carried a lance and a long, heavy sword, a *spatha*, although their main job was not to fight, merely to find the enemy.

"The rumours are true then?" Brude asked, trying to chat pleasantly so as to keep the man at ease. "The emperor really has come north?"

Cato nodded. "He has three legions and as many auxiliaries. He is determined to crush the rebellious tribes and his army is not far behind us."

Brude smiled. "Then perhaps I can help. I have travelled a fair bit around these parts and I have a fair idea of what is going on."

Cato wasn't convinced. He indicated Brude's companions. "Who are they?"

"My slaves."

Cato grunted noncommittally. "So what can you tell me of the locals round here? That's our job. To find out what's ahead. I was told there is a hostile village to the east."

"Then it is just as well that you have met me," Brude told him, "for I can tell you that you are wasting your time going that way. A lot has happened there in the recent days and things are very much changed."

"Like what?" Cato demanded. He was listening to Brude but his eyes were constantly watching the surrounding area, wary, expecting a trap of some sort.

"Perhaps we should ride back and speak to whoever commands the troops who are following you. I can give him the full story."

"Perhaps you can tell me now so I know I would not be wasting my time." Cato's voice was harsh and the threat of violence was clear in his stance.

Brude realised he would not talk his way past this man so he told him how the imperial navy had raided the village, killed many warriors and burned the houses. He explained that the rest of the villagers had fought among themselves, losing more men when the head man was challenged and killed. Now the few who were left were mostly frightened old men and women who wanted nothing but peace with their neighbours and with Rome.

"They have one of those stone towers there?" Cato asked.

The Romans had done their intelligence work well, thought Brude. There was no point in lying. If he did, he would be found out. Cato already knew about the broch. What else did he know? Keeping his face calm and trying to appear as much like the friendly trader he claimed to be, Brude said, "Yes, there is a tower but it is a bit of a ruin. The peasants will probably hide inside it if you approach. If you have some ballistae you could knock it down in a few days but I doubt it is worth the bother. If you ask them to come out and assure them you won't harm them, they'll probably hand it over to you without a fight. They just want to be left in peace."

"You seem to know a lot about it," said Cato, suspicion etched in his expression.

"I arrived there a few hours after your navy had raided the place. I spent yesterday evening, and this morning, speaking to them."

Cato chewed his lips thoughtfully. He clearly wasn't sure whether to believe Brude or not. Brude had hoped that the officer he met would be a young, inexperienced nobleman he could persuade easily but this gnarled veteran was a hard nut to crack. Turning to the interpreter at his side, Cato snapped, "Speak to the others. See if they tell the same story."

The man nodded, tugging his horse's reins. Brude said to him, in Latin, "Best speak to the woman. The man's an idiot. Doesn't know his arse from his elbow." The man ignored him and he began asking both of Brude's companions questions about events in Broch Tava. Brude's heart was racing but he forced himself to remain outwardly calm. He had been over the story several times with Mairead and Fothair. He had to hope they would remember enough to back up what he had said.

After a short while, the interpreter came back. He told Cato, "Pretty much the same story, sir. It seems the navy did a right good job on the place. They killed all their best warriors."

"The words of slaves should not be taken unless they are tortured first," Cato mused, his dark eyes watching Brude as he spoke.

"This is hardly a court of law," Brude replied. "I don't think torture is necessary. I don't want to lose my slaves."

Cato snorted. The fate of two slaves was no concern of his. "Very well, come with us and we'll have a look at this place together. Afterwards, if you've told the truth, you can come back and meet the legate. He can decide what to do with you. If you've lied...." He left his words hanging but his meaning was clear enough. His tone made it plain that this decision was not a matter for discussion. The three Boresti were surrounded by Roman horsemen and made to ride back to Broch Tava. "If this is a trap, I'll have your throats cut," Cato promised.

The ride back was an uncomfortable one. The Roman cavalrymen were tough and hard, making Brude worry about Mairead riding in their midst. He saw the tension on her face as she tried to ignore the men around her. Even Fothair's habitual good humour was dampened. He rode in stony silence, all too aware of the potential for violence.

As they approached the broch, Cato called a halt several hundred paces from the stockade. The troopers once again formed a line extending to left and right. Cato waved Brude forwards. "It looks deserted," he said flatly.

"I expect most of them are hiding," said Brude, matter-of-factly. He knew that his mother and Seoras were there, along with around two dozen others, mostly the elderly, but there was no sign of them.

The gates to the stockade lay smashed on the ground. The broch stood silent and empty but Cato was cautious. He sent a patrol of six riders round the north side, between the abandoned fields and the stockade, waiting patiently while they scouted around. They returned to report no signs of life. Then six more men were sent into the stockade. If there was a trap waiting, these men would trigger it. Brude, who had walked into the arena many times, admired the way the chosen men simply got on with the task. They were probably nervous and apprehensive but they showed no outward signs, simply walking their mounts cautiously through the broken gates, lances at the ready. Two of them stopped at the gate while the others went deeper into the village.

Time seemed to drag. Brude sat, his heart in his mouth, watching the stockade, dreading to hear the sounds of people screaming which would tell him that the soldiers were slaughtering the few villagers who remained. But all remained peaceful. One of the soldiers turned his mount and rode back to Cato. Sitting next to the Roman officer, Brude could hear every word. "There are some old folk in there," the soldier reported. "No weapons and precious little of any value."

"Have you checked the tower?" Cato demanded.

"Not yet, sir. We could do with some more men for that. And an interpreter." He shot a glance at the small man who spoke the Pritani tongue.

Cato nodded. He snapped his fingers at the interpreter. "Mata, go and speak to the peasants. Find out what you can." Then he said to the soldier, "Take ten more men and check out the tower."

Again they waited, the horses flicking their tails to ward off the flies that swarmed around them. Cato turned to Brude. "So how did you learn their language?"

"My father was of the Boresti." Brude explained. "That allows me to move among them. It's a living, but I'll never be rich. I thought I could bring them some of the wealth of Rome but most of them aren't interested in much apart from gold and silver." He hoped his tone was pitched so that Cato would hear the usual contempt of a Roman for barbarians.

"Savages, that's all they are," Cato said scornfully. "There's precious little loot to be had on this campaign, that's for sure. It's no wonder the Picti are always raiding south of the Wall. They've got nothing of value themselves."

Brude hoped his silence would be taken as agreement.

After what seemed an age, the soldiers returned with Mata, the interpreter. "Tower's empty, sir. It's been looted by the looks of it. And most of the people have gone."

Mata confirmed it. "There are only a few of them left, all too old or too stubborn to leave. They say the rest went northwards."

Cato twisted his head to stare at Brude. "What lies north-wards?"

This was the moment Brude had dreaded. This was the lie that might save the people of Broch Tava but condemn their fellow tribes people in Dun Nechtan. But Brude could think of no way of avoiding it. The Romans would learn of Dun Nechtan soon enough, if they did not know of it already. And if they went there, they might leave Broch Tava alone. He looked at Cato, using the blank expression he had learned as a slave. "There's a hill fort. It's where most of the Boresti live."

Cato considered this news. "And east of here?"

Brude shrugged. "A few small farms, the odd, tiny village. Nothing of any great note. It's mostly woodland and forest. The shoreline is either sand or cliffs. Not many people live out that way."

Cato looked meaningfully at Mata who simply shrugged. He could speak the language, but he did not know the country. Cato made a decision. "Right! That tower has to come down." He turned to the soldier who had led the advance party. "Take your contubernium and garrison the tower. I'll send some engineers to knock it down. Once that's done, you rejoin us."

The soldier nodded. "Yes, sir. Where will you be, sir?"

"With the legions. Probably somewhere to the north. Find us."

The soldier snapped a salute then he and seven other men rode back to the stockade to guard the broch. Cato rode with them to see the village for himself, taking Mata with him, but the rest of the Romans stayed where they were while Brude, Mairead and Fothair sat nervously watching. Mairead nudged her horse alongside Brude. "What's going on?" she asked.

"They are going to leave some men to guard the broch until they can send some more soldiers to knock it down."

"Why?" Mairead had lived all her life in or around the broch. The thought that it would be destroyed filled her with anguish.

Brude had no words of comfort to give her. "They know that most of the people went northwards to Dun Nechtan, so that is where the Roman army will go. They don't want to leave a stronghold behind them for anyone to use against them."

"But it's our home!" Mairead insisted.

Brude could only clasp her hand. "The people are more important than the place," he said softly.

Cato and Mata soon returned. The officer rode up to Brude. "It looks like your information has been correct."

Brude shrugged it off modestly. "So can I go now?"

Cato's mouth twitched in a grim smile. "Oh, no! You are coming back with us. The legate will want to speak to you."

The legionaries of Legio XX Valeria Victrix were marching along the north bank of the Tava when Cato's troop found them. They must have crossed the river at Peart and were heading eastwards, five thousand soldiers, with as many auxiliaries and a baggage train that included artillery. The legate, Gaius Folconius Priscus, called a halt when Cato brought Brude and the others to meet him. He gathered his officers to hear Brude's story.

"You say the Boresti will not oppose us?" the legate asked Brude after he had heard Cato's report.

"I don't think they will. Their main centre is a hill fort about twenty miles north east of here. The chieftain knows he cannot face you in battle. If you send emissaries, he will seek peace." This was the best he could do for Nechtan and his people; try to persuade the Romans to seek peace with them. He tapped a finger on the map, which the legate's aides had spread out on a small wooden table. "Your main problem lies further north. The Maeatae are a powerful tribe. They are the ones who have been sailing down the coast to raid the province. The Boresti are afraid of them, too. If you want my opinion, you would be better served going that way than wasting time on the Boresti."

Priscus stared at him icily. "When I need the advice of a merchant freedman, I will ask for it," he said coldly. "Still, Cato says your information has been good so far, so I will think on this."

"Thank you, sir," Brude said, knowing he had misjudged his man. "Do I have your permission to go south? I would prefer to return to civilisation as soon as I can."

Priscus did not even look at him. "No. You will stay with the legion. I may have need of you later. Porcius will show you where you can sleep." A young tribune snapped a salute then ushered Brude out of Priscus' presence. Brude knew enough about high-class Romans not to protest. No doubt the main topic of conversation between Priscus and his staff would be whether to trust him or not. His manumission papers had been studied carefully and his status had been accepted. Whether his trustworthiness was accepted would determine what happened next.

Porcius, young and earnest, told him to ride with the baggage train. The tribune found a quartermaster who was able to unearth a spare tent, which was loaded onto Brude's pack-horse. Porcius signed for the tent, telling Brude to stay near the baggage train at all times. Then he spoke to the quartermaster again and Brude was certain that the guards would not only be protecting the baggage but would be watching him and his alleged slaves as well.

While the legion rested for a light meal, he sat with Mairead and Fothair. They dug out some of their own meagre rations.

"They've got a few interpreters with them," Fothair told Brude. "Mostly men from the Votadini. They've been asking questions."

"What do you think is going to happen?" Mairead asked, her concern clearly showing.

"I think I have convinced them to bypass Broch Tava and head north. I suggested they avoid Dun Nechtan as well, but I'm not sure whether they'll listen. The Romans are always nervous about leaving fortresses behind them. What I don't want is for them to keep us with them, but that seems to be their intention at the moment."

"Why would they do that?"

"I expect they will want to see if I've told them the truth before they let us go. What really worries me is if they send people to speak to Nechtan. With Irb and his men having gone there, he might tell them a different story to the one we've been giving. We've told them more or less the truth but if they find out I am not a trader, we could be in trouble."

"And we cannot go back to Broch Tava either?" Mairead had never been so far from her home and the thought that the broch was to be destroyed was still troubling her, as was the fear of what might happen to the villagers. On top of all that, her greatest worry was that Castatin was being taken further away from her with each hour that passed. She was a strong woman, a woman of the Pritani, but the strain was evident in her face.

Brude's fears were proved correct. The three of them were to accompany the legion as it turned to march north eastwards towards the hills. Having brought the bad news, Porcius rode with them for the first part of the journey.

"Are we under arrest?" Brude asked him.

"Not at all," said Porcius with an affable smile. "But I'm afraid you are not free to leave either. At least, not until the legate is sure you are not part of an elaborate trap."

"I thought it might be something like that, but I'm keen to get as far away from any fighting as I can. That's why I was heading south in the first place. War is not good for business. Has your navy confirmed my story yet?"

"Indeed they have," Porcius confirmed.

The tribune seemed pleasant enough so Brude decided to take a chance. "Did they happen to say anything about some villagers they captured and took away?"

"No. Why?"

Brude gave Porcius as innocent a look as he could muster. "I had my eye on one of them, that's all. Pretty young thing."

Porcius wasn't sure how to take that, but he said, "Well if they did take any slaves, they'll be on the way south by now. There have been fairly regular batches sent back to Eboracum."

"Really? I might try there then. You know, get in and buy up the pick of the bunch before they ship them all off to Rome."

"You won't make much money on them," observed Porcius. "There will be a glut on the market. Anyway, these Picti are usually too unruly to make good slaves. I'm surprised you let your two roam around without keeping them in irons."

Brude laughed amiably. "Well, I have been fortunate, I admit. The woman had a miserable life before I got her and she's just happy to stay with me. And her brother's a simpleton. He'll do what she says."

Porcius turned in his saddle to look at Fothair and Mairead who were following close behind. Neither of them could understand what he and Brude were talking about but Brude had warned them how to act around Romans, so they both lowered their gaze when the young officer looked at them. "Well I can see why you want the woman," Porcius said. "A bit too barbaric for my tastes, though." He gave Brude a knowing look, adding with a wink, "Still, I suppose that doesn't matter in the dark anyway."

In the early evening the legions halted and the legionaries set about establishing a marching camp. Each man was laden down on the march with a spade and some wooden stakes. While some men stood guard and others set up tents, the majority began digging a ditch, using lines of small marker flags which the legion's advance party had laid out for them, showing where the camp was to be set up. They rapidly threw up an earth rampart, on top of which they planted the stakes to make a wooden palisade.

Fothair was impressed. "We should get them to rebuild the village," he commented dryly. "They'd have it done in no time." He had been amazed at how many soldiers there were. When the Pritani spoke of an army, they meant any number of warriors over thirty-five. Fothair admitted that he had not really believed the stories Brude had told of the power of Rome. Now, though, he was starting to realise just how many men the Romans could put into the field. When Brude told him that this was just one legion, Fothair could only shake his head in wonder.

They pitched their tent, watching the soldiers to see how it was done. The Romans usually had eight men to a tent, which was very crowded, but there was plenty of room for three people. Sleeping under the leather tent was a novel experience for all of them. In other circumstances, they might have enjoyed it, but a second day had passed since Castatin and Barabal had been taken and they were still trapped in the midst of thousands of Roman soldiers. They found it hard to relax and none of them got much sleep.

Brude had expected the army would march on the following day but the legion stayed in camp, and for another day after that. The soldiers were kept busy but there was nothing for Brude, Mairead and Fothair to do except sit around and wait, fretting over the delay. Brude was worried for Mairead. There were virtually no other women in the camp and he saw that she was attracting attention. His own status was not clear to most of the soldiers so he made a point of chatting to the guards who watched the baggage train. He let it be known that he had once marched with the legions in Germania. When the soldiers heard this, they relaxed their hostility enough to pass on the latest rumours. "They say that Caesar is coming to join us. He's bringing the Sixth with him," one of them told him.

"Caesar? The emperor himself?"

"Nah, his son. We've got three Caesars now; the emperor and his two sons."

"You can't have enough Caesars," chuckled one old veteran. "Emperors know they have to keep the legions happy."

"Any idea why he's coming?" Brude asked, as innocently as he could.

"I heard he's won a great victory over in the west. Sent the Caledonii running for their lives. Now he's coming over here to do the same to the rest of the barbarians."

A second soldier spat and said, "I heard he was leaving because of those blasted biting insects that come out every evening. Eat you alive, they will. When he heard they don't bother you so much over here, he decided to change his plans."

Brude politely joined in the laughter. "Do you know when he's expected to get here?"

The soldier shrugged. "Who knows? Why? You keen to meet him?"

"I'm keen to head south and get away from the war. I'm a trader, but I've got nothing to trade."

"You're all right," said another solider with a leer. "You've got your woman to keep you warm at nights."

Brude saw that the other soldiers were interested at the mention of Mairead. To stop any of them getting any ideas, he said with a laugh, "Don't get too excited, lads. She's got the pox." They laughed and the moment passed. Later, when he told Mairead and Fothair about the emperor's son coming, he decided it would be best not to tell her what he had said to the soldiers.

Caracalla, the emperor's elder son, rode into camp the next afternoon, bringing the Sixth Legion with him. They quickly set up camp nearby while Caracalla called together all the senior officers for an evening meal. To Brude's surprise, Porcius came to summon him to join the gathering. Mairead was worried by the fact that he had no decent clothes to wear to meet the emperor's son, but Brude had heard enough about Caracalla over the years to feel apprehensive about why he had been summoned. He recalled that Caracalla had had his own father-in-law executed without trial, and had been responsible for Pollio's death in the arena. Emperors were dangerous men to be around and Brude wanted to keep as far away as possible from the man who would be the next emperor.

But it was not possible. Nobody refused an imperial invitation so Brude, dressed in his shabby travelling clothes, followed Porcius to the legate's huge tent, which was already surrounded by soldiers of the Praetorian Guard, the imperial family's personal bodyguard. The Praetorians eyed everyone, even other Roman soldiers, with suspicion. They had a privileged position, close to the emperor. They earned more pay than the legionaries but hardly ever had to fight. It was a position they guarded jealously.

Porcius led Brude inside the huge tent where tables had been set around the edges in a square shape. Most of the diners sat in simple chairs but there was one, at the centre of the table facing the entrance, which was high-backed, ornate and covered with a purple cloth. There sat the emperor's son, with Priscus on his right side.

Caracalla had been a teenage boy when Brude had last seen him in the imperial box at the arena. That had been the day Josephus had died, the day Brude had gained his freedom. Now the emperor's son was a young man of twenty-four, dressed in a shining breastplate and greaves, with a purple cloak fastened at his throat. Behind him stood a Praetorian holding his helmet with its white horsehair plume. Caracalla's beard was neatly trimmed, even in the middle of a war campaign. Brude could sense his authority immediately and knew he had to be careful. This young man had a reputation for cruelty and ruthlessness.

Brude felt self-conscious, all too aware of his shabby clothes when Porcius marched him into the centre of the tables to introduce him to the emperor's son. Caracalla looked at him with interest. When he spoke, it was with all the self-assurance of a young man who was used to being in command. The officers seated round the tables were respectfully silent.

"We share the same name," Caracalla said to him. "You are a freedman?"

"Yes, Caesar. Your father freed me himself."

"Really? What for?"

"I fought in the arena at the Secular Games."

Caracalla looked at him in genuine surprise, studying his face as if trying to recognise him. "You were the Secutor who tangled himself in the Retiarius' net?"

Brude was astonished that Caracalla remembered the fight. He could never forget it himself, but the emperor and his family must have seen hundreds of similar displays in the arena. Caracalla, though, obviously still remembered it. "That was me, Caesar," Brude admitted.

"Well, I am delighted to meet you," Caracalla said, sounding as though he meant it. "I remember watching that fight and thinking you were a dead man. You took a big risk, did you not?"

"It was either that or die," Brude told him. "He was better than me."

"Apparently not, or you wouldn't be here," Caracalla said with a laugh, which was dutifully echoed by his officers. Even the men too far away to have heard the comment joined in. Then Caracalla said, "So what brings you to this god-forsaken part of the world?"

"Trade, Caesar. I was born near here and I thought I could make myself rich by bringing Roman goods to the people here."

"And have you managed that?"

"Regrettably not." Brude decided some exaggeration of events would help. "I was not popular with the village chieftains. They thought I was too Roman."

Caracalla snorted. "Savages, the whole lot of them. But now they are seeing the power of Rome. You say this Nechtan wants peace with us?"

"He certainly does, Caesar. He is very afraid of you." Most Romans liked that sort of flattery. Brude hoped that Caracalla was no exception.

"With good reason. Well, we shall soon see what he is made of. We march tomorrow and you, Marcus Septimius Brutus, will accompany us. I wish to learn more of this land and its people. Knowledge gives us power, does it not, Priscus?"

Priscus nodded dutifully. "Indeed it does, Caesar."

Brude felt his heart sinking. He wanted to get away. He had to start the search for Castatin. With every day that passed, the chances of finding the boy diminished. But there was no way to avoid an imperial command. He was dismissed with a casual wave and given a seat at a lower table where he ate as fine a meal as he could expect from a marching camp. He sipped at some wine, the first he had tasted since he had crossed the Wall. The trappings of Roman civilisation were available to him again but his son, whom he barely knew, had been taken and he felt as trapped as he had ever done when he was a slave.

Mairead was almost distraught when she learned they were going northwards. "What do they want us for?" she wanted to know.

"The emperor's son seems to think I can help them," said Brude. "I am sorry, Mairead. I do not want this, but I don't know how to get out of it."

"Just tell him!" she said.

"It's not that easy," he tried to explain. "Nobody argues with a member of the imperial family. Not if they want to live."

The legions pushed north, through the forested hills, cavalry scouts ranging far and wide in front and to either side of the marching columns. The one good thing that raised their spirits was that the Romans were heading away from Broch Tava. Brude wondered how Seoras and his mother were faring but there was no way to find out. He could only hope that they were still safe and well.

They made camp again within sight of Dun Nechtan, both legions together in a large camp. Brude was again summoned to Caracalla's tent but this time there was no meal. Instead, the emperor's son wanted to know all about Dun Nechtan, its defences and its warriors. Brude told them everything he knew, knowing that to lie would not help Nechtan or his people and could only harm his own situation if he was found to be telling less than the truth. As he spoke, aides jotted down notes while Priscus and his officers sometimes raised questions, asking him to expand or clarify on what he had said. Brude felt sick at heart, as if he was betraying his people, but if he wanted to save Castatin, to keep Mairead out of danger, there was nothing else he could do.

A sentry came into the tent and saluted. "Caesar, a delegation from the barbarians has arrived. They wish to speak to you."

Caracalla's eyes sparkled. "Do they indeed? Well, bring them in then, and let us speak. You'd best send an interpreter in as well."

Brude moved to stand behind Caracalla and the other Romans, trying to be inconspicuous. He had no idea who would be in the delegation, but he would prefer not to be recognised. Caracalla had not dismissed him, so he had to stay.

The flaps of the doorway were pulled back and three people were ushered in. Brude's heart sank again. Nechtan himself led the way, behind him his son, Eairsidh and, finally, Veleda, her long grey hair tied with a golden circlet. She saw Brude almost immediately but only the flash of recognition in her eyes revealed that she knew him. Nechtan had eyes only for Caracalla as he spoke through the interpreter, Mata, offering peace to Rome. Nechtan, Brude thought, was a clever man. His son was with him which, to the Romans, would suggest that they had the ruling dynasty in their power.

Nechtan laid his sword at Caracalla's feet but he did not grovel. He was a chieftain of the Pritani so he stood proudly while he spoke, with Mata translating his words into Latin. In what must have been the hardest speech of his life, Nechtan offered to surrender all the gold and silver in his possession, offered himself and his son as hostages and told Caracalla that the Boresti would provide warriors to act as guides to help the Romans fight the Maeatae to the north. In return, he sought Rome's protection for his people. It was a powerful plea, an offer of almost everything the Boresti had.

Caracalla listened, drumming his fingers on the arm of his chair, a thin smile playing around his lips. When Nechtan had finished speaking, the young Caesar unexpectedly turned to Brude. "Brutus, has our friend Mata translated this savage's words accurately?"

Brude, suddenly the focus of attention, and now recognised by Nechtan and Eairsidh, nodded. "Yes, Caesar. They have offered complete surrender."

"And do you think they will keep faith with me?"

Brude hesitated. He felt uncomfortable being so near to the centre of events, unsure of himself with so many powerful men around him waiting for his opinion. Priscus had reprimanded him when he had ventured to voice an opinion yet here was Caracalla, second only to the emperor, asking him what he thought.

He looked at Nechtan. He saw the pride in the old warrior and understood what it was costing him to stand before Caracalla as a suppliant. Turning to Caracalla, he said, "I have heard him described as an old woman. I do not believe he would dare do anything other than what he says."

Caracalla nodded. He rubbed his chin thoughtfully as he studied the three Boresti standing in front of him. Nechtan proudly returned his gaze, as did Veleda. The old woman, apparently oblivious to the watching Caesar, suddenly spoke to Brude. "I did not think to see you here in the midst of our enemies, Brude, son of Anndra."

"I did not think to find myself here either," Brude replied. "Broch Tava is destroyed. I was trying to return south."

"But you are caught, as are we. Now we offer our head to the foe, for cutting off the head is the way to kill a people as well as a beast, is it not? *Cut off the head and the beast will die.*"

"What is she saying?" Caracalla demanded testily.

"She recognises me, Caesar," Brude told him, "and accuses me of aiding the enemies of the Boresti. That is all."

Caracalla was annoyed. In Roman eyes, women should not speak in the presence of men unless invited to do so. Even then, their opinions on matters of war or statecraft were rarely worth listening to. "Who is this old woman?" he wanted to know.

"She is one of Nechtan's advisers," Brude said, choosing his words carefully.

"Have you told him I am a druid?" Veleda asked in a firm, clear voice.

"I have told him you are an adviser to Nechtan, but you should stay silent. Women are not expected to speak as advisers."

"You should tell him I am a druid," Veleda said, her voice firm, her eyes challenging him, daring him to say it. Brude struggled to maintain his blank expression, wondering why she was so insistent. Surely she knew what the Romans would do to her if they knew, or even suspected, that she was a druid?

"What is she saying now?" Caracalla asked him.

Brude glanced at Mata, knowing the man had understood. He could not lie because Mata would be able to reveal it, but he did not want to say what Veleda was urging him to tell the Romans. The old woman was manoeuvring him into a hopeless position. He looked at her again. She nodded and smiled a smile of grim satisfaction. He realised that she knew precisely what she was doing. Reluctantly, he looked Caracalla in the eyes and said, "She claims to be a druid."

There was an intake of breath from most of the Romans. Priscus exclaimed, "The druids were wiped out in the time of Nero!"

Caracalla turned to Mata, raising a questioning eyebrow. "Is that what she says?"

Mata nodded. "Yes, Caesar. The woman says we should tell you she is a druid."

Caracalla stared at Veleda. She returned his gaze unflinchingly. Unable to break her, the young Caesar turned to the nearest Praetorian. "Have them kept under armed guard."

The guard saluted, signalled to other Praetorians and the three Boresti were ushered out of the tent at sword point.

When they were gone, Priscus said, "She must die, Caesar."

"Of course she must," Caracalla agreed. "Whether she is actually a druid or not, she claims to be one. We cannot have druids running around, stirring up trouble against us. But she will die in the morning, in full view of the rest of the savages up on their hill. Let them all see what happens to druids."

"And the other two?" Priscus asked.

Caracalla waved a hand dismissively. "Oh, kill them too. That will leave the barbarians without a leader."

Brude and the others were dismissed. Brude felt drained and desolate. With a few words, Caracalla had condemned Nechtan and his son and there was nothing anyone could do to save them. All because Veleda had talked herself into the grave. Why?

It was after nightfall now, the camp lit by dozens of flaming torches and braziers. Brude could find his way around a military camp easily, even in the dark, but as he made his way towards the baggage area where his own tent was pitched, Mata approached him. "A word in private?" the interpreter said.

They walked slowly through the sleeping camp, side by side. "What is it?" Brude asked.

Mata kept his voice low. "I am of the Votadini. I serve because I must. It keeps our people safe from the wrath of Rome."

Brude nodded. "I understand. You live in the shadow of the Wall."

"Exactly! We all have to make compromises. Some of my fellows serve more willingly than others, of course. Rome has a lot to offer."

"As long as you do things the Roman way," Brude observed.

"Yes," Mata agreed. He paused, then asked, "Why did she say to tell Caracalla she was a druid? She knew what she was doing."

"I don't know for sure," said Brude, "but I think she is gambling that if the three of them are killed, the rest of the Boresti will be left unharmed. You heard what she said, '*cut off the head and the beast will die*'." It was the only reason he could think of.

"I thought it might be something like that. She is old and does not care, the old chieftain is willing to sacrifice himself and his son will not be the next ruler anyway, is that right?"

"Nechtan has a brother, and a nephew," said Brude, hoping he could trust the Votadini interpreter.

"A desperate gamble," Mata observed. "I will go and speak to them before dawn. Should I tell them anything from you? They obviously know you."

"I only met Veleda once and Nechtan twice, before tonight," Brude told him.

Mata laughed. "Don't worry, I will not ask them any questions about you. As I said, I understand about making compromises. I expect you have made as many as I have."

Brude instinctively liked the little Votadini. He decided to trust him to keep his word. "If you see them, tell Veleda I understood her message." *Cut off the head and the beast will die,* she had said.

As day broke, the army formed ranks outside the camp, each century arrayed neatly with armour polished and weapons at the ready. To the wings, the cavalry stood ready. Even the ballistas and onagers of the artillery were drawn up in orderly ranks, facing Dun Nechtan. A gaggle of camp followers stood to the rear, watching the proceedings with interest. Caracalla, dressed in a toga with the long folds draped over his head, officiated at the sacrifice of a young goat. After examining the entrails, he announced that the omens were propitious. The three Boresti prisoners were led out of the camp, surrounded by armed guards. They were taken to the open field where Colm and his men had camped only a few days before. Brude, watching from the ramparts of the legionary camp, Mairead and Fothair standing nervously beside him, saw Veleda survey the ranks of the Roman army. She looked at the ballistas being readied and she must have known that her plan was doomed to fail. *Cut off the head and the beast will die,* she had said. She had offered up the head of the Boresti to the Romans and they had accepted the sacrifice. But Veleda, for all her skills, did not understand the Roman mind. Brude knew with a dreadful certainty that Caracalla did not just want the head. He wanted the whole carcass.

"We should go," he said to the others. "You do not want to see this."

"We must see it," Mairead insisted. "It is the least we can do to honour their sacrifice."

Nechtan, Eairsidh and Veleda were forced to their knees. There was a fanfare of trumpets. Brude could make out the shapes of people watching from the ramparts of Dun Nechtan. Three Praetorian Guards stood ready, one behind each of the kneeling prisoners. They drew their swords and Brude recognised the preparations for the death blows. It was over quickly. The swords flashed and three corpses tumbled to the ground. The guards withdrew, leaving their victims where they lay.

Tears ran down Mairead's cheeks but the worst was yet to come. Caracalla ordered another trumpet blast and the Roman siege artillery began its work. Huge stones were flung skywards, arcing towards the top of the hill. The first shots did little damage, falling short, but the artillerymen soon judged the range and stones began to hammer at the gateway, smashing into the wooden rampart and gates. Some ballistas hurled flaming bundles of oil-soaked hides, which dropped over the walls, intended to set fire to the houses inside. Large crossbows on wooden stands were dragged to the foot of the hill. They began firing long, iron-tipped spikes which flew with astonishing speed towards the gateway, forcing the tribesmen inside to keep under cover. The awful bombardment continued until the third hour, when the gates collapsed as the battering took its toll. The infantry were immediately ordered forwards. The Twentieth Legion was in the van, marching inexorably closer to the hill. They formed into columns and began to climb the pathway towards the gate. Roman cavalry rode round either side of the long hill, to cut off anyone who tried to escape from other gates. Some stones were hurled down, over the ramparts but few of them did much harm.

"May the gods help them," Fothair whispered as a group of Boresti warriors charged out of the shattered gateway. They had suffered the hell of the bombardment and had survived. Now they wanted to strike some blows of their own. It was a forlorn hope. A flurry of catapult bolts scythed into them, sending men tumbling, punching them from their feet. Then the Roman infantry bunched their shields as they pressed upwards to meet the charge. On the tight and treacherous slope, the fighting was confined to a narrow front where numbers could make little difference. The clash of arms and the yells and screams could be heard drifting on the wind. Watching in horror, Brude remembered his own first taste of battle and how it had ended.

This fight ended the same way. The tribesmen were no match for the disciplined and heavily armoured Romans who slowly edged their way up the slope. After only a brief resistance, the tribesmen were turning, running for the gates and the Romans were after them, swords eager to continue the killing.

Brude had seen it before, in Germania. He did not want to see it again but the death of Dun Nechtan held him, fascinated. Inside the hill fort were people he knew. All the Boresti were his kinsmen, even if he did not know them personally. Now they were dying. He thought of Oengus, Irb, and the other villagers from Broch Tava who had sought refuge in Dun Nechtan. Few of them would survive this ferocious assault.

The sack of the hill fort took until mid-day. Flames and smoke rose into the summer sky. Those few who survived the slaughter and rape were led down the hill to be shackled as slaves. There were less than one hundred of them, and most of those were women. Only a handful of the men and the children were spared.

Mairead wept and Fothair's face was an ashen mask as they watched the bedraggled survivors being chained. Brude felt numb and empty. The Boresti were all but destroyed and he had simply watched while it had happened. Guilt ate at his heart. He had to clench his teeth to prevent a sob of anguish escaping his throat. Then he saw a group of Roman officers striding back towards the camp. Caracalla and his aides were returning.

"Wait here," he told Mairead. "We need to get away. I will have to speak to Caesar."

He made his way towards the gate to intercept Caracalla's party. Technically, any citizen could petition Caesar. In the past, some emperors had even been accosted in the streets of Rome by private citizens, although it was a rare opportunity in these days. He was taking a risk, especially when the Praetorians were in close attendance, and even more especially with someone as volatile as Caracalla. Brude forced the horror of the sack of Dun Nechtan from his mind, fought down the fury of his helpless rage as he put on his slave's face. He knew he had to make yet another compromise for the sake of his missing son.

Brude need not have worried about gaining a hearing. As soon as Caracalla saw him, he beckoned him over. "Brutus!"

he exclaimed, "Was that not magnificent? Another triumph for Rome."

"I congratulate you, Caesar," Brude replied. "Your army is very impressive."

"Yet another tribe falls before us. They may have wanted peace but we have learned in the past that they would turn on us as soon as our backs are turned. This way they will never get that opportunity again." He looked at Brude, his expression mirroring his expansive mood. "Was there something you wanted?"

"Yes, Caesar, if I may ask a favour?" That earned him a glare from Priscus, the stern legate, but Brude ignored him. He went on, "I would like to return south, to Britannia and eventually to Rome."

Caracalla was surprised. "Really? I had hoped you would remain here to help guide us in our march north."

"I regret I would be of little use to you, Caesar. My knowledge of the tribe north of here is no greater than yours. I only know they are called the Maeatae, which you know already." Brude could see that Caracalla was in good humour so he played his final card. "I really need to return to repay my patron his share of the profits from my trading venture."

Caracalla raised an eyebrow. "Your patron?"

"Lucius Vipsanius Festus. He was kind enough to provide me with some funds for my trip. I promised him a share in what profits I made."

"A man should always repay his patron," Caracalla nodded. "Very well, you have leave to depart. Priscus will have someone prepare a letter of safe conduct for you."

Brude had to concentrate hard not to let a broad smile break out on his face. "My thanks, Caesar."

"And twenty gold aurii for your services."

"You are too generous, Caesar," Brude protested. This time he was genuine; the sum was enormous.

"Nonsense! Priscus will see to it. Now, I am off to get something to eat." He moved on, his officers and guards trailing after him, leaving Brude wondering whether he would remember what he had just promised.

Caracalla, though, was as good as his word. Brude and Fothair dismantled their tent while Mairead packed their horses. As they were finishing, the tribune Porcius found them. He handed Brude a letter bearing the imperial seal together with a small bag of coins. "With Caesar's compliments," Porcius told him.

Brude took the letter, stuffing the bag of coins, unopened, into his pack. "Thank you."

"You are going south?"

"Yes. To Eboracum first. That is where the slaves are taken, you said?"

"That's right," Porcius confirmed.

"After that, I will probably go to Londinium, and eventually to Rome," Brude lied.

"Then I wish you well."

"And you." They clasped hands. Brude realised that he rather liked Porcius even though the young man was part of the army that had just destroyed the Boresti. It was a confusing emotion.

Brude helped Mairead climb into her saddle then he and Fothair leapt onto their horses. With a wave of farewell to Porcius, they rode out of the camp without a backward glance.

They had to go through Peart, where they found the town not as badly damaged as they had expected. There was a strong Roman garrison manning a camp at the bridge but Caracalla's letter allowed them to pass. They rode across the bridge into the village. Fothair's expression grew grim as they passed his former home. Around half of the houses had been burned to the ground but there were still some villagers there, looking sullen and downtrodden. The three of them rode slowly, not wishing to draw attention to themselves, but Brude remained anxious until they climbed the steep hills to the south of Peart. From the summit they looked eastwards to where the dark finger of the broch could sometimes be seen outlined against the sky. They could not make it out, even though it was a clear day. The Roman engineers had probably done their work by now. The broad expanse of the Tava valley was laid out below them. "Let's hope we see home and friends again soon," Brude said.

Mairead was sore from the hours of riding, as was Brude, but now that they had escaped the Roman army they knew that they had a difficult task ahead of them. Somehow they had to find Castatin and Barabal. The two young people were already six days ahead of them, so the three of them pushed on as quickly as their aching bodies would allow. "How far is this place they are being taken?" Mairead asked that evening as they lay in their blankets trying to ignore the protests of pain from their muscles.

"I'm not sure. I've never been there, but it will take us several days at least."

"What if they are not there?"

That was the question Brude dreaded. If Porcius' information was wrong, the search would be almost impossible. "I don't know. Britannia is a large place, but the Romans are usually pretty methodical about things like that. It makes sense for them to go there. It's one of the main cities. If they are walking, we should get there before them. If they are taken by ship, they could be there already."

"I am so worried about Castatin. I miss him so much," Mairead whispered. He held her close, trying to reassure her but the most comfort he could give was that they were in this together, sharing the burden.

The Antonine Wall was manned and patrolled, teeming with Roman troops. Brude thought he caught a glimpse of some wearing the uniform of the Praetorian Guard, which almost certainly meant that the emperor himself was nearby. Again, though, Caracalla's letter let them through without question. Crossing the wall, they rode southwards, climbing steep hills, ploughing through valleys, fording rivers and streams until they reached the great Wall where yet more soldiers were stationed. Fothair whistled in amazement when he saw the Wall snaking across the countryside for as far as he could see in either direction. "I wasn't sure whether to believe what everyone said about it, but it's incredible."

"You'll see more things to amaze you, the further south we go," Brude assured him.

Now inside the borders of the empire, Brude reminded them to act like slaves. He had taught them how to say, "I am the slave of Marcus Septimius Brutus." Slaves did not usually ride horses, but there was no alternative to them playing the part. They spoke no Latin and their dress marked them as obviously from north of the Wall. Because they needed to hurry, they had to ride; walking would take far too long. They pressed on, trusting to Caracalla's letter to keep them out of difficulty.

The roads were busy with wagons carrying supplies northwards for the army, while injured men and captives travelled south. Messengers galloped in both directions, usually with an escort of mounted troopers. Nobody paid much attention to three more travellers.

It took them another six exhausting days to reach Eboracum. The scale of the city was another astonishment for Mairead and Fothair. To Brude, who had seen Rome itself, Eboracum was a small place but, as the headquarters of a legion and the base for the government of all of northern Britannia, it was a busy, bustling town. The walls and gates of the fortress were strong and impressive, the streets of the neighbouring town laid out in the regular pattern of most Roman settlements, with an added jumble of traditional Pritani homes clustering round the edges of the Roman buildings. The town had the usual collection of temples and other public buildings round the edges of a forum. Throughout the town were public bathhouses, a theatre and even a wooden amphitheatre. It also had a wide variety of homes, ranging from the opulent residences of the wealthy to the three or four-storey tenements of the poor.

They arrived in a heavy downpour, rain plastering their hair and soaking through their clothes. They found an ostler near the city gates where Brude paid for the horses to be kept for them. He also obtained directions to somewhere they could rent rooms so they set off in the rain to find the landlord. Fothair and Mairead carried most of their baggage because Brude told them that was what slaves did. "You're enjoying this," said Mairead accusingly.

"I'm just playing the part," chuckled Brude. "And you should call me Master. There will be plenty of people around here who speak a language close to ours."

She stuck out her tongue at him. "Yes, Master."

"Don't encourage him," Fothair muttered.

Despite the pouring rain and having to carry a heavy load, Mairead was almost enjoying herself. She looked at the brick and plaster buildings with their red tiled roofs, pointing out different things as they passed. She walked along the paved road, splashing in the puddles and saying, "This is wonderful. It's raining and there's no mud." Brude remembered how he had felt when he first walked through the streets of Rome. Despite the rain, he enjoyed telling her what the various signs outside the shops signified.

They found the place the ostler had told them about. It was a four-storey building, the upper two floors with wooden walls because the structure would not support the weight of brick any higher than two storeys. Brude had seen many similar buildings in Rome and knew they were notorious for collapsing, or for catching fire as the occupants tried to cook on open fires in rooms built of wood. Still, they needed shelter so they went inside to find the landlord.

The man was a former soldier, named Niger, which Brude assumed was a soldier's joke since his hair was as white as any he had ever seen rather than the black that his name suggested. From behind the small counter where he was sitting, he gave them a sour look as they entered his tiny front office, apparently annoyed that they had interrupted him, even though he was doing nothing more onerous than cleaning a pair of old boots. "What is it?" he asked in a surly tone.

"You have rooms to rent," Brude replied in an equally gruff voice, deciding he could play the hard man as well.

Niger eyed Mairead and Fothair with disdain. "That depends."

"On what?"

"On who wants them and why."

Brude decided to put the man in his place. He stepped forwards, lowering his head to put his face close to the old soldier. "I am Marcus Septimius Brutus. I was a gladiator, freed by the emperor himself. I have served under Quintus Aemilius Tertius, legate of the legions of Germania, and I have just come from campaign under the emperor's son himself. These two are my slaves. I have silver to pay for rooms and no more questions. Is that good enough?"

Niger, taken aback by Brude's refusal to be intimidated and by the knowledge that, as a former gladiator, Brude could easily overpower him if the fancy took him, licked his lips. He said softly, "I've got two rooms on the first floor. Ten sesterces a week, per room. You provide your own fuel for heating."

The price was outrageous and they both knew it. Brude opened a small money pouch, counting out four silver denarii, equivalent to sixteen sesterces. He placed two of them on the counter then put the others back in the pouch. "We'll take the biggest room. You provide the fuel and get some clean bedding and blankets for us. You'll get the other two denarii at the end of the week."

Niger did not take long to think about it. "Deal!"

They climbed the wooden stairs to find that the room was actually quite good. There were four small beds and a stone fireplace for heating and cooking. There was a small wooden table with four stools, an oil lamp, a tin bowl for washing and a small selection of clay dishes and plates. The solitary window had no glass but two sets of wooden shutters; a solid pair on the inside edge, which could be closed at night, with a slatted outer pair to let light in. The wooden floor was strong enough and the brick walls had been recently plastered so the room had a fresh, airy feel to it. Even the bedding was not too bad though Brude insisted on it being replaced. Niger, persuaded by the silver, had some fresh mattresses and blankets brought in by two slaves.

Fothair lit the fire and they all changed out of their wet clothes. The room soon began to fill with the smell of damp wool and linen drying out as they huddled near the fire for warmth. After an hour or so the rain stopped drumming against the shutters. Brude looked outside. The sky was clearing and there were still a few hours of daylight. "Let's go and see if we can find some food," he said, "and some information about where the Romans are keeping the prisoners."

In exchange for another denarius, Niger gave them the locations of a few tavernas where they could buy hot food. He also told them that the captives were usually held in slave pens at the outskirts of the city. "But I hear they're using the amphitheatre to hold them now, seeing as they have so many," he said.

The city was alive with people now that the rain had stopped. In addition to Latin, many of them were speaking a Brythonic language, which was similar to the Boresti tongue. Mairead and Fothair found it hard to move through the crowded streets without staring at everything and everyone they passed. They, in turn, received some curious looks thanks to their rather wild dress and hair.

Brude found a small taverna where the owner kept hot food in great pots that were held in circular holes in his shop front counter. The pots were lowered into the holes where a small fire burned beneath them to keep the contents warm.

After their meal they went to the slave pens. They found them crowded and well guarded, with soldiers constantly patrolling the perimeter. Brude tried to bribe his way in, claiming he was interested in buying some slaves but he got short shrift and was sent packing. The slaves, it seemed, were not for sale because they were all to be taken to Rome. "No exceptions," the centurion in charge told him, "so you might as well be off." He would not even change his mind when Brude showed him the letter from Caracalla telling all soldiers to allow Brude to pass freely. "That doesn't apply here," the centurion growled impatiently. "Geta Caesar is in charge here. My orders are that

351

all the slaves will be sent to Rome as soon as we get enough ships together. No exceptions."

There was no point in arguing. Geta, younger son of the emperor Septimius Severus, gave the orders in Eboracum. The three Boresti went back to their room where Brude stared hopelessly into the fire, not knowing what to do.

Eboracum A.D. 210

The following morning they went to the amphitheatre but met with no success there either. The answer was the same: *no exceptions.*

Brude was aware that the three of them were arousing some suspicions. Although the bulk of the army was north of the Wall, Eboracum was a legionary base and Geta Caesar had made it his headquarters so there were still plenty of soldiers in evidence. Brude reckoned there was at least one cohort of Praetorian Guards plus several hundred auxiliary troops. In a remote province, with a member of the imperial family in residence, the guards were naturally cautious and Brude was asking unusual questions. With his broad shoulders and stocky build, he was hardly inconspicuous but Mairead and Fothair were drawing attention too. Mairead's striking looks and Fothair's height were enough to mark them out in any company but their clothes and language were also distinctive. To help them blend in, Brude bought some more suitably Roman-style tunics and leggings for himself and Fothair, and purchased a long Roman-style dress for Mairead. Because the weather was still poor, he also bought a hooded cloak for each of them, hoping this would help hide their features a little.

By early afternoon they had run out of ideas. "We don't even know if they are in there," said Mairead, her tone betraying her concern. "What are we going to do?"

"We can't fight our way in, that's for sure," Fothair said.

"Trying to break in is too dangerous," said Brude. "There are too many guards."

Mairead looked at him imploringly. "There must be something we can do."

Brude had only one option left. Another desperate idea in the succession of desperate ideas that had somehow got them this far. The appeal in Mairead's eyes, her need for a solution, was too strong for him not to try. "We can appeal to Caesar again."

"To the emperor?" Fothair was alarmed at the prospect.

"To his son. Geta is in charge here. As a citizen, I have the right to make an appeal to him."

"If this Geta is like his brother, that could be dangerous."

"Perhaps not dangerous, but very difficult. It's getting past all the courtiers, guards and freedmen that is the problem. From what little I have heard about him, Geta is not like his brother at all, but I have to get to him somehow."

"Couldn't you use that letter you got from Caracalla?" Mairead asked.

"That's what I was thinking, but there is no guarantee it would do any good. The two brothers hate each other. The centurion at the slave pens wasn't interested in anything except orders from Geta. The letter might create more problems than it solves."

But there were no other options available to them, so Brude set off on his own, leaving the other two to watch the slave pens and the amphitheatre as discreetly as they could, in the hope that they could catch a glimpse of Castatin or Barabal either inside or arriving with a new batch of captives. Even if they did see them, he knew that they would not be able to do anything, but if they could find out where the two young villagers were, it would be a start. At least it gave Mairead and Fothair something to do.

Brude made his way to the legionary fortress where Geta had his headquarters. Eboracum had grown up around this fortified camp, which the Romans had built over a hundred years before, on the fringes of the territory of the troublesome Brigantes. Originally built of wood, the fort had turned into a permanent legionary base and was now an impressive stone-built fortress with the Principia serving as a Governor's palace as much as a military headquarters. The emperor had used this building as his base before moving northwards. He had even named Eboracum as the capital of Britannia Inferior, the northern part of the province. It was not the sort of place anyone could simply stroll into unchallenged.

Brude was stopped at the main gate, searched, then directed to the Principia, to which he followed the main central road. Where the Principia was usually a tent in marching camps, as he had seen when with Caracalla, or perhaps a wooden upper structure on a stone or brick foundation as he had seen in Germania, this one was built entirely of stone. It even had its own column-fronted basilica. Outside the basilica was a queue of civilians who were waiting to see an official who would decide whether their case warranted referral to higher authority. Pulling his hood over his head against another shower of rain, Brude ducked into the sparse cover of the colonnaded portico outside the basilica. He joined the queue, waiting patiently for his turn. He saw some of the people turned away, while others stayed inside, presumably having been allowed to move on to the next stage.

After about an hour, he was admitted to a small antechamber where he found a stern looking clerk dressed in a toga and seated behind a table covered with parchment, quills and ink. Two guards, looking appropriately bored, stood by the back wall where a door led through to another room. The office was warm and dry and Brude was thankful to be inside after standing in the drizzle for so long. There was nowhere for him to sit so he stood in front of the desk, rain water slowly dripping off his cloak to the stone floor. The clerk gave him a weary look. "What is it you are here for?" the man asked, managing to convey the impression that he really didn't care very much what Brude wanted.

Brude pulled out the letter Caracalla had given him and began his rehearsed story. "My son was captured two weeks ago, mistaken for a war slave. I am trying to find him and get him back, along with the daughter of a friend of mine."

The clerk read Caracalla's letter carefully, studied the seal closely, then read the letter again. He glanced up and said, "You are a Roman citizen?"

"I am." Brude handed over his crumpled manumission papers. The clerk pored over these carefully. When he had satisfied himself they were genuine he handed them back and asked, "How did your son come to be captured?"

"I am a travelling merchant. I was on a long trip north of the Wall and I was staying at a coastal village. The navy raided the place while I was away one day and my son was taken. I heard all prisoners were being brought here but I cannot get in to find him."

The clerk pursed his lips. "You heard correctly. How old is your son?"

"Thirteen."

The clerk's eyebrows rose. "So he was born while you were a slave? Your papers say you were freed only six years ago."

Brude realised he had walked into a snare of his own making. If Castatin had been born after Brude was free, he would be a Roman citizen, but the child of a slave was a slave. Trying not to show his concern, he answered, "He was born before I was made a slave." Which was not true although there was no way the clerk could disprove it.

The clerk, though, was well used to people trying to argue with him. "So he was born a barbarian? That makes him a legitimate captive, I think."

"He is the son of a Roman citizen!" Brude protested. The guards stood alertly now, watching him for any signs that he might cause trouble. He relaxed his stance. "I am sorry. He is my son. I need him back. As a Roman citizen, and one who has proof of giving service to the empire, I wish to appeal to Geta Caesar." He wished now that he had made the appeal to Caracalla when he had had the chance, but he had missed the opportunity because he had been too angry at the destruction of Dun Nechtan to think that far ahead. The world of Roman politics and law was a strange and frightening one for him. For all his skill in the arena, he was helpless in his current situation.

The clerk rubbed his chin thoughtfully. "It is not a straight-forward case," he admitted after a few moments. "Very well, you may take your case to the tribune. Go through there and wait." He pointed to the door in the back wall.

"Thank you," said Brude with feeling. He gathered up his papers and went to the door, which one of the guards opened. He passed through into a second small room where he took a seat beside a couple of other civilians on one of the wooden benches that ran round the walls. He breathed a sigh of relief. He had passed the first barrier.

After a while, another door, flanked by two more guards, opened. A civilian came out, his expression hurt and confused. He was shown to an exit and ushered out, clearly having failed to get what he wanted. A clerk appeared in the doorway and beckoned the next in line to come in.

Brude waited.

The unseen tribune in the next room obviously had considerable authority. Two of the civilians who came out had clearly got what they wanted without going any further into the bureaucracy of the Roman system. The next man went in, leaving Brude as next in line. One more man had got past the clerk and been admitted to the waiting room. Brude sat rehearsing his story, hoping the letter from Caracalla, vague as it was, would help him get what he wanted.

Then his luck changed for the better. An officer of the Praetorian Guard walked in through the external door, his plumed helmet tucked under his arm. He had filled out since Brude had last seen him and had lost his boyish looks but there was no mistaking him. Lucius Vipsanius Festus, Aquila's son and Brude's one-time pupil, stepped inside. He blinked in surprise when he saw Brude, then a broad smile broke out on his face as he hurried over. "Marcus! What are you doing here?"

Brude stood, unable to keep an idiotic grin from his face. "I am waiting to see the tribune."

"Whatever for? No, wait! Let's go somewhere where we can talk in private. Come on." He saw Brude look hesitantly towards the door to where the tribune dispensed justice. "Don't worry, I'm a tribune too. Come on, we'll go to my quarters."

Earning a sour look of jealousy from the other waiting civilian, Brude followed Lucius outside. They walked round the Principia to the officer's quarters. The young Roman was in a fine humour. "I can't believe it's you. Wait till old Cleon sees you."

"Cleon is here?" Brude's spirits lifted at the thought of seeing his old friend and mentor.

"Rather against his will, I'm afraid, but things in Rome have changed so much that I preferred him to come over with me when I managed to get appointed to Geta's staff. He will be overjoyed to see you. He was even more irritable than usual after you left."

"It will be a joy to see him again," Brude admitted. "I often wished he was here but I didn't think he would be happy living away from what he calls civilisation."

"He isn't," replied Lucius. Outwardly, the young Roman was the same as he had been before, but Brude sensed that something in him had changed. The boy had become a man in the past two years. He seemed prepared to help, but he was more serious than Brude remembered. Brude suspected that, as head of the Vipsanius family now that his father was dead, Lucius had probably had a lot of growing up to do in a short time. Working as one of Geta's staff would not be without its problems either.

The Principia was a vast complex of rooms, halls and corridors, constructed from carefully carved and shaped stone blocks. Lucius' quarters were on the upper floor; a small room containing a bed, a table and two stools. It even boasted a thick pane of glass in the window. Lucius called for a slave to bring some wine and three goblets, then told him to find Cleon and tell him to come to join them. He told Brude to sit on a stool while he sat on the edge of the bed. The slave poured the wine then left, closing the door as he went.

"Keep your story until Cleon gets here," said Lucius. "That will save you telling it twice."

Brude sipped the cool wine. There was an awkward silence, an acknowledgement that something in their relationship had changed. Brude was no longer the teacher, the trainer and adviser. Lucius was a knight, one of the Roman upper classes, and moving in high circles if he was on the staff of the emperor's younger son.

Fortunately, they did not have long to wait before they heard footsteps outside. The door opened to admit Cleon. His head was almost completely bald now, and his chubby, pock-marked face seemed to have more lines and wrinkles than ever. He stopped when he saw Brude, blinking in astonishment. Then his face lit up and he rushed to embrace Brude with a cry of joy. "By Hercules, is it really you?"

Struggling to keep his wine from spilling, Brude returned the embrace as he assured Cleon that it really was him.

"I never thought to see you again when I heard you were going north of the Wall," Cleon said, his voice cracking with emotion. "I am so glad that you have escaped the war up there. But what in Hades brings you here?"

"Marcus was only waiting for you to come before he tells us his story," said Lucius. "Come, Cleon, have some wine and sit down so that we can exchange all our news."

When they had settled, Brude looked at them both. He knew he could trust Cleon with anything and he decided he had no option but to trust Lucius. According to Roman custom, Lucius, as his patron, should look after his interests, just as he should support Lucius. "Do you want the story I told the clerk downstairs or the real truth?" he asked with a rueful expression.

"You'd better tell us both," Lucius replied.

So Brude told them all that had happened to him since he had returned to Broch Tava; how he had learned he had a son and how Colm, his childhood friend, had become corrupted by his desire for power. He recounted how Colm had died because of Lutrin's treachery, and he told how Castatin, the son he had never known he had, had been taken captive not even knowing the truth of his birth. Briefly, he explained how he had been delayed by the advance of the Roman army, but had then come south looking for his son. Lucius and Cleon listened attentively in silence while Brude told his tale. When he had finished that account, he went on to outline the edited version he had given to the clerk.

Lucius thought for a moment then smiled. "Well, it's a case the legal experts would love, I'm sure, but there's an easy way to resolve it. We'll go to Geta Caesar. No matter what the law says, he can make his own decision. I'm sure we can get it sorted quickly. Assuming your son is here, of course."

"I daren't think he is anywhere else," said Brude.

"Well, the orders are for all captives to come here before being shipped off to Rome but we have few enough ships available at the moment. The emperor and Caracalla have pushed so far north they are stretching our supply lines considerably. The fleet is having to sail further north all the time. Most captives should be here, or due to get here soon."

"Do you really think Geta will let me take him back?" Brude did not dare to hope too much.

Lucius saw the concern on his face. "Don't worry, Marcus. Geta is not like his brother at all. Caracalla would probably have your son and the girl you mentioned brought out and sold off to slavery in front of your eyes just to torment you. He's got a mean streak like that. Geta's a different sort. I was lucky to get myself on to his staff."

"You have done well," Brude acknowledged. He was desperate to go, to find Geta so that he could get Castatin and Barabal back, but he knew how the Romans operated. He looked at Lucius and asked, "So what has happened since I last saw you? How are your sisters and your step-mother?" He did not really want to hear too much about Agrippina, especially with Mairead so near, but it would have been impolite not to ask. "Above all, how did you persuade Cleon to come with you?"

"My sisters are both well. Vipsania Prima has a son and Secunda is pregnant too. She often asks for you in her letters." He laughed. "She seems to think Britannia is a tiny place and that I'm bound to meet you every time I step out the door. Wait till I write back to her and tell her I have actually seen you. She'll be delighted." He hesitated slightly before going on, "As for my former step-mother, she is now my wife."

Brude was so surprised he almost choked on his wine. "Your wife?"

"Don't look so alarmed, Marcus," said Lucius reprovingly. "It's not as if she is my real mother. She's only a few years older than me, after all. About the same age as you, in fact."

"I'm sorry, Lucius," Brude apologised. "It's just that I wasn't expecting that at all. I'm sure you will be very happy."

"Yes, I am," said Lucius. "Agrippina is not just a good housewife, you know. She is very beautiful and very, well, you know...." He gave Brude a knowing wink.

Brude, who was all too familiar with Agrippina's charms, just smiled. "You are a very lucky young man," he managed to say. "I am sure there will be many who are envious of you." He caught a glimpse of Cleon who was making a point of not meeting his gaze. The old man clearly had his own views on the matter but did not want to air them while Lucius was present. Brude suspected that anyone in Rome who was envious of Lucius would find plenty of encouragement from Agrippina to satisfy their desires while Lucius was away with the army. A thought struck him. "Is she here? Your wife?"

"No, she decided that the rigours of a military campaign would not suit her. I quite agree; war is men's work. She is back in Rome."

Brude breathed a mental sigh of relief. Changing the subject before he gave himself away, he said, "Please do tell your sisters I am glad to hear they are well."

"I will," Lucius promised. "Now, let us go and see Geta so that we can get your son back for you."

The three of them made their way back down to the lower floor. They walked through some antechambers, then along a succession of corridors until they reached a guarded door, which led to the office where Geta Caesar organised the running of the logistical support for the imperial military campaign. Lucius was admitted without question. Brude followed him, with Cleon tagging along as if he was quite entitled to be there. They found a brightly lit room with large, glazed windows. Several oil lamps gave additional illumination while a blazing fire burned to keep the room warm in the unseasonably cold snap.

Geta was seated at a desk while messengers and officers brought him reports or carried away his instructions. Clerks scurried to and fro carrying scrolls and parchments or presenting Geta with documents that required his seal. The young Caesar was only twenty-one years old, clean shaven, unlike his father and older brother, with short brown hair and matching eyes. He was wearing a simple tunic of white linen with a broad purple stripe on the front and back. He smiled when he saw Lucius, waving him over. "Festus!" he called, addressing Lucius by his cognomen, "Come and rescue me from this paperwork. I am drowning!"

Lucius walked over to the table. With a smile, he said, "I'm afraid I only bring more work for you, Caesar. My friend and client, Septimius Brutus, needs your help."

Geta looked at Brude. "Does he indeed? Well, then, let us retire to my private chambers. Then we might be able to discuss what he needs without being interrupted." He sealed the document in front of him, pressing his large ring into the hot wax. Then he rose to his feet and waved everyone else away. "Let's have a short break, gentlemen. I'll take lunch in my private chambers with Festus and his friend. You can pester me with work this afternoon and all evening as well."

Wide double doors were opened in the far wall. Geta led them through to his private chamber. Cleon followed, even though he had not been invited, though Geta did not seem to mind. Brude could already sense that this young man was very different from his brother. All around Caracalla men walked in fear, never knowing when he might suddenly turn on them, while those around Geta seemed relaxed and at ease.

Slaves quietly and efficiently produced platters of bread, cheese, olives, grapes, figs and eggs along with pitchers of wine and water. Most of them left but two stayed silently in the room, standing against the wall like statues, in case Geta should need anything else.

Geta sat on a low couch, indicating that the others should do the same. "There are no formalities here," he explained to Brude. "Help yourself to as much as you want. I owe you my thanks for letting me escape that army of clerks, so tell me what it is I can do for you."

Brude looked to Lucius for encouragement. These two men were several years younger than he was, but they were very much in charge here. He felt out of his depth seated beside them. During his time in Aquila's service, he had been around enough powerful Romans to know that someone in his position was normally expected to know his place. The young man seated on the opulent couch opposite him was one of the three most powerful men in the world, however affable he might seem.

Lucius came to his rescue, outlining Brude's predicament. Brude grew concerned when Lucius gave Geta the true story, rather than the edited version, but Lucius made great play of Brude's friendship and how he had served with the legions in Germania. He emphasised that Brude had helped Priscus' legion in the current campaign but he did not mention Caracalla at all.

Geta listened patiently. When Lucius was finished, he looked at Brude with interest. "Did you meet my brother at all?"

"Only briefly, Caesar," Brude replied. "And I was one of a number of people present."

"What did you think of him?" Geta asked, his eyes warning of the potential trap waiting for an incautious answer.

Brude had heard that the emperor's two sons disliked each other and he had picked up on Lucius' failure to mention Geta's brother, but he also knew that criticising a member of the imperial family was normally a quick way to commit suicide. "I hardly spoke to him, Caesar, but he listened to what I had to say and he acted decisively. He seems to enjoy the military life and he is certainly proving very successful."

Geta laughed. "Well said, Brutus. Very diplomatic. The truth is that my brother is an arrogant pig with no virtues and many vices. You need not fear telling the truth about him here."

"I cannot possibly know him as well as you do, Caesar. But I would agree that he appears quite ruthless."

"Hah! That's an understatement," Geta said bitterly. "Rome has won her place in history by being ruthless when it is necessary, but few enjoy acts of violence as much as my brother." Then he waved a hand dismissively. "Still, we are not here to discuss my family, but yours. Whatever Festus says, though, I can't see there is any way that your son can be regarded as a Roman citizen. But you are, and you have given valuable service to the empire, even if some of it was to my brother. And, of course, Festus is a valued member of my team here. My father always says that the job of an emperor is to keep the soldiers happy, so I think we can solve this very easily by freeing your son and making him a Roman citizen."

Brude's heart surged with relief. Having met Caracalla, he had not been confident of his chances of getting anything from Geta, or even of getting a chance to make his appeal. Meeting Lucius so unexpectedly had turned a possible ordeal into an easy solution. "Thank you, Caesar," he said with feeling. "Might I ask the same for the young girl who was taken captive with him?"

Geta's eyes shone with amusement. "Of course. Cleon, seeing as you are here, you may as well make yourself useful. Get the papers drawn up. Then you can all go along to find these two prisoners."

"At once, Caesar," said Cleon, rising from the couch and somehow managing to give the impression that he had only joined them because he had expected his services to be needed for this very purpose.

"Well, it seems I only have a few more minutes away from that deluge of bureaucracy my secretaries have waiting for me," said Geta with a smile. He turned again to Brude. "So what will you do when you have them back?"

"I will take them home, Caesar. It seems that the whole of Caledonia will soon be part of the empire. My people will probably need my help to adjust." Brude had only just thought of that, but it seemed a plausible answer.

"Very good," nodded Geta. "We could do with some friends in our new province. Who knows, perhaps there will be opportunities for you to help in governing the place."

That was the last thing Brude wanted but he acknowledged the compliment without demur. In Roman society it was always good to have friends in high places and they didn't come much higher than the emperor's second son. Barring some sort of miracle, the whole of the lands of the Pritani would indeed soon be part of the empire as Septimius Severus and his sons finished off the job the Romans had left undone one hundred and twenty years earlier. Although the thought of helping the Romans impose their culture on his people was not something Brude relished, he knew he would have to help what was left of the Boresti come to terms with that new world somehow.

Cleon returned, carrying a letter, which Geta signed and sealed before handing it to Brude, with a smile. After offering his thanks, they said farewell to the emperor's son, leaving him to his afternoon of paperwork.

Lucius guided Brude back outside. They headed for the main gate, Cleon struggling to keep up with the eager pace Brude was setting. The rain had stopped but they had to avoid several puddles and wrap their cloaks around themselves to fight off the chill wind. "Does the sun never shine in this damned country?" complained Cleon.

"You get the odd day," Brude told him. "Last summer was good."

"I was in Germania last summer," Lucius said. "It seems to have been raining ever since we got here."

Their grumbles were cut short when they left the fortress because Brude saw that Mairead and Fothair were waiting for him. Mairead's expression was a mixture of eagerness tempered with apprehension when she saw Lucius but she hurried over to meet Brude. Bursting with excitement, she said, "We've found them! They arrived just a short time ago."

Brude hugged her and she clung to him, relief flooding through her every fibre. "Where are they?" he asked.

"The amphitheatre." The unfamiliar word sounded odd when she said it but Lucius understood and repeated it.

Brude made the introductions. Mairead and Fothair had picked up the odd Latin word and phrase but not enough to have any conversation while both Lucius and Cleon spoke only Latin and Greek, which meant that Brude had to interpret everything. When he told Mairead who Lucius was and that he had helped get Geta's permission to release Castatin and Barabal, she put her arms round Lucius, hugging him even though he was wearing his army breastplate. The young Roman was embarrassed at this outward display of emotion but when Mairead released him he gave Brude a knowing look and said, "I see now why you were so keen to get home."

"Indeed," agreed Cleon. He then blushed when Mairead gave him a similar hug.

"Mairead is thanking you for your help," Brude explained with a laugh.

"Castatin didn't look well," Mairead told Brude. "I tried to get Barabal's attention but she didn't see me. I couldn't go too close because there were a lot of soldiers. I didn't know what to do, so I fetched Fothair and we came to find you." The words tumbled from her in her anxiety. Her son was alive and they had found him at last. She was bursting with impatience to get him back, to free him.

The five of them walked through the busy streets to the edge of the town where the amphitheatre lay. Made from earth embankments with wooden walls and seats, it was a small arena, probably only capable of holding a few thousand spectators. It reminded Brude of his very first fight in the wooden amphitheatre at Paestum, where he had faced the black-skinned Retiarius. The guards at the main gate snapped to attention when Lucius approached. At his command, they opened the gates to let him in. Lucius suggested that Cleon, Mairead and Fothair should wait outside. "I don't expect any trouble from the prisoners, but it's best not to take any chances by bringing in civilians," he explained. Brude translated for Mairead's benefit before following Lucius through the dark tunnel that led to the arena, leaving Mairead fretting outside while Cleon and Fothair tried to make small talk despite the difference in language.

In the amphitheatre, four more soldiers under the command of a young *optio* guarded the doors at the inner end of the tunnel. Again, Lucius' rank combined with Geta's seal on the papers acted like a magic charm and the doors were opened, allowing them to walk through. For Brude it was a strange sensation walking out into an arena again, especially unarmed, but this time there was no crowd roaring a greeting, no baking sun beating down on the sand and no smell of sweat and fear from gladiators. Instead, the surrounding seats were deserted apart from a few patrolling soldiers who watched over the arena, which was full of ragged people, lying or sitting dejectedly on the hard earth, their clothes, skin and hair dirty and matted, their eyes sullen and resentful.

Lucius stopped. With a wave of his hand, he said, "I'll let you find them."

Brude began walking slowly through the prisoners, trying to ignore the silent appeal in their faces. These were his people and he wanted to free them all but he knew that was a futile dream. All he could do was find Castatin and Barabal. For the rest, as he knew all too well, there was little hope. He hardened his heart to their plight.

He checked each person, terrified that he would miss them, telling himself Mairead would not be mistaken about something like this. He made his way through the crowd carefully, wondering why they did not see him and come to him. At last he found them, near the far wall. It was Barabal he recognised but she was not looking at him. She was sitting with her back to the wooden wall, cradling Castatin in her arms, his head on her lap and his eyes closed. Brude squatted down in front of her, reaching out with his hand to feel the clammy heat of Castatin's forehead. "Hello, Barabal. I've come to take you home."

The girl looked at him, her eyes blank. Then she recognised him and she began to cry. She tried to speak but only sobs came from her tortured throat as she held on to Castatin and cried and cried.

Under the jealous gaze of the other prisoners, Brude gently moved Barabal's arms from around his son. He lifted the boy up. "Come on. He is not well and we need to make him better. Come with me." He thought at first that she would remain sitting there but she slowly pushed herself to her feet, shuffling after him, with tears still rolling down her cheeks. He made his way through the other captives, some of them looking threateningly at him as he carried Castatin towards the doors. Then Lucius came to meet him, two soldiers at his side, and the slaves made no move to stop him.

They passed through the doors, along the cool, dark tunnel which led outside. Mairead ran to meet them. "What's wrong?" she asked anxiously. "Is he all right?"

"He has a fever," Brude told her. "Let's get him back to the room. Can you look after Barabal?"

Despite her concern for her son, Mairead went to the girl. She put her arms around her, telling her she was safe now. Barabal cried and held on to her while Cleon, unable to say anything they would understand, stood silently. Lucius, unused to seeing the grief of slaves at such a personal level, looked away. The Roman asked Brude where they were staying. Brude told him. Lucius said, "We'll have to find somewhere better than that for you. Follow me. We'll go to see Caralugnus."

The strange procession attracted a lot of stares as they made their way round the edge of the city to a large, two-storey Roman house, elegantly decorated with murals and roofed with red tiles. This, Lucius announced, was the city home of Caralugnus, one of the leading citizens of Eboracum. Caralugnus turned out to be a middle-aged British nobleman who had wholeheartedly adopted Roman customs. In true Roman fashion he was busy in one of his public rooms, conducting business with some of his clients, but he quickly excused himself from them, hurrying to meet Lucius and his unusual companions. When Lucius mentioned Geta's name, Caralugnus clapped his hands to summon some servants. He ordered two rooms to be set aside on the upper floor of his home for Brude and the others. "You may stay as long as you need," he assured them. "Any friends of Geta Caesar are welcome in my home." He spoke to them in his native Brigante tongue, which they understood far better than Latin. Mairead thanked him profusely.

Brude carried Castatin up the stairs and laid him in a bed. He checked him over, heard the laboured breathing and felt the fever burning inside the boy. He turned to one of the servants. "I need a bowl of lukewarm water and some cloth, please." The servant scurried off while Mairead helped him undress Castatin. "We need to cool him down. And I need some medicine for him. When the water comes, you wash him all over. Try to get his body cool. I'll see if Lucius can get me into the legion's medical store."

Lucius was only too happy to oblige. Brude was back inside an hour, able to mix a drink for Castatin, using some medicine requisitioned from the legion's medical supplies. Mairead had got the boy's temperature down slightly but his head was still hot and he was breathing with difficulty. Brude gently lifted his head to put the beaker to his lips, talking to him, telling him to drink. He managed to get some liquid into Castatin's mouth. The boy swallowed, coughed, then took some more. His eyes flickered open and he saw Brude. "I knew you'd come," he said softly.

Castatin hovered in a fever for three days while Brude and Mairead took turns to watch him. When the fever broke, he was still weak and had trouble breathing. Brude was concerned because the chill had obviously got into Castatin's lungs. In Germania, he had seen men die when that happened. But at least the boy's fever was gone. He could only hope that time and rest would heal him completely.

Caralugnus was a concerned host and when Brude apologised for taking up room in his house, the old man brushed off his concerns. "Stay as long as you like," he insisted. "I have no family here and the place is too big for me anyway." He seemed anxious to please. Brude learned from Cleon that Lucius had told Caralugnus that Brude was an important Caledonian chieftain, an ally of Rome, and a friend of the emperor. That explained Caralugnus' generosity, Brude thought. He was tempted to tell Caralugnus the truth but Castatin would recover faster here than at Niger's rooms so he played the part of a dispossessed noble for the boy's sake.

He and Fothair had fetched their few belongings from Niger's rooms, telling the surly landlord to keep the balance of the money he had been paid already. Brude was glad to be away from Niger's place. He had shared out their money because he did not want to leave it in the lodgings while they were all out, and it was too risky to have one person carry all their wealth. Caralugnus' home was far safer.

He went to see Lucius again, handing him a bag of coins. "Your share of the profits, as promised," Brude told him.

Lucius smiled. "The money was intended as a gift, Marcus."

"I know. Take it anyway."

"My father always said you were an honourable man," Lucius said.

They settled in to their new home quickly. Barabal, washed and dressed in new clothes, with her hair brushed and combed, seemed to have recovered from their ordeal but she remained quiet and slightly withdrawn. Mairead told Brude the girl had been raped. She was still having nightmares about it, and about Seasaidh's murder. Barabal always hid in one of the rooms whenever Lucius came to see them; she saw any soldier as a threat to her. Brude was not sure what they could do but he and Mairead did their best to include her in their conversations, trying to reassure her that she was among friends.

Lucius was too busy to visit very often but Cleon made a point of coming to see them at least once a day, claiming that Lucius had no real need of him anyway. "There are more than enough secretaries and clerks in the fortress already for me to make much difference," he told Brude one evening as they sat under the shelter of the colonnade surrounding Caralugnus' peristyle garden, watching the rain splatter down.

"I can't believe you came here in the first place," said Brude. "I never thought you'd leave Rome."

Cleon looked around to check they were alone. Then he leaned close, switching to Greek as he said, "Things were not the same after old Aquila died."

"I can imagine. He was a decent man," Brude replied, his brain struggling to switch to Greek after so many months of not hearing or speaking the language.

"Indeed he was," Cleon agreed. "But he had a blind spot when it came to his wife." He paused, staring out over the garden, not looking at Brude. "Vipsania told me why you left."

Brude felt his face begin to redden. Cleon looked at him and gave a short bark of a laugh. "Don't worry, I haven't told anyone. Lucius would never believe me, even if I did tell him. And before you ask, I have no intentions of saying anything to your lovely new wife."

"She's guessed already that there was a woman involved," Brude admitted. "I am not proud of it, but it was difficult to say no to Agrippina."

"I can imagine," Cleon nodded. "I always thought she was a devious woman. She soon got her claws into Lucius when she discovered that Aquila had left nearly everything to him. She realised she could only keep the wealth through marrying Lucius. The poor boy didn't stand a chance once she turned her charms on him. It's caused a bit of a scandal in Rome, but she is only his step-mother and not much older than he is."

"And he's not so much of a boy now," observed Brude dryly.

"No indeed. He is turning into a most ambitious young man. Not the quiet child I once knew at all. His father's dreams and his new wife's urgings are pushing him into exalted circles. He aspires to the senate and I dare say he will get there. He sold all his father's business interests and invested in land, to make himself eligible. With no business to run, I had very little to do."

"So you decided to come to Britannia?" Brude could not hide his amusement.

"It was either that or stay in Rome, watching that conniving bitch try to scale the social ladder by climbing into other men's beds." Cleon shook his head. "I had no wish for that. And I suppose I did half hope to find you. Britannia looked such a small place on the maps. I had no idea it was so large."

Brude laughed. "You know damn well how large it is. It was you who showed me the maps."

Cleon chuckled. "Well, it worked anyway. Here you are. Perhaps the gods do listen, after all."

"I missed you too," Brude told him. "I am glad you came here. It is good to see you again."

"You have a family now as well," Cleon said.

"But probably no home to go back to."

"The war will not last. Another year and the whole island will be part of the empire. Then you can go home. Perhaps I might even come with you to see these houses of mud and sticks that you think are so wonderful."

The mention of the war made Brude sombre again. "There were hardly any houses left in my village when we left. The Romans destroyed most of them."

Cleon patted his knee. "I understand your concern, Marcus, but there is nothing you can do about it at the moment. You need to get your son well first. Then we shall discuss what is to be done next. One thing at a time."

Brude nodded. As usual, Cleon was right.

Castatin was up and about after two weeks but he was very weak. He coughed whenever he tried to exert himself. Brude sought advice from the Roman doctors at the legionary fort but they could not suggest anything more than rest, warmth and the herbs Brude already had. Castatin wanted to know what had happened at Broch Tava so Mairead took him aside to explain the truth about who his father really was. It was a difficult conversation and Castatin was quiet for a while afterwards before he came to Brude and said, "My mother tells me that you are my real father."

Brude, sitting in the peristyle garden enjoying a rare bout of sunshine between rain showers, patted the wall beside him, telling Castatin to sit. "I only found out a few months ago myself. It's a bit of a shock, isn't it?"

"Why didn't you say anything?"

"Because your father, I mean Colm, was my friend once and because your mother wanted it kept quiet. It would only have caused trouble. Anyway, I hadn't exactly been around for you when you were growing up."

"I'm glad he's dead," Castatin said with feeling. "He used to beat me, and my mother."

"I can understand your feelings," said Brude. "But he was not all bad. He did a lot of good things for the village. His problem was that he never learned to be content with what he had. He always wanted more."

"I hated him. I am glad you are my father."

"I am glad, too, Castatin. Now we have to learn how to be a family. It probably won't be easy for either of us. But as for hatred, try to keep that out of your heart. It does as much harm to you as to the person you hate. Perhaps it would be better for you simply to be glad that Colm is gone, not that he is dead. You would have been just as happy if he had gone off to be king of Parthia. It's his absence you are pleased about, not his death."

Castatin considered that for a moment, then asked, "Where is Parthia?"

Brude laughed. The boy was just like he had been at that age, always asking questions. "It's a long way from here. Ask Cleon to show you a map some time. Come on, Caralugnus has invited us all to dine with him this evening. In the meantime, I think a visit to the baths would be good for you. The hot steam might help you. If not, at least you'll be clean for meeting our host."

The baths were still what Brude missed most about life in Rome. The bathhouse in Eboracum was small and always busy. In true Pritani style, the locals did not bother too much with separate bathing times for men and women. The bathhouse had some times set aside for only men, and some for only women but, for most of the day, everyone mingled together, although Brude noticed that there were none of the sexual overtones Agrippina had introduced him to at the House of Venus. Not that it stopped Fothair arranging a few assignations. His height and lean, muscled body attracted a lot of attention, making him very popular with the young women.

Over their evening meal, dining from silver plates and goblets, Caralugnus regaled them with the benefits of Roman civilisation. "My grandfather insisted on living in a draughty wooden hut on a hilltop," he told them. "Our people scraped a living from the land, surviving on a diet which was bland, to say the least. And they were constantly fighting with neighbouring tribes. My father moved here when he decided to try the Roman way of life. I have to say that I am glad he did. I really couldn't imagine going back to the way our people used to live. We have the markets, we have the baths, we have roads and we have security."

Brude could see that Mairead and Fothair were both nodding in agreement. They were already starting to appreciate the comfort of life under Roman rule. Castatin had enjoyed the luxury of the baths as well. Only Barabal looked unconvinced.

"Brude and I built a house," said Fothair with his habitual grin. "No draughts at all. It even had its own well. The Romans burned it down, though. Just as well we never did build that bathhouse you were after. Imagine all that effort just for a wash, then the Romans coming along to burn it down."

Brude saw Barabal smile at that, and was pleased. She seemed to enjoy being around Fothair who was just about the only person who *could* make her smile.

"Civilisation comes at a price," Brude said to Caralugnus. "You are free to do as you want as long as what you want is the same thing the Romans want."

"I suspect that is the same whoever is in charge," replied Caralugnus.

"Maybe so, but the Romans enforce it far more effectively than anyone else. Didn't one of their own writers say that they like to make a desert and then call it peace?"

Caralugnus was impressed. "You have read Tacitus' work?"

"My friend Cleon has read it," Brude admitted. "But the other thing to keep in mind is that the poor in the empire are very poor indeed. Among the Boresti we care for our sick and elderly and nobody really goes hungry."

"The Romans believe people should work to earn their living. Festus said you had lived in Rome itself. I would have thought you would appreciate all the things life in the empire can offer."

Brude did not want to offend his host but he also wanted his friends to understand what was at stake. "The material things Rome can offer are beyond question," he said. "It is the things of the spirit that we risk losing. The soul of our people. For myself, I am not sure the price is worth paying."

Caralugnus nodded politely. "Well, each to his own. I have a cousin who still insists on living in a traditional village. He refuses to have any more to do with the Romans than he has to. But as for you, I fear you may have little choice in the matter. I hear that Caracalla is subduing all who oppose him in Caledonia."

Brude had heard that too. The official announcements were of great victories, towns taken and fierce tribes defeated, but he had also heard from Cleon that things were not going entirely the Romans' way. The Maeatae and the Caledonii were proving elusive, engaging in hit and run attacks rather than meeting the legions in open battle. "According to Lucius, it's going to be a long, slow job," Cleon had reported. In the end, though, there could only be one victor.

Caralugnus diplomatically changed the subject. Turning to Castatin he asked, "How is your health, young man? You still seem in some discomfort."

"My chest is still tight, sir," Castatin answered, "but I am feeling a lot better than I was."

"I'm afraid that it will be several weeks before he is fit to travel," Brude said. "We must impose on your hospitality for some time yet."

"It is a pleasure for me to have you here," Caralugnus replied. "Anyway, I would not recommend travelling back north just now. Not while there is a war on. Best to stay here until things settle down."

So they stayed a few more weeks, trying to keep a low profile. Caralugnus, obviously a more important figure than he let on, had many clients who visited him daily to pay their respects. Brude discovered that the nobleman had paid for the construction of a local temple for the worship of the imperial family. Their host was obviously a man of some means who was well regarded by the Romans.

Brude had wanted to be away by the time of the Lughnasa festival, which would still allow plenty of time to return to Broch Tava before the colder weather arrived. He was worried about what might have happened to his mother and old Seoras, and about the villagers who had fled into the forests with Caroc. They needed food and shelter for the winter and harvest time was approaching.

Despite his wishes, events conspired against him. By the time Castatin's health had improved enough to make travel possible, Barabal was looking pale and feeling permanently tired. Brude heard her being sick one morning but when he asked her what was wrong, she told him it was just an upset stomach. But she was sick again the next morning. Mairead told him what the problem was. "She's pregnant."

"Don't look at me!" Fothair protested in response to Brude's first reaction.

"You've been very friendly with her these past weeks," Brude commented.

"Not *that* friendly," said Fothair. "I mean, I would have, but she's been through a hard time and she just needs friends at the moment."

"She needs to know it was not her fault that she was raped," Mairead insisted, "and she certainly needs to know that the baby will be hers, one of the Boresti, not a Roman." She looked at the two men and shook her head, clearly suggesting they were not up to the task. "I'll talk to her. You two would just upset her."

Whatever Mairead said to Barabal seemed to put the girl's mind at rest but the pregnancy made her extremely unwell. She had difficulty keeping any food down and was permanently tired. Then she began to worry that her child would not have a father but, as soon as Fothair heard that, he solved the problem by telling her that he would be the father if she wanted him. She smiled and said yes, so they had a small celebration feast. The two of them spoke the words in front of Brude and Mairead as their witnesses and they were married. Fothair immediately stopped going to the bathhouse during the morning, visiting instead during the late afternoon when women were not allowed in.

Barabal, though, was too unwell to travel far, so the feast of Lughnasa came and went and the long, wet summer slowly turned to autumn, bringing biting winds and more rain. Brude resigned himself to the probability of staying in Eboracum for the winter. He was not bored because Cleon was always willing to talk, but the call of home was strong in him now. He was torn between the desire to return north with his new family and wanting to stay near Cleon.

To pass the time during their enforced stay, he took Mairead and Castatin on long walks round the city, teaching them some Latin and how to read some of the simpler signs. They enjoyed being together and life in Eboracum was easy for them, because they were staying with Caralugnus and Brude still had plenty of money. After a while, though, Mairead admitted that the attractions of the city were not so great that she would relish staying permanently.

Some days later, they got a reminder of the harsher side to life under the Romans when they saw slaves being herded onto ships that were moored on the broad river, preparing to sail out to sea and south towards Rome. Mairead put her arm round Castatin's shoulders, holding him close, knowing that if things had turned out differently he could have been among the captives being shepherded on to the galleys.

In Caralugnus' home, things were more pleasant. The nobleman often invited other people to dine with them, mostly wealthy Romano-Britons, like himself, so Brude kept up with all the gossip. As the days grew shorter and nightfall came earlier, he heard some momentous news. The emperor had returned to Eboracum, bringing his wife, who always accompanied him on campaign, together with a host of Praetorian Guards. Eboracum was, once again, the centre of government for the whole empire. It threatened to be an uncertain government, for the emperor was said to be very ill, so ill it was rumoured he might not last the winter. Caracalla had been left to continue the fighting in Caledonia.

Unbidden, Veleda's words came back to haunt Brude. *Cut off the head and the beast will die*, she had said. He recalled, vividly, the long night that he and Fothair had spent talking with Nechtan's druid in her hut. Trouble elsewhere would make the Romans leave, Brude had told her. Yet trouble was not likely to erupt with Septimius Severus as emperor, for he had an iron fist and thirty legions at his command. He had kept the empire under control for seventeen years.

But if the emperor were to die, everything would change. Brude realised that there might be salvation for his people after all. If he was prepared to pay the price as Veleda had suggested.

Eboracum A.D. 210

Julia Domna, wife of the emperor Septimius Severus, was a formidable woman. At forty years old, she was twenty-five years younger than her husband but she was every bit his equal in ambition and astuteness. Some said she was his superior in intellect. She had created a stir in Rome by insisting on accompanying her husband on his campaigns against Parthia, ignoring the tradition which kept most upper class Roman wives at home while their husbands went off to war. In a society that normally allowed women no role in public life, she was an exception, regarded by many as the real power behind the imperial throne. Cleon, always a source of gossip, said that Severus reputedly made no major political decisions without discussing them with his wife first. Rumour said he always followed her advice. She was well read, spoke Greek and Punic as well as Latin, and was interested in philosophy to such an extent that she had been known to argue with some of the famous Greek sophists who were trained in rhetoric.

She sat at the head of the table beside her younger son, Geta, leading the after-dinner conversations on whatever subject happened to crop up. Brude, sitting at the far end, beside Caralugnus, made a point of keeping quiet, content to merely listen to the conversation. He had been surprised by the invitation but Caralugnus had insisted he come along as his guest. Mairead had selected some new clothes for him, trimmed his hair and sent him off with a kiss and a look of envy. "I wish I was going," she had said. Brude had wished that he was not going.

Still, he could not help but be impressed with the way Julia Domna acted. She was elegant and poised but, while she was not unattractive, the things that were most notable about her were her wit and intelligence.

There were around thirty guests at the table, mostly local nobles like Caralugnus, although there was a handful of Geta's officers, including Lucius. It soon became evident that Julia Domna was keen to let everyone know that, even though her husband was seriously ill, she was hopeful that he would recover. She made it plain that, if he did not, the empire would still be in safe hands. "My husband has named both of our sons as Caesar," she said pleasantly. "I can assure you all that between them they have the ability to govern the empire. Caracalla is turning out to be a very successful general, just like his father, while Geta here has proved he is a very able administrator. So I am sure that, if the worst were to happen, which I pray it will not, my sons are more than capable of taking over."

Caralugnus leaned over to Brude and whispered, "What she means is that she will rule through them." He grinned mischievously, "Mind you, I think she'd make a better emperor than either of them."

Julia Domna was a charming and entertaining hostess. She made a point of speaking to each of her guests. When they had arrived, she had greeted each one, standing at the doorway, dressed in a long dress of green silk, her hair curled and piled high on her head. Brude had been introduced to her by Caralugnus as a chieftain of the Caledonii but she had obviously been well briefed. Smiling at Brude, she said, "You must be the ex-gladiator. You have done well to rise to become a chieftain of one of our allies."

Brude replied modestly, "I am the son of the former chieftain of one very small village, my lady. I was not even elected as head man before I had to leave and come down here."

"Yes, I hear there was an unfortunate mistake over your son. He is well, I trust?"

"He is fine now, my lady. Thank you." Brude was impressed at her knowledge. Her description of Castatin's capture as an unfortunate mistake was a clever piece of political wordplay, designed to ensure that he remained an ally of Rome, however insignificant he or his village were. He wondered how she would have described Cruithne's death and the burning of the village.

Her attempts to charm everyone were only partly successful because rumours about the emperor's failing health continued to circulate, despite official announcements that he was recovering.

Lying in bed that night, Mairead was full of questions about the empress. She complained when Brude was not able to give a detailed description of the empress's clothes, hair and make-up. "Why do men never pay attention to that sort of thing?" she asked him when his answers were too vague for her liking.

Mairead was fascinated by Julia Domna. Even in the short time she had been in Eboracum, Mairead had noticed how little influence women had outside the home, so she was delighted to learn that there was at least one Roman woman who exercised real power. "Is she pretty?" she asked Brude.

"Not particularly. She has a way about her that is attractive, I suppose, but she's no beauty. Not like you."

Mairead gave him a playful slap. "Flatterer! You noticed that much about her then?" Brude, though, was not concerned about Julia Domna. It was the emperor's health that occupied his mind. He found himself offering silent prayers to the gods he had ignored for many years, wishing for the emperor's death. If the emperor died, surely his sons would return to Rome? He mentioned his thoughts to Cleon the next day.

"You are probably right," Cleon agreed after some thought, "but that does not mean all of the army will go with them. They can leave their legions to finish the job."

Brude was forced to agree but Veleda's words and her own self-sacrifice had laid a compulsion on him. He needed the emperor to die. If Severus died and the Roman army stayed, Veleda's geas would have no power over him. He would have to make the best life he could, with Mairead and Castatin, under Roman rule. But if the emperor recovered, Brude would have to think of a way to kill him. He had promised himself not to kill again, but Veleda had forced him into a position where the fate of the Pritani rested on whether the emperor lived or died. And Brude was the only one of the Pritani who could do what had to be done. He wanted to forget it, to persuade himself that he had a family to care for, that he had no obligation to a dead druid, but the old woman had done something to his mind. She had laid a spell of some sort on him and he feared to go against the order of a druid. *Cut off the head and the beast will die.* As would Brude, together with his family and friends.

He had to get Mairead and the others away. He did not feel able to discuss his plans, even with Mairead, but he considered buying a wagon or carriage so that Barabal would be able to ride in comfort. The army, though, had commandeered every spare vehicle so that they could keep supplies going north by road during the winter when the seas grew too rough for their ships. Which meant they were stuck in Eboracum, with winter approaching.

Crowds gathered at the temple of the imperial cult to offer prayers for the emperor, sacrificing in honour of his image. Brude took everyone along to join in. "Questions might be asked if we are seen not to worship in the Roman way," he explained. "If someone denounces us as Christians, we might find ourselves in trouble, so it's best to go along with it." So they joined the crowd who gathered in the forum outside the temple, watching while a bull was sacrificed and the priests offered up prayers for the emperor's health.

"I thought the emperor was a man," Castatin challenged, as they made their way back to Caralugnus' home afterwards.

"He is," Brude replied.

"But wasn't that his image on show along with the other gods? I recognised the face and the curly beard."

Once again Brude was reminded of his own curiosity when he was a boy. He smiled in pleasure at Castatin's questions. He told Cleon what Castatin had asked. "Just like you," the old Greek said.

"You'd better explain it to him," said Brude. "I always struggle with that sort of thing."

Cleon was usually never one to turn down a chance to mock the Romans but the language barrier presented some problems so Brude had to try to explain it to his son. "The emperor is a man," he said, "but he has a divine quality because he is blessed by the gods."

"Why?" Castatin asked.

"Well, it is self-evident, surely?" chuckled Brude. "He would not be emperor unless he had divine qualities, would he? The very fact that he is the emperor shows that he is blessed by the gods. That means he can intercede directly with them on behalf of the people."

Castatin did not look convinced. After some thought, he said, "I heard he was emperor because he commanded more legions than his opponents when he seized power."

Cleon's eyes shone with amusement when Brude translated the question. "That is correct."

"So was he divine before he was emperor?" Castatin asked.

"Of course not!" exclaimed Cleon after Brude told him what Castatin had asked. "That would be impossible."

Castatin said, "So he only became divine when he became emperor and he must be divine otherwise he would not be emperor. Is that right?"

"Something like that," Brude agreed.

"Yes, that's about it," Cleon confirmed. "One fact confirms the other. It's very simple really."

"It sounds complicated to me," observed Castatin.

"Me, too," said Mairead, who had been listening in with interest.

Brude smiled. "The Roman religion is more about ritual than belief. You can believe what you want as long as you are seen to worship the way they do. Their gods are happy as long as the proper sacrifices are made at the appropriate time."

Cleon nodded when Brude repeated that in Latin. "That's right," he agreed. Then he looked at Brude with a mischievous sparkle in his eyes. "Have you told the boy about Epicurus yet?"

"Not yet. Our language does not have the right words to explain all the concepts."

"Then he'd better learn Latin quickly," Cleon grinned.

"You could always learn our language," Brude suggested again.

"Latin is bad enough, thank you very much."

Brude's silent hopes that the emperor's health would fail were eventually dashed. Severus recovered from his sick bed and was seen, weak and frail but still taking an active part in governing the empire. Eboracum was much busier now as emissaries came and went, travelling from all parts of the empire to see the emperor. Brude saw little of Lucius as all officers were kept busy with the countless tasks required for the smooth running of the empire, but Cleon still visited most days to keep Brude informed of what was happening. "The army is in winter quarters but they expect to complete the conquest next year," Cleon said. "Although, from what I can gather, it seems your people are being stubborn. They are refusing to fight in open battle. The Romans can't seem to pin them down. But they are still destroying towns and villages so eventually there will be nowhere for the Picti to hide."

Samhain came and went. Caralugnus held a small private celebration with a few guests. It was not the wild, open-air, fire-light feast and dance that the Boresti were used to, but there was plenty of food and wine and the servants had made some lanterns from hollowed-out turnips. By their ghostly light, Fothair told some suitably gruesome tales of the evil spirits that stalked the land during that night.

A few weeks later, the emperor invited many of the local dignitaries to a feast to celebrate Saturnalia. Cleon managed to ensure that both Brude and Mairead were included. There was a light dusting of snow on the ground as they made their way to the legionary fort with Caralugnus. Brude was uncomfortable at being seen to be so close to the imperial family but Mairead was delighted. She had bought herself a new dress for the occasion, a Pritani-style long dress of brightly coloured cloth. "Stop worrying," she told him, "there will be lots of people there. The emperor probably won't even notice you."

Mairead was right. The great hall in the Principia was crowded because the emperor wanted to demonstrate to as many people as possible that he was still very much alive and in command. He looked thin and the skin on his face was wrinkled, but his eyes were bright and he appeared to be in good humour.

Mairead's exotic appearance in her native-style dress combined with a small, freshly-painted Pritani design on her face created something of a stir. She enjoyed the evening, trying as many of the dishes as she could and talking animatedly to any of her neighbours who spoke the local tongue.

Despite apparently enjoying the Roman lifestyle, she told Brude later, "It was nice but this life is not for me. I still want to go home. Barabal really can't travel all that way, but once she has the baby we should leave."

"That probably won't be until the spring," he pointed out. "The way things are going, home will be part of the empire by then."

"Well, if we have to become Romans, I'd rather do it among my friends than here, among strangers," she said firmly.

Mairead insisted on discussing it with Barabal and Fothair who both agreed, so they at least had something to look forward to. Mairead reckoned that Barabal would have her baby around the time of the Imbolc festival, which heralded the start of the month the Romans called February. They set their sights on heading for home two months after that.

Brude could still not tell Mairead about Veleda's injunction to him. He hated keeping it a secret from her but the consequences were so dire that he could not bring himself to talk of it.

A few days after Saturnalia Cleon arrived, looking sombre. He brought bad news from north of the Wall. "I heard Lucius discussing the latest dispatch from Caracalla," he told Brude. "He says that he discovered a conspiracy among the Boresti."

Brude's heart sank. Mairead's Latin was not good enough to follow what Cleon was saying but she made out the name of their tribe. She saw Cleon's expression, so she gripped Brude's hand, asking him what was wrong.

Reluctantly, he translated what Cleon told him, speaking slowly, hating what he was saying. "There is a report that the Boresti rose in arms against the Romans. At a place where there is a river crossing, they attacked the soldiers who were guarding the bridge, killing a great number of them. They drove the garrison out and then destroyed the bridge."

"Peart," Mairead breathed. "That must be Peart."

Brude nodded his agreement as Cleon went on, "Caracalla sent a strong force to crush the revolt. His report says that all the rebels were either killed or enslaved. The Romans are rebuilding the bridge." He shook his head sadly. "I am sorry."

"Did they say who led the revolt?" Fothair asked.

"No, there were no names mentioned."

"What about our village? What about Broch Tava?" Mairead struggled to stifle a sob.

"There was no mention of anywhere else. Just the place where there was a river crossing."

That was something at least, but the dreadful news had shocked them all. Fothair's face wore a pained expression at the thought of what had happened to his hometown. Brude just stood there, feeling numb, while Veleda's face appeared in his memory and her words drummed through his head with an inexorable beat. *Cut off the head and the beast will die.*

Brude could no longer keep his thoughts from Mairead. He spoke to her that night, when they were alone in their bedroom, telling her what Veleda and he had discussed that night in Dun Nechtan. He explained to her the meaning behind Veleda sacrificing herself and Nechtan.

"She wants you to kill the emperor?" Mairead asked, reacting more calmly than Brude had expected.

"It is the only thing that might stop all the Pritani being crushed."

"Might?"

"I cannot be sure it will work. The emperor's sons will certainly return to Rome but they might leave some legions to finish what they have started. But if I do nothing, the war will continue. The Caledonii and the Maeatae will be destroyed, just like the Boresti. Veleda knew I am the only one who could possibly get close enough to the emperor to have any chance of success." He held her hand, squeezing it gently. "But I do not want to lose you a second time. Not after we have only just found each other again."

Mairead put her arms around him. They held each other in silence for a long while. He did not know what else to say but the embrace told him that she did not want to lose him either. After a while, Mairead lay back. Her expression, illuminated by the solitary oil lamp, which cast flickering shadows around the room, was calm but determined. "You know I love you," she said. "I always have. I know you were worried that I was enjoying life here too much, that I might have wanted to turn my back on what is left of our people. But this life we are living just now, pleasant though it is, is built on the work of others. I sit here with no wool to spin, no food to prepare, no cloth to sew. Slaves bring me everything I want. Above all, I cannot help but remember what happened at Dun Nechtan. The people there were of the Boresti and now any of them who survived are slaves too." She gripped his hands firmly in hers. "I understand what you meant when you told Caralugnus about the price of Roman life being too high. We are in danger of losing everything our people have cherished for generations."

Brude heaved a sigh of relief. "I hoped you would understand."

"I do. But I do not want to lose you. I am not so naïve as to think that the Romans would not take their revenge on all of us if you assassinate the emperor."

"You must all leave and hide somewhere."

Mairead nodded. "We need to get everyone together to make plans. They must understand what is at stake. We need to think of a plan which would allow you to do what you need to do without giving up your own life."

Brude pursed his lips. "I can't think of any way to do that."

"Then we will put our heads together until we *do* think of a way." Her determination and strength of will put new heart into him. If there was a way, they would find it together.

The next day, while Caralugnus was meeting with his clients, Mairead called Fothair, Barabal and Castatin into one of the other public rooms. She barred the window shutters and closed the door so that nobody could overhear. She had Brude explain what he had told her the previous evening about Veleda's plot. When he was finished, Mairead told them all, "We need to know what each of you think before we do anything else."

Barabal did not hesitate. Her pretty face was a mask of stern determination. "Kill him," she said without hesitation. She had lost her home, her freedom, her innocence and her sister. Her answer came as no surprise to anyone.

Brude looked at Fothair. The tall warrior scratched his chin thoughtfully. "I remember Dun Nechtan and Peart. I agree with Barabal, but it will mean death for all of us if we do this." He reached for Barabal's hand. "I am not afraid for myself, but we have others to think of."

Brude nodded then looked at Castatin. The boy was still two years from becoming a man but he was in this as well. Brude knew he was no fool. Castatin returned his gaze and said, "If it will help save the Pritani we must try."

"It might not make any difference," Brude warned him. "But doing nothing will certainly mean the destruction of all the tribes."

"Then we should do it," Castatin declared, clearly confident that Brude could achieve anything.

"We are agreed then," said Mairead briskly.

"Then I will do it," Brude told them. "We have to think of a way of getting the rest of you somewhere safe, so that the Romans cannot find you."

Fothair held up his hand. "You will surely die if you do this alone. You may be good enough to get close and fight your way past a couple of guards but you will never be able to fight your way through the whole Roman army to get away."

"Tell me something I don't know," Brude said ruefully.

Castatin piped up, "Maybe you don't need to fight anyone."

"What do you mean?" asked Brude, intrigued.

"If you could find a way into the palace at night, you could kill him while he is sleeping."

"There would still be guards," Fothair pointed out. "You can't just walk past them."

"Maybe you can," said Brude thoughtfully.

"How?"

"I'm not entirely sure yet. I have an idea, but we would need some help from inside the fortress."

Mairead smiled for the first time since he had told her of his plan. "Cleon?"

Brude was sure he could trust Cleon not to betray them, but he still broached the subject with apprehension. What he was asking was more than anyone would ever expect to be asked. He persuaded Cleon to accompany him on a walk to the river where they stopped, out of earshot of anyone, looking down on the busy wharves from a low hill. The day was overcast with a westerly wind blowing fallen leaves around and biting at their faces. It was not the best day to choose for a walk outside the city. Cleon was no fool and knew Brude well. "What is this all about?" he asked. "Something is bothering you."

"You'd better sit down," Brude told him, indicating a large rock sunk into the hillside. When Cleon had dutifully sat down, Brude told him about Veleda and what she had told him to do.

Cleon listened in silence. He tried to appear composed but when Brude told him what he intended, his face grew pale. "You cannot be serious!" he gasped.

"I wish I was not, but I am. The fate of my people is at stake."

Cleon clasped his hands together as if to stop them shaking. "You know what will happen to you if you do this?"

"I know, but I have a plan. Or, at least, the outline of a plan."

"I could be executed for even listening to you," Cleon moaned.

"I will not tell you if you do not want to hear it."

Cleon's shoulders slumped. "I would guess that the only reason you want to tell me is because you need my help. That means that, if I refuse to help you, you will go ahead anyway. You will do something dramatic, which will result in your death. Am I right?"

Brude nodded. "I am sorry."

Cleon let out a deep breath. "I was a slave, you know. The son and grandson of slaves. Old Aquila's father freed me in his will. I was thirty years old then, the age you are now but I knew nothing except the life of a slave. Since then I have tried to live as quietly and as comfortably as possible. Now it comes to this."

"I am truly sorry, Cleon. I should not have told you."

Cleon waved a hand dismissively. "Nonsense! It would have been far worse for me if you had not told me and ended up getting yourself killed. I don't think I could bear that. You, my dear Marcus, have a way of making people want to do as you say. It is just that what you want from me is a great deal. A very great deal."

"If I could think of another way to do it, I would," Brude told him earnestly.

"I know."

"So will you help me? Help me to do this in a way that keeps us alive?"

"Of course I will. You know, you are probably the bravest man I have ever met. I never had the courage to leave Rome and go back to my homeland. Yet, you turn your back on everything that most men want so that you can return to the wilds with your houses of sticks and mud. Then, when Rome, the mightiest power on earth threatens you, you ride through half the province to rescue your son. Now you have decided to kill the emperor himself. I wish I was unafraid like you."

"I am afraid," said Brude, "My heart beats fast and my nerves are on edge just thinking about this. I don't want to die."

"Who does?" Cleon responded. "But the difference is that you don't show your fear. Look at me, I am trembling like an autumn leaf and you haven't even told me what your plan is yet. By Hercules, I could do with a drink right now."

"Then let us go back to Caralugnus' house. We can lock ourselves in a room with a pitcher of wine. I will tell you my plan and you can tell me what is wrong with it."

Ten days after Brude had outlined his idea, Cleon began to think it might actually have a chance of success. He had told Brude he was not a brave man, and it was true. He lost a lot of sleep over what he had committed to do. But in all his life, Brude was the one person he had come across whom he considered a true friend. Born and brought up in Greece, from a long line of slaves, he had been brought to Rome when he was in his early twenties by Lucius' grandfather. He had stayed there ever since. Like many Greeks, he both admired and feared the Romans. Their civilisation was young compared to Greece, but they had imposed their way of life on almost all the known world. Greece, for the first time, was at peace, the constant inter-city warfare that had dogged Greek culture for centuries having been crushed into obedience to Roman rule. Yet Cleon had become even more Greek during his time in Rome, trying in some small way to show that he was not a Roman. Deep down he knew that Rome did not care, as long as he did what was required of him. That was what hurt him most. Even after he had been freed, he had spent his life conforming. Submitting. He feared that he was still a slave. Brude had shown him a way to change that.

Cleon thought about his ties to Rome. He had had a healthy regard for old Aquila, occasionally bordering on friendship, but it was a friendship born of mutual respect for each other's abilities rather than true closeness. As for young Lucius, Cleon felt that he owed no real allegiance to him, whatever Lucius may have felt. The young man had turned from a quiet, polite boy into a driven, ambitious individual who had little time for anyone who could not further his career. Cleon was certainly not in that category. While he was useful to Lucius as a private secretary, he was certainly not indispensable.

Yet Brude, or Marcus as Cleon still thought of him, was different. When Aquila had first mentioned the idea of hiring an ex-gladiator to train Lucius in the use of the sword, Cleon had thought the idea crazy but had gone along with it to humour the old knight. At Aquila's bidding, he had spoken to Trimalchio and, more importantly, to Trimalchio's freedmen and slaves. He had also spoken to the old lanista, Curtius. Then he had surreptitiously watched Brude from a distance on a few occasions. Everything he heard and saw suggested that the freed gladiator was not a simple brute from the wilds of Caledonia but a man who kept himself to himself, who spoke well, who learned quickly and who could be trusted. So Cleon had recommended to Aquila that he speak to the gladiator himself. Two days later, Brude had become part of Aquila's household.

He was half Cleon's age when he arrived, yet Cleon found a friend. Brude had been keen to learn as much as Cleon could teach him about anything and everything. The young Caledonian had learned to read and write and to speak Greek with a speed which astonished Cleon. He had found himself enjoying teaching the young man far more than he had ever enjoyed teaching Aquila's sons. Brude was indeed like the son he had never had.

Now Brude was determined to embark on the most dangerous venture anyone could dream of. And Cleon had agreed to help him because of their friendship and because he realised that Brude's motives were not selfish. Many emperors had met violent deaths, either by the sword or by poison, but always it had been because someone else wanted the power that being emperor brought. Brude wanted the emperor's death to end a war and to save his people. He wanted nothing more than to melt back into obscurity, far from the empire, with no dreams of power for himself. It was a humbling experience for Cleon, so used to the competitive nature of Roman society, to find someone who genuinely wanted something for the good of other people without reward for himself. Men like Caralugnus, he knew, would pay for public buildings at their own expense but they, in turn, expected to be elected to positions of authority. Nobody Cleon knew had ever truly done anything without an element of self-interest. So Brude had snared him with his plans for self-sacrifice and Cleon had agreed to help.

At first he had not known what he could do but all Brude initially wanted was information and here, Lucius was very useful. The young officer, like many Romans, often spoke in the presence of slaves and freedmen as if they were not there. He was always prepared to speak about his relationship with Geta Caesar at the slightest prompting. Cleon only had to express mild curiosity and Lucius would show off how close he was to the emperor's son by revealing the latest gossip from the imperial family.

Cleon also made a point of wandering the corridors of the Principia, speaking to any slaves and freedmen he met. He adopted the persona of an overly friendly old man who liked to talk, not a difficult task for him as he had always enjoyed gossip and was naturally outgoing. Every couple of days he would meet Brude and his companions at Caralugnus' house to pass on whatever pieces of information he could.

At Brude's request, he also managed to obtain certain small items; some sealing wax, some parchment, vellum and even a small papyrus scroll and writing implements. As a secretary, such things were easy to appropriate.

The short winter days were surprisingly mild after such a miserable summer. There was a brief cold snap in the middle of January, when the wind came from the east, bringing snow and ice in its wake, but that only lasted a few days. Generally, the weather was dull, overcast and sometimes wet. Cleon professed not to believe Brude that the sun did sometimes shine in Britannia.

He arrived at Caralugnus' home late one afternoon and was admitted without question. He paid his respects to Caralugnus personally, exchanging some minor gossip with him. Cleon knew that Brude felt badly about hiding their plans from Car-alugnus. The nobleman had been more than kind to them and they were abusing his hospitality, but he was also a Roman, even if he had been born and bred in Britannia, so they could not trust him not to betray them, if he learned of their plot.

Strolling through the atrium and on through the peristyle, Cleon saw the boy, Castatin, who reminded him so much of Brude in the way he acted and the questions he asked. The youngster ran to meet him and they climbed the steps together to find the others waiting for them in the large bedroom.

"I managed to get some more sealing wax," said Cleon, handing over a stick of the hard, red wax. "Why on earth do you need so much?"

"Practice," Brude replied with an enigmatic smile.

"Practice for what?"

"We have an imprint of Caracalla's seal on the letter he gave us when we came south," Brude explained. "Fothair is trying to carve a replica."

"You are going to forge letters from Caracalla?" asked Cleon with surprise.

"Technically, we are only going to forge the seal. You are going to forge the letters."

"Me?"

Brude laughed. "Sit down, Cleon, and don't panic. All we need is someone who can write neatly in the manner of an impe-rial secretary. Nobody will know it is your writing."

"But what am I to write?"

"All in good time," said Brude. "Now, sit down so that we can tell you what we have done. Then you can tell us what you have learned."

The discussion took a while because Brude still had to trans-late everything, but they were used to this by now. "We have found a local apothecary who stocks a wide range of herbs and medicines," Brude told Cleon. "I've bought a lot of stuff from him, whether I need it or not, but among it I got a supply of what we need. It should not arouse any suspicions."

"That is good."

"Tomorrow Fothair, Castatin and I are taking our horses for a ride in the country."

"In the middle of winter?"

"The weather's quite mild and the horses have not had a decent run for months. The ostler only has them out for a short time every few days."

"You plan to visit Caralugnus' cousin, is that right?" Brude had already mentioned this part of the plan to Cleon.

"That's right," agreed Brude. "If he is as anti-Roman as Caralugnus says he is, I am hoping he will help us. There are some things we need which will be hard for us to get here."

"Well, you had best get them quickly for I think I have found a way in for you." Cleon was pleased with himself but forced himself to speak slowly, so that Brude could translate his words for the others. "First of all, a bit of gossip. According to young Master Lucius, Geta was not all that pleased that his father recovered. It seems the emperor's son is concerned that his older brother will have an opportunity to make a name for himself as a great general, which would, of course, mean that he would be popular with the legions."

"More popular than Geta, you mean?"

"Exactly! Geta wants to go back to Rome before Caracalla builds too much of a reputation. He thought that he would get his way if his father died."

"So he wants his own father dead?"

"Lucius may be exaggerating," Cleon cautioned. "Let us assume that Geta would not be disappointed if his father were to die, although I don't think we should necessarily count on him hastening the event. The empress is very much the one in charge in the imperial family and she wants her husband alive and well."

"It would be too dangerous to approach Geta with an offer of arranging his father's death, anyway," said Brude.

"My thoughts exactly," Cleon agreed. "So, let us move on. The emperor is suffering from gout and has great difficulty walking. He has had a room prepared on the ground floor, where he sleeps now."

"Does that help?"

"It means the rooms are more easily reached, without going through the entire building."

"So all we have to do is get in."

"There is an adjoining room but it has been locked."

"Then we need a key."

Cleon nodded sadly. "I will see what I can do. But it will not be easy."

"Do what you can," Brude told him. "But don't put yourself in danger."

"Now you tell me!" Cleon laughed to try to cover his fear. "Just being around you is dangerous."

"So we may have a way in, but why the hurry?"

"Because the empress is holding a feast in twenty days' time. She wants as many local dignitaries invited as possible. The place will be full of visitors coming and going."

When Mairead heard this she protested, "Barabal's child is due any day now. We need to wait until she is well enough to travel."

"It will be the best chance we have," Cleon told them. "The emperor usually retires early, so he will be alone in his room while the Principia is full of strangers. Everyone else will be at the feast."

"We are not ready," Fothair said gloomily.

"Then, let us try to be ready," Brude announced. "We have a lot to do. Cleon is right. This sounds like the ideal opportunity. If we miss this, who knows when we might get another chance?"

Brude drove them on with a sense of urgency. Barabal's child was due at any time so she was forced to stay in the house but Mairead began spending more of Brude's dwindling supply of gold and silver in stocking up on travel clothes and making plans for departure. Caralugnus was disappointed when Brude told him they intended to leave, but he understood their desire to return home. He assured Brude that he would help in any way he could. "You have been too kind already," said Brude.

Caralugnus dismissed the notion. "Let me know if there is anything else I can do," he said. "I insist." That made Brude feel even worse about deceiving the nobleman. He felt worse still when Caralugnus made them a present of a carriage and two horses because he was concerned about them travelling with a baby. "You should wait until the springtime," he told Brude.

"Normally, we would," said Brude, "but our people need us." The gift of the carriage was far more than he had expected but Caralugnus insisted that they use it. It would make the first part of the journey easier, so Brude accepted it gratefully.

They continued to develop their plans in secret. As he had told Cleon, he rode out with Fothair and Castatin. The weather was still relatively calm for the time of year, the sky a clear, bright blue, though their breath steamed in the cold air. Caralugnus had told them roughly where his cousin lived so they headed off in search of the village, following trackways across the hills and dales. Brude had worried that they might have to try several times but they asked directions from a travelling tinker who told them how to get to the village of Moritasgus which they found by late morning.

Moritasgus was a great bear of a man who wore his hair and his moustache long, with his chin clean shaven in the British fashion. His home, a traditional Brigante village, was a cluster of roundhouses huddled alongside a stream at the foot of a hill, which was crowned with the ruins of an old hill fort. "The Romans destroyed the fort years ago," he explained, "so we built our new village down here." He was wary of them at first, because Brude looked and dressed like a Roman, but he soon warmed to them when he learned who they were. He invited them in to his roundhouse where they sat round the fire, drinking hot tisane while Brude explained what they wanted from him.

Moritasgus listened politely. When Brude was done, he said, thoughtfully, "You will not tell me why you need these things?"

"It would be safer for you if we do not," Brude told him. "For us as well. The fewer people who know, the safer we will be." He pulled a small leather pouch from inside his tunic, passing it over to the big Brigante chieftain. There was a clink of coins as Moritasgus took the bag. "A small gift," Brude told him.

Moritasgus weighed the pouch in his hand. He smiled. "Not so small, I think. Silver or gold?"

"Both."

Moritasgus laid the pouch at his side, unopened. "I thank you for your gift but there is no need of that. We will do as you ask because, despite the way you look, you are not Romans, and whatever it is you are up to, I suspect it will do them harm. We are able to do little to resist them these days. We lost many warriors, two summers past, and many villages were destroyed. My village was saved only thanks to my cousin persuading the Romans we were harmless." He smiled a wolfish grin. "I don't think they believed him, but they let us live. They settled for taking half our livestock and crops along with all our weapons."

Brude grinned. It was no wonder the Romans had not believed Moritasgus was harmless. He was a big man who exuded an air of confidence and a certainty of violence if he was crossed. Seeing him, Brude could understand why the Romans had always had trouble keeping the Brigantes subdued. "So you have no weapons?" he asked, worried that this might affect Moritasgus' ability to help.

The big Brigante laughed. "I said they took all our weapons. All the ones they could find, anyway. We have our own smith who makes tools and farming implements." His bared teeth showed that the smith made more than just that. "Now tell me, when will this happen?"

"Probably in eighteen days from now. I will send my man Fothair to you, a few days before, to confirm whether we are ready."

Moritasgus' eyebrows shot up in surprise. "That is not long."

"If you cannot get what we need a few days before, we will have to change the plan."

"It will not be easy," said Moritasgus. "But if it can be done, we will do it."

They clasped hands to seal their bargain. With that deal done, Brude began to dream that there was some hope of success after all.

Barabal's labour began on the night before the old festival of Imbolc. The men were banished to a room on the lower floor where Caralugnus stayed up with them, while Mairead and some of the older slave women took charge. Fothair paced the room anxiously, much to Caralugnus' amusement. The child was not even his, yet Fothair had promised to be a father so he worried about what was happening. Barabal had been unwell for almost her entire pregnancy and Fothair worried that the child would be a sickly one. Mairead had told him that the opposite was usually true, but he was not convinced.

Then, in the early hours of the morning, they heard a baby's cry. Soon Mairead came down, saying with a grin, "It's a girl. And she is fine." Fothair dashed up the stairs. The others followed to find Barabal, tired and looking physically drained, with the baby wrapped up tight, lying contentedly beside her. "She is beautiful," said Fothair. "And so big."

"She is strong and healthy," Mairead said. "Now you must decide on a name for her."

Fothair exchanged a look with Barabal who nodded in response to his silent question. He told them, "That is easy. We will call her Seasaidh."

Caralugnus tried again to persuade them to stay until after the feast but Brude was adamant that they would leave as soon as Barabal was up and about. "The emperor and his family won't miss us," he told Caralugnus. "I visited the temple of Apollo to ask for an augury and the signs are right for us to go." Brude had thought that the sacrificing of a small pigeon and the reading of the entrails was a bizarre ritual but Cleon had suggested it and, just as Cleon had predicted, the priest announced the omens favourable. This gave them a good excuse to leave. No Roman would ever consider arguing against favourable omens. "What if the omens aren't favourable?" Brude had asked Cleon.

"Pay the priest enough and they will be," Cleon promised him.

They went over their plan again and again. Cleon was worried that there was still a large element of luck required but he managed to solve their biggest problem for them. With seven days to go before the feast, he arrived at Caralugnus' home with a small, rectangular wooden box, which he handed to Brude with great solemnity.

"What is it?" Brude asked him.

"Open it and see. But carefully. Do not touch what is inside."

Brude gently lifted off the lid and saw that the box contained two blocks of soft wax, each of which was imprinted with the outline of a large key. He looked at Cleon who beamed back at him. "Master Lucius was duty officer yesterday. He had the key to the room which adjoins the emperor's room. I took a copy."

"We have a way in," said Brude. "By all the gods, Cleon, you are a marvel! We have a way in!"

"You still need to turn it into a duplicate key," Cleon pointed out, his voice almost bursting with pride at his achievement.

Brude handed the box to Fothair. "Moritasgus has a smith. Ask him to make two copies. And if Moritasgus has the other things we need, you can tell him we are going ahead."

Eboracum A.D. 211

So the day came at last, cold, with a biting, blustery wind sending clouds scudding across the sky. Caralugnus and his household saw them off as Mairead and Barabal, her baby clutched tight and wrapped in several layers, clambered into the coach that Caralugnus had given them. Fothair sat in the driver's seat, Castatin beside him, while Brude rode his large, brown mare. Brude presented Caralugnus with a bronze statuette of the goddess Minerva. "A small token of thanks for all your kindness," he said.

Caralugnus clasped his hand as he wiped a tear from his eye. "Good fortune to you all!"

Cleon came to see them off but there was no sign of Lucius. Brude had visited him the day before to say farewell, a risk he had not wanted to take because he did not want to chance someone recognising him later, but it would have looked odd if he had left without paying his respects to his patron, so he had wrapped himself in a hooded cloak and gone to the fortress. Lucius was polite and formal. He tried half-heartedly to persuade him to stay, but did not protest when Brude explained that his family were eager to return home to help their people adjust to life as part of the empire. Then the young Roman surprised Brude by giving him another gift of money, which he tried to refuse but accepted when Lucius insisted. "Use it to help build a proper Roman town north of the Wall," Lucius told him.

Now they were ready and there were no excuses for delaying any longer. Fothair got the horses moving, slowly at first in his inexpert hands but the coach rumbled through the paved streets and then out onto the road leading north. They were on their way home.

The weather was cold so they all wore warm clothing against the chill wind. Barabal looked tired but happy, engrossed in her baby. Opposite her in the carriage sat Mairead, her face pale. Brude was worried that the strain of what they had planned was at last beginning to tell on her. She had shrugged it off but he was grateful that they had the carriage so that she could rest while they travelled.

They made their way northwards, the road climbing steep hills and then falling down into deep valleys. Fothair's driving was clumsy and awkward but they were in no hurry so they travelled slowly and he soon got the hang of how to get the horses to do what he wanted. Inside the coach, the ride was relatively smooth as the carriage hung on its leather and rope suspension. There were few other travellers on the road at this time of year. The weather was still too unpredictable for most people to travel far, but imperial messengers galloped past once or twice and they saw the occasional wagon or army patrol.

At the twentieth milestone there was a staging post where they stopped for a short break. Brude wanted witnesses to see them heading north, so before moving on again, he chatted to the ostler who cared for the horses, which were always kept available for the imperial messengers.

Four miles later, the road descended into a wooded valley. They went very slowly down the slope. At the foot, they found a trackway leaving the road, heading west through the trees. After checking carefully that there was nobody around to see them, they turned off the road, plunging into the darkness of the thick woods. After only fifty paces they were out of sight of the road. Brude dismounted. "This is the place. Now we need to wait for our friends to arrive."

"We are here," a deep voice called from the shadows. Half a dozen men suddenly stood up from where they had lain concealed in the undergrowth. They were armed with axes and spears. All of them had moustaches with ends that drooped to their chins and they wore their hair long in the style of the Brigantes. Moritasgus stepped out of the shadows and walked over to greet Brude with a friendly handshake. "Sorry about that. We wanted to be sure it was you. This is a dangerous game we are playing."

Brude clasped the man's great ham of a hand. "Thank you for your help, my friend," he said. "We are entrusting our families to you. Take good care of them."

"As our own," nodded Moritasgus. He waved a hand, beckoning his men forwards. "We have what you wanted."

One of the Brigante warriors carried a large, heavy sack, which he emptied on to the ground. The uniform of an imperial messenger reluctantly disentangled itself from the sacking and lay crumpled on the damp grass. "I hope it fits," said Moritasgus. "You are a big fellow and it took us a while to find one we thought matched your size."

"You have done well, my friend," Brude told him. In the cold winter air he stripped off his cloak, tunic and leggings, changing quickly into the Roman uniform. It was a little tight, but he managed to squeeze into it. He kept his own undershoes and sandals and had to pad the helmet, but it was not a bad fit.

"We even cleaned the blood off it," Moritasgus told him with a grin.

Now, dressed as an imperial messenger, Brude asked his companions, "How do I look?"

"Convincing enough," Fothair told him, although he sounded worried.

"You know what to do?"

"We've been over it often enough," Fothair told him.

Mairead hugged him and gave him a kiss. "Be careful. I need you to come back to me."

He kissed her back, recognising the strain she was under and the effort it was taking her to appear strong. "Don't worry, I can take care of myself." He hoped he sounded calmer than he felt. "You can dispose of the coach?" he asked Moritasgus.

The big man nodded. "I can't guarantee they won't find it but there is a dale not far from here which is deep and difficult to get down to. We'll drag it over there. If they do find it, we'll make sure they find it looted and with blood stains all over it. We slaughtered an old sheep this morning so we have plenty of fresh blood."

"You know that if things go wrong they might still come looking?"

Moritasgus shrugged. "There are two villages nearer this place than our own. If they do come, they will search there first. And if all goes well you will be on your way before they get to us."

"Thank you. If, as you say, all goes well, we should see you tomorrow." He clasped the big man's hand again.

"Will you still not tell me what you intend to do?"

"You will learn soon enough, my friend. Best to keep it secret a little longer."

Fothair had unhitched the horses from the wagon. He produced saddles and harness from a hiding place in the trees, where he and Castatin had hidden them a few days earlier. He nodded to Brude. "Ready when you are."

Brude hugged Castatin, not knowing what to say to him. They had had so little time to learn how to be a family and now he was leaving again, on a journey from which, despite his outward optimism, he knew he had little hope of a safe return. He hugged Barabal, gave little Seasaidh a kiss on the forehead then kissed Mairead again. He thought she was close to tears.

He mounted his horse then turned to Fothair who had clambered onto one of the others, leading the third as a spare. Brude's other clothes were bundled and strapped to the saddle. "You should have run last year when you had the chance," Brude told him.

"What, and miss all this fun?"

They waved farewell, knowing that if things did not work out the way they had planned they might never see any of their family again, but there was no time to worry about that. Veleda's spell still hung over Brude and he knew that he had to attempt

404

this. Now he and Fothair had to get back to Eboracum to carry out the rest of their plan. They reached the road, turned south but, once out of the deep valley, they cut across country, riding in a great circle, passing the staging post before turning back to the road. Then Brude clapped his heels against the horse's flanks and rode at a fast canter along the paved roadway, trusting to his uniform to ensure that nobody impeded his journey. Fothair followed some distance behind, leading the spare horse.

As night began to fall he travelled more slowly. Thick clouds hid the moon and the night was dark, the road difficult to make out. The wind still gusted chill around him, carrying a threat of snow in its bitter breath. He offered up a silent prayer to all the gods he could think of to stop that. Snow would mean leaving tracks, making him easy to follow. The plan depended on him disappearing from sight. A few random spots of wet sleet spattered on his face but by the time he reached Eboracum it was late evening and still the snow held off.

He approached from the north, heading for the fortress. The bulk of the city was clustered round the south-western side of the fortress in the loop of the river so he had no need to go through the city streets. He could no longer see Fothair behind him but he trusted the tall man and knew that he would do what he had to. From here on, Brude was on his own. He swallowed, trying to get moisture into his dry mouth.

Two sentries stood on guard outside the closed gate, while others patrolled the ramparts or stood atop the gatehouse. When they saw Brude, they ordered the gate opened, without comment. Imperial messengers were never delayed. He nodded a greeting as he rode through, heading for the Principia. The building was a blaze of light with torches and oil lamps burning bright. He left his horse with the attendants then, clasping his leather message pouch, strode confidently up the steps to the main entrance.

Cleon was more nervous than he had ever felt in his life. He had vomited up the contents of his stomach and was feeling weak, his knees trembling. He had thought such reactions were just things that poets wrote about and was horrified to discover that they were real symptoms of fear. He wondered again how men like Brude could march into an arena to fight, knowing that death waited for them, or how Hector could have stood to face Achilles, knowing he could not kill him. The poems suddenly seemed inadequate in their descriptions of fear. Lucius had told him to go to bed but Cleon had insisted it was just a stomach upset and that he would be fine. "Everyone is busy tonight, Master," he had said. "I shall be on duty welcoming the guests, as I promised."

Somehow he managed to get through the first part of the evening. The guests began streaming in and Cleon organised slaves to take their cloaks while he and other freedmen checked their invitations before directing them towards the great hall, where the imperial family would join them for the feast. The last stragglers were ushered through, the large, heavy doors were closed and Cleon returned to the entrance hall where he waited, ostensibly to greet any late arrivals. The sound of music echoed distantly, muted by the closed doors. Soon, the slaves were all despatched to carry the food from the kitchens. Still Cleon waited.

The guards on the doors were bored but kept on their toes by the duty centurion who would emerge from his tiny office from time to time to check on them and to make a brief circuit of the building. When the emperor and his family were around, the Praetorians were ever vigilant.

Cleon saw one of the outer doors being opened and the silhouette of an imperial messenger strode into the hall. It was Brude, as he had promised. Cleon almost jumped up to run to him but Brude looked at him with an expression that revealed no recognition and walked on. Cleon recovered his composure but his heart was pounding, beating so loud he was certain the guards would hear it. He poured a beaker of water then made to intercept Brude. Clutching his leather message pouch, Brude strode purposefully towards the small office where the duty centurion was always stationed. He stopped when Cleon said, "Some water, sir?"

Brude took the proffered beaker, draining it at one go. "Thank you." Under his breath he whispered, "Relax. You look terrified."

"I *am* terrified," Cleon whispered in response. Then aloud, "The centurion is in here, sir."

Brude removed his helmet, knocked on the door and went in. He left the door ajar so Cleon was able to hear what was said. This was the first point of real danger. Brude had stayed away from the Principia as much as he could over the past months but there was still a risk that he might be recognised, especially with his helmet off. The officer, though, seemed to be seeing what he expected to see; an imperial messenger. "Despatches, sir!" said Brude, passing the pouch over.

The centurion, seated at his desk, took the pouch and opened it, pulling the parchment scrolls clear. He unwound one of them, giving it a cursory glance. "These are late," he said, his expression as dark as his tone. "They should have been here days ago."

"Yes, sir! Sorry, sir!" Brude had heard enough soldiers make excuses to know how they should react. "I was delayed by snow in the north, sir. Then my horse went lame. It took me a couple of days to reach a staging post to get a fresh one. Afterwards, I was waylaid by brigands and had to make a long detour to escape. My horse was shot and died under me. Blood is still on the message pouch, sir."

The centurion looked at the message pouch and saw the dark stain marking the leather. Brude knew the blood was that of the owner of the uniform he was wearing, but blood was blood. The centurion grunted, but seemed to accept the story. He gathered the scrolls and said, "Then you did well to get them here. I will see they get to the appropriate people."

"Thank you, sir. Permission to rest?"

"Granted."

Brude snapped a salute, fist to chest, then arm extended. He span on his heel and made for the door, where Cleon met him.

"Come, sir," said the Greek. "I will show you where you can get some refreshments." He scuttled away, Brude following in his wake. Cleon led him through a back corridor into the rear parts of the building, where the shadows were dark and all was quiet. He ushered Brude into a small room, leaving the door open long enough to allow him to light a lamp. Then he closed the door and leaned against it with a sigh of relief. "My knees are shaking," he said. "I can't believe you got away with that."

"Relax, Cleon," Brude told him. "The despatches were genuine, the uniform is genuine. They see what they expect to see. Now, have you got the change of clothes for me?"

"Under the bed. Put the uniform there. I will go to the kitchens to get the water." He slipped out of the door again.

Brude felt under the bed, found what he was looking for and pulled out a simple tunic and sandals. As quickly as he could, he unfastened his armour and changed out of the uniform, shoving it out of sight under the bed. In its place he slipped on the tunic and sandals.

Cleon returned a few moments later, carrying a tray bearing a fine clay jug and a silver goblet. He handed the tray to Brude. "The guard changes in ten minutes. The emperor's fresh water was taken in half an hour ago but the new guards, hopefully, won't know that."

"Even if they do, I'll blame it on confusion in the kitchens," said Brude. He was feeling remarkably calm, despite the next phase of their plan being the most dangerous. Cleon had managed to get a mould of the key they needed but he had also discovered that there was a small private bathroom between the emperor's bedchamber and the room they had the key to. Both rooms had doors connecting to the bathroom but, when the emperor had moved in, a wooden beam had been put in place inside the bathroom so that nobody could get through from the adjoining bedchamber. Lucius had told Cleon all about it when Cleon had asked what the emperor's chambers were like. Having got the key, Cleon had felt a crushing despair when he learned of the barred door. Brude had come up with this crazy idea to allow him to get in. Privately, Cleon thought he had no chance. "You have the key?" he asked, "And your potions?"

"Strapped to the inside of my thighs," said Brude. "Along with a small dagger, just in case."

"By Hercules, I don't think I want to know about that."

Cleon left again, this time remembering Brude's warning to walk slowly and calmly. He returned some minutes later. "The guards have been changed," he confirmed.

"Then let's go," Brude told him.

Carrying the tray in one hand and the oil lamp in the other, Brude set off. Cleon followed at a discreet distance, a parchment scroll in his hands, trusting to the old truth that nobody ever questioned someone carrying letters and who looked as if they knew where they were going.

Brude had memorised the layout of the rooms and corridors from a plan Cleon had drawn. He walked, head down like a slave, following the route he had been over so many times in his mind. If he got any turns wrong, Cleon, walking twenty paces behind, would call him, pretending to need a slave for some errand. But he made no mistakes, rounding the final turn to see, in the light of the burning candles mounted in brackets on the wall, two Praetorians standing at attention outside a door. Beyond the guards and around the next corner was his second target, the doorway to the adjoining room. First, though, he had to get in and remove the bar, which blocked the bathroom door.

He walked up to the guards who watched him incuriously. Slaves were commonplace in the Principia. "Fresh water for the emperor," he said in his slave voice. It was almost disconcerting how easily he had slipped back into a slave's way of behaviour.

One of the guards opened the door, standing aside to let him in. Scarcely believing how easy it was, he walked into the room. In the gloom he could make out the large bed on the far wall between two shuttered windows, the small bedside cabinet where, sitting among several other items, were a jug and goblet, just like the ones he carried. To his right, he saw the door to the bathroom. Taking his time, he went to the bedside table, took his water jug and goblet off the tray, picked up the originals and went to the bathroom door. Now he had to be quick. He saw the bar straight away, placed across the opposite door. He put down the tray then quickly lifted the bar, praying it would make no noise. Fortunately, it moved easily. He propped it carefully against the wall then went back to his tray, noisily pouring the water down the washing basin. Thank goodness for Roman indoor plumbing, he thought. Replacing the jug on his tray, he returned to the bedchamber to see one of the guards watching for him. With a subservient bow, he left the room as quickly as he could, heading back the way he had come, while the guards closed the door and resumed their posts. His pulse was racing but he felt elated. He had done it. The crazy plan was actually working. As he rounded the corner Cleon heaved a sigh of relief, then, remembering his part, said, "You! Slave! Come with me."

The quickest way to where Brude needed to be was past the guards but he needed an excuse to go that way without arousing their suspicion. Cleon gave him that excuse. The Greek began talking, telling his newly acquired slave that there were some important errands needing attending to at the rear of the building and that he would have to be quick so that he could get back to clear up after the feast. They walked past the two Praetorians, Cleon talking as they went. Then they rounded the corner and reached the door to the adjoining room. Cleon took the oil lamp and tray while Brude hitched up his tunic, pulling out one of the two keys Moritasgus' smith had made from the mould. He slipped it into the lock and turned it while Cleon kept talking in a loud, self-important voice about all the tasks needing attention. The lock clicked loudly as the key turned but Cleon coughed to cover the sound. Then Brude was in. He turned, exchanged a look with Cleon that spoke a thousand words. He gave his friend a farewell nod, then closed the door. As he locked it, he heard Cleon walk away down the corridor. Cleon's route back was long and convoluted but he could eventually reach the entrance hall without passing the guards again.

Now Brude stood in the darkness, trying to get his bearings. There was no light at all for the windows were shuttered so he moved slowly, carefully, sliding his sandalled feet across the stone floor. He followed the wall, searching for the door to the bathroom, the door he had unbarred from the other side. Completely blind, he moved painstakingly slowly so that he would not knock anything over in the impenetrable darkness. He found the first corner of the room, then a wooden cabinet, and then the second corner. Half way along the next wall was the door. He turned the handle and pushed, wondering what he would do if the door did not move but it swung open easily. He moved cautiously through and into the bathroom. Going entirely by touch, he found the bar he had removed. Gently, taking an age, he lowered it back into position, moving it barely a finger's breadth at a time so as to make no noise. It nestled securely and he breathed another in a long line of sighs of relief. Now he removed his sandals and felt for the other door. It opened with a slight creak. He stopped, afraid the guards might hear, but there was no sound from outside the room so he squeezed through, easing the door shut behind him.

The heat from the hypocaust warmed the floor beneath his feet as he warily crossed the room, feeling for the bed, making his way towards the emperor's wardrobe. This was, according to Cleon, a small room in its own right. He found the door and went in. Now all he had to do was find somewhere to hide. He had thought this would be easy but there was no light at all so he was utterly blind, having to rely solely on touch. It took a long time for him to search out the whole room. There were robes, togas, tunics and cloaks hanging around the edges of the room above rows of sandals and boots which were arranged on a low shelf. There was a recess at the rear of the room, near the shuttered window, where some wooden boxes and crates had been piled. He felt all around and discovered that there was just enough room for him to squeeze behind them and, hopefully, stay out of sight. Satisfied he could find his way around the small room, he returned to sit beside the door to wait.

Brude did not know how long he sat there but it could not have been more than an hour when a sound from the far side of the main room disturbed the eerie silence. Through the tiny crack of the nearly closed door, he could see the main door being opened, swinging silently inwards to admit a light from an oil lamp. A small, middle-aged man came in carrying the lamp. He said to someone behind him, "I will light your candle, Caesar."

Brude watched, poised to move quickly, as a second man came in. His hair and beard were still fashionably curled but greyer than Brude remembered. His skin was drawn and tight across his face, which looked pinched and tired. But although time seemed to have caught up with him, there was no mistaking Lucius Septimius Severus, emperor of Rome. Portraits and busts of this man had haunted Brude for years. Most citizens of the empire knew his face as well as they knew their own.

The emperor walked slowly to the bed, his steps small and shuffling. Two more retainers followed him. They helped him to undress while the first man lit the candle which stood on the small table beside the large bed. Brude remained alert, watching in case any of the servants came towards the wardrobe but the emperor's night gown was already laid out for him and his clothes were whisked away for cleaning. The servants said their goodnights and left, closing the door behind them, leaving the ruler of the empire lying half propped up on a mountain of pillows. The solitary candle cast a dim light, illuminating a bowl of dried figs, the goblet and jug of water and a small hand bell on the table beside the bed.

Brude peered through the tiny gap. The emperor seemed to be dozing, his eyes closed, his chest rising and falling rhythmically. There was no sound from outside the room. Brude forced himself to wait.

At last he moved. He opened the door as quietly as he could, fearing the slight creak from the old wood would waken the emperor or alert the guards. After a moment, he padded, barefoot, across the room towards the bed, feeling once more the heat from the hypocaust system rising through the tiled floor.

412

On cold nights like this, the slaves would keep the fires burning permanently. He reached the bed and looked down at the man whose actions and decisions had shaped so much of his life. He saw the gauntness of the emperor's features, heard the breath coming in laboured wheezes. He could scarcely believe he had succeeded in getting this close, undetected.

He had given himself some choices for this moment. He had his dagger and he had some poison in a small pouch. He could also use the pillows. That might be best, for he did not want to use his dagger unless he had no alternative. There would be no mistaking murder if the emperor was stabbed.

Murder. That was the problem. Brude knew he was trapped in a plot from which there was only a slim chance of escaping. He had done all he could to save Mairead, Castatin, Barabal and little Seasaidh but he knew there was not much hope for himself. Fothair had a better chance if he remained undetected but he, too, was in danger. Cleon was not immune to discovery either. If everyone knew the emperor had been murdered, his killers would be hunted down mercilessly. So it had to be the pillows.

Brude looked at the frail old man lying on the bed in the dimly lit room and knew that he should have no problem suffocating him. Still he hesitated. He had sworn not to kill unless he had to. For the sake of his own humanity he did not want to kill, yet Veleda's words thrummed through his head, an imperative he could not ignore. He remembered the years of slavery, the terror of the arena, the destruction of Dun Nechtan and Peart, Cruithne's lone stand against the Roman raiders. All of these things had happened because of this one man lying asleep in front of him. It was in Brude's power to stop any more. *Cut off the head and the beast will die.*

Indecision gripped him, froze him in place like a statue. Did he have to kill this man? Was it the only way to save the Pritani? To save himself? He stood there, wishing he could think of another way. *This is foolish*, he told himself. *You have come this far. Do it.*

Then the emperor opened his eyes.

Brude should have moved quickly, should have grabbed a pillow and rammed it over the emperor's face before he could shout a warning. He should have. He did not.

Septimius Severus looked straight at him, no sign of alarm showing in his eyes. "Who are you?" he croaked, in a voice that was little more than a whisper. "Come to kill me, have you?"

Brude looked into the emperor's brown eyes, seeing resignation and weariness but no fear. "That is my intention," he whispered back.

The emperor coughed. "Hah! I thought it would come to this sooner or later. My son sent you? Of course he did. I should have had him killed years ago, but I couldn't do that to my own blood, not even someone as twisted as Caracalla."

"I believe both your sons want you dead, but I am not here at their bidding."

The emperor still had not moved but his head cocked slightly to one side when he heard that. "Geta wants me dead too? The boy has more balls than I thought, then. He'll make a good emperor if he gets rid of Caracalla, too."

Brude was confused. He had expected shouts of alarm, summoning of guards, but the old man just lay there, his voice barely audible, speaking as if this sort of thing happened all the time. Brude said, "You value your sons' lives so cheaply?"

The emperor's shoulders twitched slightly in what might have been a shrug. "They are Romans. They know how the world works. I am trusting to my wife to keep them in line but, sooner or later, one of them will kill the other. I have done my best to make them work together but they really hate each other. And the empire needs only one emperor. The legions only need one emperor." His mouth twisted into a grotesque grin. "It's easier to get your own way with a few kind words and thirty legions at your back than with just a few kind words. And Caracalla has the legions."

"I don't care either way," said Brude, wondering what he was going to do now. This whole thing was surreal. He was here

414

to kill the emperor, yet here he was chatting to him about the machinations of the man's sons.

"And you? What drives you to do this?"

"I am of the Pritani. If your armies leave the north my people will be safe."

"You speak good Latin for a barbarian," observed the emperor.

"I was a slave for a long time. A gladiator. You freed me."

"Did I? You must have been good, then. I didn't free many from the arena. I expect you have a lot of reasons to hate me."

"More than you can know. But I hardly know you," replied Brude. "It is what you stand for that I hate."

The emperor waved an arm weakly. "Oh! No philosophy, please. That is my wife's interest, not mine. I did what I had to do. If you were in my shoes, you'd probably have done the same. You fought in the arena, so you know there are times you have to be ruthless. It might seem an easy life to you but, believe me, it's not. I'm probably almost as much a slave of the empire as you were."

"I doubt that,"

"Well, perhaps not," the emperor agreed with a weak smile. "So what happens now? Are you going to kill me or bore me to death?"

Brude felt more trapped than ever. "I don't really want to kill you but, if I don't, a lot of my friends will die." He wondered why he was telling the old man this. All it needed was one shout and the guards would run in, leaving Brude no alternative but to fight. And to almost certainly die.

"Some assassin you are," the emperor said disapprovingly. "Don't worry, I am not going to resist or call for help. I'm old and I'm tired and I have to get up to pee four times a night. I can't eat very much without throwing up and my bones ache all the time. Death would be a welcome release, believe me. I won't last out the year anyway. My sons will get their wish before long, whatever you do."

Brude looked at him in astonishment. He had seen slaves, gladiators and soldiers who had been so badly injured that they welcomed death but to learn that the ruler of the empire shared that desire was a strange revelation. "If you really mean that, I can make it painless and peaceful," he said.

The emperor raised an eyebrow. "How?"

"I have hemlock."

"The death of Socrates? There's a thought." He gestured towards the goblet on the table beside his bed. "Go ahead and mix it, then."

Scarcely able to believe what he was doing, half suspecting a trick of some sort, Brude walked round the bed. He hitched up his tunic and pulled a small vial from his pouch. He poured some water from the pitcher into the goblet, unstoppered the vial and emptied the contents into the drink. Hemlock was sometimes used as a sedative, although only in extreme cases. The difference between an amount that would render someone calm and pain free, and the amount that would kill them was very slender. Severus accepted the goblet with a nod. "How long will it take?"

"Not long. Ten minutes perhaps. Maybe less."

"What will you do then? My guards will hardly let you live, you know."

"I will leave through the next room. The guards won't see me. I am just a slave."

"Is that how you got in? Someone must have helped you. That door is barred."

Brude said nothing. The emperor had not yet touched the potion and Brude suspected he was trying to get information out of him so that he could have the conspirators arrested.

"So you have a plan and an accomplice but you are not going to tell me? I think you might be smarter than you look. Well, no matter. What do I care?" He lifted the goblet to his mouth and slowly drained it. "There. Now, tell me when I freed you."

Brude could not believe that the man was so calm. He took the empty goblet, placing it back on the small table. "At the Secular Games. In the Flavian amphitheatre. Nearly seven years ago now."

416

The emperor half closed his eyes, searching his memories. "You were the one who got himself tangled in the net on purpose!" he exclaimed. "I remember seeing that and telling my sons you were a man who had gambled everything on one throw of the dice. You got lucky."

"That was me," Brude admitted.

"Now you are doing the same again. Gambling on one throw of the dice. You think you'll be able to just walk out of here?"

"I walked in."

"You are quite a fellow, aren't you? More Roman than barbarian, I think."

"No, I am just me. A man."

"So what will happen to you after you walk out of here? Someone will talk, sooner or later."

"Let them. I will be far away, back with what is left of my people."

The emperor snorted. "Your ambition is to live in a mud hut with the other barbarians? Maybe you are not so smart after all."

"Maybe not," Brude conceded. "But it will be my choice of how I live, not someone else's."

"You have seen what Rome can offer and yet you turn your back on it," the emperor whispered. "I don't think I've ever known anyone do that. Rome brings peace, security and prosperity. What do your barbarians have to offer you?"

"Friendship, family. Rome brings death and destruction. I have seen it."

"Is your own way any better? The tribes of this island were constantly fighting each other before we brought order."

"Just because you want to rule, it doesn't mean we want to be ruled by you," Brude said.

"Everyone would rather rule than be ruled."

"In my experience, most people would rather be left alone to get on with their own lives," Brude told him.

The emperor smiled weakly. "I am not like most people. How long did you say this would take?"

Brude lifted the bed covers. He pinched the skin of the emperor's leg. "Can you feel that?" he asked.

"Not a thing," the old man replied.

Brude tried further up at the top of the thigh. "That?"

"No."

Brude let the covers down. "It won't be long now."

"Good. I am tired of this life."

"Then we will both gain from this."

"You mentioned family. Do you have sons?"

"Only one."

"Is he like my sons? Does he want you dead?"

"Not that I know of," Brude said with a slight grin despite himself.

"Then you're a richer man than I am," Severus told him. The emperor's breath was ragged now. Suddenly, without warning, his eyes were fixed open, staring at the ceiling. Brude touched his arm but there was no reaction. After a few moments Brude realised that the old man had stopped breathing. He felt the neck for a pulse but there was nothing. Gently, he closed the emperor's eyes. Whatever else he was, Septimius Severus had met his end unflinchingly and with dignity. Brude just hoped that he never grew so tired of life that he would welcome death in the same way. It seemed sad that a man who ruled the whole world did not want to live.

It was done. Now all he had to do was get out unseen.

He took the candle and went back to the wardrobe where he quickly selected a long white robe, a pair of fine leather boots and a thick woollen cloak, which he wrapped around himself, fastening it with a gold brooch that was already attached to the cloak. He checked himself in a tall mirror that hung on a side wall and reckoned he could pass for a nobleman, although a rather dishevelled one. He found a hat with a wide brim, ramming it on his head to complete the disguise. From his pouch he pulled out a gold ring, which he placed on the middle finger of his left hand, the sign of a knight of the Roman Empire. He shoved his old sandals among the rows of shoes and boots, hiding them in plain sight.

He took the candle back into the bedchamber and set it on the table. He looked at the emperor again. The death would appear to be natural so, if he could get out undetected, there should be no hue and cry after an assassin.

He took the goblet and jug into the bathroom where he washed the goblet out to remove any traces of the poison, then retraced his steps and replaced them on the bedside table so that everything in the imperial bedchamber was as it had been. He left the candle burning. Illuminated only by its solitary light, he took one final, relieved look at the body of the emperor then felt his way back through the bathroom. He tried to figure out how to put the bar back in place but there was no way he could think of so he decided to leave it. He cautiously opened the door, passed through the other bedchamber, felt for the door, which led to the hall and, taking a deep breath, slowly unlocked it. He opened it a fraction and peered out into the hallway. Light still flickered from the candles hung on the wall brackets but there was no sound. He stuck his head out, looked both ways, then stepped into the hallway. Closing the door quietly, he locked it again, then headed away from the imperial room, unsure of where he was going but glad to be putting distance between himself and the scene of the crime.

The corridors were deserted. He soon got his bearings, taking a circuitous route but eventually heading back towards the main exit. There would be guards there, he knew, but not the same ones who had admitted him as a messenger. He strode into the large vestibule, adopting a rather unsteady gait. He was relieved to see Cleon still there, sitting on a stool to one side of the hall, a rather forlorn figure. Brude staggered over to him and saw that Cleon did not at first recognise him in the gloom because of the large hat concealing his features. The guards looked at him uncertainly. Slurring his voice, trying to imitate an upper-class accent and give the impression of being slightly drunk, he ordered Cleon, "Fetch my horse, will you?" He kept walking towards the door.

The guards stood aside. One of them pulled the door open, admitting the chill night air. Brude staggered out onto the top steps. "Where's my horse?" he demanded.

"Horses and carriages are round the side, sir," Cleon told him. "I'll fetch the ostler."

"No, no," Brude said, with an exaggerated wave of his hand. "I'll go myself. I could do with some fresh air. Thought I was going to throw up for a minute there." He lurched down the steps, heading towards the eastern end of the Principia.

Cleon put an arm under his shoulder. "Here, let me help you, sir," he said. Under his breath he whispered, "Is it done?"

"It is done."

"By Hercules, I never thought you'd manage it."

"We are not safe yet," Brude reminded him. "Stop here."

They stopped. Brude leaned against the wall, glancing back to see two of the soldiers watching him. He leaned over and made a retching noise. He saw the guards turn away in disgust and then he straightened, tugged Cleon's arm and walked slowly round the corner of the building.

Once out of sight, he paused to take a deep breath. "So far, so good. But I can't afford to steal a horse. I'll have to walk out." He looked at Cleon and placed an arm on his shoulder. "Come with me."

Cleon hesitated. "I cannot. I must get back. I would be missed. If not tonight, then, certainly tomorrow."

"We will wait for you. You can join us later."

"Do not wait for me, Marcus. I am old and used to my comforts. This country of yours is bad enough here but I would not be able to live in a house of mud and sticks."

"It's not that bad," Brude told him.

"Go," Cleon told him. "Go and live your life as best you can."

Brude clasped his friend's hand, feeling a lump in his throat. "I could not have done this without you, Cleon. I will miss you."

"And I you. We have said farewell once before but, somehow, this time is harder. Go now and remember me as I will remember you and your family."

"Always," promised Brude. Then he turned and began walking, feeling a sense of loss as great as any he had felt before.

Wiping a tear from his cheek, he made his way slowly towards the west gate, keeping to the shadows as much as possible. He resumed his swaying walk as he approached the gate. The two sentries were illuminated by sputtering torches on brackets at either side of the gate. Brude wished them a pleasant good evening, slurring his words slightly. They opened the gate without question, letting him out into the dark night. Their job was to stop people coming into the fortress, not to stop them leaving. Brude turned left, heading towards the town, following the wall of the fortress, knowing there were sentries patrolling the rampart above him. In the darkness he stumbled once or twice but, after what seemed an age, he reached the first houses. Gratefully, he ducked round a corner out of sight of the fortress.

He should have felt elated at his success but he was depressed at leaving Cleon. Killing the emperor had brought no satisfaction, just a dull emptiness. But against all the odds he had succeeded. Veleda could no longer haunt him. Now all he had to do was find Fothair.

Fothair was freezing. When he had found the small depression in the low hills overlooking Eboracum, it had seemed a pleasant enough place. Here in the dark, with the bare limbs of the trees creaking in the cold wind above his head, and the winds gusting through the hollow, he hated it.

Every few minutes he climbed the low side of the hollow and looked towards the city. Some lights were still burning but he was too far away to make out whether there was anyone out and about. He doubted it. At this time of year most people stayed indoors after sundown, trying to stay warm. In an effort to keep warm himself, he ran up and down the slope but this alarmed the horses. Then he lost his footing in the dark and fell, so he settled for walking instead of running. He wondered what time it was but he had no idea. He guessed it was not yet midnight because he thought he would be able to make out the guests leaving the fortress after the feast. So far, he had seen nothing at all. He reckoned there would be a lot more moving lights when they all came outside, but then he worried that he was so far away that he might have missed them. Perhaps the feast was over and everyone had left, leaving Brude still inside. Or perhaps Brude had been caught and was already dead. He told himself he could not think that. Brude was the most capable man he knew. If anyone could get away from the fortress, it was him. Brude's biggest problem, Fothair thought, was his own self-doubt. He had been a slave for so long that he sometimes did not know just how much people looked up to him. And people did look up to him, sought his favour and tried to gain his respect. Fothair would follow Brude anywhere, would have gone into the fortress if Brude had asked him. What he definitely did not want to do was go back to Mairead and tell her that Brude had not returned. Especially in her condition.

Barabal had guessed it first. Brude had thought Mairead was just feeling unwell but Barabal had confided in Fothair that Mairead had admitted to missing her period. "She's pregnant?" he had asked.

"She thinks so," his young wife had said. "But she's not certain, so she doesn't want Brude to know yet. She thinks he will abandon his plan if he knows."

Fothair had been appalled. He thought Brude should know, but Barabal had made him promise not to say anything. Mairead's strength of will humbled him. Everyone had thought she could not have any more children. Colm had been prepared to divorce her because of it, but now, it seemed, Colm had been the problem. After so many years of misery, Mairead now had a chance of living with Brude and raising more children with him. With a word she could have stopped this crazy plan. They could have made a life together within the empire. Instead, she had said nothing. Like Brude, she had put the fate of the Pritani above her own needs. Fothair could not fathom where she found her strength.

Brude had to return. He must.

The long night passed slowly. From his lonely vantage point Fothair saw the cluster of torches as people left the Principia after the feast ended, so he reckoned that must have been around midnight. He waited, clenching his teeth to stop them chattering in the cold and slapping his arms around his body to keep his circulation going. A few spots of rain spattered on the ground but, thankfully, the wind bustled the clouds further east before any real rain fell.

He stayed near the lip of the hollow, peering into the night, trying to make out signs of movement but there was nothing. The moon was hidden by another wave of grey clouds and the earth was in utter darkness. He heard the bark of a fox and the wind brought the distant sound of an owl hooting, but there was no sign of Brude. Fothair grew more and more worried for his friend. He knew Brude had few concerns about getting into the fortress and, if he could gain entrance to the emperor's chambers, he had a plan for getting away, but there were so many things that could go dangerously wrong. The longer the night dragged on, the more Fothair worried that Brude and Cleon had both been caught.

The moon suddenly shone through a gap in the clouds. Fothair instinctively ducked below the rim of the hollow then cursed himself for a fool because he was far enough away from the fortress and the town that nobody could possibly see his head. He peered over the edge again, his eyes scanning the ground between the hill where he lay and the distant town. It was hard to make anything out, even in the moonlight, but he could see nothing moving. Then the moon was hidden behind the blanket of clouds again and all was darkness once more.

He slumped down, frustrated and concerned, yet helpless to do anything except wait. Brude had told him to stay until the first light of the pre-dawn appeared in the eastern sky and then he was to leave, making his own way back to Moritasgus' village. "If I'm not back by then," Brude had told him, "I probably won't be back at all." Fothair told himself over and over that it would not come to that; could not come to that. There must still be several hours until dawn. He waited.

Unexpectedly, he heard the snatch of a whistled tune carried on the wind. He sat up, alert, listening as hard as he could. It had come from the south west, behind him. He scrambled down the slope, across the tiny hollow and up the other bank where he looked out over the edge. He whistled the same tune, a child's ditty that everyone of the Boresti knew. There was no reply. Then he heard it again. It was definitely there, not his imagination, but it was faint and passing him on the south side. Throwing caution to the wind, he clambered over the rim of the hollow and called into the night, "Brude! Where are you?"

Silence.

"Brude! Over here!" Where was he?

Then he heard an answering call. "Keep talking but keep your voice down!"

"I'm over here. You're on the wrong side of the hill so you need to head north. Just keep coming up the slope."

Brude appeared a few moments later, a darker shadow against the dark of the night. He was wrapped in a cloak and had a broad-brimmed hat on his head. Fothair threw his arms around him in a welcoming embrace. "What are you doing coming from that direction?"

"I got lost in the dark," Brude admitted. "It was only when the moon broke through that I saw the outline of the hill and the trees and knew I'd missed you."

"Did you do it?" Fothair asked him anxiously.

"Yes."

"Cleon?"

"He's fine. He stayed."

"Then let's get the horses and get out of here. You can tell me all about it as we go."

They headed south and west, into the face of the wind, following a small stream, walking the horses so as to avoid any accidents. It was slow progress but they were south of the city and heading gradually westwards. Brude hoped that the

424

Romans would not suspect foul play but he wanted to take no chances. He and Fothair had to disappear in case suspicions were aroused by the discovery of the unbarred bathroom door, or the messenger's uniform he had left behind. They crossed the Roman road some miles south of Eboracum and headed further west into the hills, urging the horses on as the first grey light of dawn lightened the sky behind them. Brude told Fothair everything that had happened. When he was done the tall man laughed. "For a man who does not believe in the gods, you've got someone looking after you."

A.D. 211

The news raced round the fortress on wings. The emperor was dead. Lucius told Cleon as much as he knew, which was not a lot. "He must have died in his sleep while the feast was still going on. They say his candle was burned right down so he could not have put it out last night."

Cleon clucked with sympathy. "It will be a shock for the whole empire. But he was not a well man. Everyone could see that."

"At least he went peacefully. Not many emperors manage that," Lucius observed.

Cleon just nodded, keeping his thoughts private. He wanted to ask whether anyone had noticed the bathroom being unbarred but that would have betrayed Brude, so he said nothing. Instead he asked, "So what happens now?"

"Messengers are already on their way north to Caracalla. Geta is preparing to return to Rome with Julia Domna. We can go back home at last, Cleon. Once there, who knows where fate will lead us?"

By 'us' Lucius meant himself, Cleon knew. The young man was ambitious and well placed to realise his aspirations. But he was Geta's man and Cleon knew as well as anyone that there were two rival emperors in the imperial family. Attaching oneself to the wrong choice could prove fatal. He thought of Rome and he thought of seeing Agrippina and of watching her cuckold Lucius, who would be aiming for the senate, with all the political intrigue that would bring. He made a decision that surprised even himself. "If I may, Master Lucius, I would prefer to stay here."

426

"Here? In Eboracum? Whatever for?"

"Here in Britannia, Master Lucius. I find the pace of life too hard for my old bones here around the imperial court. I think I would like to travel around, to see something of the empire. I would like to start by learning more of this province."

Lucius was dumbfounded. "Well, you are free to do as you please, of course," he said at last. "But wait a while before you make up your mind. We won't be heading off for a few days yet."

Cleon agreed but, inside, he knew that the decision was made. He felt suddenly liberated and excited. Brude had been right. The price of life under the empire was high. Cleon felt he had paid it for too long.

They burned the clothes Brude had taken from the emperor's wardrobe. Brude gave Moritasgus a bag of Roman silver coins to thank him for his help. The big man did not want to accept them but Brude insisted. "I would give you some gold, but I suspect the Romans might become suspicious if you had too much of that."

"My pleasure has been outwitting those bastards," grinned Moritasgus. "Too many of our people have been seduced by the wealth and power the Romans bring. To me it is just another form of slavery. I almost wish I could come with you to your wild, free land north of the Wall."

"It's not free yet," Brude reminded him. "We may well be just another province of the empire by now."

"With the emperor dead? I think they'll have more important things on their mind than conquering your people," said Moritasgus with a laugh.

Brude hoped he was right.

They stayed at the Brigante village for nearly a month. Mairead was soon certain that she was expecting a child. She told Brude, who was stunned and elated by the news. "Are you sure?" he wanted to know.

"As sure as I can be. You'll see me getting fat soon." Her face radiated happiness.

Gently, he ran a hand over her belly, amazed that new life was growing inside her. "When?"

"Near the end of summer, I think. Plenty time for you to build us a new house."

Brude could not recall ever being happier.

Moritasgus sent men to watch the roads. After a few days, they reported the supply wagons were no longer heading northwards. Some days later, the first soldiers began marching past on their way south to Eboracum. Brude went to see for himself. He lay on a hillside overlooking the road, Castatin lying close beside him. Together, they watched the eagle standards travelling southwards.

"There are so many of them," Castatin said in wonder.

"The more there are here, the fewer there are in the north," said Brude, daring to hope that his plan had worked.

They waited three more days, then Brude decided they should begin the journey northwards. The weather was improving and young Seasaidh was strong and healthy. With the carriage Caralugnus had given them, they would make good time. Moritasgus and his men had hidden it deep in the forest but it would not take long to have it cleaned and ready.

Moritasgus gave a feast in their honour, slaughtering a bullock, which was roasted over a huge fire. Jugs of ale were consumed and the music of the Pritani filled the night air. Brude danced with Mairead then sat with her at Moritasgus' side, feeling as content as he had done for a long time. Castatin drank too much beer and fell asleep in the open air, much to everyone's amusement.

They all slept late the next day and there were sore heads all round when they did eventually rouse themselves. Now Brude was anxious to be on their way so they gathered their horses, packed their belongings and prepared to set off across the hills to where the carriage had been hidden. The day brought a promise of an early spring, despite the chill in the wind.

They were nearly ready to depart when word came that a stranger was approaching, riding on horseback. They looked to the trackway and Brude's face broke into a huge smile as Cleon, looking around with distaste at the grubby surroundings of the Brigante village, rode slowly towards him.

It took only a few days to reach the Wall. They travelled slowly but in good spirits. Most of their time was spent trying to teach Cleon how to speak the Boresti language. He endured their laughter in good spirits. "I am glad you came," Brude told him. "We have little to offer you except our friendship, though."

"After a lifetime in Rome, that is more than enough," Cleon assured him. "In a strange way, I am looking forward to it."

Cleon had brought more than just himself. The news he had heard before leaving Eboracum was that Caracalla had made peace with both the Maeatae and the Caledonii and the Roman troops were all back south of the Wall. Veleda's desperate plan had worked after all. Now the two co-emperors and their mother were on their way back to Rome, taking most of the army with them. "Good riddance to them," Fothair said with feeling.

They approached the Wall near its eastern end and were allowed through without question when Brude and Cleon, both dressed in fine clothes and wearing the gold rings of Roman knights, produced a paper bearing the seal of Caracalla authorising their journey to the lands of the Votadini on a diplomatic mission. The document looked authentic thanks to Cleon's skill with a pen and Fothair's carving of a replica of Caracalla's seal. It was good enough to see them through the Wall. With the others acting the part of their slaves, they rode through the fort and out of the gates. They headed northwards, beyond the borders of the empire.

Sitting atop the carriage beside Brude, Mairead leaned close to him. "Do you think there will be anything left of Broch Tava?" she asked. "I am worried that the people had to spend all winter in the woods."

Brude had been worried about the same thing. "Caroc is a good man. If anyone could bring them through it, he could. As long as some people survived, the Boresti still live."

Mairead snuggled close to him. Up ahead, Castatin was riding a horse, no doubt pretending he was a mighty warrior, leading the way for them. In the carriage, Barabal was nursing a sleeping Seasaidh while Fothair was trying to explain to Cleon the Boresti names for the various kinds of trees they were passing. From the sounds of things, the exercise was having mixed success.

Brude flicked the reins. "Let's go a bit faster. I want to get home."

END

Historical Note

Apart from the imperial family and other characters, such as Augustus, who form part of the background, all of the characters in this story are entirely fictitious. The main events of the emperor Septimius Severus's life as related are based on what is known about him. He did defeat Clodius to become sole emperor, he did campaign against Parthia, and he did hold the Secular Games in 204 AD. He and his sons came to Britain to restore order and subdue the northern tribes who had been raiding across Hadrian's Wall for several years. The emperor died in what is now York, in February, 211 AD. His death, from natural causes as far as is known, sent his sons hurrying back to Rome and his campaign to subdue the Pictish tribes was abandoned. The legions withdrew to the south of Hadrian's Wall and there were no more serious attempts to conquer the Picts. The emperor's sons soon fell out and Caracalla had Geta murdered, ruling as sole emperor until he was assassinated in 217 AD.

As far as places are concerned, the descriptions of ancient Rome are broadly accurate based on current knowledge. The fictional village of Broch Tava is located on the site of the modern day town of Broughty Ferry, Peart is modern Perth and Dun Nechtan is the modern village of Dunnichen. The descriptions of these places in the story are entirely fictional. Although the name of Broughty Ferry allegedly derives from it being the site of a Broch, there is, so far as I know, no trace of a Broch ever having been found there. There is a hill known as Forthill, and these two unrelated facts have been combined in the story.

The tribal names used are known only from the names given by the Romans. The Boresti are mentioned briefly by the Roman historian Tacitus but their location is uncertain, although it was probably around Tayside.